ANNA

Titles available in this series

Yannis
Anna
Giovanni
Joseph
Christabelle
Saffron
Manolis
Cathy
Nicola

Greek Translations

Anna
published by Livanis 2011

ANNA

Beryl Darby

JACH

ISBN 978-0-9554278-1-7

Printed and bound in Great Britain by
MPG Biddles Limited, King's Lynn, Norfolk

Reprinted 2012

First published in the UK in 2008 by

JACH Publishing
92 Upper North Street, Brighton, East Sussex, England BN1 3FJ

website: www.beryldarby.co.uk

For Betty, who first introduced me to Crete

Family Tree

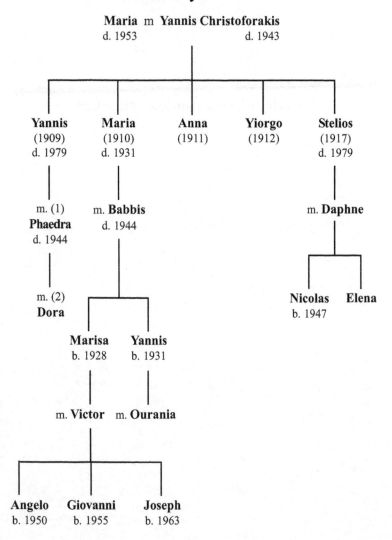

Maria m **Yannis Christoforakis**
d. 1953   d. 1943

Yannis
(1909)
d. 1979

Maria
(1910)
d. 1931

Anna
(1911)

Yiorgo
(1912)

Stelios
(1917)
d. 1979

m. (1)
Phaedra
d. 1944

m. **Babbis**
d. 1944

m. **Daphne**

m. (2)
Dora

Marisa
b. 1928

Yannis
b. 1931

Nicolas
b. 1947

Elena

m. **Victor**   m. **Ourania**

Angelo
b. 1950

Giovanni
b. 1955

Joseph
b. 1963

Family Tree

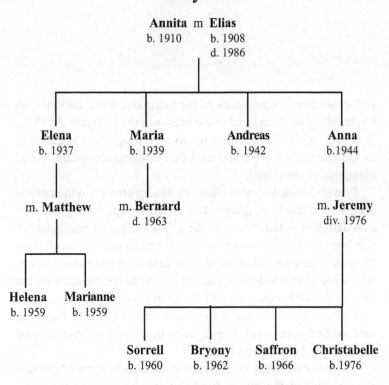

Annita m **Elias**
b. 1910   b. 1908
          d. 1986

Elena   **Maria**   **Andreas**   **Anna**
b. 1937   b. 1939   b. 1942   b.1944

m. **Matthew**   m. **Bernard**   m. **Jeremy**
                    d. 1963   div. 1976

Helena   **Marianne**
b. 1959   b. 1959

Sorrell   **Bryony**   **Saffron**   **Christabelle**
b. 1960   b. 1962   b. 1966   b.1976

Author's Note

Italian soldiers, being allies of the Germans, were stationed on Crete. Many of them lived in the homes of the villagers. At Plaka they had specific instructions not to send supplies to Spinalonga as the Germans were convinced that a resistance group would make use of the island.

Preveli Monastery was used as a headquarters and the coastal area was used to evacuate the allied troops to Egypt. The evacuation was hazardous as the allies were continually under fire from the Germans and many men and ships were lost before the evacuation was abandoned. The Australian and British troops who were unable to leave Crete set up resistance groups with the help of the archaeologists and the local people.

Pockets of resistance were based on the Lassithi Plain, an area riddled with caves. I have taken the liberty of having some caves in the hills behind Plaka.

The shooting of the local prefecture leaders in Aghios Nikolaos took place and the bullet scars can still be seen on the trees. Various atrocities took place in the villages and the Cretans risked their lives to avenge the acts of the occupying army.

All the characters in this novel are entirely fictitious. Any resemblance to actual persons, living or dead, is entirely coincidental.

1928 – 1931

Maria placed the knife she was using beside the basket of vegetables and walked from the kitchen to the main living room. Who would knock at the front door? Such formality did not exist in their small community unless the priest was visiting. She sighed, not wishing to spend time pretending a repentance that she did not feel.

'Pappa!' Maria felt her heart beating more quickly and her face paled. 'Has something happened to Mamma?'

Yannis shook his head. 'I want to speak to you. May I come in?'

Maria opened the door wider and indicated to a chair at the table. 'Can I make you some coffee?'

Yannis shook his head again. He found it difficult to know where to begin. He was not used to apologising. 'I've been thinking. I may have been a bit hard on you. You're not really a bad girl.'

Maria's eyes filled with tears. 'I'm sorry, Pappa, for hurting you. I'm not sorry about the baby,' she added defiantly as her hand went to her extended stomach.

Yannis shrugged. 'What's done is done. Is Babbis good to you?'

'Of course. We do love each other, Pappa, and Kassy has been very kind to me.'

'So she should be.' Yannis shifted uncomfortably in his seat, remembering the way Babbis's mother had confronted him with her knowledge of his past. 'I'll speak to Father Theodorakis and arrange for him to make your union official – for the child's sake,' he added.

Maria felt the lump in her throat grow and she swallowed hard. 'We'd be grateful, Pappa.'

'Nothing fancy, mind. Not the usual celebration. Just you and Babbis at a time that suits the Father. It will put your mother's mind at rest.'

'Thank you, Pappa.' The tears began to flow from Maria's eyes.

'I'll be off then.' Yannis rose from the table. 'Best you and Babbis come down tomorrow evening and see what I've arranged.'

'Do you mean it, Pappa? We can come down to the farm?'

Yannis nodded. 'Better to have someone with you when you visit your mother.'

'Oh, Pappa!' Maria placed her arms around her father's neck and kissed his weathered cheek. 'Thank you.'

He patted her shoulder gently. 'Best to forget the past and what was said in the heat of the moment. You're both welcome.' He disentangled her hands. 'I'll be off, then. I've work to do.'

Maria watched from the doorway as her father made his way up the low hill towards the cart track. She could guess what it had cost him in pride to call on her and wondered what had caused his change of heart; maybe her invalid mother's entreaties were responsible. She closed the door and leant against it, taking a deep breath. She would find Babbis and tell him the good news. Her Pappa had forgiven her.

Kassy watched from the corner of the vegetable garden as the farmer left the house and smiled grimly to herself. A bit of plain talking and some threats from her had made the stubborn man see sense. She had no intention of telling the village that he had been instrumental in the death of Olga, but he was not to know that.

Maria and Babbis walked to the farmhouse hand in hand. Both were nervous and uncertain of the reception they would receive, despite the visit from Maria's father.

'Shall I wait outside?' asked Babbis.

Maria shook her head. 'Pappa said we were both welcome.' She pushed open the door to the kitchen and was greeted by the savoury smell of yvetsi.

Anna looked up from her preparation of a cabbage salad and smiled. 'Pappa said you were visiting and I've made enough for all of us.'

Maria hugged her sister. 'I'm so happy. I'll be able to visit Mamma whenever I wish now, instead of having to sneak over when Pappa's out in the fields.'

'Come and tell her. Pappa said you were both coming, but I'm not sure she believed him.'

Maria walked through to the living room, a reluctant Babbis following, still unsure of the welcome he would receive. Maria went straight to her mother and kissed her.

'I'm sorry I didn't come this morning as usual. Anna said Pappa told you we were both coming down this evening. How have you been today?'

Maria stretched out her arm to her daughter, the other laying helplessly in her lap. 'It's good to see you both.' Her words were slurred due to her stroke, but quite distinguishable. 'I'm the same as usual.'

'Where's Pappa?'

'He'll be back shortly. He was watching for you and has gone to fetch Father Theodorakis.'

Maria looked at Babbis and pulled a face. 'I hope he won't lecture us all evening. How are you, Yiorgo and Stelios? It seems an age since I saw you both.'

Her brothers looked at her, Stelios surprised at the size of his sister's stomach. 'You have got fat,' he remarked.

'Of course I'm fat, I'm having a baby.'

Yiorgo nudged his younger brother. 'I'm looking forward to being an uncle and I know Mamma can't wait to be a grandmother.'

Maria groped for Babbis's hand. She felt ill at ease, a stranger in the house she had called home for the last eighteen years.

'Here's Pappa.' Anna sensed the tension around her and stated the obvious in an attempt to relieve the situation. 'Good evening, Father Theodorakis.'

The small, fat man, who was both priest and school teacher for the village entered the room and cast a swift glance at Maria and Babbis before approaching the woman in the chair.

'Good evening, Maria. I hope I find you well.' He spoke loudly and slowly as if she were hard of hearing.

'I'm very well, thank you. Anna is a wonderful nurse.'

Father Theodorakis nodded. 'I'm pleased to hear it. It's a daughter's duty to look after her ailing parents.' His beady eyes fell on Maria and she tilted her head defiantly.

'A drink, Father? I can offer you brandy or wine. Which would you prefer?' Yannis opened the cupboard and began to search amongst a selection of bottles.

Father Theodorakis licked his lips. 'Brandy would be very acceptable.' It was not every day that he was able to partake of such a luxury.

'Glasses, Anna, then we can get our business out of the way.'

Obediently Anna went to the kitchen, beckoning to the boys from the doorway. Yiorgo understood and rose to his feet. 'Come on, Stelios. We need to check the donkey.'

'You don't need me for that.'

Yiorgo pulled his brother by the sleeve. 'Yes I do. Come on.' He waited until they were in the kitchen and spoke quietly to his brother. 'Pappa needs a bit of time with them alone; come outside and I'll explain.'

Anna returned with three glasses and placed them at her father's elbow before retreating to the kitchen and closing the door firmly behind her.

Yannis poured glasses of brandy, placing the bottle down beside his chair leg. He was not prepared for the priest to help himself as he fancied. Another would be offered at the conclusion of their meeting.

He cleared his throat. 'Father Theodorakis knows why I have asked him here. He has agreed to say a few words over you and give you a paper that declares you officially married.'

'Thank you, sir. Thank you, Father Theodorakis.' Babbis spoke for the first time.

The priest regarded him sternly. 'I have not seen you in church for some weeks, young man. I would have thought it suitable for you to come and ask forgiveness for your sin.'

Babbis's face reddened. 'I did not feel that I would be welcomed by Mr Christoforakis. I did not want to be an embarrassment to him.'

'I would not have thought you could have caused him more embarrassment than you have already. I shall expect to see you regularly in future.'

'Yes, Father.'

'And you too, Maria. You have also sinned.'

'I have prayed long and hard for forgiveness, Father.'

'For forgiveness or an alleviation of your problem?' Father Theodorakis raised questioning eyebrows and Maria did not answer.

Yannis cleared his throat. 'You agreed to say the words that will make them officially married, Father.'

Father Theodorakis nodded. 'I have agreed, but a few words and a piece of paper does not absolve them.' He did not add that the generous gift he had received from Maria's father had immediately swept away any scruples from his conscience. 'I assume you care for each other as young people who wish to enter the state of matrimony should?'

Babbis nodded. 'I love Maria very much and I promise I will look after her to the best of my ability for ever.' He clasped Maria's hand. 'I shall always love you, Maria.'

'And you feel the same, Maria?'

'I do, Father.'

'Very well. I declare your union sanctified in the eyes of the church.' The priest withdrew a paper from his pocket and handed it to Babbis. 'This will provide you with a degree of respectability. It declares you legally married.' He swallowed the last of his brandy and looked for the bottle.

Yannis refilled the man's glass and held up his own. 'Thank you, Father. I should like you to drink to the health and happiness of the young couple.'

The priest and Yannis swallowed the liquor quickly, whilst Babbis took a cautious sip. He folded the paper the priest had handed to him and placed it carefully inside his jacket pocket.

'Thank you; I'm very grateful, we're both grateful.' Babbis took another sip of the brandy.

Father Theodorakis looked ruefully at his empty glass, but a refill was not forthcoming. Reluctantly he rose to his feet and shook hands with Yannis. 'I'll say good evening and leave you and your family to have your meal.' He waited, hoping to be asked to join them.

'Maria, tell Anna the Father is leaving,' instructed Yannis and the priest had no choice but make his way to the door.

Anna sat in the chair watching her sister nurse her newborn baby. She felt a thrill of pride. She had delivered the baby. Her very first delivery! True the Widow had been there and she could ask her advice if she was uncertain of her actions. She had checked with Maria how often her pains were coming, laid her hand gently on her distended stomach and felt the child beneath, the head safely engaged. There had been little to do then except wait and encourage Maria to push.

The small, perfectly formed head had emerged, and Anna had felt an overwhelming surge of emotion. Carefully she had supported the head until with a final slither the tiny girl lay on the sheet between her mother's legs.

'Make sure the baby is breathing first,' advised Widow Segouri and Anna wiped the nose and mouth clear of mucus, watching the slight blueness disappear and a healthy pallor take its place. 'Now hold it up and slap its bottom.' Anna did so, feeling relief as the baby drew a deep breath and began to cry.

Carefully Anna cut the cord, ensuring it did not drop on the floor, and placed the child in Maria's arms. Whilst Maria and Babbis admired their offspring Anna gently massaged Maria's stomach to release the placenta, checking with the Widow that it was complete. Finally she had washed both her sister and the baby and now she could relax.

The Widow eyed the scene. There was no need for her to stay any longer. She could go back and get a good night's sleep. 'Are you ready to take me back, Babbis?'

Babbis had borrowed his father-in-law's donkey to bring the old lady to the farm, the journey being too much for her to undertake on foot.

'I'll take you,' offered Anna. 'It will save Babbis having to make two journeys. Maria doesn't need me any more. She just needs to sleep and Kassy can keep an eye on the baby.'

Kassy nodded. She was longing to cuddle the tiny addition to the family.

'I'll come up tomorrow to check how you are, but I don't think you'll have any problems. I'll tell Mamma how beautiful she is and you can bring her down to show her next week.'

Maria smiled sleepily. The moment she had been dreading was finally over.

Maria placed her baby on the one arm her mother was able to use and stood beside her should the child start to slip.

'Isn't she beautiful?' Maria spat over her shoulder to ward off the evil eye as she spoke the words. 'And she's so good. She hardly ever cries, unless she's hungry, or needs changing, or has wind, or something.'

Babbis smiled to himself. The child seemed to him to be forever crying, particularly during the night.

'Why didn't you call her Maria?'

'Babbis thought of the name. It's half your name and a little bit of his mother's.'

'You could have called her Maria and the next one Kassianai,' argued the grandmother.

'And if I only have boys in future one of them will feel very silly with a girl's name, besides, we didn't want another Maria.' Maria tried to be patient. She had expected her mother to be displeased that she had broken with tradition. 'Don't be cross about it, Mamma. It's a pretty name.'

'Marisa. I'm not sure. It will take some getting used to. You could have called her Anna.'

Maria's mouth set in a stubborn line. 'We didn't want to call her Anna. Anna is my sister. This is our little girl. She's very special and has a special name. She's Marisa.'

'What did Father Theodorakis say when you told him?'

'He tried to pretend that he didn't know how to spell it, so I wrote it down for him and made sure he copied it correctly. She's Marisa and no one can change it. Anyway, that's enough about her name. Look at her little hands. Her fingernails are so perfect.'

Babbis moved closer to his sister in law. 'I still haven't really thanked you, Anna. You were wonderfully efficient.'

Anna blushed and shrugged. 'Thanks to Maria it was easy and I had the Widow with me. I'd also had advice from Annita.'

'I'm glad we didn't have to rely on the Widow. Her hands are so rough and crippled she would probably have scraped poor little Marisa to pieces.'

'She knows a good deal more than I probably ever will. How is Maria? She's getting enough rest and eating properly I hope. Remember she's feeding the baby.'

'My mother's keeping an eye on her. She makes her rest for at least an hour each afternoon.'

'That's good.' Anna had an idea that Kassianai was also taking advantage of the time to have her granddaughter to herself. 'I'd better take her from Mamma. It will give me an excuse to have a cuddle.'

Annita gazed about her, bewildered by the bustle before her eyes. The ship had docked and now she stood a lost and lonely figure on the large quay. All around her burly men were loading or unloading cargo on ships far larger than she had ever imagined. Plucking up her courage she walked forward to where a man was shouting orders and checking a list he held in his hand.

'Excuse me.'

He looked round, his frown changing to a smile when he saw who had accosted him. Tucking his pencil behind his ear he lounged back against a bollard. 'What can I do for you, young lady?'

'Some directions, please.'

'My pleasure.'

Annita regarded him with distaste. There was something about the way he looked at her that was repulsive. 'Can you tell me the way to the hospital, please?'

The foreman looked at her speculatively. 'If you care to wait half an hour I could take you there. It's on my way.'

Annita shook her head. 'I'm in rather a hurry.'

The man frowned. 'It's a good distance from here.'

'Which way?'

A grubby finger pointed down the road to the left. 'Follow the road until you come to a fork, take the right hand one and you'll find yourself in the outskirts of Athens. Best to ask again then.'

'Thank you.' Annita shouldered her sack and began to trudge along the dusty road. She felt very alone and for the first time began to doubt the wisdom of arriving in Athens. The road seemed to stretch away endlessly into the distance, shimmering in the late afternoon heat. Finally the fork of the road came into view and Annita walked to the right, within a few minutes signs of habitation meeting her eyes. The road was less dusty now and the air cleaner, free from the smells of the harbour. A violent hooting made her leap to the side of the road as a blue painted bus lumbered up. She waved her hand frantically and to her great relief it stopped a few yards ahead of her. Thrusting her sack up the steps before her she smiled gratefully at the driver.

'The hospital, please.'

He shook his head. 'I don't go that way.'

Annita's face fell and she turned to dismount.

'I can drop you near.'

'Yes, please.' Annita held out a selection of coins. 'Will you tell me when to get off?' She sank into the nearest seat, feeling the curious eyes of the other passengers on her, all of them appeared to be dockworkers returning from the harbour.

The houses were becoming more numerous and Annita noticed that they looked far more prosperous than those in her hometown, all having a stretch of garden in front of them and a balcony. The driver hooted and her attention was drawn to an old lady who was leading her donkey, loaded down with hay, and two goats tethered one each side, in the centre of the road. She shook her stick angrily at the driver who grinned and pressed his horn more enthusiastically, revving up the engine ready to move forward. Annita giggled involuntarily, thinking of the donkeys in her own town. Often she had been poked by the owner's stick for standing in the way.

The bus shuddered to a halt. 'This is as near as I go.'

'Where do I go from here?' Annita rose from the hard seat and lifted her sack.

'That way.'

The driver indicated with his thumb and Annita smiled and thanked him. At least she appeared to be in the centre of the city now. People were jostling each other as they walked along; shops and houses rubbed shoulders in confusion, small alleyways twisting between them and there was a spacious public garden. Annita stood and looked around her in amazement. Everything was so much bigger than she had imagined. How would she ever find her way around somewhere so vast? Spotting a taverna huddled against a tiny church she stepped out into the road, only to be hooted at as a taxi raced past her.

'I must be careful,' she reminded herself, as she crossed the road, this time without incident.

Sitting at the taverna, drinking a coffee, she watched, fascinated, by the scene. The taxis seemed to be hurtling in various directions, people ran across the road in their path, miraculously reaching the other side without injury, whilst street peddlers called to advertise their wares, shoe-shine boys accosted pedestrians, setting up their blocks and seats wherever they were, oblivious of any inconvenience they caused.

Visitors strolled, guide books or maps in hand, arguing in unknown tongues as to the direction they should take, gathering in little knots and gesticulating, until finally conceding that one of their number was right and following them docilely like a flock of sheep.

Annita was tempted to sit longer. She called to the girl who was hovering by the doorway, flicking at a table with a grubby cloth. A fixed smile on her face the girl approached.

'My bill, please, and can you direct me to the hospital?'

The girl handed Annita her bill. 'Five lepta. Are you ill?'

'No.' Annita shook her head. 'I'm a nurse.'

'Doubt if there'll be anyone there now.' She turned to go.

'Please, don't go. Can you tell me where I could get a room for the night?'

'We let rooms. You'd better ask my father.'

Annita followed the girl into the dim interior where a corpulent man sat, reading a newspaper, a cigarette dangling from the side of his mouth.

'She wants a room.'

The man looked up slowly, taking in every detail of Annita's appearance. 'In advance.'

'I'd like to see the room first and know how much.'

With a sigh he rose and led the way through the door at the back and up a narrow stone staircase, opening the door with a flourish. The sparsely furnished room held only a bed, chair and table. 'Three drachmas.'

'For one night?'

The man nodded. 'Food is extra.'

'I'll take it.' Annita felt too weary to argue. It was somewhere to sleep. Tomorrow she would find the hospital and ask the matron about accommodation.

The man held out his hand for the coins, threw a key on the table and left Annita to take stock of her surroundings. She walked to the window and opened the shutters, wrinkling her nose at the stale smell of cooking that wafted in. Kicking off her shoes she lay on the bed and closed her eyes. It had all seemed so easy when she had been at home with her parents. Now she felt very lost and frightened in this big, impersonal city. A timid tapping at the door roused her. The girl who had served at the table pushed open the door with her foot, carrying a jug of water and a bowl that she placed on the table.

'Pappa told me to bring you some water.'

'Thank you. Will you stay and talk to me for a while?'

The girl shot a nervous look behind her. 'I was only told to bring the water.'

A shout from below was heard and the girl scuttled to the door. 'I'm wanted,' she said by way of explanation and clattered her way hurriedly back down the stairs.

Annita walked slowly towards the centre of the city until she finally espied a policeman and approached him nervously, asking for directions to the hospital. At the mention of the address he stepped backwards and eyed her suspiciously.

'I'm a nurse,' Annita assured him. 'I can show you my papers.'

'There's no need.' He took a further step away from her. 'Across the road, up the hill and it's the last turning. You'll find it right at the end.'

Annita thanked him, lifted her sack and hurried across the road whilst he stopped the traffic for her. She trudged up the hill, her pace slowing as the road became steeper until it ended altogether with a branch to the right. She looked along the road. It seemed little different from the one she had just left, the street name, high up on the wall, was so worn that the letters were indistinguishable. Trusting that she was going in the right direction Annita continued to walk. The houses became meaner and unkempt, the pavement narrowed and rubbish littered the gutter. The houses petered out, but the road continued on to a large, high walled enclosure. Anticipation surged up in Annita. This must be the hospital. Iron gates, firmly padlocked, barred her way and she looked through them at the sprawling, unwelcoming building.

Reaching her hand through the bars she pulled the metal handle that hung there, hearing the bell clang in response. Two men strolled across the gravel to the gates. One of them wielded a heavy key and pulled the gates open wide enough for her to pass through before relocking them. Without a word they escorted her, one on either side, to the main door. Once inside they left her standing in the bare hall.

Wondering what she was supposed to do, Annita looked around. The walls had originally been painted a cream colour and were now grey, chipped and dirty. The wooden floor was greasy and Annita could feel her shoes sticking to it. She knocked at the first door and a disembodied voice called 'Come.'

She walked into the room, straight-backed, and a smile on her face. 'Good morning.'

The man behind the desk did not look up. 'Who referred you?'

'Referred me?'

'Yes. Which doctor?'

'No doctor. I've a letter of recommendation from the matron.'

For the first time the man raised his eyes from the sheaf of papers in front of him. 'What do you mean, girl? A letter of recommendation?'

'I've come to be a nurse. I've a letter of recommendation from the matron of the hospital where I trained.'

The eyes scrutinized her carefully. 'May I see the letter?'

Annita handed it over willingly and watched whilst the man slit the envelope and read the close writing that covered the page. Finally he looked up, a frown creasing his forehead.

'What made you come here? This is a hospital for the incurables.'

'Incurables need nursing.' Annita tilted her chin defiantly.

'Not these. They're quite capable of looking after themselves or each other. They do not need nursing as you know it. I think it would be best if I asked an orderly to find you a taxi to take you to the hospital you need.'

'No.' Annita hoped she was not going to cry. 'I want to stay here. I want to nurse incurables.'

'It's out of the question. We do not have female workers.' He handed the letter back to her, an obvious sign of dismissal.

'Would you consider making an exception?'

'Certainly not! Now, if you will follow me.'

Annita had no choice but to lift her sack and follow the man back to the main door. She felt humiliated and deflated. The man exchanged a few words with the orderly who had escorted her into the building, he looked at her in surprise and beckoned her to follow him.

'Goodbye. I hope we shall meet again.'

The man did not deign to reply and the door was closed. Annita found herself being hustled towards the gates and pushed outside.

'Down the hill.' The man pointed back the way she had come. 'Plenty of taxis down there.'

He relocked the gates and strolled back towards the sombre building leaving Annita no alternative but to haul her sack onto her shoulder and set off in search of transport. She was resentful, hurt and angry. That they should have refused her services! The idea was unthinkable. She walked on, hardly conscious of her direction and it was not until she nearly lost her life to one of the hurtling taxis that she stopped and took stock of her situation.

It took some minutes of frantic waving on her behalf before a taxi stopped and asked her destination. Gratefully she scrambled into the back and was soon revelling in the novelty of riding in a car. The hospital seemed to be miles away as they careered from one side of the city to the other before finally stopping before a high wall.

The gates were not padlocked, but propped open, a stretch of grass before the main building giving an inviting air. The door yielded at her touch and she found herself in a large vestibule, a desk in the corner where an amply proportioned woman sat knitting.

Annita approached her hesitantly. 'Excuse me, may I see the matron in charge, please?'

The woman finished the row she was knitting without raising her eyes. With a sigh she laid aside the half-finished garment and looked at the girl. 'What do you want to see her for? I can tell you where to go.'

'I have to see the matron,' Annita persisted. 'I've come here to be a nurse. I'm not a patient.'

'Oh!' The woman was obviously perplexed. 'Is she expecting you?'

'No,' Annita thought rapidly. 'I couldn't make an appointment as I wasn't sure when I would arrive.'

'Well you'll have to wait.'

Annita sat on the wooden chair just inside the entrance door. The woman returned to her knitting, the click of her needles the only noise in the quiet room. A door slammed, making both the receptionist and Annita jump. The woman hurriedly stowed her knitting into her apron pocket and smoothed her skirt. Within seconds of the door closing a man hurried across the hall.

'I shall be back tomorrow and I shall expect an improvement,' he called over his shoulder.

A small woman scowled at his back. He was such a stickler. How was she supposed to work miracles when she was short staffed? She wished his predecessor would return. Life had been a good deal easier when he had been the doctor in charge. Her eye fell on Annita.

'What's she doing here?'

'She was asking to see you, Ma'am. I told her she would have to wait.'

The matron turned towards Annita. 'I'm a very busy woman. Visiting hours are between three and four in the afternoons. There are no exceptions.'

'I'm here to apply for a job.' Annita thrust the opened letter into the matron's hands.

'What's this?'

'A letter of recommendation from the hospital where I trained.'

'Did you open it?'

'No, ma'am. I was directed to the other hospital and they opened it there.'

'What does it say?'

Annita shrugged. 'I don't know. Probably how long I was at the hospital and my capabilities. I haven't read it.'

Brown, beady eyes stared at Annita suspiciously before they scanned the sheet of notepaper. 'Follow me.' The matron led the way to a small office and offered Annita a seat. 'Tell me about yourself.'

'There's very little to tell. I come from Aghios Nikolaos. I'm nineteen now and have trained as a nurse for the last three years.'

'Why have you come to Athens?'

'I wanted to see the city,' lied Annita.

'What do your parents think about you being so far from home?'

'My parents are quite happy with my decision.'

The matron regarded her critically. 'Suppose I wrote and asked them?'

'It would take a little time, but they would write back and say they approved.'

'Do you know anyone here who would vouch for you?'

Annita shook her head.

The matron debated. It was not every day a trained nurse knocked on the door and asked for work. She leaned forward. 'Very well, I'll believe you. I'll take you on trial until I have contacted your parents. If I am not satisfied I shall dismiss you.'

Annita nodded. 'Thank you. I don't think you'll have any reason to be dissatisfied. When may I start?'

The matron raised her eyebrows. She was tempted to say "now". 'Tomorrow morning at seven. Where are you living?'

'I've nowhere yet. I was hoping you might be able to advise me.'

'There are plenty of places nearby that let rooms and they'll be only too pleased to have a respectable young nurse.'

Anna was happy and contented. She enjoyed tending her mother, looking after the house and cooking for her family. She particularly liked Sundays. She would rise early and prepare as much of the meal as she could before attending church with her father and brothers. Maria and Babbis, bringing Marisa with them and accompanied by Kassianai, Babbis's mother, would crowd into the tiny farmhouse when the service was over. Anna would prepare coffee and whilst they drank it she would return to the kitchen, usually with Maria accompanying her, to put the finishing touches to the meal.

The two girls would laugh and giggle together before returning to the living room, where Maria once again became the demure wife and devoted mother, fussing over her small daughter. The meal over, Kassianai would return to her own farm, Marisa would be placed on a small pallet on the floor to rest and her father instructed to watch over her whilst the girls washed the dishes. Yiorgo would wander out across the fields, sometimes accompanied by Stelios, but usually Stelios preferred to stay and read a book. He was to go to the High School in Aghios Nikolaos in the autumn and was determined to gain a scholarship to the Gymnasium in Heraklion as his oldest brother had done.

Maria would sit in her chair lost in her own memories. She was proud of Anna. It was not every young girl of seventeen who would be able and prepared to deliver a baby. Anna gave the credit to the Widow and the letter her cousin Annita had sent her. Maria doubted if Annita had any knowledge of childbirth at all. She had worked in the hospital in Aghios Nikolaos and you certainly did not go to hospital to have a child. You only visited the hospital if you were sick, really sick, like her poor son Yannis, who had been diagnosed with leprosy and sent to the hospital in Athens for treatment.

Thinking of Yannis made a tear creep down her cheek. Such a clever boy; attending school in Aghios Nikolaos and gaining a scholarship to the Gymnasium in Heraklion, only to have his life blighted by disease. At least he was receiving treatment for his condition, not like the poor sufferers who lived on the small island opposite their village. She sighed deeply.

Her poor Yannis. Thankfully none of her other children showed any signs of the disease, so he must have contracted it whilst he was in Heraklion. Town living was not healthy. His gland had been blocked since his attack of mumps when he was a boy, but it had not caused him any problem until the doctor had interfered with it. Another tear coursed its way down her cheek. If he had not fallen down the stairs at the Gymnasium he would not have visited the doctor. If his father had not broken his leg whilst Yannis was at home for Christmas he would not have had to work so hard on the farm; being out in all weathers had probably weakened him. If the priest from Heraklion had not brought the bad news to them she would not have had her stroke and Maria would not have had a baby without having had a proper betrothal and wedding service.

During the afternoon the girls would sit close to their mother, Anna embroidering and Maria sketching the family in their various occupations. Yannis had introduced his son in law to backgammon and the familiar click of the dice made a background to their chatter.

Maria placed her head close to Anna. 'I've a secret to tell you.'

Anna looked up at her, taking in her shining eyes and slightly flushed face.

'Are you.....?'

'Shh. I haven't even told Babbis yet, but I think so.'

Anna hugged her older sister spontaneously. 'I'm so pleased. When are you going to tell Babbis?'

'Another week or so. I want to be sure.'

'He'll be over the moon.'

'That's why I want to be sure before I tell him. You won't say anything, will you, not to anyone?'

'Of course not,' promised Anna. 'Thank you for telling me first.'

'I thought I should. I shall need your services again.' Maria smiled. 'I was so frightened last time. I didn't know what to expect.'

'So was I,' agreed Anna. 'I shall know exactly what to do this time. I've delivered three since your Marisa.'

As if on cue the child opened her eyes, rubbed them with her balled up fists and staggered to her feet. 'Mamma.'

'I'm here, little one. Come over and talk to your grandmother.'

Obediently the little girl walked over to her grandmother's chair and was lifted up onto her lap. She touched the woman's withered arm, although accustomed to it, in her small mind she could not understand why it never moved. She lifted her own arms up above her head and encouraged her grandmother to do the same. Bored with not receiving a response she wriggled back down and approached her grandfather, grabbing for the counters and dice they were playing with.

Yannis gently removed them from her hand. 'Don't want you putting them in your mouth and swallowing them. Plenty of time to learn how to play when you're older. Do you want to go for a walk with Grandpa?'

Marisa nodded eagerly and pulled at her grandfather's hand. Yannis scooped her up in his arms and made for the door. 'We'll not be that long, just up to the square and back.'

Maria smiled. The ritual was the same each week. Her father doted on the small girl and taking her for a walk up to the square meant that he could show her off to the other villagers and revel in their admiring comments.

Father Minos sat on the waterfront at Aghios Nikolaos deep in thought. His visit to Doctor Kandakis had left him perplexed. Having eventually persuaded the doctor to grant him permission to visit the island of Spinalonga he had expected the doctor to be able to give him an idea of the disabilities and living arrangements of the occupants over there. To be told by the doctor that he did not consider it necessary to visit the sick had come as an unpleasant surprise. He would have liked to talk to the young man, Andreas, with whom he had formed a friendship, but having knocked on the door of his parent's house and received no answer he felt dispirited.

He turned into the nearest taverna and over his meal he quizzed the owner regarding the whereabouts of Yiorgo and Elena, only to find they had left in Yiorgo's fishing boat the previous day, but that Andreas should be at the church. Father Minos paid his bill and walked over the hill to the church building where Andreas spent his day receiving instruction to prepare him for when he was finally ordained.

Andreas was delighted to see his visitor and when he heard the priest's intention of visiting Spinalonga the following day he begged to be allowed to accompany him. At first Father Minos was reluctant, but Andreas finally won him over and requested time off from his devotions and instruction to spend the rest of the afternoon and following day with the priest.

Father Minos asked after Andreas's sister, Annita, curious to know if she had been allowed to work with the incurables in Athens as she had planned.

Andreas shook his head. 'Apparently they don't have nurses; they look after themselves. She works in the ordinary hospital. It's such a shame Anna wasn't able to train as a nurse. She's wonderful with her mother and spoken highly of in the village. She delivers most of the babies now as the Widow is crippled with arthritis.'

'There's no improvement in her mother?'

Andreas shrugged. 'Sometimes she appears a little brighter, but she's not going to recover.'

'What about the other daughter who was expecting when I came last?'

'Maria is fine. She has a beautiful little girl and is expecting another.'

'How does her father feel about that?'

'He's completely forgiven her. He dotes on little Marisa.' Andreas smiled at the memory of his last visit and seeing the small girl tugging at her grandfather's hair; an indignity that he not only tolerated, but seemed to enjoy.

The afternoon passed pleasantly for both men, culminating in a meal together at a taverna and an arrangement to meet at the church to participate in the early service the following morning before meeting the boatman who was to take Father Minos to Spinalonga.

As the boat rounded the promontory of the island a young girl scrambled to her feet and fled up the path through an archway and was lost to their sight. By the time Manolis had secured his craft and the men had alighted the girl had returned accompanied by a man who waited by the archway. Their eyes downcast, Father

Minos and Andreas walked slowly up the path from the jetty, finally looking up as they reached the man waiting for them.

'Andreas!'

Andreas threw his arms round the man before him and clasped him tightly; tears of emotion flowing down the cheeks of both of them.

Flora smiled at Father Minos. 'Have you come to stay?'

'No, we're just visiting. Maybe you could tell people I'm here. I'd like to hold a service for those who wish for some spiritual comfort.'

Flora nodded and rushed away, calling loudly that a priest had come to visit them.

Father Minos turned to Andreas. 'I suggest you two go and chat whilst I hold a service and I'll meet up with you later.'

Andreas nodded and Yannis led the way up the path to a secluded patch of concrete. 'Tell me everything that has happened over the past few years. How's Mamma? What about Pappa and the girls? Did Yiorgo go to Aghios Nikolaos for school or did he insist on staying on the farm? How about Stelios? And how is Annita? And your parents? How do you know Father Minos?'

'Slow down, Yannis. There's plenty of time to tell you everything. I'll start from when you returned to Heraklion and disappeared.'

Yannis listened in silence as Andreas related the details of his visit to Heraklion and his encounter with Father Minos, how he had seen Yannis leaving the hospital and called to him just as he was rendered unconscious by a stone thrown by one of the crowd. Andreas went on to describe how Father Minos had insisted on accompanying him back to Aghios Nikolaos to break the news to Yannis's parents and the effect it had had on his mother.

'Will she recover?' asked Yannis anxiously.

Andreas shook his head. 'It's most unlikely. She's greatly improved. She's paralysed down one side, but able to sit out in a chair most of the day and her speech is quite understandable.

Maria married Babbis a couple of years ago, so Anna looks after your mother. Maria and Babbis have a little girl with another on the way. Your Pappa is well, he still limps, but he has no pain in his leg and Yiorgo has no plans to leave the farm. Stelios is coming to Aghios Nikolaos in the autumn to go to the high school.'

'I wonder what has happened to Mr Pavlakis,' mused Yannis. 'Tell me about Annita. How is she?'

'Annita finished her training and then decided she would go to Athens to try to nurse you. They refused to have her, but she is allowed to work at the ordinary one. I think she still hopes they may change their policies.'

'I doubt it; besides, it's no place for a woman. Can you do something for me, please, Andreas? Can you write to Annita and tell her where I am? Tell her that I release her from our betrothal arrangement and I would be very happy to hear that she has found someone else.'

Andreas nodded. He knew it was most unlikely that Yannis would ever be able to leave the island and live a normal life on the mainland. 'I'll tell her,' he promised.

Yannis drew in a deep breath to dispel the emotion he felt. 'I'd like to find Father Minos and take part in the service, if you don't mind. We can talk again later and I'll introduce you to my friends.'

Andreas and Father Minos completed the journey back to Aghios Nikolaos in silence. Andreas wondering how people could live with such deprivation and remain as cheerful and purposeful as Yannis; Father Minos more concerned with his impending meeting with Doctor Kandakis.

When the two men met again later at the taverna Father Minos was downcast. 'I lost my temper with the doctor,' he admitted.

Andreas grinned at him. 'If all you've told me about him is true I might have done more than lose my temper. I would probably have been asked to leave the church for assault. I wish

I could afford to buy the materials and medicine they need and send them over.'

'Maybe we could speak to the villagers and ask them to send some cast off clothes or bedding.'

Andreas nodded. 'I'll ask my father to talk to Uncle Yannis and ask him to send better quality food out to them in future. He could ask the other villagers to do the same. That would be a help, wouldn't it?'

'I'll have a word with him myself. I plan to visit the family tomorrow. Are you able to come with me?'

'Not tomorrow,' Andreas spoke regretfully, 'but you will call on me before you return to Heraklion, won't you?'

Father Minos sat at the table in the farmhouse. The news he had taken to the family had affected most of them in the way he had expected. Maria and Anna had cried, Yannis senior had produced a bottle of brandy, spending a considerable amount of time searching for it in the small cupboard to cover the emotion he felt, Yiorgo had shaken his hand, thanked him and returned to the fields, but Stelios had left the room without uttering a word.

Sipping appreciatively at the brandy Father Minos described his visit to the island in detail, the building that was taking place, instigated by Yannis, to try to make the houses weather proof and habitable, the poor quality food that was sent over there and the indomitable spirit of the people.

'They are determined to better their lot. It's very difficult. They have to beg the fishermen who take over the supplies for every tool they need. Sometimes their food is spoiled by the time it arrives so they go hungry; if it rains they are wet and cold as their clothing is quite insufficient for the winter months. The only fuel they have is from the wooden boxes that contain their food supplies and that has to be used for cooking. There are no fires to warm themselves by or dry their clothes.'

Yannis rose again from the table and removed a small cloth bag from the cupboard. He handed it to Father Minos. 'Buy whatever you need.'

Father Minos hesitated. 'I can't take all your savings. Yannis wouldn't want that.'

'I've plenty,' Yannis assured him. 'I can't buy goods and send them out, but you can. All I can do is make sure the food that goes out is better quality. I'll send the best of my crop in future and try to make sure the other farmers follow suit. Is there anything else they need?'

Father Minos hesitated. He was beginning to feel he was taking advantage of the farmer's good nature and feeling for his afflicted son. 'You wouldn't have a goat, I suppose? One that's in kid so they could have the milk?'

Yannis nodded. 'I'll see it's sent.'

'Pappa, could I write a letter to Yannis? I know he'd like to hear from us.'

'Certainly not,' her father snapped back at her. 'We don't want everyone knowing where Yannis is.'

Anna tilted her head. 'I'm not ashamed of him. He can't help being ill. If you won't let me write I'll wave to him every day. I'll start today by waving goodbye to Father Minos, only really I shall be waving to Yannis.' She looked defiantly at her father, daring him to forbid her.

'I'm sure it will do no harm,' Father Minos hastened to assure the farmer. 'If anyone notices they will probably think she is waving to one of the boatmen.'

Yannis gazed at his daughter and the priest sourly. If the priest supported her he was in no position to forbid her. He would just hope that she would forget after a few days.

Father Minos sat on the bus as he returned to Heraklion deep in thought. The money given to him by Yannis's father had amounted to a considerable sum, and Andreas's father had added almost the same amount. The priest had negotiated for a supply of bandages and disinfectant to be sent over to the island from the hospital immediately, followed by a further consignment each month.

From the hospital Father Minos had visited the town where he had purchased mattresses and blankets, arranging for them to be taken down to the harbour where he supervised the loading of them himself onto Manolis's boat. Father Minos had talked to Manolis on his return journey from Plaka and the boatman was only too willing to take goods to the island on a regular basis, he was quite taken with the young girl who sat on the quay and begged items from the boats when they arrived. An added incentive was the drachma he was to be paid each time for his trouble.

Father Minos's next visit had been to a builder's merchant. The man had shown surprise that the priest should want sand, cement and lime sent out to the island, along with basic tools. He shook his head. Obviously the priest had persuaded them to build a church out there, but he thought it unlikely the crippled and sick occupants would be able to accomplish the task. The builder quoted an inflated price for the materials and the priest refused, alternately cajoling and threatening until he felt he had negotiated the best possible price.

Yiorgo sat outside the farmhouse with Babbis. He ran his beads through his fingers nervously. 'Can I talk to you, Babbis?'

Babbis nodded. His brother-in-law was normally a most uncommunicative man.

'Would you talk to Pappa about the farm?'

'What about it?'

'Pappa can't work as fast as he could before he hurt his leg and Stelios is useless. Doesn't like to get his hands dirty.'

Babbis nodded again. He had noticed how fastidious Stelios had become.

'I can't ask Anna to help. She has enough to do with Mamma and the house. We've got three fields lying fallow that we couldn't plant last year.' Yiorgo swung his beads into his hand.

'I couldn't take on any more,' Babbis answered immediately.

'I'm not asking you to. I thought if we bought some more animals we could run them there and sell the meat.'

'I find it profitable,' replied Babbis cautiously.

'How many would we need to make it worth while?'

Babbis shrugged. 'I could sell you some of my yearlings. It's new young blood you need. Nature will take its course after that.'

'Would you tell Pappa?'

'Why don't you?'

'He never listens to anything I say. Insists on doing things his way.'

'I'll speak to him if the opportunity arises,' promised Babbis. 'I doubt if he'll take any notice of me either.'

'Thanks, Babbis.' Yiorgo placed his beads into his pocket. 'Maybe you could speak to him after lunch.'

Annita lay in her bed, her pillow wet with tears, the letter crumpled in her hand. She had read it through a second time before she was fully able to comprehend the news Andreas had relayed to her. Now she was not sure if she was crying because Yannis was on the island, or at her own foolishness in thinking that if she worked in Athens she would be able to nurse him. She determined, none the less, to write to him.

When she arose after a sleepless night her first instinct was to return to Crete immediately. Commonsense and her training stopped her from flight. There were patients depending upon her. Private problems had to be pushed aside. A set smile on her white face she entered the ward and read the notes that had been left for her.

The time passed whilst she worked automatically at the routine jobs, assuring patients how well they looked, that their progress was good, all the time composing a letter to Yannis in her head. By the time her duty was finished she was exhausted and the matron looked at her anxiously.

'Are you quite well?'

'Yes, I think so.' She passed a hand across her forehead. 'I didn't sleep very well last night. Probably the heat.'

The matron nodded. 'An early night will work wonders. No other problems?'

'No, nothing.' Annita turned to go. No doubt the matron meant well, but she was always trying to draw Annita into conversation on a personal basis.

The lonely girl walked from the hospital, her head bowed and her shoulders hunched. The matron shook her head. There was something both sad and perplexing about this excellent nurse. She never spoke to anyone unless it was necessary, lived alone and rarely went out. Some tragedy must have happened in her young life.

Annita was tired, both mentally and physically. She dreaded returning to her small room to be alone with her thoughts. She turned into the small taverna that almost exclusively served the hospital staff and visitors.

She managed her customary smile to the waitress who brought her coffee and doughnut to the table and then sat staring into space. The group who were chatting noisily at the other end she hardly noticed. Her doughnut sailed to the floor, landing by her feet making her start, as a young man, covered in confusion began to apologise.

'It really doesn't matter. I wasn't hungry.'

'Nonsense. I'll order another. I insist.' A pile of books was placed on the table, the doughnut retrieved from the floor and carried to the counter where the waitress produced another.

'Thank you. You really should not have bothered.'

'It was no trouble. Are you a nurse?'

'Yes.'

'At the hospital here?'

'Yes.'

'Why haven't I seen you before?'

'Why should you?'

'I know most people, but I don't know you.'

'There's no reason why you should.'

The young man looked at her and smiled. 'You think I'm being impertinent, don't you?'

'I think you could be if you were given the opportunity. You must excuse me. I have to go.'

'You haven't finished.'

'I've lost my appetite for doughnuts.'

'Please don't go. I have offended you. I won't say another word, please, finish your snack or I shall feel that it's my fault that you're hungry.'

Annita looked at him. She really felt too tired to bother. She sipped at her coffee and true to his word the young man said nothing. He opened a book from the top of the pile and began to read. Idly Annita glanced at the title 'Microbiology'. She looked at him with renewed interest. Maybe he was a student doctor at the hospital, in which case he would know most of the nurses. His face was vaguely familiar; it was possible he had visited someone on her ward. He raised his eyes from the book and smiled at her.

'You're feeling a little better now?'

'Yes, thank you.'

'And you're wondering who I am and where you've seen me before?'

'Your face is a little familiar. I imagine you must be a doctor.'

'Wrong. I'm a chemist. I work in the dispensary.'

Realisation dawned on Annita. 'Of course. No wonder you know all the nurses.'

'All except one. How have you escaped my attention?'

'Probably because I send student nurses for medicines. I prefer to stay on the ward. Now, if you will excuse me.' Annita rose, the chemist rising with her and picking up his books.

'May I walk along with you?'

'I'm returning home. I've finished my duty.'

'I've finished also and am going to the library.'

Short of going some distance out of her way Annita had no choice. As they walked the young man talked incessantly, hardly drawing breath.

'I go to the library every week, sometimes twice. Although I qualified as a chemist a year ago I'm more interested in research than dispensing. I'm trying to read as much as possible. Each time I think a disease is worth studying for a possible vaccine, cure, or even medicinal relief from the effects, I find someone has already done it and published their conclusions. I want to work on something where a cure is possible. In many ways it makes the choice more difficult as so many people will already be working on it. I'd probably be refused a grant to carry out the necessary research and it seems somewhat pointless researching someone else's research only to come to the same conclusion when there are so many other diseases around. I thought tuberculosis could be interesting; then I read about the Swiss advances and took that off my list. Which disease would you choose to research if you were in my position?'

Annita was hardly listening to him. 'Leprosy.'

'Leprosy? Why leprosy?'

'Why not?'

'Well, there's nothing that can be done for them, is there? The Oil helps a bit, but it's an incurable disease. A good deal of research has already gone into it. Hansen discovered the bacilli years ago, but there's no indication that any medicine has been developed which has any effect on it.'

'All the more reason for looking again. Goodbye.' Annita turned down a side road just before the library.

'Don't go. Our conversation was just getting interesting.'

Annita walked on unheeding.

'Please, come back.' The voice shouted after her as she continued down the road. Feet pounded on the cobbles and her arm was grabbed bringing her to an abrupt halt. Angrily she pulled her arm away.

'Please, at least tell me your name and say we can meet again.'

'My name is Annita, but I see little point in meeting again. I suggest you go to the library as you planned and find a subject to research.' She turned away and continued walking.

'My name's Elias. I'll see you at the taverna tomorrow.'

'You most certainly will not,' vowed Annita silently to herself.

Annita sat in her tiny room, chewing the end of her pen, the sheet of paper in front of her said *'Dear Yannis'* and that was all. What could she say to him? There was no point in writing all the trite, conventional sentences that usually made up a letter, nor did she want to send him an emotional outpouring. In despair she pushed the paper away. She would have to go out and have a meal, although she had no real desire to eat.

She eyed the menu displayed in a taverna a few doors away. It would do. Ordering automatically she sat facing the window, watching the passers by. What did they all find to do in the evening? She had visited the Acropolis and also the museum. Both visits had brought back poignant memories of Yannis and his enthusiastic talk of pottery and she had never repeated the experience.

Now, as she watched, she wondered as she did most evenings, where they were going. A couple entered, laughingly taking their seats and ordering wine to drink before their meal arrived. Annita bent her head over her plate and tried to ignore them. Ripples of laughter continually intruded and she grudgingly had to admit they were enjoying themselves. Annita called for her bill. There was no point in staying any longer. Her table would be needed, she had no one to sit and chat with over a bottle of wine.

As she walked towards the door she looked at the couple, realising it was the young man she had encountered earlier. Momentarily their eyes met and his lit up with pleasure. He stood, barring her way between the tables.

'This is a coincidence. Please join us for a glass of wine.'

Annita shook her head. 'Thank you, no. I would be intruding.'

'Not at all. We're waiting for some friends before going to the theatre. Maybe you'd care to come with us?'

Annita shook her head. 'I couldn't possibly. I don't know you.'

'Yes you do. We met today.'

'Meeting someone hardly constitutes knowing someone.' Annita spoke coldly.

'Have a glass of wine with us and you'll get to know us.'

Annita wavered. She had not felt so lonely since her first few weeks in the city. 'Just a glass. I haven't long to spare.'

Elias drew up a chair for her. 'This is my sister, Aspasia. She's a student.'

Aspasia smiled. 'I'm pleased to meet you. How long have you lived in Athens?'

'Almost a year.'

Aspasia chatted on, Annita answering in monosyllables, adding nothing to the conversation. Elias tried to draw her out, but he also met with no response. The bottle emptied he ordered another, scanning the window and waving wildly as a group halted outside.

'Here they are.'

They clattered inside noisily, eyeing Annita in surprise, then ignoring her as they talked amongst themselves.

'I have to go. Thank you for your hospitality.'

Elias was on his feet immediately. 'It's been my pleasure. Are you sure you won't change your mind and come with us?'

'Quite sure, thank you. I've some jobs I really must do.'

Elias held out his hand. 'Goodnight, then. Maybe you'd care to come another evening.'

'Maybe. Please say goodnight to your sister for me.'

Once outside Annita felt her depression returning. She had been foolish to refuse the invitation, the first she had received since she had been in Athens, but her pride would not let her return and accept. She must write a letter to Yannis.

Anna nursed the tiny baby, tears running down her face and dripping off her nose. She sniffed and wiped them away with the back of her hand. She should really lay him down and start preparations for the evening meal that her father and brothers would be expecting upon their return from the fields. If only she had been able to do more for her sister. She felt she had failed. Maybe if she had sent Babbis to get the donkey and cart from her father when Maria's labour had first started the hospital staff would have been able to save her life. It was so cruel. Maria and Babbis had been looking forward to their second child so much. She sniffed again and rose to her feet. The baby stirred in her arms and she rocked him gently, gradually lowering him onto her mother's bed.

Once in the kitchen she placed the meat into the pan to start to cook whilst she prepared the vegetables. She yawned widely. How she longed to go to bed and sleep undisturbed for the night. She must ask one of the women in the village how long it was before a baby no longer demanded food during the night and when she should start to give him more than milk. She felt abysmally ignorant and wondered how Maria had coped when she had Marisa. Maybe Kassianai would be able to advise her.

She really should write a letter to Andreas when they had eaten. She would have to ask him to break the sad news to his parents and ask if he could get a message to Yannis and also Annita. Her father had given up protesting about her ritual of waving and on occasions someone had waved back to her and she believed it to be her brother. She must also ask Babbis what name he wanted to give the child.

Annita wandered aimlessly along the street leading to the market.

It was her free day from the hospital and she debated how to use it. She had made her few necessary purchases and the rest of the day stretched before her. She sighed deeply. Three times she had tried to compose a suitable letter to Yannis, but it was more difficult than she had imagined. Each time she read through the pages and crossed out the paragraphs until she ended up with just a few lines.

'Hello there. You didn't meet me. I waited ages for you.'

Annita jumped. She had been deep in her own thoughts and not noticed Elias's approach. She eyed him coolly. 'I made no arrangement to meet you.'

'Yes you did.'

'You arranged to meet me. I did not arrange to meet you. Now, if you will excuse me.' Annita tried to walk on, but he barred her way.

'Come for a coffee with me now. I'd like to talk to you.'

'I have other plans.'

'Change them.'

'That's quite impossible.' Annita tried to walk on.

'Then I'll walk with you to wherever you're going.' Elias fell into step beside her.

Annita gazed round desperately. Where could she go to escape from the attentions of the young man? The solution came. Squashed, almost unnoticeable between two high walls was a tiny church, the interior so dark that the doors were left open most of the time. The walls, once richly adorned with religious murals, decorated with silver halos and amulets, were now blackened by the soot of the hundreds of candles that had been burnt there over the years. Annita stopped in the doorway.

'Goodbye,' she said deliberately.

'I'll wait for you,' offered Elias.

'I intend to spend the rest of my day here. There would be no point in waiting for me.'

She slipped inside and walked to the altar rail where she knelt and bowed her head. She asked for forgiveness for using the church as an escape and confessed that she had lied to Elias when she had said that she planned to spend the rest of the day there, hoping that if her prayers were heard she would be forgiven. For the first time in a number of days she felt at peace. The cool darkness seemed to wrap itself round her comfortingly. When she finally rose from her knees and lit a candle she glanced behind her, hoping she would not see the shadow of Elias waiting outside for her.

'I'll stay,' she thought, 'until I'm certain he won't have waited.'

Sitting on a hard chair at the side of the church she tried to compose her letter to Yannis. She could not remind him of their school days when they had lived from day to day blissfully unaware of the tragedy that was to overtake him, nor could she say she was enjoying herself in Athens, that would not only be cruel, but totally untrue. To say she was bitterly unhappy and lonely would be the truth, but would certainly not help him in any way. A hot tear coursed its way down her cheek and she brushed it away with her hand.

'Would it help to share your sorrow?' A soft voice at her side made her start. 'Would you like me to confess you?'

She shook her head. The gentle voice seemed to be reaching deep inside her, causing a searing pain in her throat and forcing the tears down her face. A handkerchief was pushed into her hand, whilst a strong arm was placed round her shoulders as she sobbed on the chest of the priest. Patiently he sat there until she managed to control her outburst.

'Now, my dear, you have shared my handkerchief, share your troubles. Whatever the cause of your distress you can tell me. I shall treat anything you say in the strictest confidence, have no fear over that.' He waited whilst she struggled for composure.

'I'm so unhappy,' she managed to say at last.

The priest nodded. 'What is making you unhappy? A young man?'

43

Tears welled up again in Annita's eyes. 'More than that?'

'Have you been foolish enough to allow the young man liberties?'

'Oh, no, no, it's not that.'

'Your parents do not approve of the young man?'

Annita shook her head. 'They were only too pleased when we were betrothed.'

The priest felt he was getting nowhere. 'The young man has changed his mind?'

'He can't marry me.'

The priest clicked his tongue. 'The scoundrel already has a wife and has been playing with your affections? The sooner you forget him, my dear, the better.'

'No, he's not married.'

The priest withdrew his arm. 'Tell me the whole story from the beginning. It can often help to talk, it clears the mind and you find the solution to the problem for yourself.'

Annita hesitated. She longed to talk to someone and she had been brought up to believe in the church.

'I was betrothed to my cousin. We were to be married when he had finished University in Athens. When he went back to High School he was taken ill and now he's on the island.' Her lips trembled.

The priest held up his hand. 'You're going to have to explain a little more fully. What island?'

'Spinalonga. It's where they send the incurables.'

'The incurables? You mean your young man is … has…'

'He's a leper.' Annita spoke the words bitterly. Words began to pour from her lips, telling him the whole story.

He listened patiently. 'Would it not be better to return to your home? I'm sure your parents would welcome you back,' he suggested.

'I don't want to go back. Everyone would want to know why I'd returned.'

'How long have you known that this young man is on this island?'

'A couple of weeks.'

'And you've kept this knowledge bottled up inside you?' Father Lambros shook his head sadly. 'Why didn't you confide in a friend you could trust?'

'I haven't any friends.'

'Nonsense. You must have friends. Other nurses, maybe some of the doctors?'

Annita shook her head. 'I've never made any friends since I came here.'

'So how do you spend your free time?'

'In my room, usually; sometimes I go for a walk.'

Father Lambros tapped his knees with his fingers. 'Now let me see if I understand. You came here hoping to nurse your young man who was ill.' Annita nodded. 'You then found that was impossible and instead of making friends with other young people you kept to yourself hoping that circumstances would alter. You have no one to turn to, no friend to spend the time with and forget your troubles. No wonder you feel so unhappy.'

'No one seems to want to be friendly with me.'

'Probably because when they tried you rebuffed them,' he chided her.

Annita shrugged, she felt resentful of his criticism of her.

Father Lambros gazed at her speculatively. 'How do you plan to spend the rest of today?'

'I'll probably go back to my room and read.'

'Would you accompany me on a visit?'

'Where?' Annita was immediately suspicious.

'I go and see my sister most days. She's a widow and appreciates someone dropping in for a chat. She has three children, but spends a good deal of her time alone now they're grown up. You may find you can be friendly with someone a little older. If you find you don't like her you don't have to go again.'

'It would be an imposition.'

'She would be delighted to see you. She must be very bored with me over the years; day after day I turn up and often fall asleep whilst she talks to me. It would be good for her to see a fresh face.'

'I'm not dressed to go visiting,' protested Annita.

'My sister isn't fashion conscious. She'll probably never notice what you're wearing.'

'I should at least go and wash.'

'I'm sure you washed this morning. There's no need for another so soon. Did you have a shawl with you? I doubt that you'll need it, but the day may turn chilly.'

Without waiting for any more excuses Father Lambros rose and assisted Annita to her feet, keeping a hold on her elbow as they left the church, both of them blinking in the brightness that met them. Annita allowed him to lead her through the streets until he stopped before a tall, dilapidated building. He pulled a bell, then pushed open the heavy door and ushered Annita through into a stone hall.

'I'm afraid we have a climb in front of us. My sister lives on the fourth floor.' He puffed heavily as he mounted the stairs behind her. 'Here we are.' He tapped lightly on the door, then turned the handle and stood back for Annita to enter.

The small, square hall took Annita's breath away. A long window let in the sunlight, falling on a bowl of fresh flowers that were placed on a highly polished chest. Beside the flowers was the small portrait of a man.

'It's me, Sultana. I've brought a visitor. May we come in?'

'You're welcome,' a voice called back and Annita followed the priest into a large, airy room.

Here the sunlight was filtered by the light curtains that covered the windows, flowers jostled for pride of place between the family pictures on small tables, woven Turkish rugs covered the polished wooden floor. Before Annita had time to take in every detail she was propelled towards the middle aged woman who was reclining on a sofa, a rug covering her legs.

'Excuse me for not rising,' she smiled at Annita. 'I have great difficulty in walking. Pull up a chair and sit beside me.' Picking up a bell from the small table at her elbow she rang it vigorously. Almost immediately the door opened and a girl appeared.

'I should like some coffee and pastries for my visitors, please.' The girl nodded and disappeared. 'There,' continued the invalid, 'she won't be long. She's a good girl. Very willing and a good cook.'

Father Lambros nodded in agreement. 'She has contributed to my downfall.' He placed his hands on his large stomach and gazed at it ruefully. 'I have to confess each week that I've eaten twice as many pastries as is good for me. I'm never sure whether I would commit a greater sin by refusing when she's taken so much trouble making them.'

The girl re-entered, bearing a large silver tray, which she placed on a marble table within reach of her mistress. They sat in silence until she returned again with a silver coffee pot. Annita all but gasped at the wealth that was suddenly before her eyes. The maid poured out the coffee into wafer thin cups and handed them round, ensuring there was a table conveniently placed for a glass of water and a plate. Annita hurriedly placed her coffee cup on the table. She was frightened she would break it if she held it any longer. Being offered the selection of pastries first she chose the smallest and also the one that looked least likely to crumble at her touch, noting with amusement that Father Lambros chose the largest baklava which was dripping with honey.

Sultana smiled. 'No wonder you put on weight when you always choose the most fattening.' She turned to Annita. 'He always did that when he was a boy. Chose the biggest and the sweetest whenever he could, and always asked for a second helping. Do you have a greedy brother, my dear? What is your name? I can't keep calling you 'my dear'. You may call me Sultana. It's so much more friendly.'

'My name's Annita.' She spoke for the first time, wishing her lips did not feel so dry or her throat so parched.

'That's a nice name. Are you called after your mother? I was,' she shuddered. 'Terrible name; I refused to give it to either of my daughters.'

'My mother's name is Elena. I was called after my aunt.'

'Do you have brothers or sisters?'

'Just a brother.'

'Is he at University or does he have a profession? Young people are so lucky these days. They're able to do as they please. When I was a girl you followed your father into his business if you were a boy, or stayed at home with your mother until you married if you were a girl.'

'He's training to be a priest.'

Father Lambros looked at Annita with renewed interest. 'You didn't tell me.'

Sultana looked at her brother triumphantly, but made no comment. 'And what do you do? Are you at University?'

'I'm a nurse.'

'A nurse! How wonderful. Are you training in Athens?'

'I've finished my training. I work at the hospital here.'

'And enjoying yourself, no doubt. Do eat up your pastry. Lambros has finished his and is too polite to ask for another until you have eaten yours.'

Annita lowered her eyes, holding her plate close to her chin, as she began to nibble at the confection. It was delicious and did not crumble embarrassingly down her blouse and skirt, as she had feared. With relief she lowered the plate a little. The moment she finished her last mouthful the plate was offered to her again and she felt obliged to choose another.

'More coffee? Why, you've hardly touched that cup. Do drink up, my dear. The poor girl will be so offended if I send back a plate of pastries and half a pot of coffee. She will think she's failed.'

Annita obeyed, sipping cautiously from the fragile cup. 'Both the coffee and the cake were delicious.'

'I'm so glad you thought so. I do insist that my companion learns to cook well. It's one of my little foibles.'

'Has she been with you very long?' Annita felt she should contribute something to the conversation.

'About six months, I think. She's nearly ready to move on.'

'Move on?'

'Once she's proficient it would be selfish of me to keep her. I shall recommend her to someone who needs a new maid or companion and she'll earn twice as much as she does with me. I shall then take a new girl from the orphanage and train her. The system works very well.'

'She's an orphan?' Annita could not comprehend what life would have been like without her parents.

'I always take orphans. What would the poor girls do otherwise? Probably end up as a cleaner or working in some low class taverna. I only wish I could take more than one at a time.'

'Who teaches them to cook?'

'They're taught a certain amount of plain cooking, then I teach them how to improve upon it and make the little delicacies that are so enjoyable. Have another pastry.' Sultana offered the plate again.

'Oh, no. No thank you. They're very filling.'

'Nonsense.' Sultana reached forward and placed one on Annita's plate. 'They slide down like air. I know you won't refuse, Lambros.'

'I'll never manage my lunch,' he smiled as his plump hand stretched out eagerly.

'Now, tell me about yourself, Annita. Where do your parents live? They must be very proud of a daughter who has qualified as a nurse.' Sultana settled herself back comfortably on her cushions.

'My parents live on Crete,' explained Annita.

Sultana raised her eyebrows. 'You're a very long way from home. What brought you to Athens? Do you have relatives here?'

Annita tilted her head defiantly. 'I wanted to see the city. It's very beautiful.'

'And what does your father do?' She leaned forward confidentially. 'You must forgive my curiosity, but I'm quite unable to go out now. I question everyone who comes to visit me in the same way. When they've gone I sit and weave little fantasies about the facts they've told me. It's my way of passing the time and quite harmless, I assure you. I spend many hours alone.'

Annita felt a lump come into her throat. 'I'm not a very interesting person.'

'When I've woven a fantasy about you, you'll be most interesting. I always say that one day I'll write them down. The sad thing is that if I did people probably wouldn't recognise themselves.'

Annita smiled. 'My father's a fisherman and my mother does embroidery for the local shops. I don't think you'll be able to imagine anything very exciting about me.'

Sultana closed her eyes. 'Oh, I can. The strong, handsome fisherman saves the beautiful young girl from drowning. She falls in love with her rescuer and marries him, having two children. One becomes a priest and the other a nurse. The dedicated nurse meets a patient...'

'Is it nearly lunch time?' Lambros interrupted his sister loudly.

Sultana opened her eyes. She caught the imperceptible frown from her brother and realised she had nearly made a mistake. 'I'll find out.' Lifting the bell she rang it again and waited for the girl to appear.

'You may clear away. Your pastries were excellent, as always, my dear. What do we have for lunch today?'

'Stuffed lamb, ma'am.'

'With plenty of garlic, I hope. How much longer do we have to wait?'

'It can be ready in fifteen minutes, ma'am. How many will there be today?'

'Four, replied Sultana firmly.

Silently the girl withdrew. Annita rose. 'Thank you so much for your hospitality.' She held out her hand.

'Where are you going?'

'It's nearly time for your meal. I mustn't delay you.'

'Sit down. I've just ordered for four. How is the poor girl to cope if I suddenly say there will be only three?'

Annita felt completely at a loss and looked appealingly at Father Lambros who simply smiled and nodded to her to resume her seat.

Overcome with embarrassment Annita sat and ate the meal that was placed before her. She should never have agreed to the visit. Father Lambros and Sultana conversed throughout the meal as though she were not present and Annita wondered if the fourth person for lunch was the maid or if someone else was expected and if so why had they not waited. As if in answer to her thoughts a door slammed and Sultana smiled.

'Here she is. Late as always. This will be my older daughter. She's in her last year at University.'

A tall, attractive girl strolled into the room. 'Hello, Mamma. Hello, Uncle. I'm sorry I'm late. It took me ages at the library to find the books I needed. Oh,' she stopped in confusion as she noticed Annita. 'I'd no idea we had a visitor for lunch.'

'This is Annita. Your uncle brought her along to visit me. She's a nurse.'

'Hello. I'm Chariklia.' She extended her hand to Annita. 'I'm studying art and I think everyone else in Athens must be doing the same. Each time I go to the library for a book it seems to be already out. Even when they're returned they never put them back in the right place so I have to search all the shelves. Is there some lunch for me, Mamma?'

'Whilst you wash I'll ring for it.'

Chariklia pulled a face in Annita's direction, then winked and left the room.

'Such a tomboy,' smiled her mother.

Annita smiled back. 'She must be very clever to be at University.'

Sultana shrugged. 'I don't think you have to be clever to study art, just able to copy a picture accurately.'

Chariklia returned. She had presumably washed her hands, but her mop of curls had not been brushed or tidied. She sat down beside Annita. 'Why did you become a nurse?'

'I wanted to help people and I'm not very clever.'

Chariklia raised her eyebrows. 'I thought you did have to be clever to be a nurse. To understand about giving medicine and how to treat people after they had operations.'

Annita shook her head. 'It's really just common sense.'

Chariklia wrinkled her nose. 'I wouldn't want to do it. Suppose someone dies!'

'People quite often die,' remarked Annita. 'There's nothing unpleasant about it. You just wash them and cover them with a sheet until the mortician arrives.'

Chariklia gazed at her wide-eyed. 'You do that?'

'Well, not often now. I ask one of the junior nurses who are training, but I have to supervise. There are far more unpleasant jobs that have to be done.' Annita blushed, remembering she was at the meal table and that her hostess was a widow. 'Tell me about your art.'

Chariklia was only too pleased to talk, breaking off from her meal frequently to show Annita a picture in one of the library books. Finally she looked at Annita. 'May I ask you something? I shan't be offended if you refuse.'

Annita nodded, puzzled.

'May I draw you?'

'Draw me? Whatever for?'

Chariklia shrugged. 'Practice, and you have an interesting face.'

Annita hesitated. 'I don't know.'

Chariklia pushed her plate aside. 'That was delicious, Mamma. If you agree I could do a few sketches of you this afternoon. When you've seen them you can decide. If you don't like them I'll tear them up.'

'If you really want to.' Annita felt obliged to agree after the hospitality shown to her.

'Could we have some coffee, Mamma, then we can start.'

Sultana smiled as she rang the little bell. 'Are you sure you don't mind, Annita? Chariklia always asks every visitor if she can use them as a model.'

'I don't mind, really. I would just like to comb my hair, though.'

'Of course. Show her around Chariklia.'

Annita followed the girl back into the hallway. 'This is my room.' She flung open a door. 'I share it with my sister.' Annita had a glimpse of two beds with matching covers, small tables at the head of each and a jumble of clothes on the floor. 'Bit of a mess. We both dashed out this morning, and Mamma insists we keep our room tidy ourselves. We're not allowed the services of her maid.' She closed the door again. 'That's my brother's room. This is the kitchen.'

The door opened and Annita gasped. Polished pans sat on a shelf, sparkling glasses in a cupboard. In the corner was a stove where a large pot of water was beginning to bubble.

'What's that?' asked Annita before she could stop herself.

'What? This?' Chariklia touched the metal contraption. 'It's the cooker. Don't you have one like it?'

'I don't have any facilities for cooking in my room,' explained Annita.

'But your Mamma must have one. How else does she cook?'

'She has an oven in the wall or she uses the fire.'

'Really! I'd love to sketch it sometime.'

'She lives rather far away. I'm sure you would be able to find one closer.'

Chariklia closed the door and opened another. 'Here's the bathroom. You know which door when you come back, don't you?'

Annita nodded and looked around the bathroom. She had never imagined such a room could exist inside a house. It reminded her of the hospital bathroom, with white tiles and large glazed bath and a toilet that had a cistern above and a chain to pull. She rinsed her hands and splashed her face with water before standing in front of the full-length mirror and combing her hair. She was struck by the drabness of her appearance and felt suddenly ashamed. Her hair needed to be cut and her shoes heeled. A new pair would not come amiss, or a new black skirt that was not bagged and shiny from sitting. Feeling very self-conscious she emerged from the bathroom and crossed the hall.

Chariklia was waiting for her, paper and pencils by her side. Father Lambros was saying goodbye and Annita had the distinct impression that he had been speaking about her as his voice rose when she entered and she noticed the glance Sultana gave her.

'Where would you like me to sit?'

Chariklia pointed to the chair by the window. 'Could you sit as though you were looking out? No, your head more this way. I can only see your ear. No, like this.' She took Annita's head gently between her hands and turned it to the angle she required, pulling a strand of hair forward so that it fell down the side of Annita's cheek. 'That's perfect. When you get tired let me know.'

Annita sat still. It was incredibly boring. Within a few minutes her neck felt stiff and her nose itched, then her ear, the piece of hair tickled her cheek and she wanted to brush it away. It seemed an eternity before Chariklia said she could move.

Cautiously Annita turned her head, her neck feeling that it would crack with the movement, and looked at the portrait the girl held up. 'That's not me,' she declared.

'Yes, it is. It's how I see you,' replied Chariklia.

Annita shook her head. 'I'm not pretty and that girl is.'

Chariklia laughed. 'Of course you're pretty. You have beautiful eyes and high cheekbones. Let me do your hair for you and draw you again differently.'

Meekly Annita handed over her comb and submitted to having her hair pulled and tugged until it was finally secured on top of her head. Chariklia handed her a book. 'Pretend you're reading. Head up a bit. That's right.'

The picture that was handed to her this time showed a different girl again. The first had looked somewhat pensive and sad, this one looked sophisticated.

'Which do you like the best?'

Annita looked from one to the other. 'I'm not sure. They're not 'me'.'

Chariklia bent over her shoulder. 'They're both you. You're just not used to seeing yourself. I could dress you up a dozen different ways, but when you looked at the pictures they would still be you.'

Annita shook her head. 'I don't know anything about art.'

Chariklia picked up one of the books she had brought from the library. 'Look, and there. The same model, she looks totally different until you look carefully, then you can see she's the same one.' Another book was passed to Annita. 'See if you can spot one.'

Obediently Annita turned the pages whilst Chariklia began to point out the ways to distinguish between one artist and another. 'Come to the gallery with me tomorrow,' she suggested. 'It's easier to see on the real paintings.'

'I'm working tomorrow,' apologised Annita.

'When's your next day off? Maybe we could go then? You could come to lunch, I could do a sketch or two of you and then we could go out.'

'Your mother might not want me to come again,' demurred Annita.

'Mamma loves visitors,' Chariklia assured her.

'I'd hate to be a nuisance when she has been so kind to me today. I've already stayed far longer than I meant to.'

'Nonsense. I've enjoyed meeting you and it means Mamma has had company most of the day. She's been sitting there listening to us chattering away and it's passed the afternoon for her. I would probably have gone out again after lunch and left her alone.'

Sultana nodded. 'It's been delightful having you here, Annita. Chariklia's quite right. I have enjoyed listening to you. Nowadays my family rush in for a meal and rush out again without stopping to talk to me.'

'Oh, Mamma.' Chariklia rose and kissed her mother on the cheek. 'Do we really treat you so badly?'

'I don't blame you. I would have done the same at your age had I been given the opportunity. You spend your evenings with me, so I'm not complaining. Come again next week, Annita, and come early so we can chat together as we did today.'

Annita found she was looking forward to her second visit to Sultana. She had bought a new skirt and washed her hair. She had thought about buying new shoes and then changed her mind. New ones would not be comfortable for some time, so she took her old ones to the cobbler and asked him to stitch the side at the same time as he replaced the heels. She wondered what time she should arrive, and finally decided that late morning would be right. She could stroll along, looking in the shops on her way.

Sultana greeted her with obvious pleasure. 'I'm so glad you came early. I reminded Chariklia that you were coming today and she has promised not to be late. I'll ring for coffee. I can't guarantee that the pastries will be quite as good. I've just taken in a new girl and she's still learning.'

'Your other maid has left?'

'Oh, no. I certainly would not let her leave until I knew the other one was going to be satisfactory. She'll be here a few more weeks.'

A diminutive girl came in answer to the bell and Annita looked at her curiously. What must it be like to work in this house where everything was perfection?

'You must answer the bell a little faster,' chided Sultana. 'Suppose I had been taken ill?'

'I'm sorry, ma'am.' She dropped her eyes and a flush crept into her cheeks.

'Now, we would like some coffee and pastries. Have you made some today?'

'Yes, ma'am.'

'Then we would like to try yours.'

A look of horror spread over her face. 'Oh, no, ma'am. They're all crumbly.'

'I should like to see them and taste them, besides, you cannot waste good, wholesome food, however unattractive it may look.'

Nearly in tears the girl left the room.

'You think I am very hard on her, no doubt?' Sultana asked of Annita. 'She has to learn. Pastries are not difficult if you follow the instructions. The next time she will be far more careful and they'll turn out a good deal better. If I were lax with her to start with she would soon take advantage of me. Now, tell me what you have been up to during the week.'

Annita searched her memory for something interesting to talk about. 'I bought a new skirt,' she ventured.

'Stand up, then. Let me look at you properly.' Annita stood and turned under the critical eye. 'Yes,' declared Sultana, 'A great improvement on your old one, but you'd not intended to go visiting that day, had you?'

Annita shook her head. 'I only went out to do some shopping.'

'What made you go into the church?'

Annita blushed deeply. 'A young man was pestering me with his attentions. It seemed the best way to get rid of him.'

Sultana wagged her finger at Annita. 'Never refuse the attention of any young man until you're quite sure that you don't want it.'

'I was sure,' answered Annita stiffly.

The door opened and the maid entered, her tray balanced precariously. She placed the coffee on the marble table and proceeded to pour and pass the cups.

'Now the pastries, my dear,' Sultana reminded her.

With trembling hand the pastries were passed and Annita chose the one that looked the firmest. Sultana eyed them critically before selecting one that crumbled to pieces under her touch. Annita felt a pang of pity for the little maid as Sultana frowned and chose another, which luckily stayed together.

'You may go,' she waved her hand at the girl. 'When you hear my brother arrive you will bring another cup and plate. There will be five for lunch today.'

'Yes, ma'am.'

'Well, despite their looks they taste good,' smiled Sultana. 'She'll pay more attention to her instructions now she's been shamed before a visitor. It always works wonders. Do you always wear your hair like that?'

'Yes, well, no,' Annita stammered, surprised at the sudden question. 'I wear it tied back when I'm on duty.'

'It would look more attractive if you wore it up, like Chariklia did it when she was sketching you last week.'

Annita blushed. 'I've never thought about it looking attractive.'

'You should. Every girl should know how to make herself as attractive as possible. You have a long neck and good eyes, but with all that hair hanging around they're hidden.'

'Did you study art when you were younger?' Annita was beginning to feel that curiosity on her part was warranted. Sultana was direct with her questions and comments.

'Goodness, no. Chariklia has talked to me and shown me pictures. Because I'm unable to leave this room all my children talk to me. I learn a good deal from them. I consider myself very fortunate to have the time. If I had the use of my limbs I'd probably be too busy rushing around doing other things to bother to listen and they would soon stop talking to me. As it is I have a tremendous amount of knowledge stored away which may be useful to me one of these days.' Sultana put her head on one side. 'That sounds like Lambros arriving.'

A bell had sounded faintly in the distance and the two women sat and waited until the priest entered the room. He appeared delighted to see Annita there again, couching his questions to her in such a way that he discovered the information he was seeking about her private life without arousing the curiosity of his sister. He scrutinized the new maid carefully and asked how she was progressing. Sultana offered him one of the crumbling pastries.

'This is her first attempt. I hope lunch will be better.'

Lambros licked the crumbs from his fingers. 'I hope it will be a little easier to eat, but I've no complaint with the lightness and flavour.'

'You remind me of my brother,' remarked Annita. 'He always finds something kind to say.'

'I always speak the truth.'

'So does Andreas,' Annita defended him.

Sultana rang her bell and requested that their dirty cups be cleared away and lunch be served promptly in thirty minutes. 'Now we'll see if Chariklia has remembered her promise.'

The minutes passed, the lunch was laid, and the three of them served when the door burst open. 'I didn't forget. It's not my fault I'm late. It's Elias. I couldn't drag him away. He was determined to turn the whole library upside down to find a book and I knew you'd included him for lunch so I insisted he came back with me.'

Sultana smiled indulgently at her daughter. 'Go and wash, dear. You're only a little late. I'm sure we can overlook that.' She turned to Annita as Chariklia left the room. 'I'm afraid they are all very bad about being anywhere on time. I was hoping

Elias would arrive before you left for the gallery, but I had my doubts that he would remember to come home for lunch.'

Annita smiled politely. She was not interested in meeting Sultana's son, and hoped she was not going to be embarrassed by his mother's attempts at match making. As he entered she did not take her eyes from her plate, and it was he who was completely taken aback.

'I don't believe it! Mamma, why didn't you tell me?'

'Tell you what, dear? Elias, this is Annita, Annita, my son, Elias.'

Annita extended her hand. 'We have met, but we've never been introduced.'

Elias touched her hand absentmindedly. 'This is the girl I was telling you about. The nurse who gave me the idea for the research and will never speak to me long enough for me to say thank you.'

'You!' Sultana and Chariklia chorused together.

Annita blushed. 'I'm not sure I know what you're talking about.'

'You must remember,' Elias turned on her. 'We met in a taverna and I knocked something over. When you left I walked with you and we talked about research. You suggested I tried to find a cure for leprosy.'

Annita's face reddened further. This could be very embarrassing for her and she could think of no way to extricate herself from the situation. 'Did I?' she replied evasively.

Elias seemed to notice nothing amiss. 'Well, I thought about it, read up on whatever I could, spoke to one of the doctors at the hospital. I couldn't believe it. Do you know,' he leaned forward on the table, almost knocking over his uncle's glass of water, 'since Hansen discovered the bacillus nothing has been done. People have studied the bacillus and talked about it, but there's no new medicine or treatment. Now I've been drawing up a paper...'

'Elias!' His uncle interrupted him sternly. 'I'm sure we're all very interested, but this is not a suitable conversation for the meal table. Your own lunch is getting cold. When the dishes have been cleared and if Annita is interested you may tell her then.'

Annita drew breath thankfully. She would make some excuse after the meal and never return to this apartment.

'I thought we were going to the gallery,' she reminded Chariklia.

'We shall, but Elias can talk whilst I draw you. You promised I could.'

'Yes, yes, I did.' There was not going to be any easy escape.

She sat patiently, obeying Chariklia's instructions. Elias talked continually, describing the paper he was writing which he hoped would convince the medical authorities that his ideas were worth investigating. Despite herself Annita found she was listening with interest.

'Do you think they will accept it?' she heard herself ask.

'I hope so. I want to do research more than anything else and this seems so worthwhile. Everyone has ignored the potential because it seemed so difficult. They knew they'd never get recognition in their lifetime, if ever. I wanted to be world famous and I'd thought along the same lines until you spoke to me. Now it doesn't seem to matter about being famous. I just want to do something to help. Do you know how they live in the hospital?'

'I don't want to.'

Elias ignored her reply. 'Being a nurse it would interest you. They believe that isolation is the best thing and hardly anyone goes near them. Food and water is sent in to them and their bodies thrown into an incinerator when they die. They're not even considered worth nursing, now I think that if...' Elias did not finish his sentence; Annita had fallen forward in a faint.

She recovered consciousness to find Elias chaffing her hands gently and Chariklia holding a vinegar rag under her nose. Sultana was advising loosening her blouse and opening a window.

'I'm so sorry,' she managed to murmur.

'Don't move,' Chariklia ordered. 'I'll bring you a glass of water.'

'No, really, I'm all right now.' She lifted her head, hoping her words were true.

'I'm terribly sorry,' Elias looked most contrite. 'I'd no idea that speaking about the conditions would upset you. I thought being a nurse...'

Annita managed to smile at his distress. 'It had nothing to do with you,' she lied. 'I'd been sitting too long in one position.'

Relief showed on his face. 'You mustn't let Chariklia keep you so long. She doesn't realise how bad it is to sit still for long stretches.'

Sultana was regarding her with curiosity. 'Come over here, my dear, and sit in a different chair for a while. We'll have a little wine. That will help your recovery.'

Annita obeyed, allowing Elias to hold her elbow as she walked the few steps to the easy chair. 'I feel so embarrassed,' she said.

'No need at all. It can happen to anyone. I don't think you should go to the gallery today, though. It would be best to stay here quietly for the rest of the afternoon, then Elias can escort you home.'

'Oh, no, that won't be necessary,' Annita assured her.

'I shall insist. Here's Chariklia. I've told Annita you'll not be going to the gallery today. She'll stay for the afternoon, but no more sketching of her today, please.'

Chariklia handed Annita a glass of water. 'When you feel better we could go to my room and look at some books or chat, unless you'd rather stay here and play backgammon or chess?'

'I'm afraid I play neither.'

'Would you like to learn?'

From politeness Annita said she had always wished to learn chess and immediately wished she had said no.

'Elias will teach you. He's very good.'

The board, beautifully inlaid with different coloured woods was taken from the cupboard and silver chess men laid out.

'I've never seen anything so beautiful,' exclaimed Annita.

'It was Pappa's,' Chariklia dismissed the admiration. 'I'll watch whilst Elias teaches you, then I'll play you. I'm not very good, so that will be fair.'

Annita had a suspicion that Chariklia would prove excellent at the game, but sat listening whilst Elias instructed her about the moves. She began to find the game intriguing and forgot her earlier dislike of the young man. He was a good teacher, explaining procedures simply and patiently, often two or three times before she fully grasped the idea. The afternoon passed quickly and Annita was surprised when the maid entered and asked how many there would be for the evening meal and at what time it was to be served.

Annita rose. 'I should go.'

'Not at all. I insist that you stay, unless, of course, you have another engagement.'

'I impose upon your hospitality too much,' protested Annita.

'Nonsense. I know how lonely it can be to live in one room in a strange town. I'd be only too pleased if you came more often. Look upon us as your family in Athens, besides, you've not met Aspasia.'

Annita smiled. 'I'm very grateful to you. I have met Aspasia, very briefly. She and Elias were on their way to the theatre.'

'And you refused to join us,' Elias reminded her.

'I didn't know you.'

Elias shook his head at her. 'I hope you'll not refuse the next time I ask you.'

Annita shrugged and refused to answer. 'Tell me more about the paper you're writing.' She felt obliged to show an interest.

'Are you sure? It won't upset you?' Elias glanced at her keenly.

Annita shook her head. This time she would be prepared. Elias talked, much of what he said she did not understand, and after a while she ventured to ask for explanation.

'I'm a nurse, remember, not a chemist. I understand what you're saying most of the time, but the long words confuse me.'

Elias grinned and drew a piece of his sister's drawing paper towards him. 'Look, this is what Hansen discovered,' his pencil flew rapidly over the paper. 'Now this is the tuberculin bacillus, see how alike they are? Now we know tuberculosis responds to fresh air, a healthy diet, rest and good nursing. By the look of the two bacilli they are related. No one has tried the same treatment for leprosy. I'm not saying it would work, because no one has examined the two together to see whether it's a superficial relationship or a basic one. If it's superficial then it's doubtful that the same treatment would give any response, but it would be something eliminated. Elimination is just as important when you're planning to investigate over a long period of time.'

'Why has no one examined them together and compared them?'

'A number of reasons. Few people are willing to take samples from lepers, or even deal with samples under laboratory conditions. Samples refuse to grow outside the body, and even if they did you'd have to continually collect new ones for comparison. There's the age old superstition that leprosy sufferers have been afflicted because they've sinned.'

'That's rubbish,' Annita replied sharply. 'Yannis...' She stopped in horror.

'Yannis?'

'A boy I was at school with. He was far too young to have committed any sins.'

'He's a leper?'

'Yes.' Annita's throat constricted with emotion.

'Is he here?'

'No.'

'That's a shame.'

'Why?'

'It could be easier to get into the hospital if you knew someone there.'

'What are you talking about?'

Elias leant his elbows on the table. 'If they accept my paper, and if they give me a grant for research, I'll want to go into the hospital for samples. I thought if there was someone there that you knew it might be easier to persuade the authorities. The patients can be pretty violent. About eighteen months ago they had a full scale riot.'

Annita felt her eyes brimming with unshed tears. 'I expect they had good reason.'

'I agree, but it was somewhat hard on those who work there. They were just doing their job; it's the authorities that are responsible for the conditions. If I could find out how leprosy is caught that might help.' Elias' eyes were shining with enthusiasm.

'How does your mother feel about you researching something that could be dangerous?'

'My mother is a very unusual woman,' Elias lowered his voice. 'I'll tell you about her some time. She's a great philanthropist, so would naturally approve. She's also a fatalist, so will accept whatever we decide to do with our lives. Aspasia wishes to become an actress and mother has agreed.'

'An actress?' Annita's eyes opened wide in horror. Only the lowest of women considered the stage as a career.

Elias laughed at her horror. 'I told you mother was an unusual woman. I also know that no breath of scandal will ever touch Aspasia, mother will see to that. We've time for another game before supper if you wish.'

Annita agreed to play. Strangely she felt more relaxed in the apartment with Elias there. Aspasia arrived before the game of chess had finished, showing no surprise to see Annita. She insisted that her mother delayed their meal until the game of chess was finished; assuring them she needed to wash and change her clothes before she sat down at the table.

The meal was more informal and amusing than the lunch had been. Annita was not sure whether it was relieved by the presence of Aspasia or the absence of Lambros. Aspasia described her day, mimicking conversations between her and others, much to Annita's amusement. As soon as she felt she could make her excuses, she did so. She preferred to walk home before it was too late, as she would have to be up early for work the next day. Elias insisted on accompanying her and for a while they walked in silence.

'Will you come and have coffee with me?' Elias broke in on her thoughts.

'When?'

'Now. I'd like to talk to you without my family around.'

Annita eyed him dubiously.

'Truly. I only want to talk to you.'

'All right, but I don't want to be too late home. I do have to be up early.'

Elias took her elbow and steered her gently into the nearest taverna and ordered a bottle of wine.

'I thought we were having coffee?'

'Wine would be more exciting. You may have coffee if you wish, but that would mean I had to drink a whole bottle of wine myself and then I'd probably be drunk. Mamma would not approve of that!'

'Tell me about your mother.'

'She's quite a character. She grew up in an orphanage, her and uncle. I gather it was pretty grim. Anyway, when she was old enough she left and took any job that brought her in enough money to live. She even managed to save a little, she knew her brother wanted to be a priest and she was determined to provide for him as well. She was lucky, I suppose. She managed to get a place as a cleaner with an old lady. Her family came to visit her and they had a son a little older than Mamma. He fell in love with her and rescued her from drudgery,' he ended dramatically.

'It sounds like a fairy story.'

'It was no fairy story. They met opposition all the way. She was dismissed and the family went back to their estates. Luckily for Mamma she wasn't a passing fancy and Pappa managed to find her. His father threatened to disinherit him, but he still defied him. They were married and lived very humbly in a tiny, one-roomed apartment. The family didn't speak for years, not until Grandpa was dying was he prepared to forgive my Pappa.'

'That is so sad.'

Elias shrugged. 'He made up for it. He left Pappa the apartment block where we live. It would have been very nice if he'd left him his money as well, but he'd gambled that away. Still, Mamma has enough to live on quite comfortably. She has the rents from the other apartments.'

'How did your Pappa die?'

'It was an accident. Mamma and Pappa were travelling by train and there was a derailment. Pappa died at once and Mamma was trapped for hours by her legs. That's why she's bedridden.'

There were tears in Annita's eyes as he finished. 'How awful.'

'It may explain Mamma to you. She's never forgotten the days when she was poor and miserable. She always takes in a girl from the orphanage and when she's finished training her she passes her on to her friends in the hope that she will make a good marriage. She believes it's very important to be happy whilst you can. You never know when happiness can be snatched away.'

Tears ran down Annita's face.

Elias gulped with embarrassment. 'I'm sorry. I would never have told you if I'd thought it would upset you so much.' He handed her his handkerchief.

'I'm just being silly,' Annita excused herself. 'I've probably had too much wine.' Her glass stood, barely touched.

Elias shook his head. 'You're just soft hearted. I hadn't even meant to talk about Mamma. I wanted to talk about us.'

'Us?' Annita stiffened.

Elias nodded. 'I don't expect you to make a decision straight away, but I'd like you to think about it.' A cold fear seemed to be gripping Annita's heart. 'When I've presented my paper, and if I'm given a grant towards research would you help me?'

The taverna seemed to spin before Annita, so great was her relief. 'Of course,' she answered without considering for a moment. 'I'll talk to you about it any time you like.'

Elias shook his head. 'I don't mean just talk. I want you to work with me, be my assistant.'

'But I don't know anything about it.'

'You're a nurse. Chemistry is very simple. I can teach you how to take a sample from a pipette and place it on a slide to look at through a microscope, or how to grow a culture in a dish.'

'If it's that simple why do you need me, or anyone? You could manage on your own.'

Elias smiled. 'I shall do the thinking and the writing. I'll need someone to remind me when it's lunchtime. I lose track of time when I'm working.'

Absentmindedly Annita raised her glass and drained it. 'I still don't see why you've asked me.'

Elias refilled their glasses. 'Because I can talk to you; I don't mean just because you're a nurse you understand about disease and research. You're sensible. You listen and ask relevant questions, you think for yourself and you make me think.'

'You hardly know me.'

'My mother's a very good judge of character.'

Elias laughed at the look of surprise on her face. 'I told her about meeting you and the way you had talked about research. When I discussed the idea with her she said 'Find that nurse. She's the right one to help you.' She had no idea it was you, I don't think she'd even met you then.'

Annita sipped at the wine slowly. 'I'll think about it. It's a big step to take. It would mean giving up nursing.'

'You could always go back to nursing if you weren't happy

working with me,' offered Elias. 'Think about it seriously, Annita. Come and visit us again next week and let me know your decision.'

Annita read the letter she had received from her brother in horror. For Maria to have died whilst giving birth was unbelievable. Poor Anna. Annita could only imagine the distress her cousin must have felt when she was unable to do anything to help her sister. It would have been better had the baby died and Maria been saved. At least Babbis would still have his wife and Marisa her mother. She shook herself. That was a wicked thought. She would visit Father Lambros in his church and ask forgiveness; she could also speak to him about Elias's proposal that she gave up nursing and worked as his assistant.

Father Lambros was comforting as always. 'Of course you will have forgiveness for a very natural thought. I'm sure her poor husband and parents have thought the same. We cannot go against God's will, but sometimes it can be difficult for us to see his purpose.'

Annita bent her head as he blessed her. 'Thank you, Father. There is something else I should like to talk to you about.'

Father Lambros folded his hands across his paunch and sat back on the chair, listening carefully as Annita told him Elias's hopes for the future and his request to her.

Father Lambros smiled. 'I see no great problem there. Elias does not know if his paper will be accepted or if he will be given a grant for research. I suggest you talk to him and become familiar with his research and what he would expect of you. If you then have to make a decision in the future you will be in a better position to do so if you are aware of all the implications. Don't worry your head about that now. There is plenty of time before Elias will know the result of his application.'

Babbis nursed his small son without a great deal of pleasure and

Marisa cast a sidelong look at her father. Something had happened that was beyond her comprehension. Her mother had disappeared, however much she asked for her she did not return. Her father no longer smiled and played with her and even her grandmother alternated between excessive affection and exasperation at her exploits. She walked into the kitchen where Anna was preparing the customary Sunday lunch.

'I want Mamma,' she announced.

Anna wiped her hands and crouched down on a level with the child. 'I know you do. We would all like your Mamma here, but it can't be. Mamma has gone to Heaven.'

'Where's Heaven?'

'I'm not sure where it is, but I know she will be very happy there.'

'Can I go to Heaven to be with her?'

Anna shook her head. 'You can only go to Heaven when God calls you. You have to stay here and look after your Pappa and baby brother.'

'Don't want to!' Marisa's lip trembled. 'I want Mamma.'

Anna felt tears coming to her eyes. How did you explain to such a young child? 'You have to be very grown up and understand that is what your Mamma would want. She would want you to be a good girl for your Pappa and grandmother and love your little brother.'

'If I'm good will Mamma come back?'

Anna shook her head. 'She's not able to come back. I'm sure she's watching you and loving you lots and lots. She'll love you even more when she sees how brave you are.'

'What's 'brave'?'

'Being brave is smiling for your Pappa, giving him a big kiss when he comes in from the fields, and not asking for your Mamma all the time. Go and give your Pappa a kiss now. Baby Yannis is far too small to give him a kiss and you are his favourite little girl.'

Anna straightened up and watched with relief as Marisa went into the living room to her father. She stood by his side and looked at the baby, then reached up and kissed her father's cheek. She stood by his side as he stroked her hair and she reached out an exploratory hand to investigate her brother.

1932 – 1937

Anna wrote a letter to Annita; still hardly able to believe the events she planned to relate to her cousin.

Dear Annita

We hope you are well. Mamma is the same. Little Yannis is quite good and sometimes he will sleep all night. Your Pappa comes to see us and sometimes brings Andreas. He says Stelios is enjoying school.

We had a surprise visitor last week. I was busy with little Yannis when Pappa told me that Yannis was in the stable. He had floated over from the island in a bathtub and then swum ashore. He wanted to see Mamma, but she didn't believe me when I told her. When I had washed her and she was sitting in her chair Pappa brought Yannis in. We all cried so much. He doesn't look like he used to. His skin is all knobbly up one side of his face but he says he feels well.

He sat and talked to Mamma for a long time, then when she was tired he told me all about the island. It sounds terrible over there, but Yannis says it is a lot better now. He said that Father Minos sends supplies over to them so they can repair their houses and the food is very good now. He said it was much worse when they were in the hospital and he wouldn't want to go back there. A doctor from Aghios Nikolaos goes over every week to see them and makes sure they have clean bandages and disinfectant.

He didn't know about Maria until Andreas managed to get a letter over to him. I think he was very touched that the baby had been called Yannis after him and Pappa. He looked at him, but wouldn't touch him. He had thought it was Maria waving to him as I had the baby in my arms. When he said that he remembered he had promised one of the women on the island that he would ask me to wave so that she would know he had arrived safely. I asked if she was his girl, but he said she was just a friend.

Whilst I was waving a fisherman came by and asked if I had seen anyone around. The bathtub Yannis had used had been found and they were searching for him. I rushed back and told Yannis and he went up into the fields to say goodbye to Pappa and Yiorgo. Pappa insisted he hid under some grass on the cart and Yiorgo took him to Aghios Nikolaos.

Before they reached Elounda they were stopped and Yiorgio was told that Yannis's foot was showing. Yannis insisted that he got off and walked the rest of the way. Pappa wasn't very pleased when Yiorgo told him but there was nothing he could do.

I went down the next day and waved as usual and someone waved back so I expect it was Yannis. I wish I could go over and see him. I'd like to see where he's living. Andreas has been over twice so I don't see why I can't go. I hope Yannis will be able to come over again and stay longer. I know Mamma would like that.

Please write to me when you have time.

Your loving cousin, Anna.

Yannis thought over what Babbis had told him about running more animals on his land. He knew Babbis was right when he said his stock needed new and younger blood. Three of the seven lambs that had been born had died and only half the ewes had conceived in the first place. The goats seemed to fare a little better, but only ten had given birth and two of them had been billies. One of them he had sent out to the island at Anna's pleading. She had pointed out that the goat sent originally would probably no longer be giving milk and unless she conceived again the islanders might as well put her in a stew.

He was not short of money; the payment he received for storing the crates that appeared regularly in his outhouses provided him with ample spare cash. He was more concerned about the future. The day would come when he was unable to work the land as he did now and Yiorgo had suggested on more than one occasion already that they employed a village boy to help them. He had turned the suggestion down out of hand. It was his land and whilst he was there he would work it the way he wanted.

For the first time he wished Anna was courting. If she were to marry her husband could be another useful hand. He sighed deeply. He did not envisage any young man asking for the hand of his daughter and taking on the responsibility of his invalid wife and his grandson. He wondered how much longer it would be before Babbis finally agreed that his mother could cope with little Yannis. Anna would be loath to give up the child now, but it could give her more opportunity to meet someone and have her own family.

He would have a look next Sunday whilst they were all at church and see if he could see anyone who might be suitable. In the meantime he must see Babbis and strike a bargain with him over the sheep and goats he had offered to sell to him. He wondered why Yiorgo hadn't suggested the idea to him earlier.

It took some weeks for Annita's reply to reach Anna and she opened the envelope eagerly. She read it through as quickly as she could to ensure there was nothing in the contents that could upset her mother, then settled herself down beside her.

'I've had a letter from Annita, Mamma. Shall I read it to you?'

Maria nodded. 'You can read it to your Pappa and Yiorgo later. They'll want to hear her news.'

Dear Anna and everyone at Plaka

I was so pleased to hear that Yannis had found a way to visit you, although I'm not sure it was very safe for him to float over in a bathtub. I don't know what the conditions are like in the hospital in Athens as I was not allowed to work there, but I'm sure he's right when he says he's happier living on the island. At least he can walk around outside and do as he pleases.

I was very upset when I received Andreas's letter saying Yannis was on the island. It appears that there was some trouble at the hospital and a number of them were sent over. I imagine they were the healthier ones so for Yannis to be amongst them is a good sign. I have tried to find out but I was told it was a government decision to try to contain the disease and stop it from spreading.

I write to Andreas regularly with my news and I have asked him to thank Yannis and consider myself no longer betrothed to him. Maybe he has met someone on the island, if so, I am very happy for him.

'He has his Phaedra,' murmured Maria.

'Do you really think so, Mamma?' asked Anna. 'He kept saying she was just a friend.'

Maria gave her lop-sided smile. 'I think she is a very special friend to him. What else does Annita say?'

I am giving up nursing in a month as I am going to start working with a microbiologist. Anna stumbled over the long and unaccustomed word. *He is researching into a cure for leprosy. I have known his family for a while now and they have been very kind to me. If I do not enjoy the work I can always return to nursing.*

Are you still looking after little Yannis? How is your Mamma?

Your cousin Annita

'Do you think she will find a cure for leprosy?' asked Anna. 'Wouldn't that be wonderful? Yannis would be able to come home.'

Maria nodded. 'He might not want to come back to the farm to live.'

Anna looked at her in surprise. 'Why ever not? It's his home.'

'Plaka would be too quiet for him now. He's used to having a lot of people around him and telling them what to do. I don't think he'd be content to work on the farm.'

Yannis glanced surreptitiously around the congregation in the tiny church. He could only see one bachelor that would be at all suitable as a match for his daughter. The other single men were either too young or too old. Davros was a possibility, not the kind of man who would have been his first choice, as Yannis was well aware that the man imbibed freely each week and could often be heard singing at the top of his voice as he made his way home from the taverna. He would visit the taverna himself that evening and try to sound the man out.

Yannis purchased a jug of wine and took it over to where Davros was sitting. 'May I join you?'

Davros shrugged by way of reply and moved his glass a little closer to him.

'Help yourself from the jug.' Yannis placed it within the man's reach.

Davros needed no second bidding and refilled his glass to the brim, smacking his lips as he leant forward and drew off a quantity of the liquid. 'Always tastes better when someone else is buying,' he grinned. 'What can I do for you?'

Yannis shrugged. 'Just saw you sitting alone and thought you might like company.'

Davros eyed him suspiciously. The man must want something. The villagers did not usually seek him out and buy him wine. They knew his reputation only too well.

'Game of backgammon?' suggested Yannis.

'Winner buys the next jug,' stipulated Davros, knowing full well that Yannis would beat him at the game easily.

'I'm not in practice these days. No one to play with. Yiorgo's not interested and Anna's too busy.'

'She's a good girl, your Anna.'

Yannis nodded soberly. 'Don't know how we would manage without her. I just hope no young man comes along and takes her fancy.'

'Don't know where they'd come from. There's no one hereabouts for her.'

Yannis pretended to consider. 'There are a couple of lads that would be suitable in a few years.'

Davros snorted. 'In a few years they'll be looking at girls their own age, not a middle aged woman.'

'She won't be middle aged. She's only twenty two now.'

'Looks older.'

'Looks aren't everything.'

'They go a long way with me. I went to Aghios Nikolaos the other week. You should have seen the girl I had there. A real looker and I doubt if she was more than sixteen. That's the way I like them.' Davros filled his glass again.

'Do you often go into town?'

'When I have the fancy.' Davros rubbed the side of his nose. 'Take what you want and no strings attached. Suits me.'

'If you were married you wouldn't need to go to town.'

Davros regarded the farmer scornfully. 'I'd still go up – probably more often – to get away from a nag and screaming brats. Don't see why anyone wants to get married. No need.'

'You've got a point there.' Yannis felt his heart sink. Not only had Davros no intention of getting married he was totally unsuitable for Anna. He was glad he had not mentioned the man to his daughter. 'Shall I get the board?'

'Yes, and another jug whilst you're at it.' Davros filled his glass yet again. This was going to be a good evening.

Anna contemplated the young man as he sat with his head in his hands across the table from her. It was a month now since he had returned to his home to find his mother lying dead on the kitchen floor. It was time he took himself in hand and thought of the children.

'Babbis', she spoke more sharply than she had intended and his head jerked up in surprise. 'Babbis, I have to talk to you.'

'Yes?'

'What are you planning to do?'

'Do?' he repeated stupidly after her.

'Babbis, you have two small children. You have to think of them. You have a farm that needs attention. You must pull yourself together. I know the death of your mother was a terrible shock, it was a shock to all of us, but you have to come to terms with it.'

For a moment Anna thought he was going to cry. 'What can I do? I can't look after the children, a house and a farm on my own. I need my mother.' He turned anguished eyes to her.

'You could get married again.'

Babbis shook his head. 'No one could take Maria's place.'

'If you sold the farm and moved to the town, maybe you would meet someone.'

Again Babbis shook his head. 'What would I do if I moved to the town? I'm a farmer.'

Anna tried again. 'What about the children?'

'I hoped you could look after them a little longer.'

'Babbis, I've had Yannis since he was born. He looks upon me as his mother and he's far more than a nephew to me. Looking after the children is no burden for me. It's you I'm concerned about.'

Babbis shrugged. 'I'll manage. I may go up tomorrow.'

Anna brought her fist down on the table with a force that made her wince. 'You will go up tomorrow. For days you've been saying maybe. If you don't go up tomorrow you'll find these doors barred against you.'

Babbis looked at his sister-in-law in surprise. 'You really mean that?'

'I mean it, Babbis. I'll come with you.'

Anna gazed after him as he left the room. Maybe she had been too hard on him. It was only a month after all.

Babbis looked around the kitchen of the deserted farmhouse. Dust was covering the shelves and floor, but not thickly enough to obliterate the rusty red mark where his mother's blood had laid congealing in a pool. He rubbed at it with his boot as though trying to remove the mark from his memory. From the kitchen he moved aimlessly up the stairs to the two bedrooms. His mother's clothes and meagre possessions would have to be thrown away. He picked up the apron that lay discarded on the chair and rubbed it between his fingers before throwing it to the floor in anger. Why had it happened? If only he had stayed with her when she had first complained of dizziness, instead of going for Anna, she would not have fallen and hit her head.

He returned to the lower floor and rummaged in the cupboard for the bottle of brandy he knew should be in there. Pulling the cork he placed the bottle to his lips and drank deeply. With a sigh of satisfaction he wiped his mouth with the back of his hand. He had needed that to calm him down. He took another mouthful of the liquid, savouring the taste as it flowed down his throat and began to course through his veins. He wondered what he should do first and took another pull at the bottle whilst he thought about it.

'That will do you a lot of good!' Anna stood there, her arms folded, looking at him in disgust.

'I was wondering where to start.'

'You can start by putting that back in the cupboard.' She took the bottle from his hand, replacing the cork and holding it up to the light to see how much remained. 'The kitchen,' she pointed. 'We'll need hot water so you'd better get a fire going and bring up a couple of buckets.'

Obediently Babbis did as she directed.

'Now go and dust off the furniture and sweep the floor. By the time you've done that the water should be hot enough for you to start scrubbing.'

Anna turned her attention to the food cupboard, wrinkling her nose as she opened it and the smell hit her with full force. It would all have to be thrown away. Methodically she removed everything that had grown a mould and wiped the shelf where it had stood. Babbis returned, a bucket of dirty water in his hand.

'Throw that out, get some clean and you can do the floor in here. I'm going upstairs.'

Critically she surveyed the two rooms. They needed dusting and the bedding would have to be washed. She stripped Babbis's bed, making a bundle by the door, then turned her attention to the mattress where Marisa had slept. They would take that back with them. It would mean she no longer had to share her mattress with Marisa. She struggled down the stairs with the mattress in her arms, then returned for the bedding.

'Babbis!' He was lounging against the doorway, the brandy bottle once more to his lips. 'I told you to leave that alone.'

'I've finished the floor.' His eyes challenged her to take the bottle away from him again.

'Then I need you upstairs. There's some turning out to be done. You'll have to tell me what you want to keep.'

Babbis shrugged. 'What's the point? Nothing will bring her back.'

'And getting drunk won't either. What would she have thought of you? You're not behaving like a man!'

Slowly Babbis removed the bottle from his lips and moved towards Anna. For a moment she thought he was going to hit her and shrank back in fear.

'I'll show you I'm a man.'

He twisted her long black hair round his hand and pulled her head backwards before kissing her hard on her lips. His free hand pulled at her blouse as he forced her back against the wall.

'No! Babbis! No!'

In vain she twisted and turned, trying to free herself from the vice-like grip that held her. As quickly as his passion had flared it abated and he released her, pushing her roughly out of his way. 'Get out,' he muttered. 'Get out and leave me alone.'

Thoroughly frightened Anna edged past him and through the open kitchen door. Once outside she took to her heels and fled across the fields towards her home.

Babbis returned from the farmhouse sometime later. He was bearing Marisa's mattress in his arms, but would not meet Anna's eyes when he offered to take it up the stairs. She thanked him briefly and laid the table for their meal, tending to her mother and fussing over the children before helping herself. She ate silently, wishing Babbis were not sitting there with them. Neither Yiorgo nor her father appeared to notice the strained atmosphere, Yannis waiting until she had cleared the table and brought in the coffee before lighting his pipe.

'Time for bed, Yannis. Go and say goodnight to your Pappa whilst I heat some water to give you a wash.'

Babbis took the small boy on his lap and ruffled his hair. He moved his cigarette to one side to avoid the boy's eyes with his smoke. 'Be a good boy. Sleep well. Pappa will see you tomorrow.'

Yannis kissed his grandparents and uncle before walking dutifully into the kitchen where he was subjected to Anna's nightly ablutions. In his nightclothes Anna carried him up the stairs and placed him on his small mattress. As she turned to go she caught her foot on Marisa's mattress and almost fell. She really would have to speak to her Pappa about more space.

When she returned to the living room Babbis rose from the table. 'Thank you for my meal, Anna. I'm going home tonight. May I come again tomorrow?'

Anna looked at him in surprise. 'Of course. You're always welcome, you know that.' Provided he was picking up the threads of a normal life again she meant her words. She was not prepared to have him sitting all day in their living room doing nothing.

Babbis nodded. 'I've spoken to your Pappa.'

Anna raised her eyebrows. She had only been gone for a few minutes, what had they talked about in her absence?

'Babbis has asked if the children can stay here indefinitely. Of course they can. He's offered to help us build on a bit at the back to make a bit more room. He said when he put Marisa's mattress into your room there's hardly a space between them.'

Anna smiled in relief. 'That would make a difference, Pappa. It would be better for the children to have their own room.'

'They can have Yiorgo's. He can sleep at the back when it's finished. When Stelios comes home he can share it with him.'

'Now Babbis has gone Yannis could sleep in with me now if it made it easier,' offered her brother. 'Just until we've built an extra room at the back.'

Anna hesitated. She needed the space, but how she would miss the small boy sleeping beside her. 'It would be a help, but suppose he woke in the night?'

'I could bring him in to you.'

'Suppose Babbis decides to come back to stay?'

'I don't think he will. He said he's made up his mind to go back to his farmhouse and make a life for himself there. He realises he can't live down here for ever.'

Elias sorted through his mail methodically. There was the usual collection of advertising material, urging him to try a new product which had been developed at great cost and would be no use in his line of research, an impassioned plea from a distraught mother, begging him to find a cure for her son and a couple of bills which he tossed aside for Annita to pay later in the day. He read again the woman's letter. Annita could compose a reply, telling her as gently as possible that there was no cure at present, but not to give up hope, then he opened the letter that bore an Italian stamp, guessing that it had come from his sister. He put it aside to read later and slit open the remaining letter from the pile, eying it suspiciously, then reading more attentively. He looked at the envelope again, it was certainly addressed to him, but the news it contained could hardly be believed. He was still gazing stupidly at the single sheet when Annita arrived in the laboratory.

'You're early,' she remarked, as she hung her shawl over her chair and picked up the bills Elias had left on her table, pulling a face as she saw the amounts. Elias did not answer her.

'What's wrong? Aren't you feeling well? Has one of the experiments failed completely?'

Elias shook his head. 'I've been offered a place at a hospital to do research.'

'That's marvellous! That means you'll be able to carry on when this grant runs out.'

'It's not here.'

'What do you mean?'

'It's in America.'

'America!' Annita felt her head reel. 'That's miles and miles away. When do you go?' She hoped her voice sounded normal, although Elias was too dazed to notice.

'I'm not sure. If I'm interested I have to reply within the month and they say they'll make arrangements.'

'I see. Shall I make some coffee?'

Elias nodded. He read the letter yet again. 'Do you think it's someone's idea of a joke?'

Annita did not answer. Her hand was shaking as she poured the strong brew and placed it on the table between them. She realised how much she would miss this young man she had worked so closely with for the past eighteen months, and she would miss the work that had engrossed her. She swallowed hard.

'Why don't you write and say that you might be interested if they could give you further details.' It was a delaying tactic and she knew it.

Elias frowned. 'It's the chance of a lifetime.'

Annita knew his mind was made up. 'I still think you should ask for more details. They may expect you to pay your own fare.'

Elias shook his head. 'Read it.'

Annita read slowly through the flattering words that commenced the letter until she finally came to the offer.

We would like to offer you a position at the above Hospital for an indefinite term to carry out your experiments regarding leprosy, the causes, effects and eventual cure, which we believe is within your grasp over the next few years given all the facilities that you need and unlimited finance. Your travelling expenses for yourself and your immediate family would be covered by ourselves, accommodation would be provided, with a monthly salary and a bonus to be paid when you find an effective treatment or cure.

Annita looked at him with wondering eyes. 'You're going to take it, aren't you?'

'I have to.' Suddenly his stupor seemed to have left him. 'This is what I've dreamed of. To be recognised. Given unlimited facilities and finance. We won't have to struggle any more, juggling the bills, wondering if we can afford another pipette. Think what it means, Annita.'

Slowly Annita nodded. 'I'm very pleased for you.'

'You don't sound it.' Elias's brow creased in a puzzled frown.

'I'm more pleased than I can ever tell you,' Annita spoke sincerely.

Elias smiled. 'America! Won't it be wonderful? We'll be able to travel and see everything we've only read about before. The Grand Canyon, New York, Red Indians; the list is endless.'

Despite her feelings Annita was forced to smile at his childish enthusiasm.

'Leave all this and let's go and tell my mother.' Without waiting for Annita to answer he grabbed her hand and began to pull her towards the door.

'You go,' she said. 'It's your news.'

'What's the matter? I thought you'd be delighted?'

'I am. I truly am for you.'

'Then what's wrong?'

'Nothing.'

'Annita, tell me the truth. I know you well enough by now and I can tell there's something wrong. Please, tell me.'

Annita avoided Elias's eyes. 'I shall just miss the work. I'd hoped to eventually find a cure with you.'

'We will.'

Annita shook her head. 'You will.'

'We both will. We'll still be working together.'

'By telepathy!'

'Don't be silly. You'll come with me.'

'How can I? It's an offer for you. Where would I find that kind of money?'

'You don't have to. It says they'll pay for my family.'

'I'm not your family.'

Elias ran a hand across his brow. 'Annita, I'm not saying this very well, but you have to come with me. I want you to come with me as my wife.'

Annita drew away from him, her hand going to the earrings that she always wore.

'I'm sorry. I shouldn't have sprung it on you like this. Come and sit down. I'd planned to ask you to marry me just as soon as we'd discovered a cure. I was so sure it wouldn't take long. Another year, maybe, then I would be able to afford to ask you. This was a complete surprise to me, but it means we could get married now. Please say you will, Annita. I can't take you with me unless we're married and I need you. I can't work without you.'

Annita drew a deep breath. 'I think you're exaggerating. Of course you could work without me. You could soon find another assistant in America.'

'I don't want another assistant.' Elias brought his fist down on the table. 'I want you, Annita, you and no one else. Let's go together to tell my mother.'

'You go, Elias. It's your news and I'd like to be alone for a while.'

'I shan't be long.' Elias took her hand and kissed it. 'I forgot to say that I love you.'

Annita waited until she was sure that Elias would be half way to his mother's house before she locked the door of the tiny laboratory and took to her heels, heedless of the other pedestrians as she pushed her way past them until she arrived at the church hoping to find Elias's uncle.

She leant in the doorway, gasping for breath and trying to compose herself before entering. Father Lambros looked up from his devotions and came to her.

'Whatever's wrong? Has there been an accident?'

Annita shook her head. She did not have enough breath to answer.

'Come inside,' he led her to a chair. 'Sit there until you've recovered.' He lowered his large bulk on to the chair next to her and waited.

At last Annita spoke. 'Elias has asked me to marry him.'

Father Lambros smiled. 'That does not come as any great surprise to me.'

Annita looked at him, her eyes moist with unshed tears. 'There's more than that. I shouldn't really tell you. It's his news.'

'Is he planning to tell me?'

'He's gone to tell his mother, so he's sure to tell you. He's so excited.'

'Then when he tells me I shall pretend not to have heard the news before.' Father Lambros smiled. 'You know you can confide in me.'

Annita smiled back at him. 'I've grown very fond of you, Father Lambros.'

'And I of you, my dear. I must admit I hoped Elias would eventually pluck up the courage to propose marriage.'

'He hasn't just asked me to marry him. He's been offered a research position at a hospital in America.'

'That's wonderful news.'

'Remember to be surprised when he tells you.'

'I will, but now let's talk about you. You're worried about going to America? I'm sure you have no need to be.'

'I'm not sure if I should marry Elias.'

'Why not? Do you have no feelings for him?'

'I don't know. I was very young and innocent when I was betrothed to my cousin. I knew nothing of life. I thought I loved Yannis and I was terribly upset and unhappy when I found out he was ill. My brother brought me a message from him when he visited the island. Yannis said I was to forget him.' Annita's eyes brimmed with tears. 'I don't know if I love Elias. I can't imagine what it would be like to work without him. When we have visited the theatre or been out for a meal I have enjoyed myself and been sad that the evening couldn't last longer. We talk, we laugh, we tease each other, but does that mean we love each other?'

Father Lambros laced his fingers together. 'Only you can decide whether you love my nephew. You are good friends and you work well together. How do you feel when you say goodbye each evening? Are you pleased to go back to your room on your own or would you prefer to spend the night with Elias? If Elias kissed your mouth would you shrink away from him or kiss him back? Would you be happy to lay in his arms, to be the mother of his children?'

Annita's face was reddening as Father Lambros spoke.

'You have to ask yourself these questions. Only then can you give Elias an answer. Maybe you could visit your parents, so that you have the time and space to think.'

'I would like to see them again. I keep saying I'll go and I haven't done so.'

'Then tell Elias that you need a little time to make your decision and go home for a while.'

Annita sat in the tiny living room of the fisherman's cottage where she had spent so much of her life. It was large by comparison with her room in Athens, but with the double bed in the corner and the adults grouped around the table there was little room to move. Her parents had been delighted to see her and they had wanted to know every detail of her life in Athens and also a description of the city.

'Would we be able to go up to Plaka one day whilst I'm here?' asked Annita. 'I'd like to see my aunt and uncle again.'

'Of course. Fancy coming all this way and not visiting them. We could go tomorrow.'

Annita shook her head. 'Not tomorrow. I want to spend some time walking around the town. I want to remember what Aghios Nikolaos is really like. I've been away for years. There must have been considerable changes.'

'Would you like me to ask for a day off to come with you?' asked Andreas.

Annita shook her head. 'I'm not likely to get lost, besides I want a bit of time on my own, just to wander around and relax.'

'You've been working too hard.' Elena shook her head at her daughter. 'That man you work for should give you more time off. You say you're often there until quite late in the evening. It's too much for you.'

'Everything is so interesting and Elias likes me to take notes as he goes along so he doesn't forget the procedure. He's very meticulous. I have to write everything he says down quickly, then when I have the chance I copy them out so he can read them easily and I have to make sure they go into the correct file. If he's in the middle of an experiment or waiting for the results we just go on working and tend to forget the time.' Annita spoke with enthusiasm.

'So when is he going to find a cure?' asked Elena.

'Oh, Mamma, who knows? Even when he does it will take some years for him to prove it and have it accepted by the medical authorities.' For no obvious reason Annita blushed. 'Tell me your plans, Stelios.' She turned to her cousin who was lodging with her parents whilst he attended school in Aghios Nikolaos. 'How much longer do you have here before you go to Heraklion?' She wanted to avoid further questions about Elias and their work that evening.

Anna and Annita sat out in the yard, leaving Elena to talk to Maria and Yiorgo to walk up to the fields for a quiet word with Yannis. Anna looked at her cousin curiously. 'What made you come over to visit your parents?'

Annita dropped her eyes to her tightly clasped hands. 'I wanted some time to myself to think. I've a big decision to make.'

'Are you coming home?'

Annita shook her head. 'I'm thinking of getting married.'

'Married!' Anna gasped. 'But you can't marry Yannis.'

Annita twisted her fingers. 'I know. I think I've known that since he was first diagnosed, but wouldn't admit to myself. I went off to Athens convinced I would be able to nurse him and at least see him. I was unhappy in Athens on my own. It was so lonely. Then Andreas wrote to me and told me Yannis had been sent to the island and I was released from our betrothal agreement. I didn't know what to do. It was then that I met Elias. We'd met by chance and he'd talked to me about the research he planned to do. He wanted to meet me again, but I refused. I bumped into him one day when I was out and went into a church to get rid of him.' Annita gave a small smile. 'I must have been guided into that church. It's very tiny and I'd never even noticed it before. It's tucked away in a back street.'

'And a voice told you to marry him.' Anna spoke sceptically.

Annita shook her head. 'The priest came and asked if he could help me. I just began to cry and finally I told him all about Yannis. He didn't say any of the usual things about time being a healer and you'll get over him and meet someone else. He asked me to visit his sister; he made it sound like a favour to him and wouldn't listen to any of the excuses I made. She made me feel so welcome and insisted I stayed for lunch. She made me promise to visit her again the next week on my day off. I met one of her daughters that day. She's an art student and asked if she could draw me.'

Anna raised her eyebrows. 'Why did she want to do that?'

'According to Sultana, that's her mother, she always asked anyone who visited. In some of her sketches I looked quite pretty and very different, depending how she had arranged my hair.' Annita smiled at the memory. 'Anyway, I went back the next week as she was going to take me to an art gallery. I wasn't sure I was going to enjoy it, but it would have been rude to refuse after all their kindness to me. Her son joined us for lunch that day and it was Elias. He talked about his research into leprosy...'

'Why is he researching leprosy? Everyone knows it's incurable.'

Annita blushed. 'When we talked the first time I suggested it to him: to research to find the cause and maybe a cure. He took me seriously, applied to the hospital and was given a grant. He asked me to give up nursing and work as his assistant.'

'You wrote and told me that.'

Annita nodded. 'I know I did. I just wanted you to know how it happened. The work is fascinating. One day we appear to have made a breakthrough, then within a week all the experiments have failed and we have to start again. It's far more interesting than nursing. I don't set up the experiments, of course. I just prepare whatever he wants and take notes about the results. I also remind him to pay the bills and when to have lunch!' Annita smiled to herself. 'He gets so engrossed in what he's doing that if I didn't stop him he would be there all night. He had a letter a couple of weeks ago, from America. They've asked him to go and research for a cure over there.'

'You're going to America?' Anna's voice was awed.

'If I marry him I will. That's what I have to decide.'

'Do you love him?' asked Anna.

Annita hesitated. 'I think so. I can't bear the thought of being without him. We've worked so closely together.'

'What do you mean – you think so?'

Annita shrugged. 'I thought I loved Yannis. I'm sure I did in a way. Having heard that I was to be his wife eventually made me want to love him, but now I look back I wonder if I was more in love with the idea of being betrothed and married than I was with Yannis. Do you know what I mean?'

Anna shook her head. She had never had to cope with the tumultuous and unpredictable emotions that seemed attached to the word love.

'What do your parents think?'

'I haven't told them yet. I wanted to talk to you. Do you think I'm wrong to want to marry someone other than Yannis?'

Anna swallowed the lump that had come into her throat. 'I suppose not – under the circumstances.'

'You don't think I'm wicked or wanton or anything like that?' asked Annita anxiously.

Anna considered. 'No. If you were married to Yannis and living here with him and wanted to go off with someone else then you would be wicked.'

'So you understand? You don't hate me?'

'Of course I don't hate you. How could I? You're my cousin. I just wish things had been different – for Yannis's sake.'

Annita nodded. 'So do I. I'd do anything to make him well again.' She frowned. 'I'm going to ask Pappa to take me over to Spinalonga when we leave here. I have to try to see him and speak to him. Do you think he'll understand?'

'I'm sure he will.' Anna spoke more positively than she felt. She hoped her brother would accept that having released Annita from her betrothal agreement she was almost certain to meet someone else and marry.

Annita sat in her father's boat, her knuckles showing white where her hands were clenched so tightly.

'You're sure, Annita?' asked her father and she nodded silently.

The visit to her relatives at Plaka had been enjoyable. Anna had been delighted to see her cousin, taking as much pride in showing off Marisa and Yannis as if they were her own children. Feeling that she had Anna's blessing on her decision to marry Elias she was now determined to face up to the inevitable.

Yiorgo sailed as close as possible to Spinalonga before he dropped anchor and cupped his hands to his mouth. 'Find Yannis,' he called to the girl who was sitting on the jetty.

Flora looked at him in surprise and ran up the path. There must be a new sufferer arriving, maybe one of Yannis's family as they had asked for him, rather than leaving them on the quay to find their own way up to the village.

Yannis followed Flora down to the jetty, rubbing his cement caked hands down his trousers. The authorities must have found someone hiding and he prayed desperately that it was no one he knew.

He shielded his eyes and looked at the fishing boat moored a short distance away. He squinted to focus more clearly. It was his aunt and uncle; the woman standing in the prow must be Annita. Surely she had not contracted the disease. He felt his heart constrict. Life was just too cruel.

They looked at each other in silence across the water, then Annita raised her hand. 'Goodbye, Yannis,' she called, then turned and stumbled her way back to the stern of the boat. 'Can we go, please, Pappa?'

Yiorgo hauled the anchor aboard and took the oars. As the boat drew away from the island he raised his hand to Yannis who waved back. They were too far away to see the puzzled frown creasing Yannis's forehead.

Elena pulled her daughter close as her tears fell and deep shuddering sobs racked her body. She could think of no words to comfort her. Finally Annita quietened and by the time they had reached Aghios Nikolaos her composure had returned.

'Thank you, Pappa. I had to go.' She turned and walked away from the harbour.

Elena made to follow her, but Yiorgo placed a hand on his wife's arm. 'Leave her. She needs to be alone.'

Annita returned to the house late in the afternoon, she seemed relaxed and at peace with herself but her mother regarded her anxiously.

'When will Pappa be home?' asked Annita.

'Quite soon, I expect. Why?' Elena had a horrible suspicion that her daughter was going to ask to be taken out to the island again.

'I want to talk to you both.'

'You could talk to me now.'

Annita shook her head. 'I'll wait until Pappa comes.'

Elena looked at her daughter and shook her head. 'America! That's the other side of the world!'

'I know, Mamma, but I've made up my mind. I'm going with Elias.'

'But we don't know him, or his family,' protested Elena.

'I'm sure you'll like him.'

'Why didn't he come over with you? He should have met your father and asked him properly.'

'He understood that I needed to come alone; besides, I haven't told him that I'll marry him yet. He's very busy trying to get everything organised. I hope he's remembered to go to the

American Embassy. I put it on his list, but he's probably lost that by now.'

'Andreas could marry you.' Yiorgo spoke for the first time since Annita had broken her news.

Annita shook her head. 'We have to get married in Athens. There is no way his mother could travel over here. You and Mamma can come to Athens easily by ferry.'

'Where would we stay?' Elena was both excited and daunted by the prospect.

'Elias would arrange a small hotel for you. Pappa could buy a new suit whilst he's there and we could go shopping and I can show you the city. You will come, won't you?'

Yiorgo nodded. 'Of course, if only to inspect this young man and make sure he's suitable.'

Annita arrived back in Athens looking tired, but happy. Her first visit was to Father Lambros who greeted her joyfully.

'How are you, my dear? Did you have a good trip?'

'I enjoyed seeing my parents and brother,' she smiled.

'And?'

'And Aghios Nikolaos seemed very small compared with Athens.'

'I'm sure it did. Has it changed very much?'

'Not a great deal. I still felt it was my home. Father, why are we talking like strangers?'

'Because I don't want to pressurize you in any way. You have a very big decision to make and it has to be your own, not one I've talked you into.'

'My parents took me to visit my relatives in Plaka and then on to Spinalonga. Yannis came down to the jetty. I know that if I did stay here there is no way we could be together, even if we still wanted to be. Each time I thought of Elias I felt so lonely. As though,' she struggled for the words, 'as though a part of me was with him. I kept asking myself if that meant I loved him and I'm still not sure, but I've decided I have to marry him.'

Father Lambros embraced Annita. 'I am so pleased you have come to that decision. I believe you do love him; you have just not given your heart a chance to experience the feeling. If you go with Elias you will be helping Yannis far more than you ever could by staying here out of a sense of loyalty to him. The work you and my nephew are doing is so valuable, so essential, that one day Yannis will thank you from the bottom of his heart.'

Yiorgo looked out at the city of Athens from the window of the cab. Had he known how vast and busy the city was he would never have allowed Annita to leave Crete. He had envisaged the city as being similar in size to the town of Heraklion, which he had visited a couple of times and now he was disillusioned.

'Do you know where we are?' he asked Annita.

She shook her head. 'No idea. I've only been down this way to get to the ferry. This is only the outskirts, wait until you see the real centre, Pappa.'

Elena was completely over-awed when they drew up in the main square before a large hotel. 'I can't go in there! The man at the door is wearing a uniform. Is he a police man?'

Annita smiled at her. 'Don't worry. You're staying round the corner in a much smaller establishment. We have to get out here as you're not allowed to drive down that road.'

Yiorgo picked up the new suitcase Annita had insisted he bought, knowing how embarrassed they would have been to arrive with their possessions in a sack, and followed his daughter down into the side road.

'What do we do?' he asked, never having been in a hotel before in his life.

'You'll be given a key and shown up to your room. I'll come with you.' She had accompanied Elias when he had booked the room for her parents and felt quite confident. 'They'll show you where the bathroom is and which room you go to for your breakfast. When you're settled I'll go and meet Elias and then we'll both come back to take you out for a meal.'

Elena clutched at her husband's hand as she followed Annita and Elias through a bewildering maze of side streets. She gasped and pointed as they rounded a corner and the Parthenon came into view.

'It's just like the pictures Yannis showed me.' She stopped and blushed with confusion.

'It's all right, Mamma. Elias knows about Yannis. I also asked Andreas to get a message to Yannis to tell him about Elias, so there are no secrets. You can take a walk up there tomorrow and look at it properly if you want. You'll really see how big Athens is then. The city is spread out before you like a book.'

Elena looked doubtful. She did not think it would be advisable for them to leave the hotel without Annita to show them their way, as they would be certain to be lost in no time. 'Maybe you could come with us?' she suggested.

'If Elias can spare me for the morning. We have an awful lot to do. I'm trying to get all his notes in order and packed ready for shipping. I've promised Aspasia that I'll shorten her dress ready for Saturday and I have to collect Elias's suit and goodness knows when I'll fit everything in.'

'I could shorten his sister's dress,' offered Elena. 'It would be one less job for you.'

'Really? Thank you, Mamma. You'll do a far better job than I will. I've only picked up a needle to sew a button on over the last few years.'

'Don't you do your embroidery?'

Annita shook her head. 'I don't have time now. Elias and I are either working or out in the evenings.'

Elena sighed. Obviously life in Athens was very different from Aghios Nikolaos.

By the end of the week both Elena and Yiorgo were exhausted.

Annita had spent most of each day with them, taking them to the famous sites, a brief visit to the museum as she sensed that neither were particularly interested in the objects displayed, shopping and visiting Elias's mother had taken up the rest of their time. Elena had delighted in the shops and Yiorgo had suffered being fitted with a suit. Yiorgo had shown little interest in either the shops or the sites he had been shown until he had discovered the fish market. To Annita's amusement he had spent a long time examining all the stalls, running with water as the ice around the fish melted, and would continually pick up a fish and examine it for freshness.

The smell was almost over-powering and Annita was relieved when he finally declared he was ready to leave. She was feeling sick and her legs were damp where a woman carrying a fish had continually slapped it against her legs as they walked around. She longed to return to her tiny room, have a shower, wash her hair and change into some clean clothes.

Now she clung to her mother as her parents waited to board the ferry.

'I'll write to you every week, Mamma,' she promised. 'Andreas can read the letters to you.'

Elena wiped the tears from her eyes. 'You're happy, Annita? Really happy with Elias and about going to America? You could always come back with us now.'

'I want to go, Mamma. Elias needs me. We have our work together.'

Yiorgo eyed his daughter doubtfully. He would have felt happier if she had declared her love for the young man she had married two days earlier. If she only cared for him because of the work they were engaged in he saw little future happiness for either of them.

Yiorgo cleared his throat. 'Take care. Don't forget we're here if you need us.'

'Thank you, Pappa. Thank you for everything.' Annita hugged

her father tightly. He had insisted on paying the hotel bill, all the wedding expenses and given her a generous dowry.

Anna listened to her aunt and uncle avidly as they described Annita's wedding and their visit to Athens. She wished she had been able to go with them. An invitation to accompany them had been offered, but she had turned it down immediately.

'I can't possibly leave Mamma. There are also the children to consider. Marisa isn't old enough to look after her grandmother and her brother.'

Elena had refrained from mentioning that their father could well have looked after them for a week and that Yannis was quite capable of looking after his invalid wife.

Elena produced a photograph of Annita on the arm of her new husband, smiling up at him.

'She looks very happy,' she managed to say, the lump in her throat choking her. It should have been her brother Yannis in the photograph. 'Are they really going to America?'

'They sail next week. It will take them almost two weeks to get there. Imagine being out on the sea all that time – no land anywhere. I'm frightened there will be a storm and the ship will sink and we'll never hear from her again.' Tears came to Elena's eyes.

Yiorgo patted her shoulder. 'I've told you. They're not going in a fishing boat. The ship they'll travel in will be bigger than the ferry. They'll be just as safe as if they were on the land.' Yiorgo spoke far more confidently than he felt. He, too, was worried about the journey his daughter was to make.

'I understand the ships go back and forth all the time, so it must be safe. Did Andreas enjoy his visit to Athens?'

Elena shook her head. 'No, he hated the city. Said it was far too big and noisy. I think he was relieved that he was only able to come for two days. He enjoyed meeting Elias's uncle, Father Lambros. They talked for hours together. Father Lambros even suggested that he went over to mainland Greece to work as a priest. Apparently there are plenty of opportunities over there, but Andreas refused. He said he was a Cretan and he planned to stay here.'

It was eight weeks before Yiorgo called again at the farmhouse with the news that Annita had arrived safely in America. He waved her letter at Anna. 'I brought her letter so you could read it for yourself.'

Anna took it from him. 'I'll read it to Mamma, if you don't mind.'

Yiorgo had no objection. It would give him the opportunity to hear what his daughter had to say yet again. There was a limit to the number of times he could ask Andreas to read it to him, although by now he knew it by heart.

Dear Mamma, Pappa and Andreas

This is just a short letter to let you know that we have arrived safely and are well. The journey across the sea seemed to take a long time. Some days it was quite rough, but I was not sick. Elias was sick for almost a week, but he has never been on a boat before.

We stayed in a hotel for the first three days after we arrived. The people here seem very nice. They said that after such a long journey we should rest before we went on to New Orleans. We then travelled for four days by train as America is such a big country.

I have not had time to see very much of the town yet as I have been busy making sure everything is in order for Elias to start his work next week. I have also had to go shopping and I am not sure how to cook some of the things I see in the shops. There is a lady next door who is being very helpful to me.

It seems even hotter here than it is in Athens in the summer. I had not expected that.

I will write to you again next week.

Your loving daughter, Annita.

Yiorgo beamed. 'I told Elena that everything would be all right and they would arrive safely. She was sure they were going to sink in the middle of the ocean.'

Anna shook her head in admiration. 'I think Annita is very brave. First she goes to Athens on her own and now all the way to America with her new husband.'

Letters from Annita arrived regularly for her parents. Her description of her life with Elias in America was far more vivid and humorous than any of her letters had been from Athens. She described her apartment and the part of the town where they lived, told them how foolish she felt when she had tried to buy something from the grocer by pointing and using sign language and then he had spoken to her in Greek.

Elias was attending classes for the language and Annita had asked to be included. When the hospital had demurred she had pointed out that she was his assistant and as such would need to be able to understand and communicate with people who did not speak Greek. She was determined to learn American English as she felt at a distinct disadvantage being only able to communicate with Elias, the grocer and his wife. They now attended classes together and were able to laugh over their mistakes in pronunciation and grammar, trying to remember a few new words each day.

Elias was planning to learn how to drive a car. Annita was excited by the idea as she had only ever ridden in a taxi on special occasions.

To Elena and Yiorgo's delight most of her letters described events that she and Elias took part in together, whether it was at work or in their leisure time. Annita described the redecorating of the living room that she called a lounge. When they had arrived it was decorated with dark cream wallpaper with pink flowers appearing to wander randomly over it. Annita had shuddered at first sight and Elias had laughed.

Annita wanted to pull the paper off and paint the walls beneath white immediately, but Elias was more cautious. He wanted to call in a decorator and have new wallpaper put on the walls. The weeks went by and no one appeared to do the job. Annita, in a fury of frustration, had begun to pull strips of it away and a good deal of the plaster had fallen off with it. When Elias came home from a meeting she was trying desperately to clear up the mess that had spread throughout the apartment. He had caught her up in his arms and turned her to face the mirror, showing her how the dust had made her face and hair white.

Fortunately he had laughed over the mess she had made and helped her remove the remainder of the paper. The following week the decorator appeared and the walls had been re-plastered and painted white as Annita had wanted.

She described the laboratory where she and Elias spent most of each day. Compared with the two rooms they had used in Athens it was vast. The main area where all the equipment was stored and the experiments took place was twice as large as her parents' house and the room next door that was used as an office was almost as big. There were proper filing cabinets to store their papers and once Annita had mastered the language she was going to learn to use a typewriter. There were other microbiologists, chemists and doctors working with them, sharing the results of their research and experiments.

Finally the news came that Elena had been waiting for avidly. Annita was expecting a baby. She and Elias were both delighted with the news and it would also mean they would move to a larger apartment that had the added benefit of being closer to his laboratory.

Yiorgo looked at his wife's ecstatic face. He wasn't getting any younger and being a fisherman did not get any easier with age. According to Annita there were plenty of opportunities for people in America. They could close up the cottage and if they decided to return they would still have a home and he could always go back to fishing for a living. Stelios was in Heraklion at the High School and he felt he had fulfilled his obligations to his cousin's children.

He counted his savings carefully, then asked Andreas to check his calculations. There was enough for their fare and a considerable amount over. He offered half of it to Andreas who refused immediately.

'I chose to be a priest, Pappa. I don't need any money. Worldly goods mean nothing to me. I have a roof over my head at the church, my food provided and a small amount given to me when I take a service. You take your savings with you. You could need every drachma you have to start a new life over there.'

'But you haven't even got a parish of your own, despite the fact that you've been ordained for a considerable amount of time,' protested Yiorgo.

Andreas shrugged. 'God will provide for me when the time is right. There are probably many others who need a parish more than I or are more fitting to take on the responsibility.'

Anna opened the letter that Davros had delivered to her from Aghios Nikolaos. She hoped it would not mean her aunt and uncle were coming to stay. Much as she enjoyed seeing them it always caused such an upheaval, even with the new room built on at the back. Mattresses had to be borrowed from neighbours and Yiorgo had to return to sharing Yannis's room. She read the words carefully, hardly able to comprehend their meaning. 'Mamma, Andreas says that his parents are thinking of going to America to be with Annita. She's expecting a baby and they want to be with her.'

Maria shook her head. 'That will cost a lot of money to go to America and back.'

'According to Andreas if they go they plan to stay there.' Anna looked at her mother with wondering eyes. 'Do you think they will go? Suppose they don't like America and uncle Yiorgo has sold his house and his fishing boat? What will they do then? I wonder if they've told Annita yet? Maybe they plan to arrive as a surprise for her. I'll write back to Andreas and ask him.'

'Are they planning to visit us before they leave?'

'Next week, Andreas says.' Anna looked at her mother in horror. 'That could be any day! I don't know how long this letter took to get here.'

'No need to write back to Andreas, then. We can ask them when they visit.' Maria sat back in her chair complacently. It was good to know her cousin would be coming to see them. Anna would enjoy cooking a few special dishes for them.

Stelios was enjoying himself in Heraklion. He had insisted that he was quite capable of finding accommodation for himself and after a few days in the town had moved into a small taverna run by the uncle of a pupil at the High School. He had inspected the taverna where Yannis had stayed and decided he would certainly not ask for a room there. The meal he had eaten had been surprisingly good, but the small child running back and forth had brought back memories of his home and a crying baby. If the girl already had one she was likely to have another and he did not wish to repeat the experience.

Having now spent a year in the town he felt completely grown up and reasonably content. He was working hard and was sure he would gain a scholarship to the University in Athens. He checked his appearance in the mirror, rubbed a few specks of dust off his boots and decided to visit the post office to see if there was an offer from the University. He was disappointed when he was handed only his fortnightly letter from Anna.

When he read the pages he felt faint with both shock and disgust. Anna had written to say there had been a wedding on the island. She gave a long description of asking their father for some chickens and how long it had taken her to catch them, and finished by saying that the boatman had brought a message back saying that Yannis and Phaedra sent their thanks. He pushed the letter into his pocket and turned into the nearest taverna, ordering a brandy, which he followed swiftly with a second.

The bartender looked at him suspiciously. 'You should go easy on that stuff at your age.'

'I've had a shock.' Stelios rose from the stool and steadied himself against the bar. He lurched out into the street and stood against the wall, drawing in deep breaths, hoping he was not going to be sick. That would be the height of ignominy. Two small boys across the road sniggered at him, passing remarks behind their hands and he scowled at them as they ran away giggling.

How could lepers possibly get married? He was sure it was against the law. If it was not, it should be. It was unnatural. He shuddered. He hated lepers, even if his brother was one. It was through him that his mother was confined to a chair, that his sister was dead and his other sister no more than a slave. An unreasonable hatred against his family made him bite his lip and drained his face of colour. When he went University in Athens he would show everyone. He would not contract any incurable disease and end up exiled on an island. He would rather die.

Die! That was the answer. When he went to Athens and was asked about his family he would say they were dead. No one would question him, they would be sympathetic over his loss and he would say he did not wish to talk about it. No taint would ever spread to him, he would make sure of that. He had to return to Plaka at the end of the school term, but he would stay only a few days, making the excuse that he had to be in Athens as soon as possible. Once he was in Athens he would never return to Crete and as far as he was concerned his family were dead. He began to feel quite maudlin at the prospect.

Anna smiled as she opened the letter with a Heraklion postmark. It was rare that Stelios bothered to write to them. To her surprise it was not from Stelios, but her cousin Andreas. She read the letter in disbelief.

'Mamma, Andreas says that Father Minos has gone to live on the island. He has permission from the authorities- and you'll never guess – Andreas has taken over his parish in Heraklion.'

Maria held up her hand to her daughter. 'Tell me again, slowly.'

Anna sat beside her mother. 'Andreas says that Father Minos visited him and said he had permission to live on Spinalonga provided he could find someone suitable to take over his parish. Andreas had to go before the Bishop in Heraklion and get his permission. He's been living up there for the last few weeks and accompanying Father Minos whilst he performed his duties. He's even been to the hospital where the lepers stay and talked to them. He says Father Minos will leave next week and go over to Spinalonga and live there for ever.' Anna looked at her mother with wondering eyes. 'What a wonderful man he must be. To give up his life in the town to go to that island and live amongst all those sick people. Yannis will be very happy, I'm sure.'

Maria smiled. 'Yannis is a good boy.'

Anna opened the letter from America eagerly. A photograph fluttered out and she gazed at it curiously. Her aunt and uncle stood there stiffly, Yiorgo had one arm round his wife's shoulders and the other around Annita. Annita was smiling happily, one hand laid protectively on her bulging stomach, the other clasping Elias's hand. He was not at all as Anna had imagined. Somehow she had expected a replica of Yannis, but he was totally different. He dwarfed Annita, being well over two metres tall, his hair appeared to be receding and he wore horn-rimmed glasses.

She turned to the letter and read began to read carefully.

Dear Anna
I have been meaning to write to you for some time, but I seem to be very busy and since I started the baby I have also

been very tired. I began to feel a little better when I stopped being sick each morning.

Elias has insisted that we employ a maid to come in to clean the apartment once a week to allow me to rest more. Mamma offered to do it, but Elias would not hear of it. I think she was quite disappointed. I have promised her that when I have the baby she can come in to help me.

Elias has passed his driving test and has bought a small car. He has promised he will teach me to drive after I have had the baby. I'm not sure if I'm excited or frightened at the idea.

Mamma and Pappa arrived safely and I think they are beginning to settle down. It is all very different for them, of course. We found an apartment for them quite close to us and there are a few people in the area who speak Greek and they have become friendly with them.

I have sent you a photograph and when I have had the baby I will send you another. It will only be about another ten weeks now and I begin to feel rather excited. Mamma has made me some little nightdresses and knitted some jackets. I have bought the other things I think I shall need, but I'm sure I shall have forgotten something. Elias has suggested that we turn his study into a nursery, but I think there is plenty of time to do that. I shall want to keep the baby close to me at first.

Of course, Elias is hoping we will have a little boy, but I really don't mind. We have decided that if it is a girl we will call her Elena and a boy will be called Andreas. I did think Pappa might want a boy called after him, but he seems quite happy with our choice.

Anna smiled to herself. Annita certainly sounded very happy and contented.

Annita lay on the sofa propped up by pillows, the baby in her arms. 'It's good to be home.'

Elias smiled fondly at her. 'I'm pleased you went into the hospital. If anything had gone wrong you were in the right place.'

'She took far longer to be born than I had expected. The woman in the bed opposite me came in over an hour later and she'd had her little boy in two hours!'

'He was also her fifth child. Each one gets quicker, you'll see.'

Annita looked at him wide-eyed. 'I'm not sure I want to have another one. I didn't realise how difficult it could be.'

'The doctors said you had her very easily. In a few months you'll have forgotten all the discomfort. Besides, I'm sure Elena would like to have a brother or sister in the future. Look at her tiny hands. Her fingers won't get caught up in that shawl and hurt, will they?'

Annita disentangled the shawl from the baby's hand. She did not share Elias's confidence that she would forget the pangs of childbirth in a few months. He did not know what it was like to feel as if you were about to be split in two, a feeling that became more intense and intolerable as the time went by, until the blessed relief of feeling something soft and slippery beside your leg and you realised the ordeal was over.

'When Mamma and Pappa arrive can you take some photographs of her? We must send one to your mother and also to my cousin.'

'I wrote to my mother last week. She knows all about her.'

'I'm sure she'd still like to have a photograph. After all, Elena is her first grandchild.'

Anna opened the thick envelope with trembling fingers. She crossed herself and hoped the letter would contain good news about Annita's baby and not a long missive about suffering and disaster to both mother and baby.

The letter was brief and a smile of amusement crept over Anna's face. Annita was finding out just how difficult motherhood was.

Dear Anna

*Just a quick note with the photographs I promised you. ELENA
– our little girl – is quite beautiful. Elias and Pappa are over the
moon and I can see she will be spoilt. Mamma is coming in every
day to help me. I am very grateful to her, as I never knew small
babies could be so demanding. How did you manage with Yannis
and looking after your mother and the house? I have to get up in
the night to feed her, but Mamma makes me have a rest in the
afternoon.*

Your loving cousin, Annita.

There were four photographs enclosed, each showing Elena in
the arms of a parent or grandparent. Anna looked at them
carefully. Elena did not look at all beautiful. Her eyes were tightly
closed, there was a slight frown on her forehead and her skin
looked very red. She was wrapped in a shawl and Anna could
not see if she had any hair. Anna smiled, remembering the babies
she had delivered. They all tended to look like that for the first
week. She hoped the next selection of photographs she was sent
would be better.

'Mamma, Annita has sent some photographs of her little girl.
They've called her Elena and she's beautiful.'

Maria took the photographs and smiled. 'I'm sure she's
beautiful to them, but she looks just like any other baby to me.'
She handed them back to her daughter. 'Now you were a beautiful
baby from the moment you were born. The whole village
acknowledged the fact.'

1938 – 1940

Stelios opened the letter from the University with trembling fingers. A single sheet of paper fluttered to the ground and he bent to pick it up, the words 'Place Refused' hitting his eyes like a sledgehammer. What did it mean? They couldn't refuse him. This was what he had worked so hard for over the last two years. He read the accompanying letter more carefully. Unfortunately his grades were just below the level he needed to be granted a place at the University. They suggested he applied to the army, as he was almost certain to be accepted as a clerical officer and with a good chance of rapid promotion.

Stelios gritted his teeth. He did not want to go into the army. He had been so confident that a place would be offered to him at the University. How could he face his friends and tell them he had been refused?

He sat sipping slowly at a glass of wine and did not see his friend Makkis until he was at his elbow.

'Can I join you? Have you heard your results? Have you got the place you wanted in Athens?'

Stelios nodded. 'Of course, but I'm not sure I shall accept it. If I went to University I would probably end up as a schoolteacher and that's the last thing I would want. I'm considering the army as a career. With my grades I should get rapid promotion and I'll probably make a good deal more money than I ever would by being a teacher.' The lies ran glibly off his lips.

Makkis frowned. 'Are you sure? Teaching is pretty safe. You're not likely to get shot at.'

'I don't envisage making such a serious mistake that the army would be forced to shoot me,' smiled Stelios.

Makkis shook his head. 'There's a lot of trouble in Europe at the moment. You never know when it could turn nasty and we could get involved. If you're in the army you'll be expected to fight and you might get shot.'

Stelios pushed his chair onto its back legs. 'I'm not talking about being a common soldier. I shall go into administration. People don't come shooting at you if you work in the offices.'

'I'm not so sure.' Makkis drained his glass. 'I'm off to tell my parents the good news. I've been offered a place on the Science course that I applied for. They'll be as delighted as I am.'

Stelios watched the young man leave with a growing sense of fury. That Makkis should have been offered a place instead of him was unthinkable. Makkis spent most of his time fooling around and making the rest of them laugh.

Stelios had been in Plaka for two days, strutting around the village and telling everyone who would listen that he had turned down a place at the University as the army insisted he would be invaluable to them. The complete re-organisation of the Greek army was going to be his responsibility, through his genius they would be invincible, whoever tried to bring war and unrest into their country. His family proudly believed him, but some of the villagers were not so sure of the posturing young man.

'Too big for his army boots already,' Davros had been heard to remark as Stelios strolled by. The boy had flushed, but pretended not to hear.

Inadvertently he looked towards the island. There were people moving around on the quay and someone was waving. He felt his blood freeze in him. It must be Yannis! Stelios turned his back to the sea. He would not wave. You did not wave to a dead man, even if he was your brother. Anna was standing there, the two children by her side.

'Wave to uncle Yannis,' she instructed them and they dutifully held up their hands and waved in the direction she indicated.

'You're sick,' he commented bitterly as he walked past her.

Anna eyed him warily. She no longer understood her young brother. One minute he seemed elated with life, full of his own importance and the next he was withdrawn and morose, unwilling even to be polite to his family.

'I'm taking the children up to see Babbis. Do you want to come?'

'No. I've better things to do with my time.'

'Come along.' She took the children's hands firmly in her own and began to walk away. If Stelios was in one of his black moods she did not want to bandy words with him.

'It's about time Babbis faced up to his responsibilities,' he called after her. 'Let him look after his own brats.'

Anna continued steadily on her way. She had a strange desire to cry. Since the day she had gone up to the farmhouse to help Babbis clean and turn out there had been a strained atmosphere between them. Each day she had walked up to the house with the children, pleased to see that Babbis was keeping it clean as his mother had and also working hard on the farm. There was a constraint between them that even the presence of the children could not eliminate. She knocked before ushering them into the kitchen to greet their father, then having bade him good morning she retired to the vegetable garden where she pulled at the weeds. An hour later she rose from her knees and knocked at the back door again.

'I must get back. Mamma will need me.'

Babbis nodded. He bent and kissed the children, holding Yannis tightly as he wriggled to place his feet back on the ground.

'Be careful! You'll hurt him.'

Babbis met her eyes. 'I've never deliberately hurt anyone in my life – except once, and I'd been drinking then,' he added softly.

Anna did not answer.

'I'd like to apologise.' He placed Yannis on the ground. 'Forgive me, Anna.'

'You gave me a shock.'

'I'd never have done it if I'd been sober. I don't drink any more.'

Anna nodded. 'I have to go.'

'I'll walk with you.' He swung Yannis up on his back where the boy crowed with delight.

They walked in silence as Babbis adjusted himself to the weight of his son. 'How's your mother?'

'Much the same. Good days, bad days.' Anna shrugged eloquently.

'When does Stelios leave for Athens?'

'Tomorrow,'

'You'll be pleased to see him go.' It was a statement, not a question.

'He can be difficult.'

Babbis nodded. 'I know. He came to see me.'

'Why?'

'To relieve his feelings, I imagine.'

'Was he very rude?'

Babbis's lips set in a hard line. 'He's a very strange young man.' He set his son down on the ground and stopped walking. 'He said it was a wicked injustice that my mother should have died rather than his own.'

'What?' Anna was horrified. 'How could he?'

'I think he's very unhappy.'

'Unhappy! What has he got to be unhappy about? He has everything he ever wanted or needed.'

'Not quite. He has no family in his eyes.'

'What do you mean?' Anna turned to face Babbis. 'He has a mother and father as well as a brother and a sister.'

'He thinks not. His mother is too ill and his father, brother and sister are too busy to spend time listening to him.'

'We would listen if he spoke sense. He either sits and says nothing for hours on end or starts an argument with Yiorgo and walks out.'

'He did say one thing that made sense.' Anna raised her eyebrows and waited for Babbis to continue. 'He said I should get married again.'

'I told you that.'

'You didn't tell me who to, though, did you?'

'Who you marry is your business.'

'It could concern you.'

Anna felt her lips tremble. 'The children! If you married again you'd take the children to live with you.'

'Naturally.'

'I hope she'll be good to them.' Anna felt a lump in her throat.

'She loves them dearly, Anna. Anna, dear Anna, I'm asking you to marry me.'

Anna sat down hard on the grass. She shook her head.

'Don't say no, let me explain. I've thought about it a good deal, before Stelios came to see me, ever since – that day.' Babbis sat down beside her. 'I realised I did need someone. I loved Maria. I can't pretend to love you in the same way, Anna, but I have a great affection for you, and I could never take the children away from you. It seems to make sense to me.'

Anna took a deep breath. 'It may make sense to you, but I'm not sure if it does to me. Anyway, it wouldn't be possible.'

'Why not?'

'Even with the new room at the back there's no space. Marisa is too old to share with her brother.'

'But you and the children would move up to my house.'

'What about my mother?'

'You could go down to her every day. She has your Pappa and Yiorgo. She won't be alone.'

Anna plucked at the blades of grass at her side. 'I don't know, Babbis. I've never thought about getting married. I've always had Mamma and the house to look after. What would Pappa say?'

'I imagine he would think it a problem solved. There's no one else here who's available for you to marry. When you've decided let me know and I'll talk to your Pappa.' Babbis helped her to her feet. 'I'd be good to you,' he assured her.

Anna lowered her eyes. 'I'll think about it, Babbis.' She took hold of the children's hands. 'Come along, it's time we went back to see your grandmother.'

The next letter Anna received from her cousin showed a little girl standing and holding her father's hand. He was crouching down to be nearer her level and appeared to be handing her something. Annita had written on the back:-

Elena – thirteen months old. (I had to get Elias to bend down or I couldn't get his head in!)

Anna giggled. It must be difficult to be so tall that you had to continually bend over to talk to people. A picture came into her mind of Elias laying in bed with his feet hanging out at the end where he was too tall to fit. She would have to ask Annita how he managed. She spread the letter out to read, a frown creasing her forehead as she did so. Annita was pregnant again.

She was annoyed that she was having another one so soon. Elias did not realise what a difference carrying a child made to her. He was very kind, but did not understand how she felt at all. She preferred being at the laboratory and working with him. To be at home all day with just a small child for company she found miserable and boring. She stressed that she loved Elena dearly and was sure she would feel the same about the next one when it arrived, but she did not want to spend all her time cooped up in the apartment.

Anna found her discontent difficult to understand. Once Yannis began to sleep throughout the night she had thoroughly enjoyed spending all her time in the house, tending to him and her mother. The problem of Annita nagged at her throughout the day and she delayed telling her mother about the letter until the middle of the afternoon.

'She didn't really want another one yet,' explained Anna. 'She misses the work she used to do with Elias.'

'I don't understand the problem,' Maria replied immediately. 'She has her mother out there.'

Anna frowned. 'What do you mean?'

'I'm sure Elena would love to look after her granddaughter and also the next one when it's a few months old. Annita could go back to working with Elias then.'

'Do you think she would?'

'She'd probably be delighted. Mothers are there to help with the family.' Maria sighed deeply. 'I wish I could have helped you more with the children.'

'You did help, Mamma,' Anna assured her. 'When they were small I could always leave them laying on your bed and know they were safe and when they were older you used to watch them whilst I was in the kitchen and call me if they got into mischief.'

Maria sighed. 'It's not the same.'

Anna wrote a letter to Annita that evening, tentatively mentioning the idea that Elena should look after the children and forgetting to ask if Elias's feet stuck out from the end of the bed. She was surprised to receive a reply within the month to say Annita had suggested it to her mother who had accepted with alacrity. Annita was to return to working with Elias in the mornings until she was closer to her time and felt it was too much for her. She was already saying that when the second child was six months old she would be able to spend a full day in the laboratory.

Anna walked sedately back from the church with her father and brother, the children running along beside their father. It was almost a year now since Babbis had asked her to marry him and he had not approached her again. She hoped he had acted on a sudden whim and would not mention it again.

'Mamma Anna.' Yannis ran back to her. 'May I go to Ourania's? Her Mamma says I can. She has a hoop and says she can make it roll the length of the street. I want to try.'

Anna nodded. When the boy had started to speak he had called her 'Mamma' and she had not felt comfortable with the name. She had tried her best to get him to call her 'Anna' but no amount of persistence on her part had made him change. As he grew older he finally compromised by calling her 'Mamma Anna' and Marisa had gradually followed his lead.

'Be back in an hour for lunch.'

'I will,' called Yannis as he ran to his friend's side.

'Can I come with you?' asked Marisa.

'Ask Ourania,' he called back and Marisa ran to catch them up.

Babbis moved to Anna's side. 'I'd like to talk to you, Anna. After lunch.'

Anna felt her heart lurch. She had a nasty feeling that Babbis was going to ask for her answer.

Yannis sat in his chair smoking contentedly. Anna's Sunday lunch had been as satisfying as usual and Babbis had spoken to him briefly beforehand. Why hadn't he thought of Babbis as a husband for his younger daughter? It was a very suitable solution. The girl had no reason to refuse him and she was an excellent mother to his children. Yiorgo's old bedroom, that Yannis now occupied, could be divided by a curtain for both children to share and Babbis could move in with them permanently.

Babbis followed Anna into the kitchen as she cleared their dirty coffee cups and glasses. He leaned against the wall as she moved around efficiently.

'Anna, can I talk to you?'

'Of course, Babbis. Are you concerned about the children?'

Babbis shook his head. 'I asked you a while back if you would marry me. You asked for time to think about it. Have you decided to accept?'

Anna lowered her eyes. 'I can't, Babbis.'

'Why not? I'd be good to you, you know that. I spoke to your Pappa earlier and he has no objection.'

Anna took a deep breath. She did not want to hurt the young man. 'I don't love you, Babbis.'

'But you like me?'

'Of course I like you!'

'Do you want more time to think about it?'

Anna shook her head. 'I still look on you as my brother-in-law. You were Maria's husband.'

'Don't you want to get married and have children of your own?'

Anna shrugged. 'Maybe, one day.'

Annita sent a long letter to Anna, with photographs of her small daughter. She sounded so much happier than when she had first announced her second pregnancy.

Dear Anna

I hope everyone in Plaka is keeping well. Elena is thriving and Mamma loves looking after her every day. I have been very busy trying to catch up on the work at the laboratory. Elias seemed to have made great strides with one of the experiments, but the notes he kept were very scrappy, not like the ones I used to keep. He said he couldn't do both and he didn't want anyone else working with him. We had to go through most of it again. It was time well spent as it proved the success of the first experiments.

I managed to persuade Elias to let me continue with my driving lessons for a few more weeks and I have passed my driving test. Elias will only let me drive the car a short distance each day as he does not want me to overtire myself. I don't find driving a bit tiring.

The hospital are very pleased with his work and when he told them we were expecting a second child they agreed to provide us with a house. We insisted it had to be in the same area because of Mamma looking after the children. We looked at quite a number before we found one that we liked and felt was big enough for us.

It has a kitchen and two large rooms on the ground floor. At the back is a utility room where I can do the washing and keep a pram for the baby. I had to keep taking Elena's up and down the stairs so that will be very useful.

Upstairs we have a bathroom and two bedrooms with a small room at the back which Elias plans to turn into a study again. We even have a proper garden with grass growing which is fenced round and safe for Elena to play in.

Elias has asked that the house be decorated before we move in and the hospital has agreed. I want to have the walls white, but Elena's little room will be pale pink. She will have to share it with the new baby so I am hoping it will be a girl. If it is we plan to call her Maria. A boy will still be Andreas.

We will have to buy some new furniture as the house is considerably larger than our apartment but there are plenty of shops here to visit and choose what we want. I cannot make up my mind whether to have curtains (they call them 'drapes' over here) or blinds. Elias wanted to leave the floors as polished wood and have rugs, but I refused. Rugs can be dangerous if you are carrying a baby. We have compromised. The floors will be polished wood during the summer months and during the winter we will have a carpet square put down for warmth. His mother does this in Athens as she has marble floors and they would be very cold. Elias is hoping to go to visit her after I have had the baby as his sister says she has not been very well. Maybe I can come and visit you in a few years when the children are older.

Mamma and Pappa send their love to all of you. I will let you know when the baby arrives.

Your loving cousin, Annita.

Anna smiled. Her mother had found the solution to Annita's problem. It was fitting that they would call a little girl Maria after her. She read the letter through again. Annita could drive a car! That surely must be very dangerous. She had visited Aghios Nikolaos once and been petrified when she had seen the traffic.

1941 – 1943

Babbis leant against the kitchen door. 'That was a very good lunch, Anna. Thank you.'

'I enjoy cooking,' replied Anna simply.

Babbis shifted his weight. 'Anna, I want to ask you again to be my wife.' He held up his hand. 'Your answer is very important to me.'

Anna felt the blood rush into her face. She turned distressed eyes to her brother-in-law. 'I wish I could accept, Babbis. It's just not possible. I love you the way I love my brothers. It wouldn't be right. You'll always be Maria's husband to me.'

Babbis sighed deeply. 'I'll ask you again when I come back.' He opened the back door. 'I'm going to have a word with Yiorgo.'

Anna watched him go with trepidation. Was he going to ask her brother to put pressure on her?

Yiorgo did not mention his conversation with Babbis when he returned a couple of hours later. He sat in a chair next to his mother and appeared deep in thought. Finally he rose.

'I'm going to the taverna. I want to speak to Davros.'

Anna felt sick. Surely her refusal of Babbis did not mean that she was to be courted by Davros? She disliked the man, who smelled continually of sweat and alcohol. Automatically she prepared the children for bed, both of them surprised that their father had not returned to bid them good night.

'I expect he had some business to attend to. I'll ask him to come up to you when he returns. He won't have forgotten,' she assured them. She had a feeling that Babbis may have returned to his farm and partaken too freely of a bottle after her refusal of him.

It was late when Yiorgo returned from the taverna, accompanied by both Babbis and Davros. To Anna's surprise none of the men appeared to have drunk a great deal and Yiorgo went straight to his father.

'We've been talking, the three of us, and we've decided we have to do something.'

Yannis looked at his son, wondering what proposal he was about to put before him.

'Marisa and Yannis are old enough to help out on the farm a bit more, besides it's easier now we're running more animals. You should all be safe enough down here. Davros knows of a resistance group that is being formed in Aghios Nikolaos and we're going to join them.'

Anna's hand flew to her throat. 'No! You can't. Think of Mamma and the children.' Her eyes went from her brother to Babbis.

'That's what we are thinking about. We don't want the Germans in our country. We've heard stories from the mainland and we don't want that happening over here. It's up to us to stop them.'

Yannis looked at his son, his emotions alternating between pride and fear. 'Have you thought this through, Yiorgo? It's not a decision to be made lightly. You could be risking your life.'

Yiorgo nodded. 'I've been thinking about it for the last few weeks. Babbis and I talked about it when we heard that Heraklion had been taken. A few more men up there and they might not have been successful.'

'So you're going to Aghios Nikolaos? What makes you think they'll come down there?'

Yiorgo shrugged. 'They may not. Davros just happens to know a couple of men there who know where the resistance groups are forming. We could end up anywhere.'

Yannis went over to the cupboard where he kept his brandy. 'When do you plan to leave?'

'The middle of this week. We can't wait around too long as Davros says they plan to move on by the weekend. Once they've gone we won't know where to find them.'

Yannis poured a measure for each man. 'I wish I was young enough to join you.'

'You're needed here, Pappa. I shall be relying on you to look after Mamma and Anna.'

Anna, her father and the children waved until the men were out of sight. Her emotions were in turmoil. Had she not refused Babbis's offer of marriage would he have been so willing to join the resistance? He had taken her to one side and spoken to her quietly and unemotionally before he left.

'I'm relying on you, Anna, to do whatever is best for the children. They are totally in your care. I want you to look after these for me whilst I'm gone.' He thrust some papers into her hand.

'What are they, Babbis?'

'The legal documents from Father Theodorakis giving the dates when Maria and I were married and when the children were born. Keep them safe. They could be needed in the future.'

Anna bowed her head. She did not want Babbis to see the tears in her eyes. He was entrusting her with them as he knew he might not return.

'I'll do my best for them, Babbis.'

'I know you will, Anna.' He tilted her face towards him and kissed her gently on the cheek. 'I'll ask you again when I get back. I'll go and speak to the children, then say goodbye to your Mamma and Pappa. I doubt we'll be gone long.'

Doctor Stavros walked briskly along the road leading to Aghios Nikolaos. The weather was perfect; neither too hot nor too chill, just right for taking a few days away from his practice in Aghios

Nikolaos and visiting Sitia. When he went over to the island this week he would speak to Father Minos and ask him to tell the people he was taking a short holiday. He deserved a rest. On many occasions he was interrupted on a Sunday during a church service with a request to attend either an accident or a difficult labour. He always felt mildly irritated when the one day he considered his own to do as he pleased was disrupted, particularly, as so often happened, the patient in question was not badly injured, only frightened, and the woman had successfully given birth.

Today had been different. The distress call had been genuine. The woman had been in labour for over twenty-four hours and finally, with his help, had given birth to healthy twin boys. Without him in attendance the outcome could have been very different. It was with a feeling of satisfaction and well being that he turned up the hill towards the square and stopped in horror. The women were on their knees tearing at their hair, beating their breasts and screaming like demented beings. From each palm tree in the tiny garden hung the limp body of a man. Doctor Stavros swallowed hard. If they were dead there was nothing he could do to help them, and if they were still alive how would he manage to tend to such a number?

He was about to move towards them when an army lorry came into view and a man jumped out as soon as it halted. He drew his revolver and fired three shots into the air. Immediately there was a shocked silence.

'Let this be a lesson to you,' he shouted. 'They will stay hanging from the trees for a week to remind you that to harbour resistance workers does not pay. Get back to your homes. I shall shoot anyone who is still in the square in five minutes.'

Petrified, the women scrambled to their feet and scuttled down the various side roads leading to their homes. Doctor Stavros shrank back into a doorway and hoped he would not be noticed. He watched in horror as the German strode towards the one woman who had remained beside a body. As he reached her he levelled his revolver and shot her through the head.

Doctor Stavros felt his stomach heave. Such barbaric behaviour was not necessary. Cautiously he slipped down the narrow streets until he was back out into the countryside and he began to breathe more easily. He found he was trembling with either fear or emotion, he did not know which. He wanted to hide. A low wall a short distance from the road would give him a certain amount of screening from anyone passing by and he hurried towards it.

He sat there, his legs drawn up beneath his chin, not daring to relax. He had heard that Heraklion had fallen some weeks earlier, but he had not dreamt the Germans would fan out over the island. He also knew that there had been mutterings about forming a resistance group amongst the men of the town and a good number of them had disappeared over the weeks. He wondered if Manolis had been shot. How would he get out to the island if there were no boatmen to take him? He berated himself for being a coward and not waiting in the square to find out which men had been executed.

Doctor Stavros sat behind the wall until the sun went down. As darkness fell he decided it should be safe to return to the town. Taking to the dark back streets he moved cautiously to the hospital and let himself in by a side door. He crept along the corridor until he reached the first of the hospital wards and was relieved to see that the patients appeared safe and the nurses still on duty.

He turned into the washroom and removed his jacket and spectacles before running his head under the tap, taking gulps of water as he did so. He slicked his hair back as best he could and rubbed his hands on the sleeves of his shirt to dry them. Jacket and spectacles replaced he picked up his medical bag and made his way down to the reception area at the front of the hospital. He would pretend to have just returned from his visit to the outlying district and have no knowledge of events that had taken place in the town that day.

He was greeted by soldiers, who levelled their revolvers at him. Slowly he raised his hands above his head, sweat beading his upper lip. He had not expected this. An exchange in a guttural language took place between them and one left, returning a short while later with a tall, blonde man who had a white scar down the side of his face.

'Your name?' He asked the trembling man in Greek.

'Doctor Stavros.'

'Where have you been?'

'In the countryside. A woman was giving birth to twins.'

The Commander nodded and spoke to the soldier who lowered his revolver.

'You live in Aghios Nikolaos?'

'Yes.'

'You work at the hospital?'

'If I'm needed.'

'You will now work for us. If we have a soldier wounded he will be sent here and given priority treatment. You will be held responsible if he does not recover.'

Doctor Stavros licked his lips. 'That would depend upon the extent of his injuries. I would do my best. I can do no more.'

'Too many fatalities and you would join the rest of your companions in the square.'

The Commander turned on his heel, leaving a very frightened doctor.

Doctor Stavros tried to concentrate on his patients. Everyone was frightened. The soldiers had returned at the end of the week and cut the bonds holding the bodies to the trees. After their departure the women had come out and claimed their loved ones, weeping without restraint as they helped each other carry the bodies back to their homes to be washed and finally buried with dignity. On Sunday the church was filled to capacity, whilst the priest, with tears in his eyes, prayed for the souls of the men who had been so brutally slaughtered. He exhorted his congregation to find it in their hearts to forgive them, but the set faces of the women told him he was asking the impossible.

'Why did they do it?' asked Doctor Stavros after the service.

'Saying we had resistance workers gathering here was a good excuse to get rid of the local government. They'd already annihilated the government in Heraklion. They'll probably do it in all the provincial capitals. It takes the power away from the local people. They have no figurehead to rally round.'

'So it wasn't all the men?'

'Most of the young ones have gone into hiding. Some may return, but it's my guess they'll make their way to Lassithi. Instead of this massacre being a deterrent it will only make them more determined to free the country of these cruel barbarians.'

'Have you any idea where Manolis, the boatman is?'

The priest shook his head. 'Have you looked in the harbour for his boat?'

'Of course. It isn't there.'

'There are plenty of secluded coves and caves he can hide up in. I wouldn't worry about him. He knows how to look after himself.'

Doctor Stavros was making his way to the hospital when he saw the soldiers marching towards him. He shrank back into a doorway, his eyes glazed with horror. Slowly he raised his hands in the air and waited.

The soldiers did not even glance in his direction and he was left sweating and feeling foolish. He waited until they had passed him before lowering his hands and clutching at the doorway for support. He needed a drink.

Doctor Stavros chose a dimly lit and deserted taverna, entering quickly and shutting the door behind him. As his eyes grew accustomed to his dark surroundings he saw the owner regarding him suspiciously.

Doctor Stavros cleared his throat. 'Have you any raki?'

Silently a bottle was produced and the doctor helped himself to three measures before his hands stopped shaking and he felt capable of speaking to the old man.

'Have the soldiers gone?'

'The Germans have gone. Left a bunch of Italians in the place.'

Doctor Stavros breathed more easily. 'I'd best be getting to the hospital, then.' The doctor placed his glass back on the bar top and turned towards the door.

'Not before you've paid me.' With alacrity the elderly man was round the counter.

'Naturally. How much?'

'Six lepta.'

'Six lepta! For three glasses of raki?'

'Prices have gone up.'

'Not that much, surely?'

The taverna owner stood barring the door. With a sigh the doctor dug deep into his trouser pocket and pulled out the coins.

'I think you'd do better to save your inflated prices for the army. You've priced yourself out of the market for the man in the street.'

As the owner stood working out the meaning behind the words, Doctor Stavros let himself back out into the sunlight. The extortionate sum he had been charged rankled and he strode along the street heedless of being seen.

No one appeared to notice him at all and he was almost at the hospital when a soldier stepped from a doorway and pointed his rifle at him.

'Halt. Where you go? Who you are?'

'I'm Doctor Stavros and I'm about to go into the hospital.'

The soldier frowned. He had caught the word 'doctor' but understood nothing more.

'I am the doctor.' He spoke loudly and clearly, pointing to his chest. 'I am Doctor Stavros.'

'Si? Come, come.'

With a rifle pointing at him the doctor was left with no choice but to accompany the soldier up to the square and be ushered into the town hall where a rapid exchange in Italian took place between his escort and a soldier seated behind the desk. Again he was looked at suspiciously, then the soldier rose, walked to a door and knocked smartly. At a word of command he opened the door and a further exchange in Italian took place, whereupon an older man, regaled in the uniform of a captain, appeared. He studied the doctor, then opened the door wider and beckoned him inside, waving his hand towards a seat.

'Please, sit. You are doctor?'

'Yes, I'm Doctor Stavros,' he had replied wearily.

'Good. Is good. We wait for you.' The captain beamed, whilst the doctor felt himself go cold. He could feel the bullets biting into his flesh as he died ignominiously tied to a tree in the square. 'Man need you. Papers, please.' From inside his jacket pocket the doctor produced his identity papers and handed them over for careful scrutiny. 'Go to hospital. Bring medicine for man here.'

'What medicine? What's wrong with him? I need to know what medicine to bring.'

The captain considered his words carefully. 'Medicine for man with trouble caught from woman.'

Doctor Stavros permitted himself to smile. 'I see. One man only?'

'One man complain.'

'Very well. Where will I find him?'

'Bring medicine here. I give.'

Doctor Stavros frowned. 'I ought to see the patient myself. It could be a mistaken diagnosis.'

'No mistake. Bring medicine here.'

'Oh – oh, I see. Yes, yes, of course.' His patient obviously sat before him. 'It will take me a little time to mix the necessary ingredients, but I'll be back.'

The captain smiled, placed a rubber stamp and his signature on the doctor's identity papers and handed them back. 'How long?'

'Two, three hours, maybe.'

'Two hours. Go.'

Thankfully Doctor Stavros left the captain's presence and continued on his way, confident that the small rubber stamp on his papers would give him immunity from further arrest and detention. He thought carefully. All the time the captain had need of him he should be relatively safe. He knew exactly what he would do, a small quantity of the effective medicine, well diluted with water, should relieve the unpleasant symptoms for some weeks, but not prove an effective cure, necessitating repeat prescriptions for some considerable time and keeping the man dependent upon the doctor.

Anna stood on the shore with the other frightened and bewildered villagers. The soldiers had marched into the village and pulled the occupants from their homes. Now they were huddled in a terrified group, cowering from the guns that were levelled at them.

At an order from their commander two soldiers launched Davros's unused fishing boat and began to row strongly towards the island. Anna stood with her heart in her mouth. Surely they were not going to attack the lepers!

It was a relief when she saw they did not leave the boat, but were talking to a small gathering on the quay. A shot rang out, followed by another and the boat began its return to the shore.

The Commander stood in front of them, his eyes raking over the small community. He was too late. The young men had obviously left the village. The elderly priest stood there, his lips moving soundlessly in prayer, an old man leaned heavily on two sticks, but one man stood erect, his hand laid protectively on his daughter's shoulder. The commander pointed to him and a soldier pulled him roughly to one side and covered him with his gun.

'Pappa!' Anna was convinced her father was to be shot before her eyes. She held a trembling Marisa and scowling Yannis to her.

The German Commander turned to face them, the scar running down the side of his face showing white against his tan, and spoke in perfect Greek. 'I am leaving soldiers in this village. I have given my orders to them and they will be obeyed. No boat is to go to the island, and no one is to leave this village without permission. There will be soldiers posted at intervals along the coast and they have orders to shoot on sight anyone who disobeys. I will have no resistance in this area. Soldiers will be billeted in the village and you will look after them until further notice. This man will come with us.'

The German Commander spoke to the soldiers in a lilting language, completely unintelligible to Anna. Two soldiers at the end of the line saluted and moved to where Yannis stood, trying hard to control his trembling limbs. The remainder of the battalion began to fan out towards the houses.

Yannis, a soldier flanking him on each side, began an ignominious march along the village street.

'Pappa! Where are you taking my Pappa?' screamed Anna.

The cold blue eyes regarded her impassively. 'There is work for a fit man in the mines.'

'But he's not fit. He has a bad leg.'

The Commander waved his revolver at her. 'Be thankful I have not shot him.'

'Please, don't take him,' begged Anna, tears streaming down her face.

The revolver was levelled at her. 'Maybe I should shoot an hysterical woman.' He shouted at two of the soldiers and they turned, walking back to where he stood and saluted.

He spoke to them again in the unknown language. 'Take this woman back to her house. Make sure two of you stay there. You,' he pointed to one of them. 'You speak Greek. I leave you in charge here. You will have use of the jeep for occasional visits to the town for supplies. Make sure the people behave themselves. Do not hesitate to shoot them. They are peasants.'

The soldier saluted again and went to Anna's side. The Commander climbed into the cab of the empty transport lorry and instructed the driver to leave. Sevas spat after him and the soldier nearest her slapped her face, leaving a red mark across her cheek and tears stinging her eyes.

Anna turned to go into the farmhouse, shepherding Marisa and Yannis before her, only to find the soldiers accompanying her.

'Stay.'

'No, oh, no, there's no room.'

'Stay,' he repeated and entered the kitchen, giving it a cursory glance before walking through to the living room. 'Who?' he pointed to Maria sitting in her chair.

'My mother. She's sick, crippled, please, don't touch her. Please, leave her alone.' Anna stood by the chair protectively.

The soldier strode forward as if Anna had not spoken, lifted Maria's hand and kissed it. 'Stay,' he said again.

'You can't stay,' Anna was struggling to regain her self-control. 'There's no room.'

The soldier clattered up the wooden stairs and looked into the two rooms, smiling with pleasure. There were two single mattresses on the floor of one and that would suit him better than having to share with his companion. He crossed to the window and looked out on the hills behind the farmhouse and sighed.

He longed to return to Italy, to the security of his home and family. Instead he was expected to stay in an almost deserted village and make sure no resistance movement was formed. How he hated the German Commander who had forced them to march until they were fit to drop and shot people at random. There should still be justice, even if they were fighting a war. Victor shrugged. Fighting, he had not fought anyone at all and he had no great wish to do so. Maybe he was lucky after all to be in this out of the way spot. He walked back to the doorway and called to his companion in Italian.

'Mario, come up and have a look.'

'Do you think it's all right to leave them?'

'Yes. The girl won't leave the old woman and her children and there's no one else around.'

Mario joined him and looked around the small room. 'Doubt if we'd have done any better in any of the other houses.'

'I don't think I've ever been anywhere quite so deserted. There's nothing, absolutely nothing.'

'There's a church and a tavern, what more do you want?'

Victor sighed. 'A few attractive girls wouldn't come amiss.'

'There's the two downstairs, three if you count the old one.'

Victor looked at Mario in disgust. 'There's a child, a middle aged woman and a grandmother. I said girls.'

Mario grinned. 'You'll just have to make do, then.' He made an obscene gesture and laughed.

Victor pushed past him and returned to the ground floor. The coarseness of his fellows had to be lived with to be believed. He stopped in the doorway.

The woman was holding her mother's hand and tears were running unchecked down the old lady's face. Anna looked at him with hatred in her eyes.

'If she's ill again it will be your fault. You had no right to take my father. He's too old, he's just a farmer.'

The Italian frowned. His Greek was very limited and Anna's outburst had been far too fast for him to follow. 'Please?'

'Leave them, Anna. There's nothing you can do. They're soldiers under orders.' Maria tried to comfort her daughter despite her own distress.

Anna laid her head on her mother's arm, not wanting their uninvited guests to see her crying. When she raised it her eyes had a hard glitter and her mouth was set in a straight line. Now over her first shock at the events she must think clearly. She had no one to turn to. She was solely responsible for her mother and her dead sister's children and she must look after them and protect them at all costs from these intruders.

She looked at the children, standing white-faced in the corner of the room and a new fear came into her heart. Marisa was nearly thirteen; showing signs of womanhood and these two coarse, foreign soldiers were not a lot older. They would not, surely they could not, she was only a child. Anna looked from one Italian to the other. If either of them dared to lay a finger on her niece she would kill him, regardless of the consequences.

Anna rose to her feet and kissed her mother's cheek. 'Come along, both of you, there's work to be done.'

Obediently the children followed her into the kitchen. She spoke to them swiftly. 'Don't say a word in front of them. We don't know how much Greek they understand. Yannis, you'd better go up to the fields, there'll be no more school today. Marisa, you stay with me.'

Yannis opened his mouth to ask for Marisa to accompany him, then thought better of it. He opened the kitchen door and sauntered across the yard.

'Where go?' a voice called after him.

'To the fields to do the work my grandfather should be doing.' Yannis called back and began to harness the donkey to the cart.

Victor spoke to his companion and the soldier followed Yannis, catching up with him at the gate to the yard. Yannis scowled. What did they think he was going to do? If they were planning to follow him around all day they would very soon be bored.

He cut at the straggly vines, whistling to show his unconcern at the turn of events and ignoring the soldier completely. Mario settled himself comfortably in the shade of a bush and lit a cigarette. Maybe it would not be so bad here after all. Their duties should be pretty light. They could be certain the old lady would go nowhere and the boy was hardly old enough to be a threat. The woman could be a different proposition, but it was unlikely that she would leave the village and doubtful that she would get very far if she tried. Things could be worse. The German Commander could have stayed and that would have meant trouble. He was so unpredictable in his moves and quite ruthless. Feeling uneasy even thinking about him, Mario looked around, then shook himself. He was just a bit jumpy in a new place.

Yannis took his time, ignoring the soldier who would come and look at his handiwork from time to time. At mid-day Yannis took some bread and cheese from the shade of the cart and munched it slowly. Mario eyed it hungrily and wondered whether he should demand to be given some. No doubt Victor had been given something to eat down at the farm.

As the sun dropped lower in the sky, Yannis collected the tools together, dumped them in the back of the cart, harnessed the donkey and began to urge her over the rough ground to the path. It was a while before Mario realised he was making for the farmhouse and he hurried after the boy.

'House?'

Yannis nodded. 'I've finished in the fields for today, but I've got to clean the tools before I get the sheep and goats a bit nearer for the night.'

Mario's brow creased in a frown. He understood a little Greek when spoken slowly and clearly, but a sentence was beyond him. 'Please?'

Yannis shrugged. If the man could not understand he would just have to remain in ignorance. He decided to try an experiment.

'I think you're a stupid soldier who hasn't a brain in his body.'

Mario grinned. 'Soldier, yes.'

Yannis grinned also. If the man had understood he would have received a cuff on the ear at least.

The donkey decided to be awkward, tossing her head and making life difficult for the boy, but Mario made no attempt to help him and Yannis was feeling thoroughly bad-tempered by the time he reached the yard. He settled the donkey, then drew a bucket of water from the pump and proceeded to wash the sticky earth from the spade and fork he had been using, throwing the dirty water carelessly to one side when he finished, narrowly missing the Italian's boots. A string of oaths came and an exhortation for more care of which Yannis did not understand a word. He shrugged.

'Only a stupid soldier would stand that close when there's a bucket of water to be thrown away. Just asking for a bath, not that it would clean the likes of you. I'm going up to the hills again now for the animals. You can come if you fancy a walk.' Yannis turned on his heel and walked back towards the fields.

Mario looked after him puzzled. He had thought the boy had returned to the house for the night, now he was going off again. There was an appetizing smell wafting from the kitchen and his stomach was rumbling unpleasantly. He did not want to miss his share. The woman was probably a good cook and his stomach craved well-cooked food after the soldiers' fare he had been living on for the past months. He hesitated, the boy would probably not be gone long, and he would be hungry also. With a sigh Mario began to plod after him.

At the brow of the first hill Yannis let out a long, shrill whistle. Mario's hand went to his gun. Had he been foolish enough to walk into an ambush, led by a child? Yannis continued to stand, silhouetted against the sunset and Mario looked around warily. There was something moving closer, he levelled his revolver, finger on the trigger, just waiting for them to take a few more steps. Yannis turned; whistling again as he did so and it was then that Mario heard the unmistakeable bleat of a sheep and heard the bell the leader wore around her neck. He smiled self-consciously and slipped the revolver back into the holster.

Yannis waited until the elderly ewe was safely between the low stonewalls, then slapped her rump, sending her forwards at a trot, followed by a flock of sheep and goats. Once he judged most of them were in the compound Yannis pulled the makeshift wooden barrier across the opening and walked away nonchalantly down the hill. Back in the yard he worked the pump vigorously, rinsing his hands and face beneath the cold water, before entering the kitchen.

Anna, her face expressionless, was ladling moussaka onto six plates, whilst Marisa cut bread into uneven slices. Yannis removed his boots, slipping his feet into an old pair of sandals that stood near the door, and walked into the living room. Mario went to follow him only to find his way barred by Anna's arm.

'Boots,' she said sternly, pointing to them. 'Off.'

Mario looked around, there were no spare sandals for him to wear. He removed his heavy boots and looked ruefully at his toe poking out from his sock. That would have to be mended before he endured another march or he would be suffering in no time. He padded into the living room in Yannis's wake and went to sit at the table. Again Mario found his way barred by Anna.

'Gun.' She pointed to the dresser at the side where Victor had placed his revolver.

Mario turned to Victor. 'We shouldn't have to give up our guns. We have nothing to protect ourselves with.'

Victor shrugged. 'You either agree to remove your gun or you don't have any supper. She refused to let me sit down whilst I was wearing mine.'

Mario looked at Anna who was still barring his way. Reluctantly he withdrew the revolver from the holster and placed it beside Victor's. 'She'll probably poison us,' he remarked morosely.

A rapid interchange of Italian continued to pass between the two men, Mario obviously complaining about the afternoon and Victor trying to placate him. Under the cover of the men's conversation Yannis spoke to Anna.

'How much Greek does he understand?' He jerked his head towards Victor.

'I'm not sure.'

'Mario only knows a few words.'

'How do you know?'

'I called him a stupid soldier and he agreed with me.'

Marisa laughed, clapping her hand over her mouth. Anna frowned.

'You mustn't antagonise them, Yannis.'

'Why not? My Pappa's fighting them.'

'You have to think of your grandmother.'

'They won't hurt her, she's old and sick.'

'You don't know what they might do.'

'I know what I'd like to do,' retorted Yannis. 'If I were old enough to fight...'

'But you're not,' Anna interrupted him quickly. 'Eat your supper.'

Yannis scowled and bent his head over his plate.

Victor looked at Anna. 'Good.' He pointed to his plate. 'Thank you.'

'Too good for the likes of you,' growled Yannis and received a cuff on his ear from his aunt.

It was four months before the Italians stopped following the villagers wherever they went. The battalion had worked out a system amongst themselves whereby two sat at the top of the beach where the fishing boats were drawn up above the water line, and two others sat at the entrance to the village. This enabled the others to spend most of their time down at the village taverna playing cards.

Anna was grateful to have them out of the house during the day so she could talk freely with her mother and Marisa. She continued to lecture her niece on her attitude towards the soldiers, exhorting her to give them a wide berth and do nothing to draw attention to herself and each day she reminded Yannis to speak politely to them, whatever he might think.

'They're still stupid soldiers,' he would reply cheerfully, then clench his fists. 'As soon as I'm old enough I'm going to find my Pappa and fight them.'

'Fine,' Anna replied. 'I'll not stop you, just be careful in the meantime.'

Anna found the continual presence of the soldiers irksome. Each time she needed to wash or tend her mother she had to ask them to leave the room and although they did so, she resented the invasion of their privacy.

Yannis seemed unconcerned with their presence. Anna insisted that he and Marisa continued to attend the village school each morning, despite his protests that he was needed to help her on the farm. Having eaten a hurried snack at lunchtime he would carry his tools up to the fields and try to do the work his grandfather would have undertaken each day. For the first month a soldier followed him wherever he went and the boy had found a certain amount of pleasure in making life difficult for either Mario or Victor. He would go up to the fields and no sooner had he started work than he would lay down his tools and run back to the farm. The soldier would chase after him, only to find that as he arrived Yannis had picked up a tool he had deliberately left behind and be on his way back up the hill. If the soldier decided to ignore his race back to the farmhouse he found Yannis did not return and had to go looking for him, only to find the boy was helping his aunt close to the house. At first Victor had been frustrated by Yannis's antics, then he decided it was easier to watch his movements through his field glasses rather than follow him around. Once Yannis found the soldiers no longer chased after him he had stopped his little game with them.

Marisa had stayed very close to her aunt for the first few weeks, but now she had unbent towards the soldiers, trying to teach them words in her own language and laughing at their pronunciation and accent. Anna would purse her lips and frown in disapproval, but Marisa only laughed.

'It makes it easier to speak to them, besides, it could be to our advantage.'

'I don't see how.'

'If we ask them to do something they can't pretend not to understand us.'

'I don't want you getting friendly with them. Remember what I told you. You mustn't be alone with them. I don't trust them. They shouldn't be here. This is our country.'

'I know that, Mamma Anna, but whilst they're here we have to put up with them, so we might as well be friendly. Victor is quite nice and funny.'

Anna shook her head. 'He's an Italian, a soldier and has invaded our country.'

'But he isn't nasty like Roberto. I'm glad he's not living here with us. Sevas said the other night he...'

'Marisa! You are not to listen to gossip. Just do as I've told you and keep away from them.' Anna had also heard from Sevas how the Italian had tried to force himself upon her and only the arrival of Victor had saved her from his attentions.

Anna was not sure who she hated most; the German commander for leaving the soldiers for the sole purpose of preventing Spinalonga from becoming a seat of resistance or the Italians for obeying their orders. She was becoming desperately worried about her brother. She knew they had a small, but continuous supply of water, but of their food stocks she had no idea and prayed fervently that their supplies would last until the order was lifted.

Since the arrival of the Italians she had not waved from the beach each day as she had done for so many years. Today Mario was sleeping and there had been no sign of Victor. She sauntered openly down to the beach; half hidden behind a fishing boat she began to wave her scarf. A hand landed on her shoulder and the scarf was wrenched from her grasp. Anna spun round to meet the angry eyes of Victor.

He shook his head at her. 'No. Commander say no.'

'I don't care what the Commander said. I will wave to my brother.' She raised her hand in defiance and a figure could be seen waving back at her.

'No,' repeated Victor. 'No signal. No resistance.'

'Don't be so silly,' snapped Anna. 'I'm not signalling. I'm waving to my brother. Brother – understand? He lives there, he's a leper, he's sick.'

Victor looked out towards the island. 'Brother? On island?'

Anna nodded, trying hard not to let Victor see she was near to tears. Slowly he raised his field glasses and studied the man who was waving back. He lowered the glasses and held them up to Anna's eyes. Anna gasped. She could see Yannis quite clearly. She could see his lips move as he spoke to someone who came and stood beside him. The sight brought tears to her eyes and she handed the glasses back to Victor, blinking rapidly. 'Thank you.'

To Anna's surprise Victor raised his arm in salutation to her brother, handed her back her scarf and walked back up the beach where he waited for Anna to join him.

'Brother – sick?'

Anna nodded. The one time Yannis had floated across from the island to visit them he had seemed quite fit. His hands were clawed, one side of his face was covered in nodules, and his neck was bandaged to hide the running sores, the original site of infection, but in all other respects he had seemed healthy.

Victor pointed to her. 'You – sick?'

Anna was tempted to say that the whole family was afflicted. She shook her head.

Victor nodded. 'Good.'

She took his words to mean he was pleased that everyone

else was healthy. Leaving him at the top of the beach she returned to the farmhouse to continue with her daily chores.

Very little news filtered through to the village of Plaka and when it did it was ignored. Whatever happened in Heraklion was not likely to affect them. Immediate problems were more pressing and demanded their attention.

There were two men in the village. Danniakis was too old to be of any use in the mines or in any other capacity and the other was the priest. Danniakis, his daughter and granddaughter had relied upon the small general store, run by his son-in-law to bring them in an income. Now the goods on their shelves were dwindling and the every day commodities they needed were hard to come by. The fish, which had provided part of the staple diet for the villagers, was no longer available due to the lack of manpower and the women were becoming seriously concerned about their future.

They gathered in little groups after the church service on the Sunday, casting sideways glances at the soldiers who stood around. The small contingent of Italians was hardly noticed now. Their presence was accepted at meal tables, their washing done and their beds changed as were the others in the household, but their idleness was resented by all.

'If they spoke Greek it would help,' grumbled Eleni. 'At least you'd be able to tell them what you wanted.'

'Or what you didn't,' muttered Sevas, who was still repulsing her lodger's advances.

'Victor would understand,' Marisa suggested timidly to her aunt.

Anna frowned. 'He doesn't speak Greek.'

'He speaks more Greek than any of the others. I could make him understand.'

'That child needs taking in hand,' warned Sevas. 'She'll end up like her mother otherwise.'

Anna's face flamed. She wished she could think of a cutting retort for the reminder that her sister had conceived Marisa before she and Babbis had married.

'They go into Aghios Nikolaos, I expect there's plenty of food to be had there.'

'Why don't we ask them to get some then?'

'They don't understand, so what's the point?'

Anna drew away from them. 'I've got two to feed. I'll have to get back.' Taking Marisa's elbow she hurried her niece through the graveyard and up the road.

'What did you have to say that for? Now they'll think you're making eyes at a soldier. At your age, too!'

Marisa's eyes filled with tears. 'I only meant to be helpful. Victor can understand much more Greek now.'

'I've told you to keep away from him, and the other one.'

'We live in the same house so I have to speak to him,' Marisa replied sulkily.

Anna placed her arm around the girl's shoulders. 'Marisa, you must understand. These young men are far from their homes and will be lonely. If you show them friendship they could misunderstand and think you're offering more. Soldiers have been known to do terrible things to women.'

'Victor wouldn't hurt me. I saw him pick Aliki up when she fell over and kiss her knee better.'

Anna swallowed hard. 'Marisa, you know I talked to you a while ago about becoming a woman.'

Marisa nodded. It seemed that no sooner had her aunt spoken to her than the dreaded signs of womanhood had shown themselves.

'You're no longer a little girl like Aliki, to be picked up and cuddled. You must conduct yourself modestly, the way a young Greek girl should, and when you're older you'll meet a nice young man who will love you and appreciate your purity. You don't want the village gossips telling him you were friendly with the

Italian soldiers when they were here. That's the way girls get a bad name and end up on the streets of the cities.'

'That seems silly. I'd tell him I was friendly with them.'

Anna gazed at her anxiously. 'Marisa, there's friendly, where you just say hello and smile, and there's friendly when you let them hold your hand and kiss you and touch you. If you let one of the soldiers become that friendly with you they'd forget that you're so young and – and – anything could happen.' Anna tailed off lamely.

'You mean he might rape me?'

Anna crossed herself hurriedly and looked at her niece. 'Whatever gave you that idea?'

'Penelope and I were talking just after they arrived. She said soldiers always raped women and I asked her what she meant. She told me all about it.' Marisa shuddered. 'I suppose if it was only one of them and you liked him it wouldn't be too bad.'

'It would be quite awful, far worse than you can imagine. That's why I'm warning you not to get too friendly with them.' Anna was relieved that Marisa knew of the danger, although she was obviously not prepared to take the threat seriously.

'Victor isn't like that,' Marisa assured her aunt.

'The best of men can behave badly on occasions,' answered Anna grimly, remembering the one time when she had fought off Marisa's father after he had been drinking.

Despite Anna's forebodings the soldiers showed little interest in Marisa or the other young girls in the village. At least twice a week a small group would depart for Aghios Nikolaos and search out the available women who lived and worked there. They would return noisily in the early hours of the morning, usually the worse for drink, but their immediate appetites satisfied.

She was becoming as concerned as the other women about the meagre supplies they were eking out. Vegetables had been plentiful during the summer and she had dried and preserved as many as possible, and they had eggs, oil, milk and cheese. She slaughtered a goat or sheep regularly to provide the village with meat, but it was the basic necessities that were becoming scarce. She began to consider the idea of asking Victor if he would be willing to bring back supplies on his next visit to Aghios Nikolaos and wondered how best to broach the subject. She waited until they had all finished eating and Victor had thanked her as usual.

'Are you going to Aghios Nikolaos this week?' she asked him slowly.

'Aghios Nikolaos?'

'Are you going this week?'

Victor's brow creased in a frown. 'Aghios Nikolaos?' he repeated.

Anna nodded. 'If you are going to Aghios Nikolaos this week I want to ask you to buy us some food.'

'Food, good, thank you.'

Anna sighed in exasperation. Victor obviously did not know what she was asking.

Marisa giggled. 'Not like that, Mamma Anna. He doesn't understand. What do you want him to buy for us?'

'I need flour, rice, lentils, coffee and salt. Some soap would be a help.'

Marisa went into the kitchen and returned with a small quantity of each article and a few lepta, which she placed on the table. She moved her hands as if holding a steering wheel and looked at Victor. 'Aghios Nikolaos?'

Victor nodded.

'In Aghios Nikolaos you buy flour,' she pointed to it. 'Need coffee, need salt, need soap.' She placed a coin beside each article and pointed again. 'You buy.'

A smile crossed Victor's face. 'I get.'

Marisa wrote the names of each article in large letters, making Victor read them back to her until she was sure he understood. He took the paper from her and wrote the names in Italian before placing it in his pocket.

'It's no good just reeling a list off to him. He needs to see what the things are to be able to put a name to them. Is there anything else you want?'

Anna shook her head. Maybe she should not have been so scathing about Marisa's friendly approach towards them. 'Let's see what he brings back this time, if he does,' she added darkly.

'He will. You can trust Victor.'

Anna was not so sure that she could when she handed over the money for the purchases. She felt it was more likely he would squander it by gambling or drinking than buying food for them. Victor had saluted, flashed his smile and said, 'I do get asked.' whilst Marisa giggled behind him.

'He is so funny,' she said after he had left the house. 'He gets so muddled up with what he tries to say. Sometimes he has to say things over and over again before I finally understand.' She sighed. 'I suppose if they stay here long enough they'll all end up speaking properly, then we'll have nothing to laugh over.'

Anna did not answer her niece. Maybe she was too old to be amused by broken Greek, or just too tired. Having attended to her mother in the morning she would climb up the hill to the pen to milk the goats, hauling the heavy containers onto the cart and leading the donkey back to the village to deliver six to the general store and taking the others back to the farm.

Marisa would be left to prepare the dough for the bread that would be baked during the day. When she finished she would search for the eggs that the chickens seemed to lay in the most inaccessible places. They would take turns in churning the surplus milk into cheese before she began her preparations for their evening meal.

During the afternoon Marisa was left tending her grandmother and the vegetable garden before searching for eggs a second time. Anna would walk up to the fields to help Yannis in any way she could before returning to the farm to finally produce a substantial meal for them and the soldiers. Every other day they would go down to the shore together to wash clothes and bedding where the fresh water spring ran down into the sea.

Anna knew she was working far harder than she had before the soldiers arrived. There was still the same amount of daily work to be done in the house, but now she had to work on the farm whenever the opportunity arose. The uncertainty of the fate of her father working in the mines, and her brothers, one on Spinalonga and the other fighting, seemed to weigh on her and slow all her actions. Daily she debated whether she would be able to persuade Victor to allow a soldier to take supplies of food over to Spinalonga, but doubted that either she or Marisa would be able to make him understand.

When Victor returned from Aghios Nikolaos she inspected his purchases, ready to find fault and criticise, but having to admit that he had completed his errand perfectly. After Anna had thanked him he handed her three letters.

'Where did you get those?' she asked in surprise. They all had American stamps and she guessed they had come from Annita. She pushed them into her apron pocket. She would enjoy reading them when Victor had left.

Victor handed her back the money she had given him for the goods. 'Soldier stores. No money.'

'I don't understand. They can't just give you food.'

'For soldiers. Soldier stores,' he repeated.

Doubtfully Anna pocketed the money. Somehow it did not seem right that he should be able to go to the town and bring back the supplies they needed without paying. Victor seemed to sense some of her unease.

'Soldiers eat. Soldier stores. Soldiers live villages. No soldier stores. Soldier stores give. Soldiers eat.'

Anna frowned. 'I think I understand. The army is willing to supply some rations to us for feeding you. Well, that's certainly a relief. Do the other villagers know?'

'Please?'

'Marisa,' called Anna, 'Come and explain something to Victor for me, please.'

Marisa appeared, amused by her aunt's final acceptance of her communication with the Italians.

'Tell Victor I appreciate the groceries he's brought us and ask him if the other villagers know they can ask the soldiers to bring them from the army stores.' Anna watched as Marisa looked up at the young man.

'Mamma Anna say thank you.' Marisa clasped her hands together and held them to her heart. She picked up first the bar of soap, then the coffee. 'Roberto get for Sevas.' She pointed to him. 'You tell Roberto.' She then tapped her own chest. 'I tell Sevas. Understand?'

Victor nodded.

'You tell Julius. I tell Eleni.' Marisa placed the soap and coffee back on the table and pointed to it. 'Sevas want soap. Eleni want soap. Sevas want coffee. Eleni want coffee. All want. You tell. Soldiers get.'

Victor grinned broadly. 'All get. I tell.'

'You see, Mamma Anna, they're not all bad.'

Anna sniffed. 'They know it's for their own benefit. If we don't have the food to give them they don't eat, any more than we do.'

Anna opened one of the letters that Victor had given her.

Dear Anna

I have not had a letter from you for a long time. I understand from the news that it may be difficult for you to send a letter, but I would be grateful to know that you and all the family are safe and well.

Andreas is thriving. Maria is growing fast and Elena will be starting school very soon, which will make things easier for Mamma. Pappa is keeping well and enjoying his shop.

Elias is very happy with the research results. It is still early days, but the treatment seems to have made a considerable difference to many of the patients.

Your cousin, Annita

Anna read the letter through a second time. Who was Andreas and what was the shop that her uncle had? She pulled out the other two letters, maybe they would enlighten her.

The first one went into great detail about the work Elias and his colleagues had been doing. They had finally found a treatment that seemed to be successful in halting the disease. She reeled off names medicines that meant nothing to Anna, and went on to describe how she was allowed to go onto the wards to talk to the patients and take notes about their condition. It is a very strange disease, she commented, some people are so badly disfigured they are quite frightening to look at, and others you would pass in the street or stand next to without knowing they had the affliction.

There was the usual news of Elena, and now Maria was also mentioned. Anna presumed Annita's second child had been another girl and a letter had gone astray. The final sentence that intrigued her was '*Pappa is looking forward to opening his shop*'.

Anna opened the last envelope eagerly and everything became clear to her as she read it through.

She wrote first about the excitement they felt regarding their experiments. At last they seemed to have found a drug that would halt the spread of the disease. It would have to be tested and volunteers at the hospital had been asked to take part in the trials. Provided the results were good, with no bad side effects, it was hoped to have the drug available for all sufferers within the next two years.

Anna crossed herself. If that were so Yannis could benefit from it. She caught her breath. Yannis might not be alive in two years time. She shook her head to banish the thought and turned back to Annita's letter.

They had been searching for a larger house and finally found one that was ideal. The two girls would still share a bedroom, leaving one for the new baby she was expecting and the other one would be occupied by a maid. Such a large house would be impossible for her to manage without help. She wanted to follow her mother-in-law's example and find a girl from an orphanage to do the work.

Her Pappa had become very withdrawn and miserable, refusing to admit that he was not happy. Finally Elias had talked to him and found out how much he missed going out to sea and catching the fish. The sea was quite close, about an hour's drive from where they lived, but Yiorgo was certainly not able to undertake such heavy work now. He had looked around in the local town and found an empty shop. After some lengthy discussions and extensive alterations he had opened it as a wet fish shop and immediately he had seemed happier.

At the end of the letter Annita had added her new address. Anna smiled to herself. No wonder Annita had not had a letter from her for a long time. She had sent letters to her cousin's original address and this letter must have taken at least six months if not more to get to her if Annita was expecting when she wrote it and was now talking about Andreas thriving.

Anna took some crumpled paper from a drawer and sat down to write a long letter in reply. She must tell Annita about her Pappa being taken to the mines, about Yiorgo and Babbis joining the resistance, the order forbidding food to be taken out to the island and the ignominy of having Italian soldiers living in the house with them. She just hoped that Marisa would be able to explain to Victor how to take the letter to the post office and send it.

Yannis gazed across the bay towards the island. He felt frustrated and miserable. Whilst his grandfather had been in Plaka he had spent long, weary hours after school trying to keep the weeds at bay in the garden of his father's farmhouse, yet now it looked no different from before. He wanted his father to be proud of him when he returned and compliment him on his industry, but his efforts were in vain. He was not mature enough to rationalise his personal failure with lack of time. Priority was given to tending the vines and vegetables on his grandfather's land and only occasionally was he able to snatch an hour or two for himself now the Italians no longer followed him around. If his aunt would allow Marisa to come up to the fields with him she could have helped, but she was kept busy down at the farmhouse. He sighed deeply. Whilst he had been feeling sorry for himself valuable time had been passing.

'You sound as though you have the worries of the world on your shoulders.'

Yannis jumped visibly. He had thought himself completely alone on the hillside.

The man lowered himself to the ground and looked up at the boy. 'Don't be frightened. I only want to talk to you.' He appeared to be a beggar in threadbare clothes, with a stubbly beard and blood shot eyes.

'Who are you? You're not from the villages hereabouts.'

A deep chuckle sounded in the man's throat. 'I'm not, but you are. You live at the farmhouse at the end of the village.'

'How do you know that?'

'I keep my eyes open.'

'Then you'll also know I've got work to do.' Yannis turned away.

'The resistance need your help.'

Yannis stopped and took a deep breath, trying to hide his elation. 'What do you mean?'

'I need some information from you.'

'Why should I give any information to you, even if I had any?' answered Yannis warily.

'You're a good Cretan, aren't you? You want to oust the Germans and have your country to yourself again surely?'

'How do I know you're not working for the Germans?'

The man frowned. 'I know you are Yannis Andronicatis and that farmhouse over there belongs to your father. You've lived at your grandparent's farmhouse since you were born as your mother died. You have an older sister and your aunt's name is Anna.'

'Anyone could tell you that.'

'They probably could, but your father, Babbis told me.'

Yannis shrugged, refusing to commit himself, much as he wanted to be considered man enough to help the resistance movement.

'I only want to ask you some questions.'

'You can ask them, but I may not answer them.'

'How many people live in Plaka?'

'Now, or before the Germans came?'

'Now.'

Yannis calculated. 'About forty if you include the soldiers.'

'Are there any village men there?'

'Why?'

'They might be able to help us.'

'In the mines, like my grandfather?' Yannis spoke bitterly.

'Oh, no; I didn't mean that. When was your grandfather taken?'

'When the Italians were first billeted on us.'

'So who are left?'

'Women and children. Old Danniakis and the priest.'

'How many Italians are there?'

'About twenty most of the time.'

'How do they treat you?'

Yannis shrugged. 'The ones that live with us are all right. I don't really know the others.'

'Do they live with the villagers?'

'Yes. Why?'

Yannis's question was ignored. 'How do the villagers feel about them?'

'Resentful. This is our country, so we shouldn't have foreign soldiers here.' Yannis bit his lip. He had tried to be so careful with all his answers.

'So they'd be willing to help us?'

'How do you mean?'

'Well, if we wanted some food, or asked them for some spare clothing they'd be willing to give to us?'

'Maybe. You'd have to ask them yourself.'

'That's the problem. I can't go near the village. I'd be challenged as soon as I walked down the road. That's where you come in. I want you to talk to them and let me know how they feel. I'm not asking them to do anything, I just want to know if we can count on their support.'

'Suppose I said everyone was willing to supply clothes and feed you, what would you do then? Send in a force of German soldiers and arrest everyone?'

The man laughed. 'You still don't trust me, do you?'

'Why should I?'

The man sighed. 'I'll come back in about a week. Let me know your answer then.' He held out his hand to the boy. 'Babbis will like to know I've shaken your hand.'

'Will you be seeing him?'

'Bound to.'

'Ask him where Yannis is. If you can tell me the answer to that question I'll know you come from him and I can trust you.'

'He knows you're here.'

Yannis smiled to himself. 'Just ask him. Now, I must get on with my work. I've wasted enough time today.'

Yannis returned to his work thoughtfully. He knew he had been cautious, neither committing himself to helping the resistance or refusing. He was convinced that if the man was spying for the Germans he had said nothing that could incriminate him or his family, but he hoped he was not. Yannis wished he was older, then he would be able to find out for himself by joining the resistance fighters in the hills. He squared his shoulders. Being a resistance fighter did not depend upon age. He could find out the answers to the questions he had been asked and if the man was genuine he would find a willing helper when he returned.

He began with the children in the village, asking them if they liked the Italian soldiers who lodged with them, leading them on to reveal the way their mothers talked about the uninvited guests, gradually building up a picture of tolerance between the two nationalities, but a desire on the part of the Cretans to see them gone for ever. Feeling confident he began to stop and talk to the women as they cleaned their doorsteps or hung their washing out to dry, always leading the conversation round to the Italians, until by the end of the week he felt he had enough information should the man decide to visit him again.

It was ten days before the man reappeared and called to Yannis from behind a bush. Yannis ignored him and finished pulling the row of carrots. Having filled the sack he pulled it to one side and walked closer to where the man was sitting.

'Time you and I had a little talk, young man.'

'You said you'd be back in a week.' Yannis spoke accusingly.

'One or two other things cropped up which needed my attention.'

'Did you meet my father?'

'I did. He was most upset to hear about your grandfather and wanted to know how you were managing.'

Yannis shrugged. 'Did you ask him where Yannis was?'

The man grinned. 'You're no fool, are you? He said he was on Spinalonga. Is that some sort of code between you?'

'No. It was just a way of proving to myself that you actually knew him and were who you said you were. You had no way of knowing about my uncle.'

'How long has he been there?'

'I'm not sure. Since before I was born.'

'How is he?'

'I've no idea. We're not allowed to have any contact with the lepers. That's why they were sent there in the first place. We're not even allowed to send food over to them any more. The German Commander decided the island would be a good place for a resistance group to hide. That's why he left the Italians here. They have orders to shoot anyone who tries to go over there.' Yannis spoke resentfully.

'I wondered why there were so many here. In most villages of this size there's just four or five. Did you manage to get any information for me?'

'A little. Everyone agrees that it's better to have the Italian soldiers here than the Germans, but everyone would like to see them leave. They've no real complaints against them; no one has been shot or even threatened. They're just not Cretans, and they're working for the Germans. If you wanted food or clothing I'm sure the villagers would help, but I haven't asked them outright.'

'Don't do so. It's enough to know that they are willing to help us if necessary.'

'What would you like me to do now? I could sabotage a jeep.' Yannis spoke eagerly.

The man shook his head. 'I don't want you drawing attention to yourself. I promised your father I wouldn't put you in any danger. A good resistance man is never noticed. He's just one of a crowd, that way he's safe.'

Yannis's eyes gleamed. 'I'll take my orders from you. What do you want me to do?'

'Keep your eyes and ears open. If you think you've heard anything of importance, remember it.'

'I could write it down,' offered Yannis.

'Never put anything in writing. That can be dangerous if the wrong person sees it. Babbis said you have no doctor in the village. The nearest one is in Aghios Nikolaos. Is that right?'

Yannis nodded. 'We haven't a doctor, but there's Mamma Anna. If she didn't know what to do she used to go and ask the Widow. Why?'

'It's as well to know. No point in coming here with an injured man if there's no doctor.'

Yannis swallowed hard. 'Do men often get injured?'

'No, but we haven't done much hard fighting yet. Don't worry. Your father will be safe enough. I shan't be coming this way again. There'll be a man called Michael in the area. He'll contact you if he needs anything. He has very blue eyes, so you'll recognise him.'

'He'll have to tell me where my uncle is before I trust him,' cautioned Yannis.

The man smiled at the eager boy. 'I'll pass the information on to him. What are you going to say if you're asked who you were talking with?'

'Just a beggar who wandered over from Aghios Nikolaos way. I gave him a bit of bread from my lunch and directed him towards the Heraklion road.'

'Did he go that way?'

'I've no idea. I went back to my work.'

'Good boy. You're learning fast. I'll leave you now anyway. It's better that I'm not seen talking to you, but always have your story ready.'

Yannis returned to the rows of carrots, a delighted smile on his face. He was a resistance worker! How he would have loved to go down to the village street and shout out the news to everyone.

Each day Yannis looked eagerly for the arrival of the man called Michael and was disappointed. The weeks went by and no stranger appeared on the hills or hid in the undergrowth to contact him and he felt resentful. Had they decided he was not old enough to be of assistance to them? He wished he had asked the man where his father was hiding so he could make his way there and join him. He considered running away during the night and trying to find a resistance group he could join, but then he thought of his aunt. There was no way she could manage the farm on her own, and his father would not thank him for leaving her. It was with a heavy heart that he dug the last of the potatoes and began to load the cart.

'Yannis.'

A man had appeared as if from nowhere and stood behind the bush where the donkey was tethered.

Yannis felt his heart leap as he looked at the man and noticed his brilliant blue eyes. This must be Michael. 'Who wants him?' he asked.

'Your uncle Yannis is on Spinalonga,' was the answer.

'He has been for years,' replied Yannis cheerfully. 'What can I do for you?'

'I was in this area and thought I'd introduce myself. I'm Michael.'

'You don't look like a Cretan,' observed Yannis.

'I'm not. My mother was a Greek from Athens and my father is from Scotland.'

'What are you doing over here?'

'I was shipped over to defend Crete. Unfortunately whilst we were defending the beaches the Germans parachuted in. We were totally unprepared. We fought, of course, but we couldn't hold them. We had the order to retreat and were told we would be picked up. Some of the ships did get in and the men were taken off, those that didn't reach the port in time had to stay behind. By then the Germans had established themselves and not all the ships got out. Those of us who had to stay have joined up with the Cretan resistance. Most of us are no good for anything other than fighting, but there are a few, like me, who speak Greek. We're prepared to take the risks. We've nothing to lose except our lives. We have no relatives here for the Germans to torture and extract reprisals from.'

'Where are you living?'

'The Lassithi caves mostly, but we're always looking for a safe area where we could make a base. Your father told us about Plaka. We thought it would be a quiet little village that the Germans would ignore. Thank goodness we sent out a scout for information before we moved any troops to the area.'

'There are only Italians here.'

'Unfortunately they're under German orders. If we cleared them out of the village a replacement would be sent, probably Germans, and they're not so lenient with the villagers.'

'So what are you going to do?'

'I'll look somewhere else, up in the hills maybe.'

'There are some caves up there. Would you like me to show you?'

Michael shook his head. 'I'll find them.'

Yannis's face dropped. 'So I'm not going to be of any use to you.'

'If these caves you have mentioned are suitable you'll be of great use to us. We shall be relying on you to persuade the villagers to feed us if we use them.'

'I haven't been to them for a long time.' Yannis frowned. 'They seemed big to me, but I was only small at the time.'

'Why were you there?'

'My uncle had lost a sheep and I went with him and my father to look for it. The silly thing had fallen through a hole in the roof, so he cut her throat and brought her back to the farm for Mamma Anna to cook.'

Michael smiled. 'Poor old sheep. Which direction do I go?'

'A couple of hills over and towards the west.'

Michael scanned the area that Yannis indicated. 'I'll be off, then.'

'When will I see you again?'

'Who knows? If I'm in the area I'll see you, or maybe one of my friends will pass by. You just continue to look after your family and go about your daily business. You're needed here. Do nothing that draws attention to yourself.'

Yannis nodded, but he felt bitterly disappointed. He had hoped Michael would ask him to do something positive that would be of assistance to the resistance group.

Marisa sat on the doorstep of the farmhouse where she could catch the last of the sun and dry her newly washed hair. She hugged her knees and rested her head on her arms. A feeling of desolation swept over her. She loved her aunt dearly, but wished she could remember her mother, who had died when she was so young. She wished Yannis had been a girl, then maybe they could have exchanged confidences and giggle together as she used to do with Penelope and Ourania. Both girls, being younger than her, made it seem so childish now, and she could not talk to her aunt, who would disapprove and lecture her. She sighed deeply.

'Problem?'

She felt the colour rush to her cheeks as she raised her eyes and looked at Victor. Her heart lurched; he was so attractive. The way his hair curled behind his ears and at the nape of his neck made shivers run up and down her spine. She managed to smile.

'I was wishing my hair would dry more quickly.'

He frowned and she realised he had not understood. 'My hair,' she held out a strand. 'Wet. Sun dry quick.'

'Hair beautiful,' he remarked, making Marisa blush even more deeply. He sat down beside her and she moved to make enough space for him to sit without touching her. 'Have letter,' he smiled and tapped his pocket. 'Mother write.'

'Mother well?' asked Marisa.

'All well,' he smiled again and sighed. 'Miss mother, brother, father.'

Marisa nodded in sympathy. She had never had a letter in her life. Occasionally her aunt had received one from America, which she explained had come from her cousin, Annita. Victor drew his wallet from his pocket and handed a snapshot to Marisa of a middle-aged couple. Marisa studied the picture with interest. They looked very ordinary people, standing stiffly before a tall building.

'House?' she asked.

Victor shook his head. He leant towards her and indicated with his finger midway up the structure. 'Apartment.' He motioned with his hands walking upstairs, panting as he did so and Marisa laughed.

Anna heard and looked out from the kitchen, seeing their heads close together. 'Marisa,' she called sharply. 'I need you here.'

Obediently Marisa rose and handed the photograph back to Victor. He continued to sit and look at it as she went inside.

'What were you doing with Victor?' asked Anna immediately.

'I was looking at a photograph of his parents. They live in an apartment and have a lot of stairs to climb.'

Anna sniffed. 'You are not to sit out there on the step with him. What would the neighbours think?'

Marisa shrugged sulkily. 'The neighbours can't even see the step.'

'Someone might pass by. I need some more parsley. There's a big clump you can pick from at the end of the garden.' Anna watched her niece as she walked away. The girl seemed to be in a dream half the time.

Yannis tethered the donkey and began to pull up the withered pea plants. He placed the sticks in a neat pile and began to load the rubbish onto the cart. He wanted to finish clearing the land before mid-day, then when the sun was at its highest he could move to the shade of the carob trees and pick the ripened pods. They would have to be added to the compost heap this year, as there would be no market for them in Aghios Nikolaos. The island was cut off from mainland Greece and no ship would arrive to transport the crop to the factory for processing. No longer a source of income, they were just a liability and he wondered if it would be more practical to leave them and use his energies to dig a field so more vegetables could be sown next spring and provide more food for themselves and the villagers. He would talk to his aunt about the idea that evening.

He took a long drink from his water bottle, wiped his mouth with the back of his hand and replaced it in a small patch of shade.

'Can you spare a drop of water?'

The words were just audible to his ears and he turned slowly to see a man laying on his stomach a short distance away half hidden by gorse bushes. His chin was cupped on his hands and he was licking his cracked lips. Yannis looked back towards the farmhouse, where there was no sign of movement or glint from the field glasses to indicate he was being watched.

'Wait a while.' He spoke as quietly as the man had before picking up an armful of dead pea plants and moving them in line with the stranger. He repeated the process until he was satisfied that anyone looking up at the fields would not be able to see the man lying there.

Yannis retrieved the bottle and held it to his lips as if drinking, before moving over to the mound of debris. He sat down and placed the bottle within reach of the man's hands. 'You can sit up if you want. No one will be able to see you.'

He heard the man drinking noisily. 'Have you got any more?'

'Not here. I'll have to go back down to the farm.'

'Any chance of a bit of food?'

'I'll try.'

Yannis picked up the empty bottle and ran down the hill. He deposited it beside the pump and let himself quietly into the kitchen. Marisa was in there and she turned in surprise as her brother entered. He placed his fingers to his lips and she nodded, turning back to her work and ignoring him. She would find out later what he was up to. He moved swiftly to the cupboard where his aunt stored their food and helped himself to a loaf of bread and large piece of cheese, pushing them inside his shirt, hoping that if he met anyone they would not notice the suspicious bulges. Once outside he refilled the bottle and retraced his footsteps up the hill.

The man was where he had left him and Yannis handed the meagre rations over to him, watching him eat hungrily.

'Thank you. You're a good boy,' he said finally. 'Is it safe for me to move about?'

'Not really. A soldier could be watching with his field glasses.'

'I need to take some water to my companion.'

'Where is he?'

'Hidden back there in the gorse bush.'

'Why doesn't he come and get it?'

'He can't. He's injured.'

'How did he get here, then?'

'He walked most of the way, but his leg's really bad now and he's becoming feverish.'

'Where are you making for?'

'Anywhere we can lay low for a while whilst his leg heals. This looked like a quiet village, so I thought I'd try here.'

Yannis shook his head. 'All the villagers have Italian soldiers living with them. No one could hide you.'

The man sighed deeply. 'I don't know what to do. He can't walk for long and I can't carry him.'

'On your own you could manage to get to Aghios Nikolaos by going over the hill. I expect they have Italians there, but being a town you should manage to find someone to help you.'

'How far is it?'

'I've no idea. I've never been there. I'll leave the bottle and go off and do some work. You can pick it up when you're ready.' Yannis rose and sauntered away from where the prickly bushes grew. Although the ground was dry and dusty there was clear evidence that someone had forced a way into the centre. It was an obvious spot for anyone to use as cover.

Yannis returned to pulling up the remains of the peas and despite being excited by helping an injured resistance fighter he was also deeply worried. If the men were discovered hiding there it would be obvious who had brought them food and water, and he certainly did not want to cause trouble for his family. For the rest of the morning he stayed well clear of the gorse bushes, although he longed to find out if the man knew his father. Thinking of his father gave him an idea and he gradually worked his way to the brow of the hill. He looked around cautiously, then ran as swiftly as possible down into the small valley where his father's house stood, empty and neglected over the past few months.

Yannis pushed open the door to an outhouse and looked around. There was a miscellany of tools, sacks, empty containers and general rubbish. He began to move the items to one side and when he judged there was enough space he walked over to his father's house. The back door yielded under his touch and he crept inside. Moving quietly he crossed the kitchen and up the wooden stairs, opening the two doors at the top and looking into each room. One was completely empty; the other still held the mattress where his father had slept for so many years. Yannis felt a catch in his throat. Maybe his father was injured, dead even, no, he would not think about that. His father was brave and clever; they would not be able to kill him. He shook his head as though to clear his mind of the unhappy thoughts, and began to pull the heavy, unwieldy mattress down the stairs.

The mattress safely installed in the outhouse, he treated himself to a long drink from the pump in the yard and filled an empty bottle with water before making his way back up the hill. He placed the water bottle close to the clump of gorse and returned to the pile of withered vegetation that he continued to load onto the cart.

The work took him closer and closer to the clump of gorse until he was finally able to dive inside and wriggle his way through to where the bushes had formed a small, dark cave of thorns. On the grass lay a man, his trousers torn and bloodied, showing a dirty leg which had been roughly bandaged. Yannis sat back on his haunches, puzzled. Surely the man he had talked with had not left his companion already to walk to Aghios Nikolaos? A rustling and cracking of branches made him stiffen, as the man forced himself back into the clearing, cursing at the scratches he was receiving as he came.

'If you decide to come in here again you'd better give me a shout first,' he remarked grimly. 'I was ready to shoot you.'

Yannis looked at him in alarm. 'Why?'

'For all I knew you'd gone off to alert some soldiers and they were forcing their way in.'

'I've come to help you,' replied Yannis stiffly. 'I know a place where you can hide out for a few days. All you have to do is get him there when it's dark.'

'A cave?'

'No, at my father's house. It's deserted and unless the soldiers are looking for you in this area they have no reason to go there. It's the other side of the hill. Can he manage to get that far?'

The man nodded. 'He'll manage. Tell me exactly where it is.'

'Just go to the top of the hill and it's in the valley below. I've moved a mattress into one of the outhouses. You take him there tonight and I'll bring you up some food tomorrow morning.'

'Are you sure it's safe?'

'It's as safe as laying here.'

The man held out his hand to Yannis. 'You're a good boy. What's your name?'

'Yannis.'

'My name's Nikos.'

Yannis clasped his hand. 'Don't try to move before it's dark. I'll be up as soon as I can tomorrow morning.'

Yannis crept into the kitchen, hoping he would not be heard. Stealthily he helped himself to cheese, bread, olives and tomatoes, which he wrapped in a cloth and pushed into his bag. He went out to the yard and placed it inside the stable before he returned, whistling cheerfully, into the kitchen.

'You're early, Yannis,' remarked Anna.

'I need to take the donkey a bit further up today. She all but cleared the patch where I left her yesterday.'

'You make sure she doesn't eat my herbs.'

Yannis grinned. His aunt said the same thing each day. 'I'll not put her anywhere near the wild herb patch.'

Yannis hurried the donkey up the hill away from the farm, the bag of food hidden inside her panniers. To his consternation there was distinct evidence where someone had forced themselves into the gorse bushes. Yannis led the donkey over and scuffed up the ground with his boots before tethering her as close as possible, hoping that the marks would be attributed to her.

From his vantage point on the hill Yannis could see the movement in the village below him as the soldiers took up their customary positions on the beach and at the rough road where the straggle of houses began. The sun glinted on field glasses as they swept the surrounding area for any sign of movement, resting on Yannis for some minutes whilst the soldier ascertained that he was working in the fields as usual, before returning them to his pocket. Yannis heaved a sigh of relief. They would not bother to look again for an hour or so, which would give him plenty of time to go to his father's house.

Taking his bag from the pannier he raced down the hill and stopped abruptly before the outhouse. He remembered Nikos's warning and knocked before he pushed at the rickety door. Nikos appeared behind him and grinned as he slipped his gun back into the holster.

'I've brought you some food.'

Nikos seized upon the bread hungrily. 'I can do with this. It was hard work getting him up here.'

'Is he any better?'

Nikos shook his head, his mouth full of food.

'Can I have a look at his leg?'

'If you like, for what good it will do.' He led Yannis to the side of the outhouse where he pushed aside a wheelbarrow piled with rubbish. Two pieces of the wooden planking had been removed giving enough space for a man to crawl in and out without using the door. The man lay on the mattress and Nikos unwrapped the soiled bandage to show the deep gash where a bayonet had pierced his companion's leg. The skin around the wound was hard and shiny, the open edges encrusted with dried blood and pus.

Yannis sucked in his breath. 'He needs a doctor. That won't get better by resting it. He'll end up with gangrene.'

To Yannis's embarrassment tears filled Nikos's eyes. 'What can I do? I can't leave him. He's my little brother and I promised my mother I'd look after him.'

Yannis sat back on his heels. 'I know someone who might be able to help. She knows lots about herbs and things.'

A glimmer of hope shone in Nikos's face. 'Would she come and look at him?'

Yannis shook his head. 'I can't ask her to do that. I'll try to find out what you ought to put on it to help it heal. I must go. I'll be back later with some more food.'

Once again Yannis raided his aunt's store of food when he took a load of dead vegetation back to the compost heap. He had avoided being alone with Marisa, lest she question him about his surreptitious afternoon visits, but he had reckoned without his aunt. He delivered the food to his father's house where Nikos accepted it gratefully and returned to the farm to stable the donkey and wash. As he entered the kitchen Anna accosted him.

'Yannis, have you been taking food from the pantry?' she asked him quietly.

Yannis reddened to the roots of his hair. 'I was hungry,' he lied.

Anna raised her eyebrows. 'Very hungry, I imagine, by the amount that has gone.'

'I'm sorry. Did it matter?'

Anna shook her head. 'We've enough food for you to have a bit extra at the moment if you need it, but I wish you'd told me. I was on the point of accusing Victor or Mario of helping themselves. It was lucky Marisa told me you'd been in during the afternoon.'

'I think it's being up in the fields all day. Actually I wanted to ask you something.' Yannis wished to divert his aunt's mind from the missing food. 'If one of the sheep cut a leg what would you put on it to help it heal?'

Anna looked at her nephew in surprise. 'Is one of them hurt?'

'No, I just wondered. I ought to know these things.'

'The juice of the ribwort would be as good as anything, or the leaves from shepherd's purse. You know what they look like, don't you?'

Yannis nodded. 'I've helped you collect shepherd's purse, and I remember you putting ribwort on me when I cut my hand on some glass. I just wasn't sure if you used the same for animals.'

'It certainly wouldn't hurt them.' Anna looked at Yannis's hands as he reminded her of the time he had come to her with his hands covered in blood from a deep, but small cut. 'It wouldn't hurt for you to put some on your hands now, by the looks of things. You're covered in scratches.'

Yannis shrugged. 'I'll do it tomorrow.'

'Come here and I'll do it for you now.'

Anna opened the small cupboard that stood beside the stone sink and took out a bottle of dark liquid. With a clean rag she dabbed at the scratches that ran up to his elbows. 'What on earth have you been doing? You look as if you've fallen into a bramble patch.'

'I think it was the pea sticks,' mumbled Yannis. 'Is supper nearly ready?' He now needed to distract her thoughts from his scratches.

As Yannis ate the meat Anna had stewed with onions he thought of the two men who had nothing more than bread and cheese. He wondered if Anna would miss the small bottle of ribwort juice if he took it up to the fields with him the following day and decided he would take a chance. He could always say he wanted to put more on his scratches.

Anna baked two extra loaves to keep pace with Yannis's increased appetite but she had to admit that however much he had eaten during the day he cleared his supper plate with relish. She wished she could say the same for her mother who was only picking at her food.

'What's wrong, Mamma? Are you feeling ill?'

Maria shook her head. 'I'm well enough, so I should be, the way you look after me. It's your poor Pappa and brother I'm worried about. Do you think Victor would be able to find out how your Pappa's getting on?'

'I don't know.' Anna frowned. 'I could get Marisa to ask him. She seems to have a knack of putting things to him in a way that he understands. In the meantime I'll make you up a tonic. It won't take me very long.'

'You're a good girl, Anna.'

Anna smiled wanly. She looked and felt far older than her thirty-one years and could hardly remember how carefree life had been for her when she was Marisa's age.

'I'll have to leave you for a while to go up on the hill to collect some of the herbs I need. I should be back in about an hour or so.' Anna took her scarf from behind the door. 'I'm going down to wave to Yannis first.'

Her trip to the beach having been successful in her eyes, as she received an answering wave from a figure on the island, she strode briskly up the hill and away from the farm. The exercise began to invigorate her and she promised herself that she would do it more often. Arriving in the hollow where she could expect

167

to find some of the herb she was looking for growing, she clicked her tongue in annoyance. The donkey must have been there, trampling and spoiling all of it. She would have a few words to say to Yannis about that. Now she would have to walk the further half a kilometre to Babbis's farmhouse and raid the garden there. She should really take back any of the vegetables that were going to seed before they spoilt completely and wished she had thought to bring a sack with her. There would probably be one in an outhouse and she could check that all was well in the farmhouse whilst she was there.

The door opened at her touch and she stepped into the dusty kitchen. She wondered when Yannis had last been to the house as there were finger marks on the shelves and footsteps leading through to the living room. Anna walked in, automatically pushing a chair into place as she passed and brushing the crumbs from it. She frowned. Was Yannis coming to his father's house to eat his food at mid-day?

At the top of the stairs she stopped and looked into the empty rooms. Where had the mattress gone? She would have to ask Yannis if he knew.

She sighed resignedly. Yannis had a way of avoiding direct questions. She retraced her steps, closing the door carefully. She did not want a stray animal making its way inside. She walked across to the outhouse and pushed at the door, meeting with resistance. Something must have fallen and be blocking it. She pushed again, managing to move it a few inches. As she paused to catch her breath she felt a strong arm around her neck and something hard pressing into the small of her back.

'What do you want?' The grip on her neck was relaxed slightly to allow her to answer.

'I came for a sack.' Her heart was beating so fast she thought she would faint.

'A sack?'

'I was going to collect some vegetables.'

The man removed his arm and turned her to face him, levelling the revolver at her.

'Who knows you're here?'

'No one.'

'So you came to steal some vegetables?'

'I'm not stealing.' Anna was indignant. 'I have every right to be here. This house belongs to my family.'

'So where are they?'

'At the farmhouse down by the shore.'

Slowly Nikos lowered his revolver. 'Did the boy tell you we were here?'

'No.' Anna's mouth set in a straight line. So this was why Yannis had been asking for extra food and asking what he should put on a cut. 'How long have you been here?' she asked.

'A few days.'

'Who knows you're here?'

'Only you and the boy.'

'You shouldn't have asked him to help you, he's only a child.'

The man laughed harshly. 'We're with the resistance. We depend on all loyal Cretans to help us, whatever their age.'

'Don't you know there's a battalion of Italian soldiers down in the village? If they find you they'll shoot you, and us as well, I expect.'

'There's no way they're going to catch me here. If they come snooping around, I'll disappear. Are you the medicine woman?'

'I know a bit about herbs.'

'Would you have a look at my companion?'

'What's wrong with him?'

'He's got a flesh wound, trouble is, it's festering. He can't walk until it clears up, so we're staying here.'

'Where is he?'

The man jerked his head towards the outhouse. 'In there.'

'Show me.'

Nikos pushed aside a wheelbarrow and exposed a hole in the wall. 'You'll have to crawl through.'

Anna looked at the hole in exasperation. 'Did you cause that damage?'

'I blocked the door in case someone came. I needed another way in and out. The boy told me about the soldiers.'

Anna crawled through the hole, Nikos following her. She waited for her eyes to adjust to the dim light before moving to where the man lay on the mattress. She wondered if Yannis had told them to help themselves or if it had been his own idea to make them as comfortable as possible under the circumstances.

Nikos unwrapped the soiled bandage and Anna gazed at the wound. The skin was stretched and shiny, purplish with green and yellow streaks hardly disguised by a brownish liquid that had been liberally applied. Anna bent and sniffed at the leg. Intermixed with the smell of dirt and infection was the scent of ribwort.

'This needs to be properly treated. It needs draining for a start and then the dead flesh needs to be cut away.'

'Can you do it?'

'Me? I'm not a doctor. I've a little herbal knowledge, that's all.'

'Where's the nearest doctor?'

'Aghios Nikolaos.'

'Could you fetch him?'

Anna shook her head. 'It's a long walk; besides, we're not allowed to leave the village. Even if I could go I have a sick mother to look after.'

'What about the boy? Maybe he could go?'

Anna shook her head. There was no way Yannis should risk going for a doctor, yet the man on the bed would probably die within the next week or so unless he received medical help.

'I have to get back. I told my Mamma I'd only be about an hour and if the soldiers come looking for me and I'm not there they'll start to come up into the hills.'

'Why should they look for you?'

'We have two of them living in our house.'

'That's what the boy said. All the villagers have soldiers living with them.' Nikos sighed. 'I'll ask the boy to go to Aghios Nikolaos. He seems able to move about freely enough, and he's not frightened of a few Italians.'

Anna's face blanched. 'You can't, you mustn't. He's too young, besides, I'm responsible for him until his father returns.'

For the first time Nikos smiled. 'If it were him laying here you'd get that doctor fast enough, wouldn't you? What's the difference?'

Anna hesitated. What was the difference? 'I mustn't endanger Yannis.'

'Then you go.'

'I can't. I'll be missed. Let me go home now and I'll try to think of something. Trust me.'

'Short of keeping you a prisoner up here, which would probably start the whole village looking for you, I've little choice. If any of those Italians show up I'll know why and you'll wish you'd never been born, you and your mother,' he threatened.

'I'll say nothing,' promised Anna.

'And you'll get that doctor?'

'I'll try, somehow I'll try.'

'We'll be grateful, Alecos and I.' He spoke softly and smiled gently at her. 'He's my little brother.'

Shyly Anna returned the smile. 'I'll try to think of something.'

'Just a moment.' Nikos pulled away the obstructions blocking the door, making enough space for Anna to slip through. He watched from the gap he had created whilst she hurriedly picked the herbs she needed. She ignored the vegetables she had intended to collect; they could draw attention to the fact that she had been to the house. Running over the rough ground as fast as she was able she reached the hollow which had been her intended destination, there she slowed to a walk and continued down the hill.

How could she possibly go to Aghios Nikolaos and ask a doctor to visit the injured man? The journey was too hazardous for either Yannis or Marisa to undertake, and she did not want to leave the children alone in the house with the soldiers. She wished she had never gone out to collect the herbs to make her mother a tonic. Her mother. That was the answer. She would make up a light sleeping draught for her; then tell the soldiers she could not wake her and feared another stroke. If she was convincing enough one of them might even offer to go to the town for her.

Full of apprehension, she entered the farmhouse, relieved to see that her mother appeared to be dozing and Marisa was still down at the seashore doing the washing. She chopped the meat that was to be part of their meal that evening, planning carefully. She needed to get a message to the doctor that afternoon so he would come out that evening, but she did not want him to arrive too soon. She would not be able to take him up to the farmhouse until it was dark.

The bell in the church tower tolled, making her start and she realised that within a few minutes Victor and Mario would be arriving and wanting a midday meal.

Hurriedly she gathered the ingredients she needed and pounded them together, all she had to do now was to administer the potion. Her hands shaking, Anna poured the dark mixture into a cup and woke her mother gently. 'Drink this, Mamma. It will make you feel better. Then I'll bring you some soup.'

Unresisting Maria drained the cup and handed it back. 'You're a good girl, Anna.'

Anna felt the blood rush to her face. Suppose she had given her mother too much and she did not wake up? No, she would not contemplate such a terrible thought. As Mario and Victor entered she was placing bread, cheese, olives and tomatoes on the table.

'Help yourselves,' she said. 'I'm just going to heat some broth for my mother.' She spoke so calmly that she surprised herself.

'Here we are, Mamma. I've crumbled some bread in for you. If I put it there will you be able to manage? Mamma?' Anna leant over her mother. 'Mamma!' Her voice rose higher. 'Oh, no! Mamma, can you hear me?' Anna took hold of the old lady's wrist and felt the pulse, to her overwhelming relief it was throbbing strongly.

Victor and Mario stopped eating and looked at her. Anna turned to Victor, her eyes wide and worried. 'Marisa. Get Marisa. Marisa washing.'

'Mamma ill?'

'Mamma very ill. Get Marisa.'

Without further questions Victor left the house and hurried down to the shore. He knew just where Marisa was as he had stood and watched her as she laughed and chatted with the women whilst they slapped their clothes on the flat rocks.

'Marisa! Marisa! Come. Anna!'

Marisa looked up at the breathless soldier. 'What's the matter?'

'Anna say. Mamma ill.'

Marisa looked at the pile of wet washing, wondering if she should gather it up and take it with her. Victor took her wrist. 'Come.' He pulled at her urgently.

Unresisting she allowed Victor to hold her wrist until they reached the farmhouse and he opened the door, pushing her in before him. Anna was bending over her mother, chaffing her hands and speaking to her gently.

'What's happened?' Marisa was clearly frightened by the scene before her.

'Your grandmother's been taken ill. She may have had another stroke. I can't rouse her. Go up and find Yannis. Tell him to come down at once. He'll have to go to Aghios Nikolaos for the doctor.'

Marisa did not hesitate. She ran across the yard and up the path towards the fields where Yannis could be seen working. She shouted and waved until he finally heard her and began to make his way in her direction. Breathlessly she relayed her message to him and he ran ahead of her.

'What do you want me to do?' he asked immediately.

'You'll have to go to Aghios Nikolaos and get a doctor. Ask him to come back here to see your grandmother. Marisa, ask Victor for a pass for Yannis to leave the village.'

Yannis looked perplexed. 'I'll not be back before tomorrow. Even if I took the donkey it will take me hours.' He gnawed at the side of his thumb. 'Isn't there a soldier going into town who could take a message?'

Marisa looked at Victor. 'Soldier go in jeep.' She mimed a steering wheel with her hands. 'Aghios Nikolaos. Fetch doctor.'

Victor's face lit up with a grin. 'Si, Si. I find.'

Mario glared at him. 'You went earlier this week. I'm due to go before you go off again.'

Victor shrugged. 'Go if you want. Just remember it's an emergency. You won't be able to go out and enjoy yourself, you'll be coming straight back, with the doctor, I hope.'

Mario hesitated. 'All right, you go. Your Greek's better than mine. I could have trouble finding the man.'

Anna sat at the table and wrote a few lines. She doubted very much that any soldier could read Greek, but she dared not write the truth. Signing herself as Yannis's sister she hoped the doctor who had attended the lepers on the island before the war would treat her message as an emergency. She would be able to give her mother another dose before the doctor arrived, but certainly no more. Yannis was still gnawing at his thumb, hoping his aunt would not ask him to go into town with the soldier.

Victor held out his hand for Anna's note. 'Where doctor is?'

'Aghios Nikolaos.'

'Where doctor is?'

'Ask at the hospital. In Aghios Nikolaos. Ask at hospital or taverna. Where is Doctor Stavros?'

'Si, Si. I ask. Where is Doctor Stav-ros?'

Marisa nodded. 'Remember, Doctor Stavros.'

'Si, Si. I quick go.' Victor placed Anna's note carefully in his pocket and buttoned down the flap. He saluted Anna and they could see him hurrying down the road to where the jeep was parked.

Once he was out of the house Anna had a great desire to laugh. Provided the doctor came reasonably late in the afternoon her ruse would have worked. Mario returned to his meal, eating self-consciously as Anna hovered over her mother and Marisa returned to the washing.

'Maybe it would be better if I brought the animals down early,' suggested Yannis tentatively. 'I'd like to be here when the doctor comes.'

Anna shook her head. 'There's no need for that. You stick to your usual routine, and I want a word with you later, Yannis. I collected some herbs this morning and thought I might make you up a brew to curb your appetite a bit.'

Alarm showed on Yannis's face. 'There's no need for that. I'm just growing fast.'

'We'll talk about it later,' Anna replied grimly.

Yannis sidled into the kitchen, expecting his aunt to be too engrossed with the welfare of his grandmother to pay any attention to him as he raided the cupboard, but he was wrong.

Anna closed the door firmly behind her. 'Yannis. I have to talk to you.'

'I ought to get back to the fields.'

'That can wait awhile. What have you got in that bag?'

'Just a snack.'

'Show me.'

Reluctantly Yannis unwrapped the loaf of bread and lump of brawn he had filched.

'Why didn't you tell me you were taking food to them?'

Yannis hung his head.

'Didn't you realise you were endangering all of us? If the soldiers found out they'd probably shoot us.'

'That's why I didn't tell you,' mumbled Yannis. 'I thought if I was the only one who knew they'd only shoot me.'

'Oh, Yannis, Yannis. You silly, courageous, little boy.' Anna spoke with a catch in her voice and tears in her eyes. 'They'd never believe you were the only one who knew. You must never, ever, do such a thing again.'

Yannis raised distressed eyes to his aunt. 'But they're resistance. We have to help them. They're fighting and losing their lives to try and get rid of the Germans.'

'I know that, but you mustn't try to help them alone. If you had told me I could have sent for the doctor earlier.'

Yannis looked at his aunt in disbelief. 'You mean grandma isn't sick?'

Anna placed her finger on her lips and shook her head. 'She doesn't need the doctor, but I had to think of a good excuse to get him here. I've still got to persuade him to go up to your Pappa's farm.'

'How did you find them, Mamma Anna?'

'I went to gather some herbs and they've been trampled. I knew there were some in the garden so I went up there. I thought I'd bring back some vegetables and went to the outhouse to look for a sack to put them in.'

Yannis grinned. 'When they've gone I can bring back some of the vegetables. I need to tidy it up a bit.'

'You mustn't try to do too much, Yannis. You're only a child still.'

'When my Pappa comes back I'd like to be able to show him how well I've looked after his farm.'

'Your Pappa will be proud of you, however the farm looks. We've got to think, Yannis. How are we to get Doctor Stavros to go up there without the soldiers suspecting anything?'

'Do you think the doctor will come this evening?'

'I hope so.'

'Will he go back to Aghios Nikolaos afterwards?'

'I don't know. If it's late he may stay the night.'

'If he does I could take him up there.'

'Don't be foolish. What excuse could you give to take the doctor up to a supposedly deserted farmhouse?' Anna shook her head. 'He'll have to leave here and make his own way up there.'

Yannis pursed his lips. 'I can't see him being very happy about that. How will he know the way?'

'Happy or not, that's the way it must be. We have to protect ourselves. You must think of your grandmother and sister.'

Yannis placed his arms round his aunt and hugged her. 'I'll remember. Thank you, Mamma Anna.'

Anna patted his arm. 'Off you go; tell the men we're hoping a doctor will be with them soon, and, Yannis, not a word to Marisa.'

'I know how to keep a secret.' Yannis winked at her and picked up the bag of food, stuffing it under his shirt.

All the way to his father's house Yannis tried to think of a plan to get the doctor to visit the men under the cover of attending his grandmother. He was glad she was not really sick, but wondered how his aunt had managed to get her to play a part. He approached the outhouse whistling to attract attention and sat down with his back to the door. Within minutes Nikos joined him, hungry and worried.

'Alecos is getting worse.'

'Don't worry,' Yannis assured him. 'Mamma Anna has sent for a doctor, in fact one of the soldiers has gone into Aghios Nikolaos to fetch him.' He grinned. 'I said they were stupid.'

Nikos gazed at him in concern. 'That means they know we're here.'

Yannis shook his head. 'My grandmother's ill. That's why the doctor's coming. The problem is, how to get him up here without the soldiers suspecting anything.'

Nikos munched the bread and brawn slowly. 'How well do you know this countryside?'

'Pretty well.'

'Over the other side of the hill, on the route to Heraklion, there are some small caves. Suppose some of your sheep strayed and whilst you were looking for them you thought you saw some people in the caves. Would the soldiers go and look?'

'I expect so.' Yannis's eyes gleamed with enthusiasm. 'We could try. If the doctor doesn't come up you'll know they didn't fall for it, or he wasn't willing to take the risk. The only problem is, I'd have to go with them, at least part of the way, and there'd be no one to show the doctor the way here.'

'Wouldn't the woman bring him up?'

'She might, part of the way, at least.'

Nikos took Yannis's small, brown hand in his own. 'You're a brave boy. Wherever I go I'll ask for Babbis from Plaka and when I meet up with him I'll tell him what a fine son he has.'

Having brought most of the sheep down and stabled the donkey he entered the kitchen, hoping Anna would be there. He had to speak to his aunt and return to the sheep as quickly as possible. He opened the door of the living room and frowned when he saw Mario was sitting there.

The soldier looked up and smiled. 'Good evening.'

'Good evening, Mario,' Yannis answered automatically. 'Mamma Anna, how is grandma? Has the doctor been yet?' He jerked his head in the direction of the kitchen.

'She's no worse, but there's no sign of Victor or the doctor yet.' Anna rose from her chair beside her mother's bed and walked into the kitchen with Yannis.

'Come outside,' he whispered, then added in a normal tone. 'What time will we have supper? Are you going to wait until they get here?'

'I was just about to come out to pick some beans. There are just about enough left.' Anna followed her nephew out to the kitchen garden. 'What are you up to, Yannis?'

'Nikos gave me an idea for getting the doctor up to Pappa's house. If I say I searched for some sheep on the other side of the hill and saw some people in the caves there the soldiers ought to go and investigate. Whilst they're over there you can take the doctor up.'

Anna bit her lip. 'I don't know. It's dangerous, Yannis.'

'We've got to get the doctor up there somehow. I can lead them over the hill in the opposite direction and keep them away for a couple of hours. That should give you and the doctor plenty of time to get there and back, unless you can think of anything better.'

'You can't suddenly say you've lost some sheep and go off and look for them! They'd wonder why you hadn't realised when you brought them down.'

'I'll tell you I've lost them in a minute and you tell me to go back and look. I'll hide up on the hill and when I see the jeep come back I'll rush in and tell my story.'

Anna looked at her nephew doubtfully. He was only a child and seemed to have no concern for the danger he could be placing them all in. 'Suppose they don't believe you?'

'Then we'll have to think of something else.'

'But what will happen when they find there's no one up there?'

Yannis shrugged. 'Maybe I was mistaken or maybe they've gone. What difference does it make?'

'I still think it's dangerous, Yannis.'

'Please, Mamma Anna. We can try, and it was Nikos's idea. He thought it would work.'

'All he wants is a doctor and never mind the consequences to anyone else,' replied Anna, grimly.

Yannis looked at his aunt, his eyes large and pleading.

'All right, we'll give it a try, but you're not to get mixed up with anything like this again.'

Yannis grinned. 'I knew you'd help. Let's go in and I'll tell you about the missing sheep.'

Anna shouted at Yannis, who appeared sulky and reluctant, finally leaving the room and slamming the door behind him. Mario looked up questioningly.

'What?'

'Sheep lost. Yannis find.'

'Please?'

Anna sighed. She found this continual need to explain in broken Greek so tiring. 'Sheep, baa, baa, lost.' She shaded her eyes with her hand and looked around the room.

Mario nodded. He was more interested in the coming meal than a lost sheep and was certainly not offering to help in the search. He sat comfortably in his chair, his legs stretched out before him and a glass of wine at his elbow. He wondered what was keeping Victor in Aghios Nikolaos and cursed himself for not insisting on going. He could have stayed over and made his own way back the following day. At least there was a bit of life in the town, not like this straggle of houses at the end of nowhere. He recalled the girl he had met the last time he was there, with her merry eyes and willing acceptance of his overtures, until they had at last staggered up some rickety stairs to a mattress. He had enjoyed her and was determined to seek her out again as soon as the opportunity arose. He eyed Marisa speculatively as she sat quietly beside her grandmother. If her aunt were not so strict and sharp eyed he could flirt with her a little to relieve his boredom, and who knew where that might lead. Anna interrupted his reverie by bringing in their supper and he joined the two women at the table eagerly.

They ate in silence. Marisa was genuinely worried about her grandmother, whilst Anna was worrying that Yannis's plan, which seemed so simple, would fail, leaving them at the mercy of the soldiers when the two fugitives were found. Maria showed no signs of waking and Anna made no attempt to rouse her. If only Victor would return soon, then the waiting would be over. As if in answer to her unspoken prayer she heard the grind of wheels and doors slamming as the jeep drew up outside and discharged both the doctor and Victor.

Smiling with relief Anna opened the door. 'Doctor Stavros? Thank you for coming out.'

Doctor Stavros's gaze swept round the room, alighting on Maria. 'Has there been any change since you sent for me?'

'None, Doctor,' answered Anna truthfully.

'I don't know if I will be able to help her at all.'

'Perhaps if you examined her,' suggested Anna. 'Marisa, take Victor and Mario into the kitchen. You can give Victor his supper, he can eat it there, but leave enough for Yannis and the doctor.'

Marisa nodded. Anxious though she was over her grandmother she did not feel she should stay and watch the doctor's examination, or that Victor or Mario should stay in the same room either.

'Come,' she said to them, and pointed to the kitchen. Obediently they followed her and she shut the door firmly behind them.

Anna held her finger to her lips and looked at Doctor Stavros. 'Please listen to me,' she whispered. 'There's nothing wrong with my mother. There's a wounded resistance fighter up in the hills. My nephew will be in soon and he'll draw the soldiers off in the opposite direction. Whilst they're gone I'll take you to where the men are hiding.'

Doctor Stavros's mouth opened and shut. He rubbed his hand over his forehead. 'I can't...' he began loudly, then dropped his voice as Anna hushed him. 'I can't go running off into the hills! Whatever made you think of such a wild scheme?'

'It isn't very far and we have to help them. Pretend to examine my mother. One of the soldiers will drive you back to Aghios Nikolaos later.'

Doctor Stavros shook his head and was about to refuse when loud voices could be heard in the kitchen. The door opened and Yannis burst in.

'Mamma Anna, I've seen some men up in the hills.'

'Men? What kind of men?'

Yannis took a deep breath as though he had been running hard. 'I went looking for the stray sheep; they were over the other side of the hill. I was just driving them back when I saw a movement. I thought it was another sheep, then I could hear voices, and the men went into one of the caves there.'

'Have you told Victor and Mario?'

Yannis nodded and winked. 'They're going up to look for them. Mario's gone down to the village to get the others. I'm going up with them.'

'Oh, no, Yannis.'

'I have to go. I'm the only one who knows where they are.'

'But you haven't had your supper yet.'

'I'll have it when we get back. I doubt that we'll be more than a couple of hours.' Yannis winked again and shut the door.

Anna turned to Doctor Stavros. 'Please, doctor.'

'What have you done to your mother?' he asked suspiciously.

'I gave her a sleeping draught. She should wake up in a little while.'

Doctor Stavros gave Anna a hard look. 'I hope for your sake that she does. Who are these men you are willing to take such risks for?'

'I only met them today. One of them has a bad leg wound; it will go gangrenous unless it's treated and his brother's desperate for a doctor. My own brother is with the resistance and I wouldn't want to think he'd died because a doctor wouldn't take a chance and visit him.'

'And if I refuse?'

Anna shrugged. 'I can't make you go, but the villagers will be pretty disgusted when they hear that you left a resistance fighter to die.'

Doctor Stavros sighed deeply. 'You leave me little choice. I'd better examine your mother whilst I'm here.'

Anna stood to one side, her ears strained to catch the sound of the soldiers leaving, until Doctor Stavros stood back.

'As you say, she'll probably wake soon. Her pulse is strong, so you've done no harm. How did you know how much to give her?'

Anna smiled. 'I learnt a good deal from the Widow when she was alive. She told me about the herbs and which ones to use for different ailments.'

'So why don't you give this man one of your brews?'

'He needs to be cut and the poison drained first. I can't do that. I don't know how and I haven't the implements.'

'You surprise me.' Doctor Stavros spoke sarcastically. 'You seem quite capable of everything else. Well, shall we go?'

'I'll find out if the soldiers have gone.' Anna opened the door to the kitchen. Marisa lifted a woeful face to her aunt.

'Do you think they'll be all right? Yannis seemed quite excited, but it could be dangerous, couldn't it?'

'There's nothing at all for you to worry over. I want you to stay here with your grandmother whilst I show the doctor a short cut to another house he has to visit. I'll wait for him and bring him back. I'll try not to be too long.'

Marisa nodded. 'Is grandma going to be all right?'

'Perfectly,' Doctor Stavros assured her. 'She may rouse herself whilst we're gone. If she does she will probably be very thirsty. Give her plenty of water to drink, but no food before I return.'

'Suppose Victor and Mario come back before you?'

'They won't.' Anna spoke more confidently than she felt. 'We won't be very long.'

Doctor Stavros followed Anna out across the yard. Anna touched his arm and placed her mouth close to his ear.

'Not a word. Sounds travel at night.'

In the gathering darkness Doctor Stavros nodded. He had certainly not bargained for this when he had agreed to come to the village. He tried to follow Anna without stumbling across the rough ground and by the time they had reached the top of the hill he was breathing heavily. Anna gave him no chance for a rest, but hurried him down into the hollow where Babbis's house stood.

'We're nearly there,' she spoke quietly. 'The soldiers should be at least a kilometre away in the opposite direction. The man is in the outhouse. I've no idea how they got here, or how one came to be wounded. If you can drain his leg and leave me instructions for treating him we will try to keep them hidden until he's fit to move. Be careful. There are two steps down here.'

Anna took his hand and indicated the steps, continuing to lead him to the outhouse. She tapped quietly on the door and waited. The door opened a crack and Nikos pulled it wider to allow the doctor and Anna admittance.

Anna shivered. This was madness. At any moment the soldiers could realise they had been tricked and return to the farm to find her and the doctor missing. It would take them no time at all for them to realise she had taken him to a wounded man, a man who was their enemy, and force the information of their whereabouts from Yannis.

'Is there a light?' asked the doctor.

'I'll find an oil lamp.'

In the darkness she slipped across to the house and opened the door. As she did so she remembered she had taken the lamps down to the farm. Frantically she rummaged in a drawer until her fingers felt some candles. It took her further time to find a box of matches and she hoped they would not be damp and refuse to strike.

Doctor Stavros was standing where she had left him and Nikos took the candles and matches from her; striking one carefully and shading it with his hand before touching it to the wick. He stuck the candle in the ground and lit another from it.

Doctor Stavros placed his bag on the floor and knelt beside the injured man. He unwrapped the dirty bandage and sniffed.

Thankfully there was no unpleasant odour of gangrene to assault his nostrils. 'Light another candle.' he ordered.

Nikos lit another and placed it as close to his brother's leg as he dared whilst the doctor removed a bottle and a wad of cloth.

'Take this,' he said to Nikos. 'Sprinkle a few drops on the pad and hold it over his nose and mouth when I say. We don't want him screaming. Anna, I'll want a pad held beneath that wound to catch the poison as it comes out, and then a clean one soaked in iodine when I say.'

Anna nodded. She had no qualms about assisting the doctor. She knelt quietly as he made a deep cut into the shiny, red, flesh and watched as the greenish-yellow liquid spurted out. Doctor Stavros squeezed and more of the pus oozed, until finally the wound began to dribble blood. The doctor stitched the gaping wound together as best he could before he took the clean pad, soaked in iodine, from Anna and applied a bandage.

'I'll leave you to clean up,' he said to Nikos, as he tied the bandage firmly. 'And I can't promise anything. I've done what I can under the circumstances.'

'I'm grateful, Doctor, and to you, Anna. At least he has a chance now.'

Anna stiffened. 'How do you know my name?'

'The doctor called you Anna.'

Anna pursed her lips. 'I'd like you to forget that.'

'I've already done so,' Nikos smiled at her. 'If I never see you again, remember how grateful I am to you.'

'I'll be up tomorrow,' replied Anna tartly. 'Someone will have to change that bandage. Snuff out the candles and we'll be off.'

Anna hurried the doctor back down the hills towards the farm, finally breathing a sigh of relief when they entered the farmhouse and finding only her mother and Marisa there.

'Where've you been?' asked Marisa. 'You've been gone for ages – and your shoes are all mucky.'

Anna looked down and sucked in her breath. Both her shoes and Doctor Stavros's boots had small brown lumps of animal excrement stuck to them where they had walked over the dark hillside.

'Sit still,' she ordered. 'I'll get a cloth to clean them.'

She kicked her own shoes into a corner of the kitchen and had just finished rubbing the doctor's boots clean when she heard the soldiers returning. She threw the cloth into the corner with her shoes and turned to Marisa with a warning look.

'Not a word. We've been here with you the whole time.'

Marisa looked at her aunt in surprise and opened her mouth to protest.

'I mean it, Marisa. You're to say nothing. I'll get some supper ready for you doctor. It was good of you to wait until they returned.'

By the time the soldiers had dispersed to the village and Yannis, Victor and Mario entered; Anna had their food simmering and plates on the table. There was nothing to indicate that she had arrived back at the farmhouse only a short while before.

'Did you find them?' she asked of Yannis.

'We must have missed them. They'd been there, though.'

Anna's eyes opened wide.

'There was the remains of a fire. They must have been moving on towards Heraklion when I saw them.'

'What makes you think that?' Anna was surprised to hear that anyone had sheltered in the caves.

'Well, there's nowhere at all to hide over this way. It's my guess they'd come over from Lassithi and just stopped to have a meal.'

Anna nodded. She was relieved that something had been found to bear out Yannis's story, but hoped it would not mean the soldiers would start to scour the surrounding hills or they would be bound to discover Babbis's farmhouse and its occupants.

'What did the doctor say about grandma?' asked Yannis.

'I'm sure she'll recover. It was only a slight relapse.' Doctor Stavros looked at the boy. 'I hope it won't happen again.'

Yannis shrugged and grinned. 'Who can say?'

Doctor Stavros safely on his way back to Aghios Nikolaos with Mario, and Victor down at the taverna discussing the events of the evening with the soldiers, Marisa rounded on her aunt.

'What were you up to with the doctor? Where did you go?'

Anna hushed her niece. 'Keep your voice down, Marisa. Victor understands a good deal more Greek than he speaks now, thanks to you.'

'He's down at the taverna. He can't hear us.'

Anna looked round warily. 'You never know who's listening.' She dropped her voice to a whisper. 'There's a wounded man in the hills. He needed a doctor.'

Marisa gasped. 'And you took the doctor to him? That was terribly brave of you.'

'It was probably more foolish than brave. I just thought it could be your Pappa or uncle Yiorgo laying there and I ought to help.'

'Wasn't it lucky that grandma gave us a fright so that the doctor had to be called? Why didn't you tell me earlier?'

'There was no time, besides, it was better that you didn't know.'

Marisa considered her aunt's words. 'Did Yannis know?'

Anna nodded. 'It was Yannis who found him.'

'In the caves, where he took the soldiers?'

'No, that was just an excuse to get them out of the way.'

Marisa's lips quivered. 'I think you're mean. You let Yannis help and you don't even tell me! It's not fair, just because I'm a girl.'

'It has nothing to do with you being a girl,' snapped back Anna. 'It was common sense. If anything had happened to Yannis and myself, someone had to be here to look after your grandmother.'

'Was grandma really ill or was she helping you too?'

'You saw your grandmother for yourself. You know we couldn't wake her.'

Marisa looked doubtfully at her aunt. 'Does grandma know?'

'She knows nothing. She doesn't even remember being ill – and you're not to tell her. You're not to tell anyone about the doctor and I going out. If you're asked we sat with your grandmother until the soldiers and Yannis came back from the hills. He waited until they returned to ensure they were unhurt. After they'd told their story and eaten they took the doctor back to Aghios Nikolaos.'

'Will the man be all right now?'

'I don't know.'

Marisa's eyes widened in horror. 'How can you find out? He might be worse, then you'd have to get the doctor again.'

Anna sank down at the kitchen table. 'Please, Marisa, stop questioning me like this. Just forget about it.'

Marisa shook her head. 'I can't. You said it could have been Pappa or uncle Yiorgo. I want to know how the man is. If he's worse he could die up there in the hills on his own.'

'He's quite safe. He has his brother with him.' Anna spoke wearily, reaction to the strain of the evening setting in and making her feel close to tears.

'But you must find out how he is.'

'I'll find out tomorrow. You can stay here and look after your grandmother. If Victor or Mario want to know where I am you can say I'm gathering herbs to make a potion to help her to recover.'

Doctor Stavros sat in the jolting jeep as he returned to Aghios Nikolaos and pondered over the events of the evening. The soldiers had taken him to the house where they were billeted and there should be no suspicion voiced that he had attended an injured resistance fighter. The woman had certainly been resourceful, ensuring that the old lady would sleep for some hours, and the boy had courage, taking the soldiers up into the hills on a wild goose chase. He wondered how deeply involved they were and decided it would be better for him not to know. He had looked over the bay towards the island of Spinalonga and wondered how the sick people over there were managing without his regular visits. Maybe he could approach the Italian captain and persuade him to allow him to resume his weekly trips. Waving goodbye to Mario he let himself into his house, looking forward to a good wash and couple of glasses of raki.

With an assurance that he did not feel, Doctor Stavros confronted the Italian. He had been correct in his assumption that the captain was his patient and the man had finally confided in the doctor that he had a weakness for beautiful young women and indulged himself whenever possible in his home country and abroad.

'How are you feeling, Captain?'

'Feel good. No problems. Good Doctor.'

'I want a favour from you, now.'

The Captain frowned. 'What is 'favour'?'

Doctor Stavros leaned forward. 'I want to visit Spinalonga. I have sick people there who need me.'

The captain shook his head. 'Aghios Nikolaos, yes, villages, yes. Spinalonga, no. Commander say no.'

In vain he tried to argue that his visits to the island were a necessity, a soldier could accompany him each time, but the captain was adamant. He did not want to bring the wrath of the German Commander down on his own head or put any of his men at risk from the disease. Tactfully, Doctor Stavros refrained from telling him that they were more likely to catch a venereal infection by their casual associations with the loose women of the town than leprosy.

Anna longed to rush up to Babbis's farmhouse the following

morning to check on the injured man, but steeled herself to behave normally. She made her customary trip down to the beach and waved to the island, which seemed quiet and deserted and the church bell could be heard tolling mournfully. No answering wave was to be seen and she returned to her mother.

'I'm going up to the hills now, Mamma. Marisa will be here to look after you. I want to pick some more herbs. The infusion I gave you seems to have helped.'

Maria nodded. For some reason she felt very weary and was having a job to keep awake for very long at a time. She doubted that any medication would help her, but would not dream of hurting her daughter's feelings by saying so.

Anna hurried up the hillside, stopping on the brow of the hill to look down at the village. There was no sign of any movement and reassured, she continued on her way. Stopping in the garden she gathered the herbs she needed, then crossed to the outhouse.

'Nikos,' she whispered and the door was pulled open for her.

Nikos smiled. 'I hoped you'd come early. He seems better.'

Anna nodded. The figure on the mattress was no longer sweating and his high, unnatural colour had lessened. Swiftly she unwound the bandage and looked at the wound. Still discoloured, and obviously tender, the swelling was reduced and it looked considerably healthier than the previous day. Anna crushed a handful of leaves between her palms and placed them directly on the open flesh, placed a clean pad over them and re-bandaged the leg.

'Here are a couple of leaves,' she said. 'You can see what they look like and can pick them yourself from the garden. They need to be changed every day and should help the inflammation.'

Nikos looked at her gratefully. 'How long before he can walk again?'

Anna shrugged. 'I don't know. Where were you making for?'

'The hills around Lassithi.'

'I doubt if he'd manage that.'

'We can always hide up on the way.'

'How did it happen?'

Nikos grinned. 'We heard the German Commander was taking a little trip and we thought we'd surprise him. He had more men with him than we thought. We put up a good show, but had to retreat without him.'

'Will you try again?' asked Anna curiously.

'Probably.'

'What's so important about him?'

Nikos's face took on a look of pure hatred. 'He's the most evil man you can imagine. He came over here before the invasion, posing as a Frenchman, speaking perfect Greek and pretending to be a friend. He marched the Government to a river valley outside the town and shot them, then took control of Heraklion and rounded up all the traitors, as he put it. Everyone who had considered him to be a friend when he was there earlier was questioned about the information they'd given him. If it was proved right they were shot and if they'd told him wrongly they were shot. No one was safe.'

'But why?'

'He didn't trust them. He said if they told him their country's secrets they were traitors to Crete, and if they lied to him they were traitors to their German masters. He liked to torture and humiliate them.' Nikos shuddered. 'The day he killed my father made up my mind. I'd rather die fighting than wait for him to come for me, and if I can get him along the way it'll be all to the good.'

'You mean you'd kill him?'

'Cheerfully and with pleasure, so would many others.'

'But if you did surely Germany would just send a replacement for him?'

'Very likely, but each time we got rid of a commander it would be one less German in the world.'

Anna frowned. 'He's the man who sent my father to the mines

and stopped the supplies going to the island.' She too, would be willing to kill him.

Nikos did not answer her. 'Did you bring any food with you?'

Anna nodded and took it from her bag. 'Has your brother eaten anything?'

'A little.'

'I've brought some broth. He'll need his strength if he's got to walk.'

'Can you send some more with the boy?'

'I'd rather he didn't come here.'

'I doubt you could stop him. Don't worry. He's very careful. I want to hear all about the dance he led those soldiers last night.'

'That could have been very dangerous for him.'

Nikos shook his head and laughed softly. 'I'd agree with you if they were Germans. The Italians aren't so bad. Besides, I knew there would be some ashes there to prove out his story.'

'How did you know?'

'I left them there. The last place we stopped and lit a fire was in those caves.'

'Do you live in the caves at Lassithi?'

Nikos grinned. 'They're home from home. We're well organised up there.'

'How do you mean?'

'We have proper bedding, regular food, and we know we're safe.'

'You'll be glad to get back.'

'I certainly will. I appreciate the help you've given us, but once I'm back there I'll be a good deal happier.'

'What will happen to Alecos?'

'He'll be well looked after until he's strong enough to go out and fight again.'

'Suppose he doesn't want to fight?'

Nikos looked at her incredulously. 'Of course he'll want to fight. Every Cretan wants to fight. Give your boy a couple of years and he'll be up there with us.'

Anna shuddered. 'Please don't suggest it to him. He's only a child.'

'He's a child now, but it won't be long before he's a man. You'll see.'

Yannis was cutting grass as near as he dared to the top of the hill. Anna had forbidden him to visit his father's house before she had been up there to check on the progress of the injured man and he found he was continually looking in that direction to see if she was returning. As she approached he could tell by the relief on her face that all was well.

'Can I go up now?' he asked eagerly.

'Wait until I'm back at the farm, and be careful. Don't stay too long,' she cautioned him. 'It's just possible the soldiers will want you to take them back to those caves to do a daylight search. You don't want them finding you at your father's farm.'

'I'm sure Victor would have told me this morning if he wanted me to take them up again.'

Anna pursed her lips. 'He may not have thought of it until he talked with the other soldiers. Just wait a short while to be sure. Be patient, Yannis. Alecos won't be going anywhere today.'

'How long will it take before he's well enough to move?'

'That depends how quickly his leg heals. I just hope they go soon.'

Sulkily Yannis agreed to wait until he saw her enter their house. If she returned to the yard with a soldier he was to stay within sight of the farm until he was certain they were not going to ask him to come down.

It seemed an age to Yannis before his aunt entered the farmhouse and he wondered how long he should wait before it would be safe to leave the fields. He continued working doggedly, cutting the grass and loading the cart, deciding that once the load was complete he would have given time enough for Victor or Mario to come and look for him. He looked down towards the shore and saw the glint of field glasses as they swept the hills looking for any sign of movement. They trained themselves on Yannis for a few minutes, then swung further to the left.

As soon as Yannis saw they were no longer looking in his direction he slipped behind a low stone wall, watching for them to come back his way. He waited for them to return again to his position and could see by the way the sun was shining on them that they were searching the hillside for him. After a while he stood up and placed some stones on the wall, allowing them a good view of him for some minutes, before ducking back down out of sight.

He continued the charade for over half an hour, by which time the soldier on duty seemed to accept that the boy was doing a job that took him out of their sight for a while, and directed the glasses towards the hill where the caves were situated. Once Yannis was certain they had lost interest in him he ran behind the gorse bushes and was brought up short by the man sitting there, nonchalantly resting in the sparse shade.

'Who are you and what are you doing here?' he asked, hoping the man would not sense his fright and hear the loud beating of his heart.

'You don't need to know who I am. Yannis is on Spinalonga.' Brilliant deep blue eyes looked at him. 'I just want you to take a message to some friends of mine.'

'What friends?'

'One of them has an injured leg and his brother has been caring for him. I've been asked to send them a message.'

'What kind of message?'

'Just tell them "tomorrow tonight". They'll understand.'

'And where will I find these friends of yours?'

'In the usual place.'

'So why don't you tell them yourself?'

'I've been watching you playing games with the soldier down

there. It's better I stay out of sight, besides I need to take another message somewhere else.'

'How will they know it isn't a trap for them?'

'Tell them the man with blue eyes told you. Do you remember the message?'

Yannis nodded. 'Tomorrow night.'

'Good. Go back out on the hill for that soldier to check on you again. I'll leave it for you to decide when it's safe to take the message.' The man edged his way slowly towards the far side of the clump of gorse.

Nikos was sitting on the side of the mattress, waiting for Yannis to arrive. 'You're late today.'

'The soldiers are watching the hills. I had to play a little game with them for a while. Once they lost interest in me I came as quickly as I could, but I dare not stay too long. How's your brother?'

'Getting better by the hour.'

'I'm glad to hear it. I've got a message for you, from the man with blue eyes.'

Nikos looked up eagerly. 'That's Michael, our commander.'

'He said "tomorrow night".'

'That's really good news. That means they're going to get us out of here.'

Yannis frowned. 'How did they know you were here?'

'A group of us left together. When I realised Alecos couldn't walk much further I insisted they went on to Lassithi without us. They knew we would be in this area.'

'How are they going to get you out? Alecos will need to be carried.'

'You don't need to worry about that. Just make sure you and your family are safe indoors.' Nikos dismissed the question as of no consequence. 'Tell me how it went last night when you went to the caves.'

'The soldiers fell for my story of seeing people, and do you know what, they found the remains of a fire in one of the caves.'

Nikos grinned. 'I'm not surprised. We stayed there for a night on our way here.'

'You knew?'

'Of course I knew. I wouldn't have suggested it otherwise. I wouldn't want any harm to come to you or your mother.'

Yannis looked at Nikos with new respect. 'How old do you have to be to join the resistance?'

'Well,' Nikos scratched his head. 'You don't so much join as belong. Those who went up into the hills to get away from the soldiers can't just hide away like cowards; they've got to do something. There are some English and Australians up there and they got us organised. They know who they want to get and we know the country. We take them where they want to go and have a few guns ready to help them.' Nikos tousled the boy's hair. 'I know what's in your mind, boy, but forget it. You're more use down here.'

'What do you mean?'

'To the soldiers you're a little boy. No one takes much notice of you. You can move about, do more or less as you please. More use than having a price on your head and having to move around after dark to get what you want.'

Yannis's face fell. 'I'll be twelve soon.'

'You're still a boy. Tell you what I'll do. When we get back I'll tell our commander how brave you've been. You just sit tight and if there's a job for you someone will find you, like he did today.'

'Whenever I'm needed I'm ready,' promised Yannis.

'Shake, fellow resistance worker.' Nikos held out his hand. 'Have you brought any food with you?'

When Anna visited the farmhouse to change Alecos's dressing the next day she was relieved when Nikos told her they would be leaving that night.

'Alecos isn't fit to walk very far,' she warned him.

'He won't have to. Some friends are meeting us and between us we'll be able to carry him.'

'How do they know where you are?'

'I expect a little bird told them, don't you?'

Anna looked at him, puzzled. 'What do you mean? No one knows you're here except the boy and I.'

'And the good doctor.'

'Oh! You mean he knows who the resistance are in Aghios Nikolaos?'

'I can't think of anyone else, can you? I expect he passed a message through, so they're coming to get us out.'

'Who told you they were coming?'

Nikos winked. 'Another little bird, I expect.'

'You mean Yannis. Someone gave him a message to bring to you,' Anna spoke bitterly.

'Don't be hard on him. You should be proud of a boy like that. Just make sure you spend the evening inside tonight.'

'What's going to happen?'

Nikos shrugged. 'We're leaving. That's all I know, but better for you to be safe indoors. Now, have you got any messages for anyone?'

Anna bit at her lip. 'Do you know Babbis and Yiorgo?'

'Plenty of them.'

Anna sighed. 'If you come across two men from Plaka just tell them we're safe and well.'

Nikos nodded soberly. 'And may you stay that way.'

'Will you promise me something, Nikos?' Anna looked at him, close to tears where fear was clutching at her heart.

'If I can.'

'Don't let the boy go with you.'

Nikos laughed. 'I've already told him he's not old enough to come with us.'

Anna felt herself go limp. 'He planned to go, then?'

'He asked if he could, but I told him he was more use here.'

'You mean he's working for you?' asked Anna in horror.

'Not as such, but he's here if he's needed.'

Anna shook her head. 'I don't like it. He's too young to become involved.'

Anna felt nervous. Surely if a group of men went to Babbis's farmhouse they would be noticed by the soldiers? How would they be able to run away carrying an injured man? She insisted Yannis brought the animals down early that night and refused to allow him to go outside and do any jobs.

'You're looking very tired, Yannis. I think you should have an evening inside. You work far too hard for a boy of your age. Spend the evening playing cards with Marisa.'

Yannis looked at his aunt suspiciously. She was not usually this solicitous. Although she treated him like a boy she expected him to work as hard as a fully-grown man. 'What are you up to, Mamma Anna?'

'Nothing at all.' Anna assured him. 'I think it would be good if we all spent one evening a week relaxing.'

Yannis grinned. 'I'm not going with them,' he assured her.

Anna glanced at him sharply. 'I know, but I still want you inside this evening.'

Yannis shrugged. 'If you say so.'

Anna relaxed visibly. She had expected Yannis to protest and find some excuse to go out.

'I'll ask Victor and Mario if they want to play cards with us.' He winked at his aunt. 'At least we'll know where they are.'

Anna watched the trio as they sat at the table and played a simple card game amongst much hilarity. Victor was cheating openly, with a wide smile on his face as Yannis continually challenged him. Mario had refused to join them and left for the taverna as he did most evenings. Yannis wagged his finger at Victor.

'You cheat. I should have won that game.'

'Cheat? What is cheat?' Victor placed his hand protectively over the pile of matchsticks that sat beside him.

'You keep looking at my cards so you can win.'

'Me, win.' Victor smiled more widely than ever. 'Me good.'

'You – cheat.'

'Cheat? What is cheat?'

Yannis laughed. 'I'm sure you know what a cheat is. As we're only playing for matchsticks I'm not very worried. I'll certainly not play you if there's a lepta at stake.'

Victor smiled again, picked up the cards and dealt them out deftly. He continued to look openly at the cards both Yannis and Marisa held before playing his own, but when they attempted to look at his he covered them with his hand.

Anna sighed. This was the way life had been when she was a girl. The evenings spent playing cards or backgammon amongst laughter and happiness. She closed her eyes, wishing she could go to bed. She was probably more tired than anyone. Although Marisa tended to her grandmother and did a good deal of the cooking and washing, Anna spent most of her time out in the fields. The work was arduous and back-breaking. Her hands were stained with the earth, the skin cracked and rough. There was no way she would be able to do any embroidery for a considerable amount of time, even sewing a button on Yannis's shirt snagged the cotton. This was the way life had been for a few weeks when her father had broken his leg and they had all had to help, out in all weathers. At least that had come to an end, but she could see no end in sight for their current struggles.

A muffled sound came to her ears and she jerked her eyes open. It came again and she realised the room had fallen silent. Victor was already rising from the table to take his revolver from the side table.

Running feet could be heard outside and Mario burst in through the door, shouting for Victor and speaking rapidly in

Italian. Victor nodded, went into the kitchen for his boots and prepared to follow his soldier companion. He turned back briefly to the family and held up his hand.

'You stay.'

'What is it?' asked Marisa.

'Sounded like gun shots.' Yannis rose from the table and went to the back door.

'You're not to go out,' Anna shouted shrilly at him. 'Yannis, did you hear me? I forbid you to go outside.'

Yannis returned, a contented smile on his face. 'There seems to be a fight of some sort going on up in the hills, over by the caves, where I took the soldiers the other night. The Italians are puffing their way up the hillside as fast as they can. I wonder what's going on up there, Mamma Anna.' He raised his eyebrows quizzically at her.

Anna permitted herself a small smile. She should have realised the resistance would cause a diversion to enable them to take the two men safely out of the area.

'I think I shall go to bed. Marisa, you should do the same. I'll see to Mamma.'

Once Marisa had left the room Anna went to Yannis's side. 'Promise me you'll not leave the house, Yannis, please.'

'I promise, Mamma Anna. I wouldn't be much use to them. I haven't got a gun.'

The look of horror on Anna's face sent Yannis into a peal of laughter. 'I was teasing you, Mamma Anna.' He gave his aunt a hug. 'I promise I'll not go out. Besides, a good resistance man obeys his orders and Nikos told me to stay here.' He swiftly dodged the blow she aimed at him.

Shaking her head in despair over her nephew; but confident that he would not leave the farmhouse Anna turned her attention to her mother.

Anna, with the help of Marisa, had moved her mother outside

into the early autumn sunshine, and now she weeded the vegetable patch whilst her mother dozed. A feeling of being watched made the skin crawl on her neck and she looked round swiftly, expecting to see one of the Italian soldiers. There was no one. Anna shrugged. The events of the previous week when the men had been hidden at Babbis's farmhouse had made her jumpy. She resumed her weeding, although the feeling of being watched persisted. She rose and drew water from the pump, struggling back to the vegetable garden with the unwieldy watering can. Three times she went back and forth, resolving to mend the hosepipe that evening.

On her fourth trip a noise from the shed attracted her attention and she placed the heavy can on the ground. There was certainly something in the shed and she looked around for a suitable implement to defend herself with and seized a length of wood. If a rat was in there she would soon chase it out.

Cautiously she pushed open the door, her eyes on the ground, expecting to see a rodent rush past her feet. Instead a pair of boots met her eyes. Feeling the breath constrict in her chest, Anna tried to step backwards, pulling the door with her. A strong hand fell on her arm and pulled her inside.

'Don't be frightened. I'll not hurt you.'

Anna went cold; the pounding of her heart was painful in her chest. 'Who are you?' she managed to ask.

'I came to say thank you for helping my men.'

A surge of relief flooded through Anna and she was able to take stock of the man who stood before her. She looked into the deep blue eyes and saw nothing but kindness and amusement lurking within. 'What do you want?'

'Nothing. I just wanted to meet the brave young woman who had risked so much to help an injured man and thank her. You'll be pleased to know Alecos is back on his feet, due to you.'

Anna blushed, not knowing what to say in reply. She looked again at the striking blue eyes. 'You're not a Greek, are you?'

'I'm an officer in the British army. I volunteered to stay behind after Heraklion fell, as I'm able to speak Greek fluently. I'm afraid my eyes give me away every time.' He smiled at Anna and she could not help but smile back.

'I've never seen eyes that colour before.'

'I had never thought about them until I came over here. They do make me stand out. Thank goodness I don't have the red hair to go with them!'

'Red hair?'

'My father came from Scotland and he had red hair. Luckily I inherited my mother's dark hair. She was Greek.'

'And she taught you Greek?'

'She always spoke in Greek to me. She said it could be useful to me if I ever had the chance to meet my relatives.'

'And have you met them?'

The man shook his head. 'They live on the mainland. Maybe I shall be able to visit when our business here is finished and the war over.'

'Do you think it will be over soon?'

'I've no idea.' He sighed heavily and shrugged. 'I'd like to think so.'

They stood in silence, Anna's gaze riveted on his blue eyes. Finally she spoke, her voice trembling a little 'You took a chance coming here during the day with the soldiers around.'

'I was very careful,' he smiled again. 'You didn't see me and you were working only a few yards away. You go back to your weeding and you won't even know I've slipped away.' He held out his hand to her. 'I'll say goodbye now. I'll call again next time I'm passing.'

Anna touched his fingers with her own as her mother began to call. 'Anna. Anna.'

'My mother. She must need me.' She dropped his hand swiftly and let herself out from the shed, walking back to where her mother sat.

'What have you been doing in there so long?'

'I thought I heard a rat. I went in to look for it. What did you want me for?'

'Could you bring me a drink? I'm parched.'

With a pang of guilt Anna hurried into the kitchen for a glass of water and handed it to her mother. 'You're not feeling too hot, are you? I could help you back inside.'

'I'd rather be out here watching you than cooped up in there on my own not knowing what's going on in the world.'

Yannis, once over his first disappointment that the two men had departed without him, was philosophical. They had promised to find him if he could be useful and all the time he was able to continue with his normal routine the less likely anyone was to suspect him in the future.

Before he herded the animals back to their enclosure each night he tried to spend a short time at his father's farm, struggling to repair a fence or rebuild a wall, despite knowing that the task of running two farms was beyond him. He wished his aunt would let Marisa go up into the fields with him each day, but she was adamant that his sister stayed at the farmhouse where she was able to watch over her. Anna insisted they could manage, provided they grew sufficient vegetables and looked after the animals; they would have enough food for their immediate needs and those of the villagers.

During the summer months she had been proved right. The most time consuming and arduous job had been to keep the land watered, but now it was time to start sowing ready for the next crop of vegetables and the soil had to be turned.

Anna had completed the vegetable garden with the help of Marisa. Now she had insisted that she helped Yannis in one of the lower fields.

Yannis looked at his aunt's drawn, tired face and felt angry and resentful. 'You shouldn't have to do this.'

'Someone has to dig the ground ready to plant next year's vegetables or we won't eat,' she replied grimly. 'You can't do it alone.'

'Mario or Victor ought to help. They eat our food, you wash their clothes and cook for them, and what do they do in return? Nothing.'

Anna smiled at his vehemence. 'We get basic stores from the army. They get those for us.'

'That's our right. We didn't ask them to come here. The army ought to pay you for having them. I'm going to ask them to help you.'

'Yannis, you mustn't.'

'Why not? I'm going to find them now and insist.' Yannis swung away, leaving Anna to return to her digging feeling decidedly disturbed.

Yannis found the two Italians lounging in the sun and approached them warily, for all his brave talk to Anna.

'Would one of you come and help Mamma Anna, please?'

Both men frowned. It was pleasant standing in the sun ensuring no boat approached the island.

'What to do?'

'She's trying to dig one of the fields ready to plant the vegetables. It's far too much for her to manage. Could one of you come and help?' Yannis mimed sticking a fork into the ground and tossing the earth, then wiping his brow and panting.

The two men exchanged glances. 'On duty.'

'One stay. One help Mamma Anna? After all, you eat the food,' he added.

Mario shifted from one foot to the other. 'You go, Victor.'

'Why should I?'

'You eat more than I do.' The men argued back and forth in Italian. Yannis looked at them in disgust.

'All the time you stand here arguing Mamma Anna's working. She looks after you for nothing. You could at least do some digging for her by way of saying thank you.' He walked away, feeling he had acted foolishly, resisting the urge to turn back and shake his fist at them. A hand fell on his shoulder.

'I come.'

Yannis's face broke into a delighted smile as he turned and saw Victor. 'It really is too much for her,' he insisted. 'Mamma Anna tired.'

Victor was forced to agree. Anna was doggedly continuing with her digging, but each time she pushed the fork into the ground she took longer to do so and withdrew it with less earth clinging to the prongs. Victor took the implement from her hands.

'Coffee,' he said. 'I dig.'

'I can manage.' Anna tried to take the fork back, but Victor fended her off easily.

'Yannis right. We help.'

'No!' Anna tried again to take the fork.

'Anna, please. We no ask come here. I know you not like. We go fight where sent. I not ask come here, but it good live here.'

'I'm sure it is. It's like living in a hotel,' answered Anna bitterly.

'You cook. I dig.'

Anna felt tears stinging at the back of her eyes. She did not want the Italian to help, but she recognised the necessity.

'And what will the rest of the village think? The soldiers helping me on my farm.'

Victor shrugged. 'They think – pouf.'

Anna shook her head. 'Not pouf! I will get a bad name. When you leave they will make me leave. Where would I go? What about my mother?'

Victor gazed at her, understanding her dilemma. 'You think?'

'I know.' Anna gave him a withering glance, released her grip on the fork and walked back down to the house. Victor threw the fork to the ground and followed her.

'I help. Mario help. Emmanuel help. All help. All help you and others. Make all right?'

'Maybe.'

Victor smiled. 'We do.' He sat down at the table. 'We talk.'

Anna did not answer, but busied herself making coffee, finally placing a cup in front of him.

'You sit,' he commanded.

Anna hesitated.

'You sit, please,' he said again and reluctantly Anna sat opposite. 'You, I like. Marisa, Yannis, Mamma, I like. Mario like. We lucky, live here in home. Other soldiers lucky to live in homes. I talk to soldiers, say we help. Do work of men gone. Keep village good.'

Anna smiled. 'And if the other soldiers say no?'

'I say yes. I say Commander say we do.'

'Why should they believe you?'

'I say see Commander in Aghios Nikolaos and he say.'

'Why should you want to help us, Victor?'

'I like go my home. Think of Mamma, think of Pappa. Big mistake join army. No like fight. Live together, be friends. Yes?'

Anna shook her head. 'Think of my Pappa. He is in the mines. You bring him home.'

Victor frowned. 'Me, say yes. Commander say no. Shoot men if try to leave.'

'Surely they wouldn't shoot him if you went and asked for him?'

'Need papers from Commander. No papers, not go.'

Anna sighed deeply. 'My brother; on the island. He could be starving. Take food out to them.'

Victor shook his head. 'Commander find out. Shoot me, shoot you, shoot everyone in village.'

'Just for taking them some food?' Anna spoke incredulously.

Victor nodded solemnly. 'Commander bad. Like shoot gun. Shoot all government, shoot doctors, shoot teachers, shoot anyone not like.'

'There must be something you can do.'

'I help. Soldiers help.'

'Suppose the Commander finds out.'

Victor shrugged. 'Commander not give order not help.'

Anna shook her head. 'You make it sound like a game.'

'No game.' Victor drained his coffee down to the dregs and rinsed his mouth with water. 'Help now.'

Yannis returned with a cartload of firewood that he stacked carefully into a shed, ensuring the pile would not fall the first time a log was removed. He smiled at his aunt.

'You see; it was just a question of asking.'

'It wasn't quite that simple, Yannis. Victor and I had a talk and we've come to an arrangement. He's going to get the other soldiers to help in the village with some of the jobs the women can't do.'

'That's even better. I know Danniakis is worried about his roof, and there's no way he or Eleni can get up there to repair it.'

Anna frowned. 'It doesn't seem right, somehow, to accept help from them when they're the enemy.'

'Look on it as making use of them. They've spent all their time doing absolutely nothing since they've been here, so from now on let's make sure they're kept busy.' He thanked Victor as he passed him on his way to the higher fields and the soldier grinned and wiped the sweat from his forehead.

'Big work. Soon finish.'

Yannis nodded. 'See you at supper.' Whistling cheerfully, he continued his way up the hill, inspecting the vines automatically as he went for any sign of blight or mould that would spread rapidly and decimate the small vineyard.

Whilst Victor stuck doggedly to the task of turning over the heavy, sticky clods of earth he turned the problem of food for the island over in his mind. Who could he trust? Emmanuel, certainly not; Filippo, Julius and Mario were a possibility. It would need two men to handle the rowing boat drawn up to the top of the beach and he needed to be certain that whichever men were on sentry duty that night would not shoot at him. He considered his best approach to them. He could throw caution to the winds and tell them outright what he wanted to do, or he could try leading the conversation round and try to ascertain the extent of their compassion.

He decided he would speak to Mario first and sat with him after eating their meal, choosing his Italian words carefully.

'Have you ever been out in a boat?' he asked.

'Of course. How did you get over here? We came by boat.'

'I mean a small boat, like the one down on the shore.'

Mario shook his head. 'I lived in Milan. Not much use for boats around there. What's in your mind?'

'I think we ought to go out to that island. For all we know there could be a landing place on the other side and that could be where the resistance are hiding out. We'd look pretty stupid when the Commander found out and we had to admit that we'd never been out to look.' Victor was pleased with the inspiration that had suddenly come to him. He had originally planned to suggest a fishing trip.

Mario nodded. 'Maybe Filippo knows how to row. He lived by the sea. You wouldn't plan to land, would you?'

Victor shook his head. 'I'd just like to have a look and see what the seaward side is like.'

Victor watched as they drew closer to the island. He had been able to see through his field glasses the people who sat on the shore fishing, whilst others appeared to be searching the rock pools. He had often lent his glasses to Anna when she waved from the shore, but the high walls of the Venetian fort obstructed his view of any other activity that might be taking place. Filippo and Mario rowed past the jetty where a woman waved to them. Slowly Victor raised his hand and waved back.

She stood and held out a hand to them in supplication, then moved it to her mouth, repeating the action. 'Food,' she called. 'We need food.'

Victor scanned the arm of land that ran out towards the island from Olous. There had never been any sign of activity on the barren hillside, but he did not want to be ambushed as they passed through the narrow channel between the island and the mainland.

Filippo halted in his rowing. 'Do you want to go on? It's pretty dangerous here. There are rocks just below the surface.'

Victor nodded. 'Take it slowly.'

He continued to scan both shores with his glasses. A small, deserted beach could be seen on Spinalonga, the Venetian wall running down to it. As they entered the channel he could see another beach and an expanse of barren land leading up to an archway that presumably led into the fortress. He held up his hand and the men stopped their rowing. Carefully he turned to look back the way they had come. He could see the soldiers stationed on the shore, which must mean they could also see this stretch of beach, but from where he was he could not see the village of Plaka.

'Continue,' he ordered.

Once through the channel the sea became a little choppy and both Victor and Mario were uneasy. Neither of them could swim and if the boat overturned their chances of survival were slim. Victor touched his crucifix surreptitiously and said a silent prayer for their safe delivery. Filippo appeared unconcerned as he studied the rocks beneath the sea and steered the boat a little further out to ensure they had clearance.

Victor raised his glasses to his eyes again. The cliffs fell down almost sheer to the sea, the walls of the Venetian fort rising above them. It was most unlikely that anyone would be able to land safely and climb up from such an inhospitable shore. There was no sign of movement and Victor felt fairly certain that no one except the most desperate of men would try to gain access to the island from there.

They rounded the end of the island and Plaka came back into view once more. The shoreline still steep and forbidding until they were opposite the village where the steepness had given way to low rocks and once again people could be seen. They held out their hands to the boat as it began to draw away and return to the shore.

Anna entered the shed and pulled a sack from the pile. Yannis could take that up to his father's house when he went up for the donkey and bring her down the remains of the vegetables.

'Anna.'

Her name was spoken so softly she was not sure if she had imagined it. She stood frozen, the sack held tightly to her chest.

'I need to talk to you.'

'That's impossible. The soldiers are in the house. They could come out here at any moment.'

'Meet me later in the hills. I'll be waiting.'

'Where?'

'Go to the gorse clump. I'll find you.'

Anna's mouth felt dry. She walked stiffly from the shed and back into the kitchen, throwing the sack into the corner. From the pot of coffee she poured a cup and dunked her bread thoughtfully.

'Don't I get a second cup this morning, then?'

Anna jumped at the sound of her mother's voice. 'I'm sorry. I was just thinking.'

'What about?'

'The jobs I plan to do today. I'll go and collect some vegetables from Babbis's place. Whilst I'm gone Marisa can go down to the shop. She can make out a list.'

'Make a list! She should be able to remember.'

'I'm sure she can, but it's good for her to practice her reading and writing.'

Maria sniffed. 'Be better if she practised her cooking. The bread she made last week was as hard as a rock.'

'That wasn't her fault, Mamma. The oven went out whilst it

210

was cooking. Now, do you want me to cut the crust off this bread for you?'

Marisa was pleased she was going to the shop. It would give her the opportunity of speaking to some of the other villagers, and also to Victor, without her aunt watching her. She picked up her shawl and basket.

'I can't think of anything else we need, but if there's any soap or matches you could buy some to put in the store cupboard.' Anna watched as her niece left the house, then poured some water into a glass and took it to her mother.

'I've brought you a drink. Marisa has gone down to Danniakis's shop and I'm going up for the vegetables.'

Maria nodded. 'I'll still be here when you get back.'

'So I should hope! I may stop to gather a few herbs, but I won't be away too long.'

Anna returned to the kitchen and placed a wedge of cheese and half a loaf into her basket before leaving the house. Walking slowly she scanned the hills as she followed the rough path until she came to the fields of straggling vines. There was no sign of anyone, except Yannis gathering dead wood from around the olive trees. She waved to him as she continued towards the gorse bushes. She was wondering whether she should wait or continue on to Babbis's house when she heard a low whistle.

Turning swiftly, Anna could still see no one, but the whistle came again. Intrigued, Anna moved forwards towards the bushes.

'Sit down,' a low voice commanded her, 'and look out towards the island.'

Anna did as she was told. 'Why do you want to speak to me? Are you hurt?'

'Not at all, but I do need a bit of help. Can you get a couple of pairs of trousers for me, please?'

Anna nodded. 'That should be easy. You can have some of my father's.'

'Fine. I'll be here tomorrow. Bring what you can.'

'Don't you need any food?'

'I can forage for that. Why? Have you brought me some?'

'It's not much.'

'Lay it on the ground and I'll pick it up after you've gone.'

Anna emptied her basket and heard the man suck in his breath. 'Cheese and bread! I've been living off apples and raw vegetables. This will be a treat. Thank you, Anna.'

'How do you know my name?'

'I heard your mother calling you, remember?'

'What's your name?'

'Michael.'

'I'll bring you some more food tomorrow and leave it here with the trousers.'

Marisa hurried down to the village shop. Provided she did not linger too long she should be able to have a word with Victor on her return. The village had an artificial air of normality about it. The children were in school, the elderly priest had agreed to all the girls attending each day along with the boys, much to their mothers' relief. It was comforting to know their offspring were under the eye of the school master and not likely to draw the attention of the soldiers to themselves. The women were busy about their cooking and cleaning, but the men who should have been calling to each other from their fishing boats or working in the fields were missing.

Danniakis sat outside his little general store gazing with rheumy eyes across the sea and clicking his beads between his fingers. It was all wrong. His daughter should not have to move the heavy barrels of olives, the containers of oil and the sacks of flour and rice. It was a man's job. He was acutely aware of his own helplessness, as the slightest exertion to his over-sized frame brought on an attack of breathlessness and an excruciating pain in his chest. Even moving out into the sunshine was a tremendous effort and he wished his daughter would not insist that it was good for him. He sighed, hearing his breath rattle around inside his lungs. No wonder they had not taken him to work in the mines. He was no good to anyone any more and the sooner his daughter had one less mouth to feed the better.

He watched Marisa swinging down the street and wished he were young again. She was certainly good looking, the way her mother had been. She greeted him cheerfully.

'Good morning, Danniakis, how are you?'

'All the better for seeing you, my dear,' he wheezed. 'What brings you?'

'Mamma Anna's sent me with a shopping list. She's hoping you might have a bar of soap to spare.'

'Can't say.' He shook his head dolefully. 'Can't run the place as I used to. Have to leave it up to her now. She'll tell you what she's got and what you can have. Things aren't like they used to be.'

'Have you heard any news?' asked Marisa anxiously.

Danniakis shook his head. 'There isn't any news. No news of anything. No news of our men, no news of what's happening or what they're doing. Nothing.'

'I'm sure we'll hear something very soon,' replied Marisa comfortingly.

'The only news I want to hear is that these foreigners have been sent packing.'

'They will be. They can't stay here forever. They must want to get home to their families.'

Danniakis cleared his throat and spat on the ground. 'Scum, that's what they are. Forcing themselves on us, living in our homes and eating our food. Pretty girl like you wants to watch out for herself. Soldiers can't be trusted.'

'Victor and Mario are all right. I trust them.'

'Then you shouldn't. They're no different from the Germans.'

'They've treated us decently. Victor told us about drawing supplies from Aghios Nikolaos and he's been helping my aunt with some of the heavy work.'

Danniakis sniffed. 'Don't trust him. He'll want something in return, you mark my words.'

'He says he's grateful for the way we look after him. He's asking the other soldiers to help in the village, with the work the women can't do.'

'That so? Well my daughter could do with a bit of help, so why haven't we seen any of it?'

'I'll tell Victor when I get back. He probably thought that running a shop you didn't have any heavy work.'

'There are sacks and barrels that have to be moved. How do they think that gets done? By magic?'

'I'll tell him,' promised Marisa, anxious now to make her purchases and seek out Victor. She patted Danniakis on the shoulder. 'You look after yourself, and don't worry.'

Before he could reply she walked into the shop and waited for her eyes to become accustomed to the dim interior. She looked around the small general store hoping to see something that was plentiful, but the empty shelves told their own story.

'Good morning, Eleni. I was wondering if you had any flour and maybe a bar of soap?'

Eleni pursed her lips. 'I can't let you have more than a couple of pounds of flour, and there's no soap. Have you heard any news?'

'No. I asked your father the same question. He said you needed a bit of help.'

'Help? What do I need help with?'

'He said moving the sacks and barrels was too heavy for a woman. Would you like me to ask Victor to ask one of the soldiers to do it for you?'

'I'm not as friendly with those soldiers as you are.'

'I'm not particularly friendly with them,' Marisa blushed deeply as she said the words. 'Yannis asked Victor to help Mamma Anna with some heavy digging and he said they were willing to help anyone with the jobs they found difficult.'

'And what do they get in return? They can take their eyes off my little Ourania.'

'Victor said they would be doing it in return for letting them sleep in the house and feeding them. He doesn't like being here as a soldier. He wants to go home.'

'Shouldn't have joined up, then, should he? You can tell him from me that when they bring me supplies from Aghios Nikolaos they can put them down in the cellar instead of dumping them outside like they did the last time, and when I want something they can bring it up. If they're so willing I can use them. The fence out the back needs repairing and there are two tiles off the roof. Get those jobs done and a bit of lifting and carrying and I might feel a bit more friendly towards them.'

Marisa smiled. 'I'll tell Victor. He'll ask one of them.'

'I don't want that useless lump Emmanuel around, and I don't like that Roberto who lodges with Sevas. I don't like the way he looks at me – or at Ourania for that matter.'

'I'm sure Roberto doesn't mean to worry you. It's just his way.'

'Way or not, I don't trust him. My Ourania's too young to think about men yet, besides, I'm not having her getting friendly with any Italian soldier. She's been brought up properly.' Eleni glowered into the embarrassed face of Marisa, daring her to contradict.

'Of course she has,' agreed Marisa. 'Can I have the flour? Have you got any pasta, and what about matches? I ought to get back. My grandmother's on her own.'

'Where's your aunt?'

'Getting some vegetables from my father's house.'

'Your Yannis should do that. It's not safe for a woman to go up to the fields.' Eleni began to ladle the flour from the sack into the scale.

'Yannis does so many jobs he can't cope with any more. I think Mamma Anna is safe enough.'

Eleni sniffed in disbelief. 'You wouldn't get me going up there. Anything could happen.'

Marisa looked at the over-weight, swarthy woman and had a desire to giggle. She swallowed hard. 'How much do I owe you?'

'Forty lepta, although how long I'll be able to hold my prices down I don't know. Each time I get something the price has gone up. I don't see why it should. Just because there's a war on they use it as an excuse for everything.' She sighed heavily. 'How's it all going to end, that's what I want to know?'

Marisa placed her money on the counter. 'I'll ask Victor to find some soldiers to give you a hand and do those repairs, not Emmanuel or Roberto,' she added hastily.

'I'll believe it when I see it. Tell your aunt I'll see her at church on Sunday.'

Marisa nodded. 'I will. Thank you, Eleni.'

Relieved to be out of the shop, Marisa hurried home where she could see Victor digging vigorously. Without waiting to place her purchases in the kitchen she hurried across the yard and up the hill towards him.

He leant on the fork and smiled at her. She was growing so beautiful that she took his breath away.

'Victor, I've been talking to Eleni and she could do with some help down at the shop. The sacks and barrels need to be moved, there's a fence to be mended and also the roof. She doesn't want Emmanuel or Roberto to do it, so I said I would ask you to ask one of the soldiers.'

'Please?' Victor's brow creased in a frown, understanding little of Marisa's rapid speech.

'Oh Victor, I thought you could understand Greek now,' she reproached him.

Victor shook his head. 'Understand not all.'

Marisa stood beside him and spoke slowly and clearly. 'Eleni at shop, needs help. Move sacks, move barrels, mend roof, mend fence.'

Victor nodded. 'I do.'

'No,' Marisa frowned. 'Not you. Not Roberto, not Emmanuel. Another soldier.'

'Why not me those men?'

'Eleni does not like them. You help us. Another soldier help them.'

Victor smiled. 'I ask. Maybe Filippo?'

'Filippo would be fine.' Fervently Marisa hoped Eleni would have no complaint with the choice.

'I ask.'

'Thank you, Victor.' Marisa picked up her bag.

Victor reached out and took the bag from her, sending a tingling through her whole body as their fingers touched. 'You go?'

'I have to go. Grandmother is alone.'

'Why alone?'

'Mamma Anna has gone up to the fields. For vegetables.'

Victor raised his eyes to where a small figure could be seen walking down the track.

'I must go,' breathed Marisa.

'Anna come. You stay.'

'No, I have to go,' insisted Marisa. 'Mamma Anna cross.'

'Why cross? You talk to me.'

Marisa shook her head. How could she explain her aunt's fear of the soldiers, a fear that Marisa found quite irrational when in the company of the good looking young Italian. 'I must get back to my grandmother.' She stretched out her hand for her bag of shopping.

'I bring.'

'Thank you.' Although the bag was not heavy she appreciated his gesture. She turned and began to walk quickly back down the field track to the house. She knew her aunt would have seen her talking and want to know why she had spent so long with him, but she had her excuses ready.

217

'Marisa,' he called after her.

She turned and looked into Victor's smiling eyes. 'You teach Greek, good Greek for me?'

Marisa smiled back at him. 'Of course I will.'

Anna returned to her home feeling vaguely excited. Taking trousers up to the fields with her was simple after her previous task of getting the doctor to come from Aghios Nikolaos. If she was challenged she could always say they were to be used as rags to clean the tools and leave some dirty pieces of cloth around to bear her story out. She wondered why Michael had asked her to go up to the hills to meet him. He could quite easily have asked for the clothes during the few moments they had spent together in the shed.

'Did you bring the vegetables?'

Anna gave a guilty start. She had completely forgotten them. 'I thought Yannis could bring them back when he brings the donkey down.' The lie rolled glibly off her tongue to her mother.

Having quizzed her niece thoroughly about the time she had spent with Victor, she set her to making a batch of bread. Taking advantage of the soldiers' absence Anna went up to the bedroom that had been commandeered by Victor and Mario. The trunk where she had stored her father's clothes stood untouched in the corner. As she lifted out his Sunday suit, carefully folded, she felt a lump come into her throat. It had been somewhat tight on him the last time he had worn it, but she doubted that it would be when he returned home. She laid it on the bed and dug deeper, pulling out shirts, trousers and socks, rolling them into a bundle and taking them into her own room.

Desperately she looked for somewhere to hide them until the next day. Her trunk she shared with Marisa and they were sure to be found if she left them there. She decided their bedroom was impractical, then the solution occurred to her. Swiftly she stripped the coarse sheet from their mattress and bundled the clothes inside. It would just be a bundle of dirty washing, sitting in the corner of the kitchen to be done the next day.

Marisa saw her aunt place another bundle of washing in the corner and sighed. She hated washing and there was always so much of it. She always ended getting water all over the kitchen floor during the winter months, but at least then the water was warm. It was too cold to use the sea now, but still mild enough to work outside and she would be expected to use the water straight from the pump, making her hands end up red and sore. She covered the dough with a clean cloth and left it to prove whilst she went in search of pencils and paper. If Victor wanted to learn Greek properly there was no time like the present to start teaching him.

Supper over, the dishes washed, and a pot of coffee sitting in the centre of the table, Marisa turned to Victor.

'Now we do Greek.'

'Si? You teach?'

Marisa nodded. 'We'll start with the letters. I'll write them and tell you the sounds. Then you write them and tell me.'

'Please?'

'Oh, Victor! Never mind. You'll understand as we go along.'

For over an hour Marisa sat, painstakingly writing the letters of the alphabet and insisting Victor copied them until he finally shook his head.

'Go now. Taverna.'

'But, Victor, we've only just started. If you stop now you'll have forgotten everything by tomorrow.'

Victor smiled. 'Taverna. Mario, Filippo, Julius at taverna. Victor go taverna.'

Marisa pouted at him and banged her pencil down on the table. 'You'll never learn if you go to the taverna each evening,' she called after him.

Anna frowned. 'I don't know why you want to teach him anyway.'

219

Marisa tilted her chin defiantly. 'I knew you wouldn't understand. Victor asked me to teach him Greek. Besides, you said it would be good for me to practise my reading and writing.'

'I didn't mean by teaching an Italian. If he learns Greek properly we can never have a private conversation, he'll be able to understand everything we say.'

'So what are we going to want to talk privately about?'

Anna shrugged. 'I don't know,' she admitted lamely. 'But I don't want you getting too friendly with them. There'll be talk in the village.'

Marisa tossed her head. 'I don't care what the villagers say.'

'Well you should. When the time comes for you to think about becoming betrothed you don't want a family to refuse you because you have a bad reputation.'

Marisa bit her lip, she seemed to be struggling to keep her self control. 'I'd rather not get married than be betrothed to any of the village boys.'

'You'll probably change your mind in a year or two.'

'I won't. They're all younger than me anyway. I don't want to get married to a baby.'

Anna sighed. 'I know it's difficult. All the young men are away fighting, but they'll come back and be ready to settle down. They'll have had enough excitement to last them and be only too glad to stay in one place with a wife and home of their own.'

'Well they can take me off their list of possible wives. I can't think of a single one I'd want to spend the rest of my life with, besides, Pappa will be back then and he won't make me marry anyone if I don't want to.'

Yannis looked at his rebellious sister. 'You have to do as Pappa says.'

Marisa gave him a withering look. 'You may have to, but I shall choose the man I marry – if I ever do get married,' she added, feeling tears coming into her eyes. She rose from the table and placed the paper and pencils in the cupboard. There was only one man who filled her thoughts day and night and he certainly did not come from the village.

Anna sorted the washing carefully, placing the clothing she was taking up to the fields into a sack. Marisa was already drawing water from the pump into the galvanised bathtub.

'I'm going up to the fields for some more vegetables. You should have finished that lot by the time I get back.'

Marisa nodded. She would have preferred to be the one to go up and collect a sack of vegetables. Anything would be better than spending the morning with her arms immersed in the cold water. She wondered why her aunt had changed the sheet from her bed. It had been clean on no more than three days before, at least it would only need a dip in the water, unlike Yannis's trousers and socks that always seemed to be covered in mud.

On the pretext of checking on her mother before she left, Anna returned to the kitchen. She wrapped two loaves of freshly baked bread in a cloth and tucked them under her arm. Hoping Marisa would not question her as she carried the loaded sack out of the yard, she turned at the gate and called back to her niece.

'I'll not be long. Keep an eye on your grandmother.'

'Of course.'

Anna hardly heard her reply, already she was thinking of her assignation with Michael. She wished she knew how long he planned to stay in the area and if she would be expected to provide food for him all the time. She walked to the gorse clump and placed the sack under a bush, continuing on over the hill to where Babbis's farm lay. She dug the last of the potatoes that were going soft and beginning to sprout. They would be useless for cooking, but if they were stored and kept dry the goats would be glad of them during the winter months. She worked quickly, hoping Michael would appear and she could tell him where she had left the clothing and food. Finally she could delay her return no longer and began to hurry back over the hill.

She passed the gorse clump and resisted the urge to check and see if the items she had left were still there, continuing down the hill.

'Anna.'

The voice from nowhere made her jump and she stopped in her tracks. 'I expected you to be in the gorse. I've left the clothes and bread.'

Michael lay behind a low wall. 'It's a good idea never to be where you're expected to be. I saw you pass, but thought it better to stop you on the way down. I suppose there aren't any old boots or shoes with the clothes?'

Anna shook her head. 'There are socks, shirts and trousers.'

'Not to worry. I'll get some elsewhere I expect. You've been a great help.'

'Are you moving on now?'

Michael smiled at her. 'Anxious to see the back of me? I'm not going just yet. We've decided we quite like being here.'

'We?'

'My friends and I.'

Cautiously Anna looked around. 'Where are your friends?'

Michael waved his hand. 'Around and about.'

'I can't see anyone.'

'Good. If you can't see them I doubt if the Italians can either.'

'What are you doing here?'

'Just settling ourselves in. Making ourselves comfortable. Finding friends. Tell me, do those Italians ever leave the village?'

'Almost every night two or three of them go to Aghios Nikolaos.'

Michael nodded, a speculative look in his eyes. 'What time do they leave?'

'About four usually.'

'And come back when?'

Anna shrugged. 'Quite late, sometimes very late, sometimes not until the next morning.'

'That could be useful. I'll see you tomorrow. Off you go, now. Goodbye.'

Obediently Anna picked up the sack of potatoes as Michael moved higher up the hill in the shelter of the wall. She assumed he would expect her to bring him more food the next day, although he had not mentioned it, in fact, looking back over their conversation, he had told her very little.

Victor examined the outhouses. There were a quantity of sacks that contained potatoes and carrots that Anna had cleaned and packed away ready for the winter months. He tested their weight, they were heavy, but not impossible to lift and two men would be able to manhandle a sack between them with ease.

He waited until Anna and Yannis were up in the fields and Marisa busy with her grandmother. Then he called Mario and between them they carried a sack of potatoes followed by another of carrots down to the shore and pushed them beneath the rowing boat.

'I'll speak to Filippo and we could take them out tonight, there's no moon.'

Mario looked at him doubtfully. 'We were told not to take supplies out to them.'

'You could hardly call a couple of sacks of vegetables supplies.'

'Suppose the sentries shoot at us?'

'I'll make sure they don't. I'll tell them we want to go out to the island to check out any movement there after dark.'

'If it's dark you wouldn't see any movement anyway,' protested Mario.

'If you were expecting anyone from the resistance you'd have to leave a light to show them where to land.'

'We've never seen a light from here.'

'It won't hurt to check. If you're unwilling to help then I'll find someone else.'

Mario shrugged. 'If the Commander finds out I shall tell him I was under orders from you.'

Yannis sat disconsolately on the patch of concrete that Kyriakos had called his home for so many years. The hunger pangs that were continually with him were nothing compared to the anguish in his heart. Even the fear and loneliness he had first experienced when diagnosed were nothing compared to the pain he was suffering now. First it had been Phaedra, becoming weaker by the day, until she finally drew her last breath whilst holding his hand. Then it was Anna. Silly little girl, disobeying him and using a knife to carve pictures when there was no more paper for her to draw on.

Conditions were becoming desperate. The first eighteen months had not been too difficult. They had cooked communally, saving the left overs from a meal to make a soup that would be their main meal the next day. Rice, lentils and pasta had been strictly rationed until they finally ran out and they were dependent upon the vegetables they had stored and the produce from their small gardens.

The eggs from the chickens had been saved for the hospital patients, but gradually the hens had ceased to lay. One by one their necks had been wrung and the scraggy carcasses had been boiled at least twice until nothing more could be gained from the bones. These they had crushed and pounded until the resulting powder had been fine enough to thicken a soup in the belief that it would give them some added nourishment.

The same fate had befallen Panicos's goats. As they failed to reproduce and ceased to give milk the thin beasts were slaughtered, their stringy meat dried for future consumption and their soft internal organs eaten before they could rot. Even their skin had been boiled to extract the last molecule of meat.

Now the vegetables from their gardens were almost exhausted and there was no seed for planting further supplies. The only produce that seemed to flourish was Flora's geraniums. Yannis smiled wryly. If only she had wanted something edible, even nasturtiums would have been more practical. There would be nothing to eat until the evening, and that would depend upon someone having caught a fish or risked negotiating the slippery rocks in search of a few edible shellfish. He wondered how much longer those who did make the hazardous journey would have the strength to continue. Already Makkis had fallen into the sea and not had the strength to clamber back onto the rocks.

The mournful tolling of the church bell reminded him that another funeral would be taking place that morning. No longer were coffins made for the deceased. Wood for the cooking fires was becoming scarcer and he envisaged a time when those who were strong enough would be digging up the bodies in the graveyard to use their coffins as kindling. It was doubtful if anyone would have the strength to wield a spade, but they would have to try.

He wiped his hand down his dirty trousers. There was no spare water for washing and they had resorted to using the sea for both their clothes and their bodies. Reluctantly he rose to his feet. He would have to take his turn with the others to help carry the coffin to the church and then up to the tower where all the dead were now placed. The empty coffin would be brought back to the church to be used for the next soul who had finally succumbed to the deprivation they were all suffering.

From respect for the dead he felt he should wash his hands before taking his turn with the coffin. With dragging feet he made his way to the square and through the tunnel to the small beach crunching across the shingle to dip his hands in the sea and rub them over his face. Stumbling he retraced his steps across the shingle and then he saw, laying almost at the foot of the Venetian wall, two sacks.

Yannis stood and looked at them. Where would they have come from? They did not look wet, so could not have been washed up by the sea. A surge of hope ran through him. Maybe a passing fisherman had thrown some of his catch over to them. Carefully Yannis undid the neck of the first one and was surprised to see potatoes, the second one held carrots. No fisherman would have caught those in the sea.

Frowning, Yannis returned to the square, looking for anyone who appeared strong enough to help him to carry the sacks. He did not really care where they had come from. At least they would be able to have some soup for a few days.

Yannis harnessed the donkey to the cart and gave her a flick on her rump with a twig. She looked at him reproachfully and began to amble down the hill towards the track.

'Yannis.'

The voice came from behind a wall and he knew it belonged to the man with startlingly blue eyes.

Yannis grinned in delight. 'What do you want me to do?'

Michael smiled at the boy's eagerness. 'I hear some of the Italians go into Aghios Nikolaos in the evenings. Are any going tonight?'

'I know Guiseppe is. I expect a couple of the others will go with him.'

'Where does he lodge?'

'In the end house, with Aspasia.'

Michael nodded. 'I want you to find out which soldiers are going into the town each evening and tell me which houses they live in.'

'Is that all?' Yannis looked disappointed.

'That will do for the time being.'

It became a habit for Anna to wrap two loaves each day, take them up to the fields and leave them hidden amongst the gorse bushes. Sometimes Michael was there to receive them and thank her, but most days she saw no sign of him or anyone else in the hills. Since his first request for trousers he had asked for nothing more from her, and apart from the ritual of the loaves, he might not exist except in Anna's imagination.

Unknown to her, Yannis saw him each evening as he gathered the sheep and goats down for the night. He would examine walls, vines and olives trees until he heard Michael's voice and the boy would tell him which Italians were leaving the village for a night out in Aghios Nikolaos. Michael would thank him and disappear and Yannis would continue on his way.

It was Yannis who took the news to him that the German Commander was about to make an inspection of the Italian troops ranged along the coastline.

Michael smiled. 'That's the news we've been waiting for. Any idea when?'

Yannis shook his head. 'Julius went into Aghios Nikolaos last night and he heard about it there, according to Victor. It could be just a rumour to keep the Italians on their toes. They're a pretty slack lot; they spend most of their day doing nothing. What are you planning to do?'

'Nothing that concerns you.'

'Are you going to fight them?' Yannis's eyes glowed.

Michael ruffled his hair. 'Not in the way you're thinking.'

'I'll let you know if I hear anything,' promised Yannis. 'Besides,' he added, as Michael was about to speak, 'I have to come up to get the animals each night.'

'You're not to take any risks.'

Yannis grinned. 'I couldn't leave the poor things up here all night, now could I?'

He walked away up the hill, leaving Michael to shake his head over the departing figure. He wondered if all boys of that age had such devious natures.

1944 – 1946

Each day Yannis asked Victor if he knew when the Germans were coming and each day Victor shook his head. 'Why you want know?'

Yannis debated whether to be heroic or sensible in his answer. Commonsense won. 'So I can keep out of his way.'

'Please?'

Yannis sighed. 'He come. I hide.'

Victor nodded soberly. 'Good, yes. You hide, Marisa hide. Where hide?'

Yannis shrugged. 'Stable, fields.'

'No good. You find.'

'Then I'll run away and join the resistance.'

'Resistance? Where resistance?' Victor gripped Yannis's shoulder. 'Tell where resistance.'

Yannis shook himself free. 'I don't know. In the hills, in the mountains.'

Victor gave Yannis a hard look. 'No speak to Commander of resistance. No speak go to them.' Victor's voice dropped to a whisper. 'Commander kill resistance. You not know resistance.'

Yannis refused to meet Victor's eyes. 'I have to get to the fields.'

Anna could not sleep. She did not know what frightened her more, the thought of anything happening to the children and her mother, or the thought of something happening to her whereby they were left to fend for themselves. There was no one she could share her fears with, not wishing to alarm any of her family, and of Michael there had been no sign for over a week. She hoped news of the impending visit of the German Commander had reached him and he and his men had moved out of the area where they would be safe.

Yannis began to wonder, as did the Italians, if it had been a rumour spread to make them tighten up their security. Each day saw them marching along the road and sentries were evenly spaced along the beaches, instead of passing the day gambling together in the taverna as they had in the past. The evening visits to Aghios Nikolaos became less frequent and on two occasions Victor had accompanied Yannis up to the fields.

The Germans marched into the village at dawn, their tread purposeful as they spread themselves out and opened the doors of the villager's houses. Each house was thoroughly searched, the occupants held cowering in corners, a rifle pointing at them. Everyone was interrogated and each declared their total ignorance of any stranger in the district, either now or earlier, until Yannis volunteered the information about the search, which had taken place some six months previously.

'Why were you in the hills?' the Commander barked his question.

'I'd lost some sheep.'

'So?'

'I had to look for them. I was in the hills and saw some men.'

'Which men?'

'I don't know. I just caught a glimpse of them. I came straight back and told Victor and Mario. They went up to the hills with me to look for them.'

'And did you find these men?'

'No, sir, but they'd been in the caves.'

'Caves? What caves?'

Yannis pointed vaguely towards the headland. 'Over the other side there are some caves. Do you want me to take you there?'

The Commander looked at the Italian soldiers lined up before him. 'Why was I not told about this before?'

Victor began to explain. 'We went with the boy and searched for hours and found nothing. There had been a fire in one of the caves, but no one was there. We went up again a few nights later as we heard shooting coming from that direction.'

'What did you find?'

'Nothing.' Victor shrugged. 'There was no sign of anyone. The shooting must have been further away than we realised.'

'Have you been to these caves since then?'

Victor shifted his weight from one foot to the other. 'I haven't.'

'You didn't think it worth your while to check another time: during daylight, perhaps? You idle lot of ruffians. If you were part of the German army I would have you shot. You spend all day gazing out to sea at an island and do not see what goes on behind your back. I know there are resistance workers in this area and I will find them.' His gaze swung back to Yannis. 'You, boy, will take me to the cave. I will decide for myself who was there.'

Yannis shook his head. 'I can't. I have to take the donkey up to the fields and let the animals out. Maybe this evening when I've finished working.'

'You will come now.'

A German soldier took up a position on either side of the boy and he was marched out of the house.

Victor looked at Anna sadly. 'I take donkey. I do sheep.'

'No!' She rounded on him angrily. 'If you'd reported your failure to find anyone in the caves at the time this would not have happened. Now they've taken Yannis. What will they do with him?'

'Please?'

'Oh, get out of my way.' Anna pushed past the Italian, threw her shawl across her shoulders and strode across to the stable. She felt very close to tears and extremely frightened. She now hoped Michael had not left the area, although she had no clear idea how he would be able to help.

Her hands trembling, she placed a halter around the neck of the patient animal and began to lead her up the hill. She had almost reached the gorse when she remembered she had not brought the customary bread. She walked more slowly, scanning the area carefully for any sign that Michael was hiding in there, repeating his name softly in the hope that he would hear.

Anna continued up towards Babbis's farm and fastened the donkey securely, checked there was water in the bucket and pulled away the barrier that had penned the sheep and goats for the night. As she pushed it against the wall she wheeled round in relief at the sound of Michael's voice.

'I need to talk to you.' She pretended to examine a sheep before giving it a smack on its rump to send it on its way. 'They've taken Yannis,' she leant against the wall, her lips quivering and tears beginning to spill from her eyes. 'They've taken Yannis,' she repeated.

Michael frowned. 'What do you mean? Who's taken him and where?'

'The German Commander. They arrived at dawn and searched everyone's house. They say they're looking for strangers in the area. Yannis told them about the caves and they've gone to look there.'

'Which caves?' There was sharpness in Michael's voice.

'The ones where Yannis took the Italians whilst I brought the doctor up here. I should never have agreed to help.' Anna began to cry in earnest, racking sobs that shook her whole body.

Michael held her in his arms. 'Hush, now Anna. Calm yourself. Yannis is in no danger.'

'Of course he's in danger.' Anna spoke angrily between her sobs. 'He's been taken by the Germans.'

'Be sensible. He's gone to show them the way to some caves. He's doing his duty as a good Cretan citizen. They'll not harm him for that. The Italians will corroborate his story and he'll be home before you know it. I promise you no harm will come to him.'

'How can you promise! He's only a boy, a child.'

Michael sighed. 'Please, Anna, trust me. My men will watch him all the way and if there's any sign of trouble they'll get him out.'

'Your men? What men? I've never seen any men, I've only seen you.'

'I can assure you there are plenty of us around. Nothing will happen to him. All my men know him by sight and if they thought he was in danger a couple would show themselves. The Germans would take off after them and the others would spirit Yannis away and back here. Your Yannis is very brave. He's leading them on a wild goose chase of their own choosing.' Michael chuckled. 'They'll find no one there, but the chances are they'll leave you alone in the village.'

Anna sniffed. Michael's words and arms were comforting. 'I couldn't bear it if anything happened to Yannis.'

Michael squeezed her gently, then released her to dry her eyes on her apron. 'Nothing will happen to him. I swear it.'

Yannis returned to the farmhouse just as Anna was about to give up hope. The German Commander, grim faced and weary, barked orders to his soldiers before climbing into his jeep and heading back for Aghios Nikolaos. Yannis looked at his aunt with amusement in his eyes.

'It was a stiff climb and all for nothing.'

'I thought you were going over the brow and up the valley.'

Yannis grinned. 'We did, but I took them by the scenic route and dropped down from above. You should have heard them puff and pant. I'm off to get the donkey.' Before Anna could answer he was gone, whistling cheerfully as he ran across the yard.

The door to the kitchen opened, startling Anna as she lifted the heavy pot of stew from the fire. The muzzle of the gun pointing at her made her tremble and she placed the pot on the ground before she spilled the contents.

'What do you want?'

The gun waved at her, and she stood rooted to the spot, too petrified to move. Sounds from the living room came to her ears and she longed to know what was happening. The door opened and the Commander appeared.

'You may join your family.'

The gun at her back, Anna walked into the room where Yannis and Marisa stood protectively before their grandmother.

'Now, we will take another look. You thought we had left and you were safe now to bring your visitors from their hiding places. Now we will find them.'

Anna shrugged. 'There are no visitors here, unless you count the Italian soldiers.'

'We will see for ourselves.'

The clatter of boots overhead confirmed that the house was once again being thoroughly searched. A man appeared from the yard and shook his head. The Commander wheeled round to face Anna again.

'I know there are resistance round here. Someone has to be feeding them and I wish to know who. If they are not staying in the village they must be in the hills. Maybe there are more caves which we have not been shown.'

Anna shook her head. 'There are no caves here.'

'No? How long have you lived here?'

'All my life. I was born here.'

'So you would know the countryside? You could take me to these caves.'

Again Anna shook her head. 'The only caves I know of are the ones where Yannis took you. They are the nearest ones to Plaka.'

'I do not think so. Why should there be caves in that hill and not in this one?'

Anna shrugged. 'I've never seen any.'

'What about you, boy?'

'Not round here. I took you to the only ones I know.'

'My soldiers will search and they will find them.' The steely blue eyes swept over the group who did not flinch.

Anna lifted her chin defiantly. 'May I continue with the supper now? My mother and the children are hungry.'

'You will wait.'

'They're hungry. Yannis hasn't eaten all day.'

'Hunger pangs will not hurt them.' The Commander turned to his German soldiers and barked a command. 'They will look a little more closely outside. Maybe you will remember if you have seen any caves as you become more hungry.'

For over an hour Anna and the children were forced to stand beside Maria's bed, the Italians standing in a corner by the door and the Commander seated comfortably in a chair. Finally the soldiers returned and a rapid interchange of German took place, the Commander frowning at their words.

He pointed his gun directly at Anna. 'It is strange, is it not? We know there are a number of outlaws hiding in this area. Everyone denies knowledge of them. No one has seen them. They have not hidden in an outhouse; no food has been stolen; yet we know they are here. Who is looking after them?' The cold blue eyes went from face to face. 'When we discover who has helped them they will wish they had admitted it.'

An uncomfortable silence fell. Anna wished her heart was not beating so loudly, sure that the German would hear it and be convinced of her duplicity. Yannis studied his boots, his stomach rumbling unpleasantly, whilst Marisa felt for her grandmother's comforting hand.

'So, you are not prepared to admit to helping these enemies? You are fortunate this time. We have found nothing. We will find where these men are hiding and we will also find those who are hiding them. You may not be so fortunate the next time.' He clicked his fingers, rose and swept out of the door. The German soldiers followed him, whilst the two Italians stood rigidly to attention and saluted.

Anna looked at Yannis and Marisa and frowned, hoping they would interpret her sign correctly. 'I'll re-heat the stew.'

Victor followed her into the kitchen. 'I sorry. You good. Yannis good. No one hide here.'

Anna did not answer. She felt incredibly weary. The strain of waiting for Yannis's safe return with the Germans and the sudden and unexpected evening visit from the Commander had thoroughly unnerved her. She heaved the pot back on to the fire and leaned her head against the chimney, fighting the tears that threatened to overwhelm her. Finally she took a long, shuddering breath, regained her composure and dipped her finger into the mixture to test the heat, licking it clean. Victor followed suit and grinned.

'Good.' He rubbed his stomach. 'I take.'

He lifted the pot from the fire and placed it on the table for Anna to serve generous helpings into the bowls with shaking hands. 'Marisa,' she called, 'come and carry these in for me.'

Her eyes large and frightened, Marisa carried the dishes back to the living room and busied herself with helping her grandmother to break up her bread.

'Do you really think there are resistance workers round here?' Her eyes swept across her aunt and brother.

Anna shrugged. 'Who knows? They're not our concern.' She frowned at Marisa. 'Eat your supper before it gets cold.'

Anna's sleep was troubled that night. She dreamt that she opened a cupboard and found a German in there, wherever she went in the house a soldier lurked and the familiar faces of her family became distorted to represent the blonde German officer with the cold, blue eyes. She woke at sunrise, feeling weary and resentful of the cause of her disturbed night. She must see Michael and ask him to move away from Plaka before any harm came to the village or its inhabitants.

Michael shook his head at her request. 'Not at the moment. We were so close last night and still we lost him.'

'What do you mean?'

'Whilst Yannis led them off to the caves we organised an ambush. We were going to catch him on the track between Olous and Aghios Nikolaos, but then he doubled back, hoping to catch us.'

'You mean you asked Yannis to take them to the caves!'

'Not at all. It just seemed an opportunity not to be missed. Think about it, Anna.' Michael took her hand in his. 'We could have had a pitched battle in the centre of the village, or we could have ambushed them on their way to the caves. Either way the villagers would have suffered terrible reprisals and we none of us want to endanger your lives. They're still looking for us, so we can have another try later on.'

'You mean they'll come back here again?' Anna turned frightened eyes towards her companion.

'Probably. They'll try to catch you unawares. They're not as easily fooled as the Italians.'

'Suppose they find you?'

Michael shrugged. 'We'll fight.'

'They have rifles.'

'So do we, and we have something they certainly haven't.'

'What's that?'

'The loyalty of the Cretan people.'

Anna sighed deeply. 'If it weren't for Mamma and the children I wouldn't mind.'

'I don't think you need to worry about that lad of yours. He's all about. I'd better go. There's a boat coming round the headland, probably another search party.' As Michael spoke he gave Anna's hand a last squeeze and slipped behind the low wall. Anna sat alone.

The Germans continued to arrive at the village unexpectedly, wearing the nerves of the occupants and the Italians to shreds with their continual harrying. Each time Anna or Yannis went up to the fields they were accompanied and the movement of all the villagers was under continual observation, until even the German Commander had to admit he had found no evidence for his suspicions. Still unconvinced, he led his troops from the village and towards the town of Aghios Nikolaos, vowing that he would be back.

Cautious and uncertain, Anna sat down on the wall, which had been her last meeting place with Michael, but no one came. Maybe with so much troop activity in the area he had moved away. She felt sad that she would not see his merry blue eyes or feel the pressure of his hand in hers when he reassured and comforted her. She shook herself impatiently; it was no use feeling sentimental about a foreigner who she might never see again.

The mournful tolling of the bell drew her attention to the island and she strained her eyes, hoping to catch a glimpse of someone moving over there. She crossed herself and began to walk back down the hill. She would visit the church, light a candle and say a fervent prayer for her brother before going down to the beach to wave to him.'

'Anna.' Michael's voice came from the sheep pen.

'Michael!'

'I need your help, Anna. I've some injured men.'

'Where are they?'

'I'll take you to them. Walk to the far side of the gorse. I'll meet you.'

Without a second thought Anna obeyed his instructions, wondering what kind of injuries she would find and if she would be capable of dealing with them. She ought really to go back and collect some herbs, but there was no sign of Michael, and she had an idea that her request would be refused. As she hesitated she could see Michael sitting in the shade of the tangle of gorse.

'Come and sit beside me,' he ordered. 'I'm trusting you, Anna, with my men's lives. I don't want to find a German reception committee the next time we come out.'

Anna did not answer. The enormity of her actions began to dawn on her and she began to shiver apprehensively. Michael stripped off his jacket and placed it across her shoulders.

'Put that on. You don't want to tell everyone you've been pushing your way through a gorse bush.'

Obediently she slipped her arms into the long sleeves and began to follow Michael deeper into the prickly bush. After only a few yards a dark hole appeared.

'I'll go first. It widens out after a few feet.'

Trustingly Anna crawled into the narrow opening after Michael, her hands occasionally touching his boots. The dark, confined space was making Anna feel claustrophobic and panic was welling up inside her. She was about to say she could go no further when she realised she no longer had the earth touching her head and sides. Suddenly Michael was beside her.

'You can stand up now. Hold onto my belt and I'll lead the way.'

Taking a firm grip Anna stumbled along after her guide in the intense darkness.

'I'll make some light.' Anna felt Michael bend forward and strike a match to light a rag and kerosene torch.

'This is the difficult bit. Can you climb a ladder?' He held the torch aloft and Anna could see a makeshift ladder propped against the cave wall leading to a dark opening above.

Anna nodded.

'Come on then, but take it carefully.'

Michael held the ladder firmly.

'Up you go. I'll follow when you've reached the top. You're quite safe.'

Doubting very much that she was, Anna gingerly began the climb until her hands could no longer feel a rung above her. She felt around the smooth rock until her fingers met with a projection and trusting that it was rock and not crumbling earth she pulled herself up onto her knees and then stood upright. As soon as she did so she was in utter darkness again, as Michael extinguished the kerosene torch. No more than a few seconds elapsed before Michael joined her. He took her hand and began to lead the way along the twisting passage. Anna shivered, despite the fact that she was still wearing Michael's jacket.

'Not far now,' he reassured her.

'Where are we?'

'In the hill just up from your farm.'

'I never knew there was a cave here.'

'I just hope it doesn't get too damp in here when the rains start. We don't want to be washed out. This way.'

He led her across the cave and into another passage. A kerosene torch was burning and she could see mattresses and bedding at the side, some of them occupied by sleeping forms. Michael took a battery torch from a niche in the rock and handed it to her.

'You'll see better with this. Here are your patients. They're all Greeks, so you'll have no problem.'

Anna nodded and sank to her knees beside the first man, noting the bandage, stained with blood, across his shoulder.

'What happened?'

'Bullet in the shoulder. Only a flesh wound.'

Anna felt the man's forehead and took his pulse. 'Who bandaged you?'

'My mate. Used his shirt.'

'Does it hurt?'

'Bit stiff.'

Anna nodded. 'I'll not touch it yet. Let me see the others.'

Michael led her to the two other mattresses where she examined her patients. One was no worse than a sprained ankle, but the other had a bullet lodged in his thigh. She drew Michael to one side.

'The ankle's nothing. I can bring some healing herbs for the flesh wound, but I can't touch that bullet. You need a doctor.'

'I thought as much.'

'Can one of your men get into Aghios Nikolaos? I'm sure Doctor Stavros would be willing to come out.'

'Are you sure? We don't want to run ourselves into a trap.'

'Who will you send? I'll tell him what to say.'

Michael paused and thought. 'Lambros would be the best man; he knows the area. Come and meet him.' Michael took the torch from her and switched it off. 'We have to be careful to save the batteries.'

Anna blinked as she was once more in the flickering light of the kerosene torches and followed Michael over to the corner of the cave where a middle-aged man sat cleaning a rifle with a scrap of rag. Anna sat beside him whilst Michael informed him of his errand.

'You have to find Doctor Stavros. Tell him Yannis's sister needs him again. The old lady is sick.' Anna made the man repeat the sentence three times before she was satisfied that he would remember the exact words. 'I can't be sure he'll know the way from the village. I took him to Babbis's house at night.'

'Lambros will wait for him and bring him back. We don't really want him wandering through the village and asking his way.'

Lambros looked at Anna sourly. 'I don't agree with women being here. This is man's work.'

Anna smiled, hoping to have a mellowing effect. 'I agree with you. Once you've brought the doctor you'll have no need of me.'

Lambros rose, pushed the pieces of his rifle beneath the mattress, tied a scarf round his head and stuck a revolver into his belt. 'I'll be back.'

Anna looked at Michael in concern. 'How are you going to get the doctor in here? Or are you going to take the man out? I can't see the doctor being willing to crawl through that tunnel.'

'There are other ways. That's just the nearest entrance to your farm. It's quite well hidden, and if the Germans did find the way through we'd pull up the ladder. If they came in through another entrance we'd simply go out that way.'

'I've lived here all my life and never known about it.' Anna shook her head in disbelief.

Doctor Stavros was finally run to earth at a waterfront taverna where he sat morosely drinking raki. Lambros had enquired after the man discreetly of various shopkeepers and had been directed to his house, only to find no one responded to his knocking. Soldiers were everywhere in the town and Lambros had been forced to dive down side streets, hiding in shops and doorways to escape their attention. Now he stood before him and spoke quietly.

'Doctor Stavros?'

The doctor nodded.

'I need to speak to you. Tell me to stop begging and go away. I'll be at your house.'

The doctor frowned. 'Why can't you speak to me here?'

Lambros looked around nervously. 'Soldiers. I'll wait at your house.'

Doctor Stavros raised his voice. 'Stop begging you dirty old man. Go away and leave me alone.'

Lambros slunk away; looking dejected, and returned to the house of the doctor by a circuitous route. He hid behind the wall which ran down the side of the road and waited, not knowing how long it would be before the doctor returned. Finally he heard a voice call out 'good evening, doctor' and the greeting was returned. He emerged from his hiding place a few moments later and pushed at the doctor's door, which opened beneath his touch. He stood inside uncertainly.

'Well, come in, man, if you're coming,' the doctor spoke irritably.

Lambros walked into the room from where the voice had emanated. 'I'm sorry to trouble you, but I've been asked to bring you a message and take you back with me.'

Doctor Stavros raised his eyebrows. 'What makes you think I would go anywhere with you?'

'Yannis's sister says she needs you again. The old lady is sick.'

'What?'

'The girl said you would understand. Those were her exact words.'

'What girl?'

'I don't know her name. She came to have a look at some injured men and she said a doctor was needed to take a bullet out. She told me to come to you and give you that message.'

Doctor Stavros frowned. 'Are these men at the farmhouse?'

Lambros shook his head. 'I can take you to them.'

'How do we get there?'

'Over the hills. We'll start as soon as it's dark.'

Doctor Stavros frowned. 'And how long is that going to take us?'

Lambros shrugged. 'It took me about three hours to get here. It will take a bit longer in the dark.'

Doctor Stavros consulted his pocket watch. 'We've time for some food before we go, then. You'll join me, I presume.'

Lambros nodded. He would appreciate a decent meal that was freshly cooked.

The doctor and his guide left the house as the sun began to set. Doctor Stavros led the way into a dark, narrow alley, walked swiftly to the end, turned left and entered a courtyard.

'What...?'

Doctor Stavros held his finger to his lips and hushed Lambros. He listened intently for a few moments, then placed his lips close to the man's ear. 'I know this house. If anyone was following us we could go inside and no questions asked. Follow me when we leave and we'll end up on the outskirts of the town.'

Walking quietly and keeping in the shadow of the walls they skirted the Italian sentries who were smoking and talking together, bored by the monotonous duty. A jeep arriving made the doctor and Lambros shrink back into the shadows, but it was waved through unquestioningly, ribald remarks shouted to the soldiers as it passed.

They walked along the rough road leading to the town of Neapolis until the houses of Aghios Nikolaos were out of sight. Lambros slipped down into the ditch and signalled for the doctor to do the same. Cautiously Lambros surveyed the area. It was deserted; no one had followed them. He touched the doctor's arm and indicated they were going to begin taking a detour into the hills. Doctor Stavros nodded and followed his guide up a path that was steep and littered with loose stones, making them slip continually. Lambros climbed easily, carrying the doctor's medical case whilst the doctor panted behind him. Once over the summit Lambros turned and grinned at the perspiring man.

'That was the easy bit. There's no path now.'

Forcing their way through low growing prickly shrubs, which caught and tore at their trousers, they made slow progress as they walked across the hillside to give a wide berth to Olous and the salt mines.

'It must have taken you more than three hours to get to Aghios Nikolaos,' complained the doctor.

Lambros shrugged. 'Maybe,' he agreed. 'Maybe four.'

Doctor Stavros tried to calculate the time in his head. He was sure they had been walking for more than three hours and they seemed hardly nearer now than when they had stood on the summit of the first hill. He shook his head. At this rate he would never manage to be back before dawn and how would he explain his absence from Aghios Nikolaos if anyone asked for him?

'Isn't there a quicker way?'

Lambros turned sad eyes towards him. 'We go this way.'

Over the brow of another hill the going became easier until they reached a rocky outcrop, which forced the doctor to his hands and knees as he tried to scramble over it. Lambros stopped.

'Wait here. I'll be back.'

Thankfully Doctor Stavros sank to the ground, his breath coming in painful gasps. As he breathed more easily he wondered where his guide had gone and the awful fear came to him that he had been deserted. He rose to his feet and strained his eyes in the darkness, longing to call out, but not daring to do so. He took a few stumbling steps forward and looked again, then some more steps.

'I told you to wait.'

'I thought you'd left me.'

'I said I'd come back. Come on.'

Obediently the doctor followed again, the darkness seeming to swallow him up.

'Stand still.' A scraping and scrabbling sound followed the command, then he was pushed forward a few paces and a flickering light came nearer.

'Follow me.' Lambros walked forward confidently, the doctor following him uncertainly until the light increased and he was able to see his way. Unerringly Lambros twisted and turned through the passages until they reached the cave where Michael sat with the injured man. He rose and extended his hand to the doctor.

'I appreciate you coming. Anna told us you were the man we needed. She's had a look at Makkis, but wouldn't touch him.'

'What's wrong with the others?'

'Sprained ankle and a flesh wound. It's just the bullet she won't touch.'

Doctor Stavros nodded and looked down at his grimy hands. 'I ought to wash before I do anything.'

'Fine. Follow me.'

The doctor found himself in a cleft at the back of the cave where water dribbled continually down the wall.

'That's the best we can do.'

Doctor Stavros pursed his lips. This was not what he had in mind. Michael held a rag to the wall until it was soaked and then squeezed the water into a container. When it was half full he passed it to the doctor. Doctor Stavros dipped his hands cautiously into the icy water and accepted a grubby cloth to wipe them. He returned to where the man sat propped against the wall of the cave.

'I suggest you lay down on your good side. I'll probably have to probe a bit which I warn you will hurt. Can you administer chloroform?' he asked of Michael.

Makkis eyed them both warily. 'How long is it going to take?'

'Only a few minutes,' Doctor Stavros assured him.

'I'll do without the stuff then.'

Doctor Stavros frowned. 'I'd rather you used it. I don't want you moving at the wrong moment. It could send the bullet in deeper.'

'I'll not move.'

The doctor looked at Michael for assistance.

'How about if I sat beside you with it ready just in case? If you want it you'll only have to take the pad from me.'

'Sit if you want. I'll not need it.'

Doctor Stavros removed his jacket and rolled up his sleeves. From the case he had carried with him he took a bottle and a pad, which he handed to Michael. He placed tweezers, scalpel, needle and thread on his handkerchief on the ground beside him in clear view of his patient. Removing the makeshift bandage he examined the injured thigh and tutted under his breath.

'I'd be happier if you used that chloroform. It's pretty deep and it's done a bit of damage on the way in.'

'I'm all right.'

'Very well. Don't say I didn't warn you.'

Doctor Stavros picked up the scalpel and made a slit in the man's skin, using the soiled bandage to wipe away the blood as it gushed to the surface. He felt the man tense beneath him. Beads of sweat were breaking out on Makkis's forehead and he made a sudden grab for the pad of chloroform, breathing it in greedily. With a nod of satisfaction the doctor cut again and pulled back the flap of skin to expose the muscle where the bullet was lodged. Taking up the tweezers he managed to get a purchase and pulled sharply.

'Here it is.' He dropped the foreign body on to his handkerchief and re-examined the hole, which was already beginning to close together. 'Looks clean enough. I'll put in a couple of stitches and bandage him. Give him a drop more chloroform to keep him quiet whilst I finish.'

Michael held the pad beneath Makkis's nose again. The sickly smell was making him want to retch and he had an idea that was the reason behind Makkis's original refusal.

'That's done.' From his pocket Doctor Stavros withdrew a bandage, poured iodine over the wound and bandaged the leg firmly. 'Shouldn't give any trouble. He'll be walking on it again within a week. Not too far, mind. Don't want him overdoing things for a while.'

Michael replaced the cap on the bottle of chloroform and handed it back to the doctor. 'You wouldn't consider leaving that with us, I suppose?'

'What for?'

'There's always the chance of a bad injury. It could help someone get through the worst whilst they waited for you.'

Doctor Stavros handed it back. 'I should have thought and brought more with me.' He added six rolls of bandage from his bag and a bottle of aspirin. 'Keep them safe. Now, where are my other patients?'

He unwrapped Dimitris's shoulder and declared himself satisfied that the injury was no worse than he had been led to believe, and insisted that Lucas walked on his ankle.

'Resting it will only make it swell more. Wrap a wet cloth round it, keep moving and it will right itself. Is Anna coming up tomorrow?'

'I expect so.'

'Good. She can change the soiled bandages when necessary. You won't need me any more.'

Michael held out his hand. 'We're indebted to you. I hope you won't mind if we call on you again if necessary.'

'I'm the only doctor for a good many miles around, but I'd rather you didn't make a habit of it.' Doctor Stavros polished his glasses and yawned.

'Would you like to rest before you return?' asked Michael solicitously.

Doctor Stavros looked round the comfortless cave. 'I'd rather get back. I'm hoping no one called for me in an emergency and found I was missing. I might have some explaining to do.'

Lambros led the way back to the hillside, making the doctor wait whilst he placed some dead vegetation and kicked some stones around to disguise the entrance to the hiding place. They climbed steadily to the summit of the hill where Lambros stood and listened. The sound of gunfire could be heard in the distance.

Lambros grinned. 'That should keep everyone occupied for a while. We should be able to take a short cut.'

Doctor Stavros breathed a sigh of relief and plunged on after his guide down to where a reasonable shepherd's path ran round the side of the hill, saving them the stiff and rugged climb up one side and down the other. They skirted Olous, but not so widely this time, and dropped down onto the road between Aghios Nikolaos and Neapolis only a short way from the outskirts of the town. The doctor bade his guide farewell and Lambros melted back into the dark hillside, leaving the weary doctor to walk the remainder of the way alone.

Anna was woken before dawn by the sound of tramping feet and the soldiers entering the house. This time the Commander was not with them, but the soldiers were clearly ill at ease and nervous. Mario and Victor were escorted outside and stood with a German pointing a revolver at them.

'We search.'

Anna was held at gunpoint beside her mother, whilst Yannis and Marisa were brought to stand beside her.

'What do they want this time, Mamma Anna?'

'I don't know. Just do as they say and we'll be safe.'

'Where are Victor and Mario?'

'The soldiers took them out.'

Marisa bit her lip. 'I'd feel safer with them here.'

A soldier waved his gun at the two women and Anna hushed her niece.

For three hours they were made to stand in the cold room, the silent soldiers watching their every move, escorting them out to the yard when they insisted they could wait no longer to relieve themselves, and not even having the decency to turn their backs whilst they did so. Anna felt humiliated and annoyed at their treatment.

Finally the door was thrown open and after an exchange of words the soldiers filed out, the last one letting his gaze linger over Marisa speculatively.

Anna collapsed into a chair at the table and placed her head in her arms, Marisa began to cry and Yannis slammed the door violently behind them.

'Who do they think they are to treat us like that?' he asked furiously.

Anna raised her head, her eyes dark rimmed and her face strained. 'Mamma, are you all right?'

Maria smiled. 'Of course I am. I could do with a change of sheets, and a cup of coffee wouldn't come amiss. They've gone now, Anna. There's nothing to fear.'

Victor and Mario returned to the house, hurrying upstairs to don their uniforms before returning to the living room. Anna rounded on them angrily.

'What was that all about?' she asked. 'We were held at gunpoint for hours and the house was searched again.'

'Please?'

'Oh, Marisa, explain to him and find out what's been going on.' Anna felt too weary to cope with Victor's limited Greek.

Patiently Marisa spoke to him. 'Soldiers.' She mimed being asleep, then having a rifle pointed at her. 'Long time. Soldiers look.' Again she mimed them looking in cupboards and chests.

'Si, Si.' Victor looked worried. 'Resistance. Bang, bang to Commander. Soldiers bang, bang. Resistance,' he clapped his hands to parts of his body as though wounded. 'Bang, bang in night. Where? Where go? Soldiers look.'

'Did you understand that, Mamma Anna?'

Anna nodded. 'Well, they're certainly not here.'

Victor turned his dark eyes on her. 'Not here,' he agreed. 'Where go?'

Anna felt uncomfortable beneath his penetrating gaze. She shrugged and turned away. 'I'm going to feed the chickens. Marisa you can change your grandmother's bed. Thanks to those soldiers there are extra sheets today.'

Anna longed to go up to the hills to find out if the doctor had visited the caves, but she dared not leave the farm. From the yard she could see soldiers moving around on the hills as well as on the waterfront and she hoped that Michael and his men would not be found.

Victor waited until Anna had left the room. 'Marisa, I sorry. Soldiers bad. Marisa stay here. Be careful.'

Marisa looked at Victor. 'Where were you and Mario?'

'With soldiers. Stand by sea. Soldier with gun.' He swung an imaginary rifle from side to side.

'You were under arrest? Prisoner?' Marisa gasped in horror. 'Why?'

'German soldiers not trust Italians. Maybe help resistance.'

Marisa could not help smiling at the thought.

Gradually the village returned to its somnambulant state and when there had been no sign of the German soldiers for two days Anna judged it safe to venture up the hill to the gorse patch. She sat on a low wall and waited for Michael to appear. The time passed slowly and finally she dared stay no longer, disappointed she retraced her steps down to the farm. Throughout the day she would look towards the hill, until by the afternoon she could contain herself no longer.

'I'm going up for some herbs, Mamma. Those stupid soldiers have trampled mine into the ground.'

Maria eyed her daughter. 'Be careful, Anna. They are not always as stupid as they would like us to believe.'

Anna tilted her chin defiantly. 'There's nothing wrong with collecting herbs.'

'Nothing at all. I hope it doesn't take you too long to find them.'

Anna drew in her breath. 'What do you mean? To find them.'

'The herbs, of course. What did you think I meant?'

Once again Anna returned to the gorse patch. To her horror the bushes were broken down, the dark hole that led to the cave exposed for all to see. Anna gazed at it. Had the resistance men been found? Surely they would have heard shooting, or if they had been captured the Germans would have marched them through the village. Anna tried to recall all Michael had said about the cave having another entrance. She certainly did not feel brave enough to crawl through the hole and find her way in total darkness to the ladder and climb it without him as her guide.

For some time she stood there, her thoughts in turmoil. She finally decided she would walk over the hill and into the valley where Babbis's house stood with a melancholy and neglected air and see if there were signs that the Germans had been there. Despite Yannis's attempts to keep the weeds down the kitchen garden was completely over-run, the vegetables having seeded themselves, adding to the mayhem. She crept inside, fearful that a German soldier would jump out at her, but relieved to find it empty, although there were signs that people had been there by the footsteps on the dusty floors and cupboard doors left open. From the upstairs windows she scanned the hillside, but the only movement was from the sheep and goats as they wandered from one patch of pasture to the other.

Anxiety was gnawing inside her for Michael and his men. She thought of his deep blue eyes and felt a lump come into her throat. He had sounded so confident that they would not be found. She remembered there was an outcrop of rock a short distance away where her father had collected stones to make some of the walls on the farm. It was quite possible that the weather had exposed a cave and the resistance had found it.

She moved back and forth over the rough, uneven ground, finding nothing. Finally in despair she sat on a rock and plucked listlessly at the grass. She could not wander for hours over the hills in the hope of finding their hiding place.

An arm went around her throat and she was thrown roughly to the ground, nearly knocking her senseless. As she opened her eyes she met the lascivious look of a soldier and the muzzle of a revolver. Her fingers curled around the blades of grass beneath her as she made to move. The harsh voice that grated on her ears she ignored, but the rough hand that pushed her back down she shrank from. She understood not a word he was saying to her, yet she was frightened, the sweat trickling down her back. His fingers bit into the flesh of her shoulder, whilst he replaced his gun in the holster and began to unbuckle his belt. The full horror of her situation dawned on her, yet she seemed powerless to move or scream. He relinquished the grip on her shoulder and ripped her blouse open to the waist. Frantically she tried to cover herself.

'No, please, no,' she managed to whisper.

Ignoring her plea he began to unbutton his trousers. Anna shut her eyes. She must be dreaming and soon would awaken from this nightmare. As he bent towards her he appeared to lose his balance and toppled onto the ground beside her, falling across her legs. Then she screamed, only to have a hand clamped across her mouth.

'Quiet. It's over now. You're quite safe.' Slowly the hand was withdrawn and she took a deep shuddering breath.

'He was, he was...' The words would not come out and Anna began to shiver uncontrollably.

Unceremoniously she was pulled to her feet. 'Come on, move. You can't stay here.' She was pulled roughly across the uneven ground.

'Where are you taking me?' Anna began to struggle to free herself from the firm grip.

'To Michael.' He pushed and dragged her over the rough ground and finally into a cleft in the rock. 'Stand still until your eyes are accustomed to the darkness.'

Still shivering uncontrollably Anna could make out a dim passage.

'Follow me.'

Stumbling, Anna followed the man until the passage widened into a cave and he released her arm.

'Wait here.'

Gratefully Anna sank to the ground, her teeth chattering and deep sobs racking her body. Strong, comforting arms were placed around her and she allowed herself the luxury of laying her head on Michael's chest and sobbing. He stroked her hair gently and waited until she was calm before questioning her.

'I was looking for you. I didn't dare come up before. There were Germans everywhere. They made us stand in the living room for hours whilst they searched the house again. They're sure the villagers are hiding injured men. I wanted to find out if the doctor came and how the men were. I saw what had happened to the gorse and the cave entrance was visible. I wanted to find out if you were safe.' Anna began to sob again.

Michael's face was grim. 'They're watching from the hills. Where do you think the soldier that molested you came from? He'd probably been watching your every move.'

Anna's hand flew to her mouth. 'Have I put you in danger? Will they find the cave?'

'I doubt it. Panicos was watching. That German was more interested in you than he was in finding us.'

'But when he's found outside? What will they do?'

'He won't be found for quite a while,' Michael assured her. 'He's already being moved to a far less conspicuous place. They'll know we were responsible and add it to our list of crimes, but if they can't find us they can't do very much about it.'

Anna became aware of Michael's arms still round her and stirred. 'I ought to get back. Mamma will be worried.'

'Can you come and have a look at the men before you leave? Just to reassure them.'

Anna bit her lip. Now over the worst of her fright she only desired to get back to the comparative safety of the farmhouse. 'I can't. My blouse.' The colour rushed to her cheeks, remembering it was ripped to her waist revealing her breasts.

'I'll find you a shirt. Stay here. I won't be a minute.'

Michael returned swiftly and held it for Anna to slip her arms into the sleeves.

'It's far too big.'

'I'm a big man.' He smiled and Anna managed to smile back at him. 'Feeling better now?'

Anna nodded. 'Thank you for looking after me.'

'I wouldn't want any harm to come to you, Anna. Promise me you'll not wander off anywhere again. If I don't come to the gorse or seek you out there will be a good reason and you must just be patient.'

'I promise.'

Michael tilted her chin upwards and kissed her gently on her mouth. 'When you're ready I'll take you safely to your door. Now, as you can see, Manolis is doing well, hardly a limp. The doctor said Makkis would be on his feet within a week. He left us some bandages and I'd appreciate it if you'd have a look and redress his wound.'

'Of course.' Anna knelt and inspected the injured thigh. 'It looks fine. Nice, healthy skin all around. I'll put a clean bandage on, but there should be no problem there. I'll have a look at that shoulder whilst I'm here.'

'Whilst you're dealing with that I'll get ready.' Michael slipped away, leaving Anna to change the bandages and assure the patients that their wounds were healing.

A handsome German officer escorted Anna back to the farmhouse, saluting her in farewell at the door. 'Do not wander so far in the hills again. My men will not be so lenient in future.'

Anna had a desire to giggle as she said 'Yes, sir,' and slipped inside the door, hoping to reach her room and change from the shirt into a blouse before she was noticed. It was later than she had realised and Marisa stared at her curiously over the vegetables she was preparing.

'Why were you with a German?'

'I went up to your father's house. I wanted to see if it had been damaged by a search. The Germans are in the hills and they thought I was spying, although what there is to spy on up there I don't know.'

'In Pappa's shirt?'

'I was chilly. I put it on over my blouse.'

Marisa looked pointedly out of the window at the autumn sunshine and back at her aunt before picking up a potato and peeling it swiftly. Anna, knowing how guilty she looked, offered no further explanation. Now she would have to face her mother.

'You were gone a long while. I was getting quite worried,' remonstrated Maria gently. 'Did you find what you were looking for?'

Anna felt her face redden. 'I went a bit further than I'd intended. I won't be a moment.'

Thankfully she escaped up the stairs where she stripped off the shirt and torn blouse, hastily donning another in its place. She pushed the blouse beneath the mattress. That could be thrown away tomorrow and she could return the shirt when she went up to the hills. On impulse she hugged it to her. It was Michael's shirt.

Anna waited with trepidation for another visit from the Germans when the body of the soldier was found, but none came. It appeared they had finally decided that Plaka was innocent of sheltering resistance workers and were concentrating their efforts elsewhere. Michael met her regularly at the gorse bushes, to receive the loaves of bread she took up each day and often asking her to visit the caves to tend to injured men. They would linger together, hidden by the gorse bushes or sit behind a wall, holding hands and talking softly, until Michael would kiss her goodbye and Anna would hurry back to the farm, her cheeks glowing and her heart beating fast at the memory of his touch.

The winter passed, cold and wet, with little to celebrate at Christmas. There had been no news of Yannis senior since he had been led off to work in the mines, and the only news that came regarding Yiorgo and Babbis was from other resistance workers who said they had seen them in various places. No presents exchanged hands, as Anna insisted there could be no celebration until the war was over. Shyly Victor had presented Anna with four small bars of chocolate and indicated that there was one for each of them.

Christmas morning saw the whole of the village in church, accompanied by the Italian soldiers, who were as fervent in their prayers for an end to the war as the Cretans. The service over, they filed out solemnly to return to their homes and treat the remainder of the day like any other. Anna hurried away, wondering what excuse she could make to visit the hills that afternoon, whilst Marisa lingered in the church to say a private prayer and light a candle.

Victor and Mario decided to join the other soldiers in the taverna for the afternoon and Anna announced her intention of going for a walk. Yannis and Marisa looked up at her from their game of backgammon, in surprise, as the day, although dry, had a cold wind blowing.

'I won't be very long. Just up the hill and back. I need some fresh air. I'm not used to being indoors all day long.'

Yannis nodded understandingly. Although it was Christmas Day and Anna had insisted that the only work should be with the animals, he felt ill at ease sitting around the house.

Anna hurried up the hill, the wind buffeting her, numbing her fingers and toes. The mournful tolling of the bell from the church on the island reached her ears and she hoped fervently that it was calling the islanders to prayer and not announcing a funeral. The bell, at one time a comforting sound on a Sunday and occasionally during the week, now went so frequently that it sent shivers down her spine.

She turned into the shelter of a wall and waited, hoping Michael would have been told by a lookout that she was on her way. She passed a fruitless quarter of an hour and decided she dared not linger any longer. There could be many reasons why Michael had not come to meet her, but after her unnerving experience with the German soldier she had never dared to venture close to the gorse bushes to look for him. Shivering with the cold she made her way back to the farmhouse and the comfort of the fire.

It was three days before Michael met Anna again and when he did appear his sallow skin and dull eyes worried her.

'What's wrong?' she asked immediately.

'I haven't been feeling too well,' he explained. 'The lack of sunshine, I think. When you're living in a cave you begin to depend upon a few hours out in the sun.'

'Are you sure you're not ill?'

Michael shook his head. He did not wish to tell her he had been vomiting intermittently since Christmas and was beginning to feel weak, with a pain niggling away inside where he had obviously strained himself.

'I'll make you up a tonic,' promised Anna. 'It won't make up for the sunshine, but it should help.'

Michael carried her hand to his lips. 'I don't know what we'd do without you, Anna.' He leaned back against the wall, hoping the giddiness that had come upon him would pass. 'I must get back,' he excused himself. 'I'm expecting some new arrivals at any time.' He turned Anna towards him and kissed her gently. 'You go back down. I'll see you tomorrow.'

Despite being disappointed that their meeting had been so brief, Anna did not argue. 'I won't forget the tonic,' she promised, as she left him.

Michael watched her for a few moments, shivering violently. He hoped he would have enough strength to crawl back down the tunnel and climb the ladder.

Anna made up a quantity of the tonic she thought would help Michael. If he was feeling the effects of living in a sunless cave no doubt the other men were also and they could all benefit from the herbal medicine. She corked the bottle tightly, wrapped it separately from the loaves just in case it should leak, and walked happily up the hill.

She was surprised when an anxious Manolis met her. 'Michael is ill,' he stated the fact simply.

Anna felt her mouth go dry with an unnamed fear. 'What's wrong with him?'

'Stomach pains, sickness, fever.'

'Maybe he's eaten something bad.'

'Maybe. You come and see him.'

Anna bent over Michael and felt his hot forehead. 'How long have you felt like this?'

'About a week. I can't keep any food down.'

'I'm going to feel your stomach,' she warned him as she loosened the belt on his trousers and began to undo the buttons.

Michael smiled feebly. 'If I were feeling better I would say something very ungentlemanly.'

Anna felt herself blushing and hoped he had not noticed. 'Tell me when it hurts. Just there?' she asked as Michael winced and she could feel the hard swelling beneath her hand. She sat back on her heels. 'That's your appendix.'

'It can't be. Not now,' he groaned.

'I'm sure it is. You need to see a doctor and have it taken out.'

'Could Doctor Stavros come?'

Anna shook her head. 'He can take out bullets and stitch people up, but he couldn't possibly do that kind of an operation here. You need to be in a hospital.'

'Anna, I'm an Englishman, a resistance worker. I can't just go into a hospital, have an operation and walk out.'

'You can't be left to die, either.'

Michael struggled to sit up, groaning with the effort. 'Can't you give me some medicine to take the inflammation down?'

'It wouldn't help. You need to have your appendix out before it bursts.'

Michael closed his eyes. 'What can I do?' he asked himself. 'What can I do?'

Anna bit her lip. 'You have to go to a hospital.'

'And how do I get there? I can't walk.'

'I'll take you in the cart. I'll think of something.'

'You can't do that. There are guards along the road. You'd be stopped and they'd find me. What would happen to you?'

'I'm going to pretend you're my husband.' The idea had just come to Anna. 'Your men will have to carry you down to the road and I'll meet you there tonight after dark. Ask some of your men to create a diversion to draw the Italians away from the area.'

'Anna, this is madness. There only has to be one slip.'

'Leave it to me. If we're stopped, don't say a word and keep your eyes closed.' Anna bent and kissed his cheek. 'Trust me, Michael.'

Anna had spoken to Michael with more confidence than she felt. She had to think of a good excuse to leave the farm for twenty-four hours and she was not happy at leaving her mother and the children alone with the Italian soldiers over night. She stopped in the field where Yannis was working. This time she needed his help despite her previous unwillingness for him to be involved with the resistance.

'I have to go to Aghios Nikolaos tonight. There's a sick resistance worker. He needs to go to the hospital and he can't walk in over the hills.'

Yannis sucked in his breath. 'You're taking an awful chance, Mamma Anna.'

Anna's mouth set in a stubborn line. 'I need you to help me. Come down to the farm this afternoon and tell me the donkey's hoofs need paring. The only place I can get that done is Aghios Nikolaos. I'll insist that I leave this evening.'

'Wouldn't it be better if I went?' asked Yannis.

'No. I have to do this myself.'

'How are you going to get through the checkpoints? If the soldiers see anyone in the cart they'll know he's a resistance man and arrest him.'

'They'll create a diversion and if I'm stopped I shall pretend he's your father. Don't ask me any more questions, Yannis. The less you know the better. All I want you to do is bring me the message about the donkey and make sure Victor or Mario is there when you tell me.'

Only Mario returned to the house for their mid-day meal and Anna waited anxiously for Yannis to appear. When he did so he looked worried and began to speak to his aunt in rapid Greek.

'I have to take the donkey into Aghios Nikolaos. Her hoofs are bad. I should have checked her ages ago, but grandpa always saw to them and I just didn't think. They're badly overgrown and must be painful for her.'

Anna frowned. 'Will she be able to walk that far?'

'She'll have to be taken slowly. I'd planned to finish digging that far field so that it's ready for planting, but it will have to wait.'

'I'll take her,' Anna offered immediately.

Yannis shook his head. 'Even if you started now you wouldn't be there until the evening. Then you've got to find a farmer who can do it. It's better that I go.'

Anna shook her head. 'I'll take the cart. I can sleep in it over night and find a farmer first thing the next morning.'

'Maybe Mario could give you a pass?' suggested Yannis.

Anna looked cautiously at the soldier. She wished Victor were there.

'Mario, please may I have a pass to Aghios Nikolaos?'

Mario frowned. 'Pass?'

'To go to Aghios Nikolaos. With the donkey.'

'Pass? Aghios Nikolaos?' Mario shook his head. 'Victor give pass.'

'Surely you could give me one? Victor would understand.'

'No pass. No paper.'

'Where is Victor?' asked Anna.

'Aghios Nikolaos.'

Anna shrugged. 'I'll wait for an hour or so to see if he returns. I'll speak to Aspasia and see if she'll be willing to come up and stay the night with you.'

'I'm here, Mamma Anna. I can look after grandma,' protested Marisa.

'I'll be happier to know that Aspasia is around.' Anna glared at them both. 'It often takes two people to help your grandmother.'

Yannis kicked his sister's ankle under the table. 'Whilst you speak to Aspasia I'll get the cart ready. I'll put some straw in the bottom and a couple of blankets. If you plan to spend the night in the cart it will be pretty cold.'

Trying to look more confident than she felt, Anna led the donkey slowly along the rutted cart track and away from the village. She had delayed her departure as long as she could, insisting that she left a meal prepared for Aspasia and fussing over her mother. Once out of sight of the farmhouse she strolled gently. She did not want to be too far from Plaka when night fell, nor could she hang around the village without questions being asked.

Finding a sheltered spot on the road where she could draw the donkey and cart almost out of sight Anna sat huddled in a rug and waited. The time dragged as she watched the watery sun coursing gently across the sky, and she prayed fervently that no Italian patrol would come that way and see her. They would certainly want to know why she was waiting and when they could find her doing no wrong they would send her back to the village. The donkey raised her head and stepped backwards, looking back reproachfully at Anna as she bumped into the shafts. Night fell suddenly and with it came scudding clouds, which covered the moon leaving her in total darkness.

The donkey moved her feet again restlessly. 'What's wrong?' Anna looked into the darkness warily. The touch on her arm made her catch her breath and she wheeled around in alarm.

'We're here,' a low voice informed her.

'Put him in the cart and I'll be off.' Anna found it difficult to speak where her throat had become parched with fear. She threw off the blanket and scrambled to the ground.

The men manhandled Michael as gently as possible onto the straw and Anna covered him with the blankets. He was sweating profusely and groaning intermittently. Lambros looked into Anna's frightened eyes.

'You're not bad – for a woman.'

'I'll do my best,' Anna promised.

Lambros nodded. 'We'll be keeping an eye on you. Be careful.'

Anna nodded and took the donkey's head, trying in the darkness to avoid the worst of the ruts and bumps. In Elounda she stopped to allow the donkey to drink, then continued slowly up the hill, hoping no one from the village would stop her and question her errand. She hoped that Michael would not talk in English if he became delirious, or shout and draw attention to them.

From Elounda she dropped down towards Olous, which she knew would be heavily guarded because of the salt mines and the forced labour employed there, hoping they would believe her story. She was almost in the village when she heard the sound of gunfire. Soldiers seemed to appear from everywhere and rushed past her, making for the hills.

Anna continued slowly on her way, feeling more confident now. The resistance had caused the promised diversion and were drawing the guards away from the road. She was nearing the outskirts of Aghios Nikolaos when a jeep approached her and she stopped at the side of the road to let it pass.

The jeep came to a halt and the passenger alighted and approached her.

'Papers.'

Anna broke into a torrent of hysterical Greek, pointing to Michael and beating her breast.

The Italian called to the driver. 'You understand a bit of Greek. I've got a woman going demented here. Come and tell me what she's on about.'

'I speak little.'

The Italian came to Anna's side. 'Please. You tell. Very slow.'

A look of horror came over Anna's face as she recognised Victor standing easily before her. Her mouth opened and shut wordlessly.

'Please. Tell, very slow.'

Anna swallowed hard. 'My husband. He is very sick. In the stomach. Needs the doctor in Aghios Nikolaos.'

Victor nodded. He drew the rugs back from Michael's body and looked at the prostrate form, legs drawn up in pain and hands clutched to his stomach. Gently Victor moved them, opened his shirt and loosened his trousers. To his surprise there was no sign of a bullet wound.

'Sick here?' Victor pointed.

'Very sick. Needs doctor.'

Slowly Victor nodded. 'Husband?'

Anna tilted her head defiantly at him. 'Yes. Babbis Andronicatis. Marisa's pappa.'

'Papers.'

Anna handed over the page of crabbed writing which had made Babbis and her sister Maria officially man and wife. He looked at it, quite unable to read a single word except the names. He folded it neatly and returned it to her waiting hand.

'Pass.'

Trembling with fear, Anna took the donkey's bridle and began to lead her forward. She had gone no more than a few yards when she heard feet pounding after her.

'Halt! Halt!'

Anna stopped, the sick feeling in the pit of her stomach threatening to overwhelm her.

'I come.' Victor walked at her side, not uttering a word until they came to the checkpoint at the entrance to the town, when he began to shout in Italian.

'Let this woman through. Her husband is very ill and she's taking him to the doctor. I've checked her papers. No need to hold her up again.'

A voice came back to him. 'Are you sure? Have you checked the body?'

'I've checked everything. Let her through. We don't want a dead man on our hands.'

'Depends who he is.'

'He's only a farmer from up on the hill. I know them by sight.'

They reached the two soldiers who were barring the road.

'Let's have a look.'

The blanket was drawn back roughly and Michael was pushed onto his back, his stomach and chest exposed for the soldier's scrutiny. He groaned loudly and drew his legs up as far as he was able. The soldier threw the blanket back over him.

'Not surprised he's got guts ache with the food in this country.' He stepped aside and Victor walked a few more yards with Anna.

'Be careful, Anna,' he breathed. 'Good luck.'

Anna did not answer, she was not even sure she had heard him correctly. Blinking rapidly to stop herself from crying she hurried as fast as she was able, hoping Michael was not being jolted too unbearably.

Timidly Anna knocked at the house where she had been told Doctor Stavros lived, hoping he would be at home, although no light was showing in his window. Three times she knocked and was just about to turn away in despair when she heard a movement inside.

'Who wants me?'

'I have a very sick man with me. He needs to go to the hospital. Please, open the door.'

'Do I know him?'

'Yes – and you know me. I'm Yannis's sister.'

The door was pulled open and Anna was dragged inside. 'Don't wake the street, girl.'

'He's sick, very sick. He needs the hospital.'

Doctor Stavros pushed her down into a chair. 'You haven't

brought a resistance worker into town, have you?' he asked in horror.

Anna nodded. 'I had to.' Her head drooped wearily. 'I think he needs his appendix out. He's very ill.'

'Who is he?' Doctor Stavros took off his glasses and polished them.

'Michael.' Anna's voice was almost a whisper.

'Michael! Good God, girl, don't you realise the danger – to him and yourself?'

Anna nodded dumbly.

'How can I admit him to hospital? All the admissions are screened. If there's any suspicion that they're resistance workers they are watched over and taken off for questioning as soon as they're well.'

'He'll die if you don't operate.'

'I can't admit him to the hospital.'

'Please, doctor. I risked my family to bring him here. His men are relying on you to help him.'

Doctor Stavros frowned. 'You're a brave girl, Anna, but I can't help.'

Anna looked at the doctor in despair. 'Give me some morphine and a knife and I'll do it myself, out there in the cart.'

'Don't be so foolish. He'd never survive.'

'I don't know what his men will say when I return and tell them you refused to help.' Anna spoke bitterly and looked around the room. 'Where will I find a sharp knife? All the time he's left outside he's probably getting more sick and a soldier could find him.'

Doctor Stavros looked at the distraught, but determined woman. 'You would really try to operate on him yourself?'

'I would. At least I would have tried to save his life.'

The doctor picked up his coat. 'You leave me no choice. Can you walk a bit further?'

Anna nodded. She felt light headed with relief as she left the house and once more took hold of the donkey's rein.

The doctor left her at the side door to the hospital, promising to return. When he did so he had a stretcher with him.

'You'll have to help me get him onto the stretcher and carry him in.'

Anna found the weight of Michael difficult to deal with and she was struggling to keep her grip on the end of the stretcher by the time they were through the door.

'Put him down. I'll get some help.'

Anna waited until he returned accompanied by an old man. He instructed the man to take one side of the stretcher and Anna the other. As speedily as possible the doctor traversed the corridor and entered a room that was obviously used for operations.

'Get out, Anna, You shouldn't be in here.'

'I could help you,' she offered.

Doctor Stavros shook his head. 'It's better that I use one of my nurses that I can trust.'

Resignedly Anna dragged her weary self back to where the donkey and cart were standing outside. She led the donkey up to the square where she was able to drink from the trough, then returned to a side road. Exhausted she climbed into the cart and lay on the straw wrapped in the blankets, the residual warmth of Michael's body comforting her.

Within a few minutes she was asleep, the rising sun did not wake her, or the people passing by on their way into the town. She did not stir until her donkey answered a fellow and pulled at the rope that tethered her.

Stiffly she climbed down and walked back to the hospital, pushing open the heavy front door. No one gave her a second glance and she stood uncertainly in the hallway, finally deciding to look for Michael herself. She opened doors and traversed long passages until she finally entered a ward where the beds lined the walls. She walked up to each, scanning the faces of the occupants, until finally stopped by a nurse.

'I'm looking for someone,' explained Anna.

The nurse frowned. 'No one new has come in here.'

'Is there another place where I could look?'

The nurse shook her head. 'There's nowhere else. Maybe he was taken to Heraklion?'

Anna felt her heart constrict. 'Where is Doctor Stavros?'

'He's not here until the afternoon.'

Defeated, Anna turned away, tears running down her face as she stumbled from the ward. Michael was dead. She should never have subjected him to the long and tortuous ride, but taken the doctor to him. It was her fault. She sniffed dolefully and rubbed her hand across her dribbling nose. She could not wail or beat her breast to show the extent of the loss she felt. She must just disappear and hope they would not look for her.

Somehow she found a taverna and ordered coffee and a roll, remembering she had not eaten for hours. After two more coffees her head began to clear. She must take the donkey to a farmer and have her hooves pared back to give credence to her errand, then she must seek out Doctor Stavros and thank him before returning to Plaka and telling the men hiding in the hills they had lost their leader.

'There you are!'

Anna did not realise the words were directed at her until the doctor sat down opposite and called for a raki.

'I've been looking for you everywhere.'

'Michael's dead. You don't have to tell me. I know.'

'What? When? Who told you that?'

'He's not in the ward with the others, he's dead.'

Doctor Stavros reached out and took Anna's hand.

'He's not dead, Anna. I swear that when I left him he was sleeping. You were right about his appendix. A few more hours and it would have ruptured and there would have been no hope of saving him.'

Anna lifted dark, pain filled eyes to the doctor's face. 'He's still alive?'

Doctor Stavros nodded. 'He'll need careful nursing for a while, but there's no reason why he shouldn't make a full recovery.'

Anna let out a long breath, then her tears began to spill. 'I thought he was dead. I was sure he was dead.'

Doctor Stavros waited until she had regained her composure. 'I'm telling you the truth, Anna. I suggest you return home where you're needed. There's nothing for you to do here.'

Anna led the donkey back into Plaka, her heart thumping loudly as she neared the farm. She knew Victor had recognised her and she was certain some German soldiers would be waiting for her. There was no sign of activity at the farm, adding to Anna's conviction that Victor had already denounced her and the family had been taken.

She pushed open the kitchen door and crept towards the living room where the murmur of voices could be heard and a low laugh. She peered round the doorway to see her mother and Aspasia sitting amicably together. Anna forced herself to move forwards and speak normally.

'I'm back, Mamma. Is everything all right?'

'Of course. Marisa looked after me and it's been nice having Aspasia to chat with. We've been talking over the old times, before you were born, when we were girls together. Those were the good days.' Maria sighed, then took stock of Anna, who had sunk into a chair, the colour drained from her face. 'What's wrong with you, girl?'

'I'm – I'm just tired. It was a long walk.'

Aspasia rose. 'I'll get you some coffee. Have you eaten?'

Anna shook her head. 'Not since early this morning. Where are Marisa and Yannis?'

'Yannis is up in the hills and Marisa went down to the shop.'

Anna frowned. 'I didn't see her.'

'Here.' Aspasia placed a cup of coffee on the table with a large piece of cheese, and the end of a loaf. 'Eat that and you'll feel better. Then you can tell us all about Aghios Nikolaos. Are the Germans there or just Italians?'

Marisa left the village shop and walked along the beach to where Victor was standing. With her aunt away she could chat to him for a while before returning with the bar of soap, which had been her excuse for the errand. She leant beside him against the upturned boat and smiled.

Victor regarded her gravely. 'Anna?' he asked.

'Aghios Nikolaos,' she answered. 'I expect she'll be tired when she gets back. It's quite a long walk.'

Victor made no attempt to struggle with the meaning of the sentence. 'Who Maria Andronicatis?'

Marisa looked at him in surprise. 'My mother.'

'Where mother?'

'My mother's dead. You know that, Victor.'

'Where Pappa?'

'I don't know.' Marisa shook her head sadly. 'I wish he'd come home, him and uncle Yiorgo. I hate this war. I'm frightened. Whenever the German soldiers come I'm scared they'll take me away, or Yannis or Mamma Anna.'

Victor frowned. 'No fright. I here.'

'You're a soldier too, Victor. No one asked you to come here. We were happy, just happy living here and farming. We were no trouble to anyone, then you came and the Germans, and all we hear is of killing and war.'

'Marisa. I soldier. Obey orders.'

'And if the Germans said to shoot us all you'd obey your orders.' Marisa turned to him, her eyes blazing.

The puzzlement and hurt showed in Victor's eyes. 'Marisa, I friend.'

'You're no friend. Soldiers are not friends.'

Marisa began to walk away, hoping Victor would not realise she was crying. She had not meant to speak to him so harshly.

He had done nothing to deserve it. He caught her easily and pulled her down to the ground in the shade of the boat. Holding her shoulders he shook her gently.

'Marisa, I friend. Always friend.'

Marisa kept her head averted, the tears spilling from her eyes. Victor placed his hand under her chin and turned her face towards him. Bringing his face down close to her, he kissed her long and full on her mouth. Despite her distress Marisa found herself responding and relaxing in his arms. Still holding her he began to caress her hair, cushioning her against his chest as she quietened.

'No fright,' he murmured. 'Victor here. Victor friend.' He kissed her moist eyes, her damp cheeks and found her lips again, meeting no resistance from her. His kisses became more insistent and urgent and Marisa responded willingly.

'Victor friend. Victor love Marisa.' He enfolded her in his arms, stroking her hair and murmuring endearments to her in Italian. He slid his hand up her skirt. Marisa closed her eyes and drew a deep, shuddering breath.

'No,' she whispered. 'No, Victor, please, no.' Her words contradicting her body as she pressed herself closer to him.

Slowly Victor shook his head and released her.

Marisa felt hot tears of frustration at the back of her eyes. She pulled herself reluctantly from Victor's embrace. 'I have to go.'

Victor looked at her heightened colour and rapid breathing. He took a deep breath himself. 'Victor love Marisa,' he said again as he kissed her, this time less insistently, realising the emotional danger to both of them.

He released her and Marisa scrambled to her feet, stumbling up the beach to the path that led to the farm, only to stop abruptly as she saw the donkey tethered beneath the tree, the cart unhitched and standing idly.

She smoothed her hair back from her face, ran her hands under the pump and splashed her eyes with the cold water. No doubt she would have some explaining to do.

Marisa could not understand why her aunt had not questioned her regarding her trip to the shop. She was sure her dishevelled appearance would be commented upon and she would be called upon to give a full explanation. That night she lay awake on the mattress she shared with Anna and recalled Victor's kisses. She shivered with delightful anticipation as she remembered his hand touching her leg beneath her skirt and blushed in the darkness at her forwardness. This was what she had been warned against, but it had taken all her self-control to refuse his advances.

Anna tried to avoid Victor and he watched her with troubled eyes. He wished his Greek were good enough to tell Anna that he would say nothing of her trip to Aghios Nikolaos, although he was curious to know the truth. Was the man in the cart her brother-in-law, and if so where had she been hiding him?

He tried hard to remember the Greek Marisa had taught him to put his thoughts into words, but found it impossible. He worked with more concentration when she gave him Greek lessons and pleaded with her to help him each day.

Maria noticed the change between her granddaughter and the soldier. A look would pass between them, they would sit close together and their hands would touch at the slightest excuse, but she said nothing to her daughter. Besides, Anna did not look well, the dark circles under her eyes betrayed her lack of sleep, she jumped at the slightest noise and seemed suddenly frightened by a word from the Italians. Maria sighed. Who would have believed a few years ago that their life would have changed so dramatically? Confined to her chair, she let her thoughts drift back to when they were one large, happy family, with no thought to the future and what it might hold. She worried about her sons. Yannis she doubted she would ever see again, even if he survived on the island, Yiorgo could well be killed, and Stelios had gone from her life forever. In the quiet of the afternoon she held conversations with them in her mind and Anna often found her mother with a lop-sided smile on her face, mouthing words to herself.

The wet and windy days of the winter confined them to the house when the essential jobs on the farm had been completed each day. Anna found herself looking towards the hills, wondering if the caves had flooded, as Michael had feared. She tried not to think of Michael. Upstairs the shirt that had belonged to him lay amongst her other clothing, but of him or the other resistance workers she had seen not a sign, and she had ceased to take the bread up each day when she found it mouldering where she had left it on previous days.

For a month Doctor Stavros kept Michael in a small side room, the door of which was locked and only the doctor and a trusted nurse held the key. Should it be opened it appeared to be a storeroom, boxes stacked from floor to ceiling. Michael's progress was slow and Doctor Stavros lived in fear of the day when the soldiers would decide to search the hospital thoroughly and the man would be discovered. He wished he could ask some of Michael's companions to remove him, but he had no idea of his way to the cave and he dared not get a message to Anna.

Michael seemed quite unconcerned when Doctor Stavros voiced his fears. 'I can move around now. If they decide to do a search I can hide.'

Doctor Stavros pursed his lips. 'There's nowhere to hide. If they decided to do a full search they would turn out all the cupboards and chests, insist upon seeing the papers of every patient and hold us all at gunpoint until they were satisfied.'

Michael grinned. 'Do they search the water tanks on the roof?'

Doctor Stavros looked at him in amazement. 'You'd never get up there.'

'You'd be surprised what a desperate man can do! There's a drainpipe outside the window and I should be able to haul myself up that far. You might have to stitch me up again afterwards, but I doubt if they'd think of looking up there. These soldiers are Italians, remember, not Germans.'

The doctor eyed him dubiously. 'If you're well enough to climb up there you should be well enough to leave. Have you any friends who could collect you?'

'Plenty. They just need to be asked.'

'Where can I find them?'

'Try the market. Ask for the orange seller from Mardati. Tell him the hospital needs some good quality fruit and to bring his cart round early in the morning.'

'Suppose I don't find him?'

Michael shrugged. 'Then you'll have to go the next day.' He leaned back against his pillows. 'I'm sure it's more comfortable here than wherever they'll take me to finish recuperating.'

'For you, but not for me, my friend.'

Victor spent long hours sitting at the table writing assiduously or staring into space with a look of intense concentration on his face. Each evening he would sit with Marisa and she had to admit that his Greek had improved beyond recognition. He finally found the confidence to approach Anna.

'Please, I want talk with you.'

Anna looked up impatiently. She still found his attempts at communication with her difficult and painstakingly slow. 'Yes, Victor?'

'Maria Andronicatis – Marisa's mamma?'

Anna felt her heart constrict. This was it, then. He had lulled her into a sense of false security by saying nothing for so long and now he meant to denounce her.

'Yes.'

'Pappa with resistance?'

Anna shrugged. 'Maybe.'

'Not pappa you take in cart. Who man in cart?'

Anna did not answer. Her brain was reeling. Should she deny all knowledge of the identity of the man or say he was Babbis?

'Anna, I friend. I help. Tell soldiers let you through. Make no trouble. Man well now?'

'I don't know.' Anna answered hesitantly. 'I left him at the hospital.'

'Who man in cart?' persisted Victor.

'I don't know. I found him ill on the road.'

Victor eyed her unconvinced and shook his head. 'Why you have paper? Why you say husband? Not find man, arrange to meet.'

'He was ill, very ill. He needed to be in hospital. There was no time to wait for you to return from Aghios Nikolaos.' Anna spoke slowly, hoping he would not notice how her hands were shaking.

'Not do again, Anna. I friend. Say nothing.'

Anna felt the blood rush to her face. 'Thank you, Victor.'

'What for supper? You cook good.'

The door crashed open as two German soldiers entered, their rifles covering the family sitting at the table eating their meal.

'You. Come.' The rifle pointed to Anna.

Her face ashen, Anna rose to her feet and looked up to see striking blue eyes. The colour flooded back into her face and she swallowed hard. 'What do you want?' She could hear her voice trembling.

'No questions. Come.'

Victor's hand went to his belt, but he had long ceased to wear his gun around the house.

'It's quite all right,' Anna spoke calmly. 'There's nothing to be alarmed about.'

'I'll come with you,' Yannis had also recognised their visitor, and began to rise from his chair.

'You stay.'

Scowling, Yannis resumed his seat as Anna walked through the kitchen and out into the yard, the door closing firmly behind him.

Michael smiled at her. 'I'm sorry if I gave you a fright, but I knew the Italians were there. I came to say thank you.'

'Michael! Oh, Michael.' The words Anna wanted to say stuck in her throat.

'Walk to the stable. We can talk there.'

Her legs trembling, Anna obeyed, walking with her head held high, as if in defiance. The donkey gave her a curious glance before returning to her masticating. Michael replaced the rifle he had been carrying over his shoulder and took Anna in his arms.

'I'll never be able to repay you, Anna. We're not in this area any more, but I had to see you. You saved my life, and God knows at what risk to your own.'

Anna leaned against his chest, breathing in the musty smell of the German uniform. 'I never thought I'd see you again,' she whispered.

Silently they stood together, not needing words to communicate their feelings for each other. Michael kissed her long and tenderly.

'I'm being taken back to England, Anna. I wish I could take you with me.'

'It's not possible. I can't leave Mamma and the children.'

'I love you, Anna.' He held her tightly to him, his face buried in her hair. 'If only you weren't married. I'll never forget you, never,' he whispered.

'I still have your shirt,' murmured Anna inconsequently.

'Keep it, along with my heart, my beloved Anna.' He kissed her fiercely. 'I must go. Every minute I spend here puts you in danger and makes it more difficult for me to say goodbye. Pretend to be frightened when I shout at you.'

Reluctantly Michael released her, threatening her again with the rifle as he marched her back to the farmhouse and into the living room. There was no need for Anna to pretend. The guttural words that were thrown at her in the harshest of tones made her cringe. Michael clicked his heels, saluted and strode rapidly out, his companion following, leaving the Italians looking at each other bemused.

'What he want?' asked Victor as the door closed.

Anna did not answer. She was sobbing uncontrollably in her mother's arms, Maria stroking her hair and trying to calm her. Marisa and Yannis looked at each other. This was not like their aunt.

'Mamma Anna, did he touch you?' Marisa's voice was shrill with fear.

Victor raced up the stairs and returned with his rifle in one hand and a revolver in the other. 'I follow. I shoot soldier who hurt Anna.'

'No!' Anna was on her feet. 'He didn't hurt me. He only searched the stable. I was just frightened.'

Yannis looked at his aunt in amazement. Since when had she been frightened of Michael?

Slowly Victor shook his head. 'Man in cart! He do hurt Anna.'

Anna turned imploring eyes on the Italian. 'Finish your meal, please, all of you, finish eating.'

Yannis had grown considerably during the last year. He had the beginning of dark stubble on his cheeks and chin, and felt himself to be a man now. He wished the resistance would come back to the area so he could join them. He had considered making his way to the Lassithi Plain where the main body of men were known to be hiding, despite all attempts by the Germans to flush them out, but his aunt begged him to stay with tears in her eyes. He did not understand why any mention of the resistance should upset her so much and he wondered if she had news of his father or uncle that she did not wish to impart. When Yannis finally dared to ask if that was the reason she shook her head, a smile touching her lips.

'I've heard nothing from them at all. I just pray each night they will be safe and come back to us soon.'

'You would tell me, wouldn't you?' Yannis persisted. 'I'm a man now and I'd have to make decisions.'

Anna looked at him in surprise. 'What decisions?'

'How to run two farms in the most profitable way possible, who to approach regarding Marisa's betrothal, things like that.'

'What! Marisa's betrothal! She's no more than a child.'

'Mamma Anna, she's seventeen. These things take time. We ought to think about them now.'

'And who would you have her betrothed to?'

'That's the problem. There's no one in the village who I'd be happy with, maybe if I went to Elounda.'

'Now you listen to me, Yannis. You think you're a man now, but before any decision is made about your sister's future or the farm you'll wait for your Pappa to come back.'

Yannis gazed at his aunt mutinously. It was all very well for her to say wait, but his Pappa might not be coming back and his sister had to get married some time. If they waited too long there would be no one available. He tried to talk Marisa round to his way of thinking, but she was adamant.

'You can do what you like about the farm, Yannis, but leave me alone. I'll marry who I want, not who you say.'

'You'll have to marry whoever Pappa says, and if Pappa doesn't come back you'll have to marry who I say.'

Marisa turned on her younger brother in a blaze of anger. 'I will not! Mamma Anna hasn't been made to get married, so why should I? You just want to get rid of me, then if Pappa doesn't come back you can have the farm all for yourself.'

'Marisa!' Yannis was truly shocked, such an idea had never occurred to him. 'I'm just thinking of you.'

'Then don't!'

She slammed the door and ran from the house until she was half way to the sheep pen. She should be safe from prying eyes there and able to cry in private. There was something very wrong with her. She did not want to get married to any of the local boys who were near enough her own age, but she did want to be kissed, kissed and kissed and kissed. She was wicked to have such thoughts. No nice, properly brought up girl thought things like that. She could not be a very nice girl; she was probably no better than the girls in Aghios Nikolaos who went with the soldiers. Twisting her hands into the tough grass and beating her feet in frustration she did not hear footsteps, but sensed she was being watched. Swiftly she turned her face upwards to see Victor standing there, all concern. He lowered himself down beside her.

'Marisa not happy? Marisa sad, Victor sad.'

'Why should I be happy when my brother's trying to marry me off to the first person he thinks will be suitable? Why should I have to get married if I don't want to?'

'Marry? Who get married? Slowly, Marisa, Greek not good.'

Marisa drew a long shuddering breath. 'Yannis thinks he ought to arrange my betrothal.'

'Betrothal? What betrothal is?'

'Arrange for me to get married.'

Victor looked stricken. 'Who you marry?'

Marisa shrugged. 'Yannis will probably find four or five young men who he thinks will be suitable, but I won't, I won't.' She beat her fists on the ground.

'You have to marry who Yannis say?'

'Not yet.' Marisa shook her head. 'I'll wait until Pappa comes back, or Uncle Yiorgo or grandpa. Yannis won't be able to make me do anything then.'

'In Italy,' Victor chose his words carefully. 'Man marry girl he love. No allowed in Greece?'

'Oh, allowed, if both families agree.'

'And if not agree?'

'You either marry someone else and forget him or wait until you are old enough to do as you please.'

Victor reached out and took Marisa's hand. 'You wait for me, Marisa?'

Marisa looked at the Italian in disbelief. 'Do you mean that, Victor?'

'I love you, Marisa. Always I love you. First day I see you I love you.'

'Don't be silly, Victor.'

Victor carried Marisa's hand to his lips. 'You only girl in whole of Crete or Italy for me. I try tell you, but my Greek no good. On beach I try tell you.'

'Oh, Victor.' Marisa's voice was a whisper.

'I love so much I want.' He took her face in his hands. 'One day you say you want. I very happy that day.'

'Victor, I want now.' Marisa looked into his eyes. 'I love you, Victor.'

'I love so much I want now, but we wait. Victor love Marisa.' He kissed her, pushing her back on the grass. 'Love Marisa very much. We kiss, we touch, but we wait.'

News of the war filtered through very slowly to Plaka, usually brought back by the Italians after their regular visits to Aghios Nikolaos, but Anna took very little notice of the village gossip. She was more concerned about the mournful tolling of the bell from the island. She knew sacks of vegetables had disappeared from the outhouse and the disappearances coincided with Victor's sudden whim to check for resistance on the island at night. She was grateful, but she could not see a few vegetables going very far between the occupants. Surely they would all be dead soon from starvation, then the only time the bell would be heard would be when the wind blew strongly.

She visited the beach three or four times each day in the hope of seeing her brother's answering wave, but she went in vain. Victor would lend her his field glasses and she watched people crawling slowly over the rocks in their search for seafood, but from the distance she could not discern if her brother was amongst them. Resigned to the inevitable, Anna tried to alleviate her misery with hard work on the farm, but she did not have her father's quick eye for spotting leaf moulds and blight and whole areas would be devastated.

Yannis was frustrated. He wished he had listened more attentively to his male relatives when they had tried to impart their knowledge to him. To care for the sheep and goats seemed far easier than trying to drag a living from the soil. He tried to talk to his aunt, explaining that the animals cost next to nothing to keep, but seed and plants had to be bought. Didn't she think it wiser for them to forget the carob, olives and grapes and just grow enough vegetables to feed themselves? Anna would not budge in her opinions.

'It's my Pappa's farm. We'll keep it as it is until he comes back.'

Yannis had tried to reason, but Anna had insisted that he nurtured the remaining vines and olive trees until the men of the family returned.

Marisa used any excuse to escape from the house to enable her to share a few stolen minutes with Victor. The happiness shining in her eyes and the tender glances that Victor bestowed on her did not go unnoticed by her aunt. Although Anna was concerned and ensured they were rarely alone for more than a few moments, she did not have the heart to confront her niece. The memory of her own feelings for Michael were too close to the surface and she shed many a sad tear when she was alone.

Victor still helped on the farm with a will, but Mario spent less and less time in the village, until he returned elated, and gathered the soldiers together to break the news.

'The war is over. We'll be going home.'

The noisy reception that greeted his news brought the villagers from their houses. The Italians rushed to them, embracing their reluctant hosts as friends, kissing them and shaking their hands.

Anna was both relieved and grateful when Victor agreed to her request that some of the Italians rowed over to Spinalonga with supplies for the besieged island.

It was with trepidation that Victor watched as the few men who were sitting on the rocks, a fishing line dangling hopefully in the water, began to negotiate their way slowly and carefully towards the quay. Father Minos sank to his knees and said a prayer for their salvation as he saw the skeletal inhabitants struggling down to collect their first substantial food for months.

Victor clicked his tongue. He called out to the soldiers, who were sitting silently at their oars. 'Get out and help them. Carry those who haven't the strength to walk.'

His men eyed him warily and made no move. 'Help them, I said,' he called again and leapt over the side of the boat. He scooped a man who had collapsed up in his arms and began to carry him up the ramp towards the village.

'Where take man?' he asked of a woman sitting by the side of the path.

'Hospital.' She pointed up the slight incline and Victor carried his light burden onwards. The door to the hospital was open and inside he could see the rows of mattresses, occupied by still forms.

'Where put man?' he called.

A wraith-like form rose slowly from a mattress. 'Put him there. I'll see to him.'

Thankfully, Victor laid the body as gently as possible onto the mattress and backed out of the door. He had no idea if the man was still alive, whether anyone other than the man who had spoken to him was alive, and he had no wish to linger and find out.

He returned down the path towards the quay, where the soldiers had carried the boxes of food up the ramp and left them in a disorderly pile. He looked around for help. They could not stay there or much of it would spoil. Watched by a disbelieving gathering of islanders the soldiers sorted the boxes at his direction, until he was satisfied that he had done as much as possible. Some of the eggs that had been sent were broken and a container of milk had been upturned.

'We must return to Plaka,' he called out in Italian to the soldiers.

The soldiers willingly obeyed his order, moving to one side and filing up ready to march away. Father Minos touched his arm.

'Thank you.'

Victor looked at the priest in his tattered and filthy robe. He looked as frail as the other people he had seen. Despite having the food they so desperately needed would they have the strength to eat it?

Victor frowned. 'Go now. Come tomorrow.'

Anna waited in an agony of apprehension until they returned. 'Did you see my brother?'

Victor shrugged. A number of skeletal forms had struggled down to the jetty and raised a hand in thanks to them.

'Maybe. Tomorrow I ask.'

With that Anna had to be content.

Manolis moored his boat in the harbour at Aghios Nikolaos and sought out Doctor Stavros.

The doctor scowled at him. 'So where have you been?'

Manolis slid into the seat opposite and ordered a beer for himself. 'Making myself useful. I saw what happened here and decided I didn't want to end up on a tree. I thought I'd go up to Plaka and stay there for a bit. I was just rounding the island when a boatload of Germans appeared. I stayed out at sea for the rest of the day and when I decided it was safe to go round to see Flora I was shot at. I came back here and found it was seething with Italians. I spoke to some of the other boatmen and they said no one was going to be allowed out without an escort. I waited until dark and sailed back down the coast to Preveli and joined up with the resistance.'

Doctor Stavros regarded him more favourably. 'So what did you do?'

'Helped to ferry the army out to the waiting ships. That was pretty scary. The German planes flew over and kept bombing them. Hundreds of men were lost. We never knew when we would come under attack. When we could do no more I hung around and spoke to their leader. He said I could be useful transporting fighting men to deserted coves for them to land and take the Germans by surprise. I was pretty relieved that he didn't ask me to actually do any fighting.' Manolis grinned. 'What about you?'

Doctor Stavros shrugged. 'I ended up treating injuries, along with my usual duties.'

'How's Flora?'

'As well as can be expected. She's still alive.'

'What do you mean?'

'No one was allowed to go to Spinalonga, not even with an escort.'

Manolis eyes widened. 'What happened to them? What about their food?'

'They managed as best they could. A considerable number have died.'

Manolis swallowed the rest of his beer. 'Are you planning to go out today? I can take you over. I'll be leaving in about ten minutes.'

Doctor Stavros shook his head. 'You'll have to give me an hour. I need to get some supplies ready.'

Manolis waited in a fever of impatience until Doctor Stavros finally appeared on the quay. Hardly waiting for him to be settled Manolis cast off and started the motor, despite the stiff breeze that was blowing. 'I'm going through the canal. It will be quicker that way.'

Doctor Stavros shrugged. There really was no immediate hurry.

Victor drew Marisa apart from the turmoil. 'You wait for me?'

Marisa nodded. 'I'll wait, Victor. It will seem like forever, but I'll wait.'

'I promise I come back. When you of age I come and ask your Pappa.' He kissed her gently. 'Tonight I kiss you as I want and no one say no.'

Marisa clasped her hands behind his neck and pulled his face down close to her. 'Victor, I want now. I love you too much to wait for years.'

Slowly Victor unclasped her hands and shook his head. 'No, Marisa. I want so much, not ask me.'

'Please,' she begged.

Again he shook his head. 'Few days, few weeks I go to Italy. I leave my Marisa in Crete. I not leave bambino with her. I come back. We make ten, twenty bambinos.'

Marisa pressed herself against him. 'I want your bambino,' she insisted.

'You want, I want. Your Pappa not want. He kill me when I come back.'

Hot tears of frustration pressed against Marisa's eyelids. 'I want, Victor.'

'Not ask me. Please, not ask me.' To her surprise she could see tears in his eyes. 'I love Marisa too much.'

Victor sought out Anna as soon as the official orders for the Italians to leave Plaka were received. He shifted from one foot to the other self-consciously, holding Marisa's hand.

'What do you want, Victor?'

Tongue tied Victor looked at Marisa for help.

'Victor and I want to get married. We want to get married now.'

Anna looked at Victor coldly. 'Is she carrying your child?'

Sadly Victor looked at Marisa's aunt. 'I love Marisa. Not make trouble for her. Love her, want to marry her.'

Anna took a deep breath of relief. She shook her head. 'You cannot marry Marisa. She is a Cretan girl and you are Italian.'

Marisa's eyes filled with tears. 'Please, Mamma Anna. We love each other.'

Again Anna shook her head. 'You think you love each other. Victor has been a soldier over here, lonely without his family and friends. When he returns to Italy he will soon forget us. He'll find a nice Italian girl and you will have a Cretan marriage.'

Victor shook his head. 'I not marry Italian girl. I marry Marisa.'

'Marisa is too young to get married. She's only seventeen.'

'My mamma was only eighteen when I was born,' protested Marisa.

'We won't go into that,' Anna dismissed the subject of Marisa's conception before Maria was married to Babbis. Her sister had been the talk of the village for some time.

'Please, Mamma Anna, let me marry Victor.'

'Your Pappa is the one to give permission when he returns, not me.'

'But we don't know when Pappa's coming back,' Marisa turned anguished eyes on her aunt. 'By the time he returns Victor could be back in Italy.'

'You can write to him and let him know what your Pappa says. Once life gets back to normal over here you will soon forget each other.'

Marisa caught her breath in a sob and Victor held her in his arms. 'I will not forget my Marisa. If Pappa say no I will wait. Wait until you can say yes without Pappa. Not cry, Marisa, please not cry.'

'It's not fair,' she sobbed. 'All we want is to be together.'

'Be sensible, Marisa,' Anna spoke sternly. 'Even if you did marry Victor now you would not be allowed to go to Italy with him and he would not be allowed to stay in Crete.'

'Aunt Anna right. Marisa, believe me. Always I love you. I come back. I promise I come back.'

Marisa lifted her tear-streaked face. 'You won't forget me?'

'Never forget Marisa. Love Marisa too much to forget.'

Anna turned away. Michael had said he would never forget her. Tears came to her eyes as she thought of him and she wondered if he would come back to Crete. She left the kitchen, where Victor was still consoling Marisa, and went up to her bedroom. She took Michael's shirt from amongst her clothes and held it to her, wishing she were holding him in her arms, and cried bitterly.

The Italians seemed genuinely sorry to be leaving the small village where they had spent the last few years. Despite the hostility they had encountered when they first arrived a mutual tolerance had been reached, leading to a certain amount of friendship and affection on both sides by the time they left.

An oppressive silence seemed to follow their departure. The villagers were waiting for their loved ones to return to them and were having difficulty in coming to terms with the sudden emptiness of their lives. They gathered at the taverna and began to recount the various ways in which the Italians had helped them, the conversation inevitably leading to how they had fooled and outwitted them to help the resistance whilst they lived nearby. Anna listened in surprise. She had no idea all her neighbours had provided food and clothing.

'Used to come and sit by my fire, he did,' chuckled Sevas. 'Always knew when Julius would be away. I don't know how, but he never made a mistake.'

Yannis took a sip of the wine he had been allowed. 'I used to tell them when I went up for the animals each night.'

All eyes turned in his direction. He grinned, delighted to be the centre of attention. 'I used to ask Victor who was going into town. He never realised why I wanted to know.'

The women shook their heads in admiration and some disbelief, whilst Anna turned on Yannis.

'You didn't tell me.'

Yannis shrugged. 'Some things are best kept to oneself, aren't they, Mamma Anna?' He raised his eyebrows and looked quizzically at her.

Anna found she was blushing and hoped the women had not noticed.

'I gave them a mattress. Told Emmanuel I'd burnt it. Don't know where he thought the smoke went!'

To Anna's relief the conversation had moved on.

'I let them have my husband's best boots. I hope he won't mind when he gets back.'

'I met their leader,' Sevas leaned forward confidentially. 'He wasn't Greek. Said he was English, but he spoke Greek.'

'You mean Michael.' Anna spoke automatically and felt herself reddening again.

All eyes turned to look at her. 'How did you know him? You had two Italians with you. He couldn't sit by your fire.'

'I used to go to the caves if anyone was wounded.'

'What was he like, then?'

'Tall, broad-shouldered.' She remembered the shirt still amongst her clothes. 'He had very blue eyes.' She spoke with a catch in her throat.

'I heard Michael had died.'

Anna's eyes swivelled towards the woman.

'When did you hear that?' she asked, hoping her voice sounded normal.

The woman shrugged. 'I don't remember. Some time back, when one of his men came for eggs, I think.'

Anna sucked in her breath. 'When they were still living in the hills?'

'Yes, must have been then. They've none of them been around for a good while now.'

'And a good thing too. Sooner or later we'd have had those Germans back again. They knew they were here. Never did catch one of them, though. We were too clever for them. All we want now is our men back and we can forget all about it.' Sevas smiled complacently.

Anna hoped her smile did not appear too false as she agreed with them. How could she ever forget Michael?

Davros was the first of the villagers to return to Plaka. He had lost a leg and was fitted with a wooden stump that stuck out before him when he sat down. Time and again he regaled the villagers of his heroics that had resulted in its loss, each time the story becoming more far fetched until they began to disbelieve his exploits. Of Babbis and Yiorgo he had heard rumours, but had no news of their whereabouts, and it was another month before Yiorgo finally opened the farmhouse door.

Anna walked to Olous for news of her father. The closer she came to the town the more an icy fear seemed to grip her heart and she was not surprised when she was told he had died within the first six months of his captivity. She shook her head sadly and shed bitter tears on her return journey. The look on Anna's face as she entered the farmhouse told Maria the news she had been dreading. Without restraint she beat her breast and wailed, Anna and Marisa joining her, although they were neither of them sure if their grief was for the elderly Yannis or for their own private tragedies.

Marisa walked around, her eyes red-rimmed from weeping, whilst Anna was tight-lipped and seemed to be in a sad world of her own. Maria tried to encourage her daughter's confidences, but Anna kept her own counsel. Maria tried to direct her thoughts elsewhere.

'Has there been any more news of Yannis?'

'He's still in hospital over there.'

'Ask Davros to take you over to visit him. You could make some of your soup.'

Anna bowed her head guiltily. She should have thought and gone before. Her brother needed to know that his father was dead, and would be anxious about his mother and brothers.

1947 – 1949

Yiorgo shook his head sadly as Anna imparted the news of their father's death to him. 'I would never have left if I had thought you were in any danger down here.'

'I'm glad you did,' Anna replied swiftly. 'Had you stayed you would probably have been shot or sent to work in the mines with Pappa. We were fortunate that the Germans didn't stay down here. The Italians actually helped us after a while.'

'They helped you?'

'They worked on the farm and made repairs to some of the houses when it was necessary. It was Yannis's doing really. He told them they should do something for us in return for being looked after.'

'How have the children taken the news of their father's death?'

Anna shrugged. 'They've neither of them said very much. I think they realised when you arrived back alone.'

'They can be proud of their father. When Babbis saw what had happened to the villagers on the other side of Crete he was determined to avenge their deaths, whatever the cost. He was tormented by the thought that the same things could happen to Marisa and Yannis.'

Anna nodded, but did not ask her brother to elaborate. She had no wish to hear the details of the torture, rape and mutilation of the citizens that had taken place, whole villages burnt to the ground, their occupants with them.

'Yannis wants to pull down his father's house.' Yiorgo wanted to change the subject.

'He suggested that to me. Said it would be easier and less costly to run more animals. I said he must wait until you returned to make a decision like that.'

Yiorgo smiled at her. 'He's a good boy. It's an idea worth considering.'

'I think he was hoping I would agree and then Victor and Mario would have helped. They really were quite nice.'

Yiorgo looked at her scathingly. 'How can you say that about enemies.'

'They stayed here with us. I suppose we became quite used to them. Victor even managed to get some food over to the island occasionally.' Anna twisted her fingers nervously. 'He and Marisa became very friendly.'

'Is she pregnant?' asked Yiorgo immediately.

Anna shook her head. 'No, but she says she's in love with him.'

'Stupid child. I hope you've spoken severely to her.'

'Before they all left he came and asked if he could marry her.'

'You refused, of course?'

'Naturally. I agreed they could write to each other. I imagine after a few months he will find an Italian girl and that will be the end of the matter. Marisa will be hurt, but she'll get over him.'

Yiorgo nodded. 'I'll have a look around and see who's available.'

Doctor Stavros had been horrified on his first visit to the island. At least three quarters of the population had died and those who were left were clutching to their life by a thread. Each day Manolis delivered large canisters of soup to the hospital and the doctor had cajoled two fishermen to go with him and help to heat and distribute the nourishment.

To his surprise, after the first couple of weeks, Father Minos was striding around vigorously checking on the welfare of his self-elected parishioners and Spiro had insisted he was fit enough to run the hospital. Another month saw more of them able to look after themselves with some degree of adequacy and there were no more than the usual number of hospitalised cases, all of whom he expected to recover fully from their ordeal. Once he knew the situation with any degree of certainty he would have to contact the government about their living conditions. They could not be expected to undertake the manual work of repairs as they had done before the war and would need a considerable amount of help to combat the dilapidation that had occurred over the past years.

He wrote a long and impassioned letter to Andreas and asked him to explain the problems facing the islanders to the newly formed government. Andreas pleaded and exhorted them to help until he was finally told to go to the island himself and assess the situation. When he reported back to them they would consider the necessity of sending aid.

Maria was delighted to see her nephew from Heraklion. He satisfied her questions regarding Yannis's state of health, assuring her that he had regained his physical strength. He made no mention of the fact that her son had taken to drinking heavily in an attempt to forget the death of his wife.

He produced a letter from Annita and withdrew the photographs she had sent to him. Maria and Anna pored over them with interest.

'This is Elias,' he pointed, 'and of course you recognise Annita. She has four children now, three girls and a boy. Here's my mamma and pappa. It was taken outside his fish shop.'

'Your pappa has got fat,' observed Maria. 'Your mother looks much the same.'

Anna walked up the hill to Babbis's farmhouse and took a long look at the outside. The decision reached by Yiorgo and Yannis to demolish it made sense, and the building would no longer be there to remind her of the tragic outcome of her nephew's birth. Inside she looked around. There was really nothing of value. Over the years she had helped herself to the kitchen utensils and the house had been left neglected, gradually falling into disrepair.

She climbed the stairs, feeling them sag beneath her weight. There was nothing in either room except a large, empty chest. She wondered if it was worth the effort involved to take them back to the farm. Downstairs the cupboards yielded little. An overlooked bottle of wine, two broken glasses, a cracked cup, but standing upright at the back her hand contacted something hard and cold. She pulled it towards her, a flat metal box with a clasp at the side. Intrigued Anna lifted the lid and peered inside, feeling like a thief as she saw the sketches it contained. Carefully she removed them, laying them on the floor as she examined each one. There was Babbis, eating his meal, working in the fields, holding Marisa as a tiny baby, his mother, her mother, father, brothers, even herself, each one showing the strong, simple lines which were so characteristic of her sister's art.

She replaced them carefully. Although Maria had sold a few of her sketches they held no monetary value for Anna, but to Marisa and Yannis they would be priceless. Carrying the unwieldy case she walked slowly back to the farm. The men could do as they wished with the building now.

Yiorgo looked at the pictures in surprise. 'Babbis never told me about them.'

'Maybe he felt they were too poignant a reminder.'

'What are you going to do with them?'

'Give them to Marisa and Yannis, of course. It will be up to them if they want to keep them.'

Yiorgo picked up one of his father and himself. 'If they were willing I'd like to keep this one for myself.'

Anna studied it critically. 'You're the very image of Pappa. It could be of you and your son.'

Yiorgo smiled with her. 'Uncanny. I see what you mean. Did you find anything as interesting as this when you turned out Pappa's cupboard?'

Anna looked at her brother in surprise. 'It never occurred to me to look. It's just as he left it, his tobacco and even most of the bottles of brandy are still there.'

'Maybe we ought to have a look.'

'I'll do it tomorrow,' promised Anna.

Anna spread the contents of the cupboard on the table. Two spare wicks for the oil lamps and a cracked chimney, her father's tobacco pouch, three unopened tins of tobacco, a small black book, a dozen bottles of brandy, the best white china and something soft wrapped in oilskin and tied with string.

Yiorgo pushed the broken chimney to one side. 'That can go. It would probably shatter the first time we tried to use it.' He slipped the tins of tobacco into his pocket. 'I can use those. No point in leaving them in there to moulder.' He flicked open the pages of the book. 'What do you think this is?'

Anna peered over his shoulder. 'I've no idea. It's full of figures and dates.'

Yiorgo tossed it to one side and turned his attention to the oilskin package, slitting the string with his knife and unfolding the material, gasping in amazement at the sight that met his eyes.

'Where did Pappa get that!'

Anna looked at the bundle of notes. 'Is it money? Real money?'

'It's money, all right. Thousands of drachma.'

Brother and sister looked at each other.

'What shall we do with it?' asked Anna eventually.

Yiorgo scratched his head. 'I don't know. I'll have to think about this.' He picked up the small black book again. 'Maybe this will tell me.'

Yiorgo pored over the book for a week until he managed to make any sense of the entries. His Pappa had certainly been a dark horse. All those years of shifting heavy crates and thinking they were produce for the island. What a simpleton he had been! No wonder his uncle Yiorgo had been such a frequent visitor to the house and had enough money to follow his daughter to America. The proceeds from being a middleman, able and willing to store contraband goods, had certainly been lucrative. He counted the notes carefully, nearly fifty thousand drachma. He was a rich man. The realisation shocked him. It was not his money. It belonged to his mother. He bundled the money back into the oilskin and went to sit beside her.

Maria listened to him gravely. 'You're a good boy, Yiorgo. Spend it wisely.'

'Oh, no.' Yiorgo spoke firmly. 'It was Pappa's money, so it should all be yours.'

Maria smiled at him. She had no desire for money. What would she spend it on? Money could not buy her husband or daughter back, or a cure for her leprous son on Spinalonga. 'I don't want it, Yiorgo. Divide it up between yourselves however you wish.'

Systematically he began to sort it into seven piles. He would put aside a sum for his mother regardless of her wishes. It could go back into the cupboard until it was needed. He would save a share for his brothers, Yannis and Stelios, assuming he was still alive. Marisa could have her share when she married and Yannis could have his when he became of age. He wondered what Anna would do with her portion. Finally he returned seven named packets to the cupboard and told his mother of his actions.

Maria nodded with approval. 'You look after it for them and don't let them waste it on nonsense.'

Andreas returned to Heraklion with a long list of requests from Doctor Stavros and Father Minos. He dreaded his inevitable meeting with the government and the hours he would spend wrangling over minute details before he had any success. He was amused to see that many of the most expensive items had 'agreed by Mr Pavlakis' written beside them and at the head of the list was a generator. Andreas doubted if any of the old records of the assistance agreed by the government remained, but he saluted Father Minos for his astuteness.

He tried hard to regain the rhythm of his life now he no longer suffered disturbed nights by being called to administer absolution to those who had been fatally wounded or to spend long hours trying to bring a little comfort to the bereaved. He felt a prick of annoyance when his early morning devotions were interrupted by a hammering on the church door and a boy, panting hard, asked him to go to the hospital.

'Been an accident. They want you.'

Andreas gathered up his robes and hurried along the streets to the hospital in the wake of the youth. He walked into the ward, trying hard to still his thumping heart and regain his breath. One look at the young soldier told Andreas he was too late and he fell to his knees. The doctor waited politely until he rose.

'Who is he?' asked Andreas.

'I've no idea. He was hit by a lorry I should think. Picked up on the Heraklion road. Going home, I imagine. Maybe there's something on him.'

Methodically the doctor turned out the young man's pockets. His wallet contained a few notes along with some photographs, the subjects being total strangers to both men, and his official discharge paper.

Andreas took it from the doctor. 'At least there is somewhere we can write. I'll copy down the address, then you can send this with the rest of his belongings.'

Andreas looked again at the discharge paper. It was signed by Stelios Christoforakis in Athens. He sucked in his breath. It was possible, just possible that this man was his cousin. It would be worth a letter to him to find out.

Stelios read the letter from Father Andreas in annoyance. The death of the soldier was no concern of his. He wrote the customary words, asking for his condolences to be passed on to the man's family. He said they had a son of whom they could be proud, although he had no idea of the man's record. As far as he was concerned that was the end of the matter.

To receive another letter from the priest in Heraklion at first surprised and then angered him. He should have ignored the first letter. Now he sat at his desk, biting the end of his pen and wondering what he could say that would put an end to the correspondence.

Dear Andreas,

You are correct in your assumption that I am your cousin. I have been far too busy during the war to correspond with anyone. There was also a question of security, which I am sure you will understand.

I see little point in writing to Plaka, as there is only Anna who might be competent enough to write back. I have recently married and have no leave due to enable me to pay them a visit.

Please pass on my good wishes.

Stelios

Andreas read the letter in disgust. He would have to tell his aunt that her youngest son was alive and he would elaborate a little about the security Stelios mentioned to explain his lack of concern for them.

Maria was delighted with the news. 'Maybe he can come and see us next year. He could bring his wife with him. We should meet her. She's one of the family now.'

Anna looked at her cousin steadily. 'He won't come, will he, Andreas? He doesn't want to know us.'

Andreas felt uncomfortable. 'We'll have to wait and see. He's in the army, bound by rigid discipline. When everything is back to normal he'll probably be able to pay us a visit.'

Anna pursed her lips and shook her head. 'Are you going to write back to him?'

'I shall reply. I can't force Stelios to do the same.'

Andreas spent a week writing a letter to his cousin. He said how delighted Maria had been with the news that Stelios was fit and well and hoped he and his wife would be able to visit them. Andreas added that in view of Maria's age and state of health Stelios should seriously consider a visit before it was too late. He told his cousin about the death of his father during his enforced labour in the mines, and how many on Spinalonga died from starvation, but that his brother, Yannis, was still alive. He extolled Anna's virtues, looking after her mother devotedly and bringing up Maria's children.

He said that Marisa had become a beautiful young woman and what a fine young man Yannis had turned into. How hard the boy had worked on the farm during the war, only to be disappointed that his father had not returned to compliment him. He described how his parents had decided to follow Annita to America, that she now had four children and none of them had any intention of returning to Crete. Finally, unable to think of anything more he sealed the letter and took it to the post office.

Anna visited Yannis each week and she passed on the news from Andreas regarding Stelios.

'It's a shame he didn't decide to become a doctor,' said Yannis. 'I might have managed to get some answers from him.'

'What do you mean?'

'There's a new drug available; it's described as a cure for leprosy. I've asked Doctor Stavros for it but he says it's not being used in Greece. I'm writing to the government and demanding they give it to us. If Stelios had been a doctor he might have been able to help.'

'Do you mean that, Yannis?'

'Of course, if Stelios hadn't…'

'No, I mean about a new treatment. Tell me about it.'

'I'll read you my letter to the government,' Yannis picked up the closely written pages, 'then you'll understand.'

Anna thought it most unlikely she would understand, but she was willing to sit and listen if it would please her brother. 'Why don't you write and ask Annita about it?' she suggested. 'She should know.'

Annita opened the letter from her brother. It was considerably thicker than usual, then she saw the pages, covered in small, spidery writing and realised it was from Yannis. She read it curiously. According to Yannis the government were refusing them the new drugs that might be able to alleviate their suffering. Indignation rose in her. After all the hard work Elias had put in to develop them!

She showed the letter to Elias, who pushed his glasses up on his forehead.

'What do you expect me to do? I have no influence with the Greek government.'

'He's not asking you to confront the Government. He's asking if you can send him the results of the tests and experiments that you've had published over here. He could send those on to the medical authorities. They'd have to take notice of him then.'

'He wouldn't be able to understand them, and I doubt if anyone in the government would either. They've been published in English.'

'I could translate them into Greek for him,' offered Annita.

Elias smiled at her. 'It would be a massive work.'

'I don't mind. I could work on it in the evenings when the children are in bed.'

'We'll work together as we always have. I'll find the relevant articles and you can translate, but I warn you, it will take months.'

As Annita smiled at her husband she remembered Father Lambros's words to her. "One day Yannis will thank you from the bottom of his heart."

Daphne looked around the two rooms she and her husband had rented. She could hardly wait until they moved into the larger appartment that Stelios had found. It would be so good not to have to queue outside a bathroom that was shared between two apartments, but have their own. Maybe it was their cramped surroundings that was troubling Stelios.

She picked up his jacket that he had discarded carelessly on a chair and smoothed out the creases. There was a bulge in the pocket and she pulled out the soiled handkerchief, a letter fluttering out with it, the pages scattering across the floor. As she collected them together the name at the end caught her eye. "*Your cousin, Andreas.*"

Daphne frowned. Her husband of a few months had told her he had no relatives. A cousin counted as a relative, a cousin was almost as close as a brother. Maybe it was an old letter that he carried with him from sentiment. She looked for a date and in doing so read the first line.

Your mother was so delighted when I told her you were safe and well and recently married.

Daphne bit her lip. The letter was obviously not an old one. Her curiosity overcoming her she began to read and when she had finished she sat with the pages in her hand. How could she tell her husband that she knew he had a family?

From his position by the Venetian walls Yannis watched the small procession wending its way up to the cemetery, thankful that he had managed to reach the farmhouse and see his mother for the last time. He touched the charm she had given to him to ward off evil when he first went to Heraklion. She had been so proud of him and he had loved her dearly. With tears in his eyes he made his way down to the church to seek comfort from Father Minos.

Anna found the void left by the death of her mother almost intolerable after all the years she had cared for her. Yiorgo and Yannis would disappear off to the fields each day, leaving her and Marisa with plenty of time to cope with cooking and cleaning. She expanded the vegetable patch and tried to cultivate the wild herbs she had previously gathered from the hills, pleased that most of them seemed to be thriving in their new habitat.

Letters arrived regularly to Marisa from Victor and he declared his undying love for her. He described his life in Turin, how he had found his family after the war, and how difficult it had been to find any employment. He had finally decided he would attend college and become an engineer. The course would take him three years to complete and then he would return to Marisa. She would have to be patient, but by then she would be old enough to marry without her uncle's permission.

Yiorgo had suggested a number of young men whom he thought might make a suitable husband for her, but Marisa was adamant. 'I marry Victor or no one,' she declared. 'I don't care if you send me to Leros. I'll stay there until my dying day, but I'll not agree to marry a man I don't care for.'

To her surprise her aunt seemed to agree with her. 'I wish it wasn't Victor you're so enamoured of. It would be much easier if you could meet a Cretan.'

'You won't let uncle Yiorgo make me get married, will you?' Marisa had turned distressed eyes to her aunt. 'If he tries to betroth me to anyone I'll run away.'

Anna shook her head. 'You'll not be forced. It wouldn't be right to marry a man you didn't love. It wouldn't be right for you to run away either,' she added grimly.

Marisa regarded her aunt curiously. 'Why haven't you got married, Mamma Anna?'

Anna gave a half smile. 'Maybe I haven't met the right man. I've always been busy looking after everything here.'

Marisa would sit and chatter to her about the news that Victor had sent from Italy in his frequent letters, whilst they sat and sewed together, but to Anna it was trivial and inconsequential. Of Michael she had heard nothing and her heart ached with longing each time she buried her face in his shirt before carefully refolding it and placing it back amongst her clothes.

She began to visit Yannis twice each week to fill her time, listening to him as he railed against the government for their lack of action on the part of the inhabitants of Spinalonga.

Andreas read the letter he had received from Stelios and shook his head. It was curt to the point of rudeness. Did the young man have no feelings?

Thank you for advising me of my mother's death. I'm sure it is a relief to Anna to no longer be burdened with her care.

The share of the money you sent to me will be very useful as our first child has just been born.

Yannis waited in a fever of impatience for an answer to his letter to Annita, expecting a reply immediately with the information he had requested. He was quite unprepared for the parcel that finally arrived for him, full of newspaper cuttings, reports and medical papers written by Elias. He sorted them methodically and read the translation of each article carefully, discarding some that appeared repetitive; until he decided he had as much relevant material as possible to place before the medical authorities. It was with a feeling of triumph that Yannis finally sealed the envelope and sat back to await the answer.

'They'll have to do something now,' he announced to Spiro.

Finally a specialist from Heraklion arrived to take tests from everyone and the results from those would depend whether the sufferers were suitable candidates for the new treatment. To Yannis's surprise the doctor was his friend Nikos, who had been a fellow student at the High School in Heraklion. He was disgusted when Nikos returned to say the first results had been inconclusive and the procedure would have to be repeated.

Now, after a third series of tests and still not having heard the results, despite writing continually to the government, Yannis was losing patience. He wrote to Andreas, pleading with him to investigate the delay. Andreas was evasive and Father Minos kept telling him he must be patient. He was determined to take action. He made the hazardous journey across the stretch of water to his village and confronted his brother, finally persuading him to go to Aghios Nikolaos to purchase a motorbike. Despite his misgivings Yiorgo carried out his brother's errand and had watched in trepidation as Yannis sped off down the road towards Heraklion.

A week later Yannis parked the motorbike in the yard and entered by the kitchen door. Anna was making pastry and looked up timidly as he came in. 'What was that awful noise?'

'The motor bike,' Yannis smiled. 'Aren't you pleased to see me?'

'Of course I am. Were you successful?'

'Partly. I have hopes, anyway. Finish doing that, then sit and listen to me,' Yannis ordered.

Anna covered her dough and began to heat the water for coffee. 'Do you want me to fetch Yiorgo before you start?'

'No, I'll tell him later. If I keep saying it enough times I might finally believe it myself.' Yannis leaned forward. 'Anna, I haven't got leprosy any more.'

Incredulity and disbelief were written all over Anna's face as she looked at the white nodules on her brother's skin and his misshapen hands. 'But, Yannis, you have, you can see you have.'

'I'm burnt out now,' announced Yannis proudly.

Anna frowned, trying hard to come to terms with the news. 'What do you mean? I don't understand. Have you had the new treatment?'

Yannis shook his head. 'It's nothing to do with the treatment. I don't know how, but over the years the leprosy has stopped. It's not getting any worse. That's why Athens kept asking for more tests. They didn't believe it any more than I did when Andreas first told me.'

'Andreas told you? How did he know?'

'He'd been told by Nikos, the doctor.'

'Oh, Yannis – and he didn't tell you before!'

'I understand now, Anna. He knew I would tell everyone they were no longer lepers and you can imagine what could happen then.'

Anna shook her head.

'They'd all want to go running off to their families and there would be terrible problems. They'd be arrested, their families might not want them, they might not even find their families and then what would happen to them – they'd be beggars. Andreas pointed all that out to me. I would never have thought of it.'

'So what is going to happen to you all?'

For the first time Yannis began to look doubtful. 'I'm not sure yet. I went to a council meeting with Andreas. That surprised them, I can tell you. I think between us we managed to convince them that I was serious in my demands for decent treatment.'

'They won't take you back to the hospital in Athens?' asked Anna fearfully.

'I shouldn't think so. I've asked for treatment for those who are still sick and freedom to move around as we please for the rest of us. Nikos has even promised to help us fight for our rights and is going to petition the government for us to have visitors. I went to his house last night for a meal and met his wife and children.' Yannis's face lit up with a smile. 'For the first time in years I feel like an ordinary person.' He frowned. 'I thought you'd be pleased, but you don't seem very happy about it.'

Anna sighed. 'Of course I am. I'm just worried about Marisa. She's determined to get married to Victor, the Italian soldier who was billeted here. She asked me if they could get married before he left and I told her it was out of the question. I thought once he'd gone home they would forget about each other, but they've been writing regularly and now he's coming over next week. She says if we won't let her get married she'll run away with him.'

Yannis frowned. 'What's he like, apart from Italian and a soldier?'

'He's no longer in the army, he's an engineer. He seemed to be pleasant enough when he was over here. In fact,' Anna lowered her eyes, 'He helped me get a sick resistance man to the hospital. He could easily have turned me over to the Germans or shot me out of hand.'

Yannis looked at his sister in admiration. 'You never told me about this.'

Anna shrugged. 'It was a long time ago.'

'So tell me.'

'There's not much to tell. There was an Englishman up in the hills, he was organising resistance locally and he was taken ill with a bad appendix. I took him into Aghios Nikolaos in the cart and bumped into Victor at a check point.'

'Go on.'

'I pretended he was my husband, Babbis, but of course Victor knew he wasn't. He tried to find out later who he was, but I never told him.'

'And what happened to the Englishman?'

A spasm of pain crossed Anna's face. 'The operation was successful. He went back to England before the war finished.'

'It was very brave of you.'

'Everyone helped. Yannis took food up to a wounded man until I found him and managed to get the doctor. He used to tell the resistance which Italians were going into Aghios Nikolaos for the evening. He even took the Germans on a wild goose chase up in the hills so that Michael's men could try to catch the German commander.'

'Michael?'

'The English man.' Anna's face flamed.

Yannis pretended not to notice. 'Did Marisa help?'

'She never told Victor what we were up to, but she knew. One time Doctor Stavros and I came back with our boots covered in sheep droppings and we weren't supposed to have left the house.'

'This Victor sounds a bit of a simpleton if you were able to do things under his nose,' frowned Yannis.

Anna shook her head. 'I don't think he's at all simple. He was kind and hated being a soldier. We could never have kept the farm going without his help. He managed to get a few supplies over to you when he thought it was safe to do so and as soon as the war ended he ordered his men to take supplies over every day.'

'It sounds as though he saved my life! How old is he?'

'Twenty four.'

Yannis placed an arm round his sister's waist. 'Don't worry, Anna. I'll have a chat with her when she comes in.'

Anna looked at her brother suspiciously. 'You're not to encourage her.'

Yannis sat out in the yard with Marisa in the last of the sunlight and quizzed her thoroughly. At first she answered sulkily, telling him she was no longer a child to be told what she could and could not do, then she gradually unbent.

'He was so kind, uncle Yannis. He knew Mamma Anna and Yannis were helping the resistance, but he just pretended not to notice. He would have been in trouble had the Germans found out that he helped us on the farm. He made the other soldiers help the villagers so they wouldn't accuse Mamma Anna of being too friendly with them and having problems when they left.' Marisa smiled at the memory of Mario trying to persuade the donkey to walk for him.

'He felt terrible about you being on the island and no food getting to you. He used to give his field glasses to Mamma Anna so she could see you when you waved. He would have liked to visit you, but even he was in awe of the German Commander, and couldn't be sure that one of his men wouldn't report him. Did you know they were supposed to shoot us if we disobeyed them? They never did, of course, Victor was in charge and he wouldn't let the soldiers hurt anyone. All he really wanted was to go back to his family in Italy. I liked him when he first came. He wasn't terribly polite because he didn't know much Greek. I helped him and now he speaks and writes quite good Greek,' she ended proudly.

Yannis nodded sombrely. 'I wish he were a local man. You may not be happy living in Italy, you don't speak the language and you'll be too far away to run home.'

'Victor has been teaching me Italian in his letters. I won't be unhappy,' smiled Marisa. 'Not with Victor.'

The first time Marisa visited Spinalonga in the company of her aunt she looked around fascinated. 'It looks little different from the village,' she remarked.

'Why should it?' asked Yannis. 'When the Turks were here they built a village. We just took over what they had left behind and repaired it.' Yannis made light of the appalling conditions they had encountered when they had first arrived. 'Now, tell me of the plans you have made with Victor.'

'We plan to get married in September. Mamma Anna still doesn't really approve, but I can always come back. Uncle Yiorgo has given me my share of Grandpa's money. I'm very rich.'

'Does Victor know about that?' asked Yannis sharply.

'No, not yet.'

Yannis nodded. 'Then he can't be accused of marrying you for your money. If I were you I'd keep quiet about it.'

'Victor wouldn't take it away from me.'

'I'm sure he wouldn't steal it from you, but he could ask for a loan, and then be unable to pay it back. Put it into a bank, Marisa, and forget about it for a few years. You'll be surprised how quickly it grows, then you'll have something for your old age.'

'I'll bring Victor over as soon as he arrives,' promised Marisa. 'I'm sure you'll like him.'

Victor sat comfortably in Yannis's house and talked about his life in Italy. Yannis listened, impressed by the young man his niece had insisted on marrying.

Yannis sighed. 'I wish you were a local man for her aunt's sake.'

'Aunt Anna bravest lady I ever meet. She help resistance. I know why she go to the hills so much, very brave.' Victor twisted his fingers. 'I say nothing. Pretend not to know.'

'Anna told me you were responsible for the sacks of vegetables we found on the jetty occasionally. We were very grateful, they probably saved some of us from starvation.'

Victor nodded. 'I have respect for you. I want to help in war, but we shot if disobey orders. I be careful, pretend to look for resistance on island. I do not like war. I am sick when people scream.'

'You feel ashamed of yourself for feeling like that?'

'No, not a man.' Victor smiled sheepishly.

'You've no need. I was sick when I had to help the doctor operate. He had very little morphine and we had to hold Flora down.'

'I never do that.' Victor spoke emphatically. He turned as Marisa opened the door, followed by Father Minos.

'Father Minos has suggested we have another wedding ceremony over here. That way Uncle Yannis can come.' She looked at Victor, her eyes glowing and a flush of happiness in her cheeks. 'I think it is a wonderful idea.'

'And wedding party?' asked Victor.

'We could have that over here, too, couldn't we Uncle? We can bring everything over in the boats and set it out in the square during the morning.'

Yannis smiled at her enthusiasm. 'You may find that some of your guests don't wish to come over here.'

Marisa tilted her chin defiantly. 'I don't care. If they're not prepared to come over here I don't want them at my wedding.'

Yannis exchanged glances with Victor. 'She is used to having her own way,' Yannis warned him.

'Not always with Victor,' the young man assured him, whilst Marisa whispered 'Ten bambinos' in his ear and they hugged each other.

Anna sat between Yiorgo and Yannis watching happily as the men danced and the women handed around the sweets and savouries they had spent many long hours baking.

'I could hardly believe it when Marisa said she wanted to get married over here as well as at Plaka, and then have her wedding feast over here. I never thought the villagers would come.'

Yannis smiled at her. 'I think they've begun to realise that we're not ogres and demons. I only hope that some of them will continue to visit us. It can get pretty boring with the same old faces and limited space.'

'I found that when I was fighting. I felt crowded the whole time, never able to get away on my own into the fields and the hills. I've decided that I prefer my own company.' Yiorgo looked guiltily at Anna. 'I appreciate coming home in the evening and having a chat, but I'd hate to find myself face to face with someone all day long.'

'When you meet the right woman you'll change your mind,' Yannis assured him. 'How's the farm doing?'

'We're just about back on our feet. Yannis and I are able to manage on our own now.'

'Is Yannis happy as a farmer?'

'He's never said he wanted to be anything else. I suggested going on to High School to him and he laughed at me. Said he'd had enough of books and learning.'

'Silly boy; no learning is ever wasted. Is he slow?'

Yiorgo shook his head. 'Certainly not. I leave all the accounts to him nowadays. He's much quicker at figures than I am.'

'What about banking?' suggested Yannis.

'I don't think he'd want to be shut away in an office all day any more than I would. He's all right, Yannis. Don't worry over him, besides, he's got a girl. Hadn't you noticed?'

Yannis looked around for his nephew. 'Where is he?'

'Probably found a quiet corner to be alone with her. He won't have gone far. She's a nice little thing. Grand-daughter of Danniakis.'

'What do you think of her, Anna?'

'She'll do. She's a good girl. Been brought up properly and will make a good wife.'

They lapsed into silence, each occupied by their own thoughts until Yannis pulled Yiorgo to his feet.

'Come on, we should be dancing. Marisa will think we're not enjoying ourselves.'

'I haven't danced in a long time,' protested Yiorgo.

'Then you should. We dance regularly over here. Don't look at me like that. Why shouldn't we enjoy ourselves?'

'I just can't imagine it, that's all.'

'Look around you.'

Yiorgo did, and watched with mixed feelings as cripples were dancing arm in arm with healthy villagers, whilst those who had lost their limbs were clapping or banging rhythmically. He felt strangely sad at the macabre scene and drained his glass.

'I'd better find Yannis,' he said by way of an excuse, and pushed his way through the bystanders to the quietness that lay beyond.

Despite the festivities Victor managed to draw Anna to one side. He kissed her affectionately and held her hand.

'I thank you, Aunt Anna. You were like mother to us when we live with you. Cheese and spinach pie. Never I forget that.'

Anna wagged a finger at him. 'Now I know why you have married Marisa. Cheese and spinach pie!'

Victor smiled at her. 'Always I love Marisa without pie. Aunt Anna, two things I want ask.'

'Yes?'

'You not be cross?'

Anna smiled happily at her new nephew. 'Why should I be cross?'

Victor shrugged. 'Marisa and me, I, me, we want you come to Turino. See us happy. See Italy. Maybe bambino next year. Come and see.'

'Oh, Victor. I don't know about that. I've never been further than Aghios Nikolaos in my life.'

'You come. Marisa want. I know.'

'Maybe, Victor. I'll think about it.'

'And Aunt Anna, who man in cart?'

Anna's face whitened and her hand went involuntarily to her throat. 'That's long forgotten, Victor.'

Victor shook his head. 'Always I want to know. Man like German soldier come to you and he man in cart. You cry very much when he go.'

Despite her resolve Anna felt the tears come into her eyes. 'I suppose you have a right to know. You helped to save his life.' Anna looked at Victor fearlessly. 'He was an English resistance worker. He was ill with his appendix and I had to get him to the hospital. He came back wearing a German uniform so he could say thank you and goodbye.'

'Is true?'

'Quite true. I have nothing to gain by lying to you.'

Victor slapped his thigh and laughed. 'I thought he Marisa's pappa. I know you help. I know you go to hills. My men say 'we search hills', I say 'no people there, waste time.'

Anna smiled with him.

'Why you say he husband?'

'I thought it would be easier to get through. I had my sister's papers, so I used them.'

'Very dangerous, Aunt Anna.'

'I thought you might shoot me.'

'Never shoot you, Aunt Anna. He come back now?'

'Now? Why should he?'

'For Aunt Anna.'

Anna felt herself blushing.

'Aunt Anna risk very much for friend. Aunt Anna love friend very much.'

Anna heard her voice breaking. 'Don't be silly, Victor. I hardly knew him.'

For a moment Victor gazed at her mockingly, then raised her hand to his lips. 'I hope Aunt Anna always my friend.'

'Oh, Victor, you are silly.' Anna was really crying now and Victor handed her his handkerchief.

'Everyone always cry at wedding,' he assured her.

1950 – 1954

Anna began to spend more and more time over on the island with her brother. She found the life over there more companionable than in her own village and said as much to Yannis.

'It's not a real life, Anna. You can decide to go to Aghios Nikolaos tomorrow if you want and no one will stop you. I can't.'

'I've only been to the town a couple of times. I didn't enjoy it.'

'That's because you didn't know where to go. Annita and I used to walk to the top of the hill and look down at the pool. You could see all of Aghios Nikolaos from there.'

'Yiorgo went in last week on your motorbike. He says they've built a lot of new houses, apartments he called them, so I suppose they're like the ones you have over here.'

Yannis wrinkled his sunken nose. 'I'd rather live in a house. I like to be able to shut my door.'

'You can in an apartment.'

'It's not the same.'

'I had a letter from Marisa two days ago. She's living in an apartment, although they hope to have a house eventually. She sent me a picture of it. She seems happy enough there.'

Yannis gazed at the featureless building. 'She's only happy there because Victor's with her.'

'You think it was right for her to marry him, then?'

'Time will tell, but I believe that he truly loves her.'

'That's obvious. She can twist him round her little finger,'

Anna agreed readily. 'I do like him, but Yiorgo still feels she should have married a Greek.'

Yannis shrugged. 'Words of wisdom from a confirmed bachelor.'

'He's like Pappa was, a born farmer.'

'Even farmers get married. Pappa did.'

'Maybe he's waiting for the right girl to come along.'

'Well if he waits much longer he won't have much fun when she does come. What about you, Anna? It's time you thought of yourself.'

'I'm happy enough. I miss Marisa and mamma, but ...' Anna shrugged.

'I thought, maybe, if Babbis had come back, you and he...?'

'No,' Anna shook her head sadly. 'He wanted to marry me to give his children a mother, but he only ever truly loved Maria and I was not in love with him.'

'Why don't you go and visit Marisa? Maybe Victor has a handsome uncle.'

'I've never wanted to get married.'

'Never?' Yannis was surprised as the colour rose to Anna's face.

'Girlish thoughts, never anything serious.'

'What was his name?' persisted Yannis.

'I've told you, there was no one,' Anna snapped.

'I think there was.'

'Mind your own business, Yannis.' Anna rose to her feet. 'I ought to be going. Davros will be ready to go back.'

'Oh, Anna, I'm sorry. I was only teasing.'

'I know, but I don't like to be teased.'

Yannis put an arm round his sister. 'Actually, I'm glad you're not married. If you were you wouldn't have time to come over here to see me.'

Yiorgo watched the two men as they measured and wrote down their findings. That was enough. They were moving further and further onto his land.

'Hey, what do you think you're doing? Get off my farm.'

Instead of retreating to the cart track as he had expected they walked towards him.

'Mr Christoforakis?'

'Yes.'

'We're from the government.'

Yiorgo waited. Being from the government did not give them the right to trample across his land.

'Maybe there is somewhere we could talk?'

'My sister's out,' he announced, using the excuse not to take them to the farmhouse.

The older man spread a map of the area on the ground, a smaller one beside it. 'This is Aghios Nikolaos, Olous, Elounda and Plaka.' The man pointed to the four places. 'Up here,' he indicated a wavy red line, 'is the road to Heraklion, down there to Neapolis. There is your farm.'

Yiorgo said nothing. The lines meant nothing to him.

'Now this map,' he placed the smaller map onto the larger, 'shows the extent of your lands. The government would like to buy some of that land from you.'

Yiorgo shook his head.

'It's my land.'

'Yes, Mr Christoforakis, we know it is your land. Have you been to Elounda recently?'

Yiorgo nodded.

'Then you know the government is constructing a road, a road with a hard surface, from Aghios Nikolaos to Elounda.' He traced the line on the larger map. 'The government plans to extend the road along to Plaka.'

'We've got a road.'

'You have a cart track, Mr Christoforakis. When it rains you have a mud track. No vehicle could get along here.'

Yiorgo was thoroughly puzzled. 'Why would they want to?'

'Maybe I'd better start at the beginning,' the man smiled

showing yellowing teeth. He took a packet of cigarettes from his pocket and offered one to Yiorgo.

'Now, since the war, events have moved much faster in Crete than they used to. Everywhere there is construction. Crete wishes to expand her industry and improve the living conditions of her people. More goods will be coming into this country and they will have to be moved to the towns. To move them there will be lorries and a lorry needs a road, not a cart track.'

Yiorgo shrugged. 'We don't need lorry loads of goods here. There's only a few houses and we can go to Elounda.'

'I agree, but we are not thinking just of the people who live in Plaka. Look at the map for a moment, see the road from Heraklion.'

He pointed with a finger stained with nicotine. 'The road goes to Aghios Nikolaos, then has to travel along the coast until we reach Plaka. Think how much quicker and easier it would be if there was a road here.' He indicated the space on the map between the main road and Yiorgo's farm. 'The goods destined for Plaka, Elounda, and Olous could be brought directly over the hill. It would save considerable time and money.'

'And you think I'm going to give you my farm!' Yiorgo shook his head. 'You put your precious road somewhere else.'

'No, no, we do not expect you to give up your farm. The government wishes to buy a small amount of your land. Just enough to build the road. The rest would still belong to you.'

'How much?'

'The land involved,' the man took a pencil from behind his ear and drew on the map, 'would be no more than that. Possibly a little less when the construction was completed.'

Yiorgo looked at the strip that was indicated and shook his head. 'My sheep run there. What would happen to them?'

'The government would fence the road on both sides. There would be no danger to your sheep.'

'I'd have to move them back and forth across the road. No, I'll keep my land.'

'Mr Christoforakis, I have to tell you that this road will be built.'

'Not on my land.'

Slowly the man nodded. 'The government is offering to buy the land it needs, but should you refuse they will simply take the land away from you and give you compensation. You really do not have a choice Mr Christoforakis.'

Yiorgo's face suffused with a dull red. 'Get off my land.' He rose to his feet. 'And if you know what's good for you don't come back.'

'Now, please, listen to reason. Many small farmers have had to relinquish a little of their land. They have all profited by the sale. Think what you could do with the money.'

'Money! I don't need your money. I don't need anyone's money. Go away. Get off my land before I take my shot gun to you.'

The man rolled up the maps with deliberate calm. 'We'll be back, Mr Christoforakis. We'll be back.'

Yiorgo looked after the two men. He was visibly shaken. Could they really take his land if he did not agree to sell? It was his. His father had always said he would have the farm. He walked down to the farmhouse and poured himself a generous measure of brandy, despite the early hour. He would have to think about this.

Anna was surprised when she returned from Spinalonga to see her brother sitting with a half empty bottle of brandy before him.

She crossed herself rapidly. 'What's happened? Is it Yannis?'

Yiorgo shook his head. 'They want to take my land. My land! It's criminal, that's what it is, criminal.'

Discreetly Anna removed the bottle from his reach. 'Who wants to take your land?'

'The government. They want to take my land and build a road. What good is a road? You can't grow crops or run sheep on a road.'

'They're building a road at Elounda.'

'That's what they said. All the way along they're going to build it and up the hill – across my land.'

Anna frowned. 'Surely they can't do that if you don't let them?'

Yiorgo banged his fist on the table. 'They say they'll buy the land from me, but if I refuse to sell they'll take it. It's my land,' he repeated stubbornly.

'Maybe Yannis will know something about it,' suggested Anna.

'What will he know! He's only a boy.' Yiorgo stalked out of the kitchen and slammed the door behind him.

Yannis returned to Plaka feeling very pleased with himself. Now all he had to do was persuade his uncle to let him have the money. He was quite unprepared for the scene that met his eyes when he walked into the kitchen. Yiorgo had returned to finish the bottle of brandy and Anna was desperately trying to persuade him to eat some food.

'What's wrong?'

Anna wrung her hands. 'They want to take your uncle's land.'

'Who does?'

'The government.'

'What for?'

'A road.'

'But the cart track doesn't belong to him.'

'They want to make a road over the hill.'

Yannis nodded. 'How much do they want and how much are they willing to pay?'

'I don't know. I wasn't here.'

Yannis looked at his uncle for enlightenment, but none was forthcoming. 'Maybe we could talk about it after supper,' Yannis said pointedly, and Anna hurried to put a plate of food before her nephew.

Yannis mopped his plate with his bread and decided it would not be the right time to put his own plans before his uncle. The man was not drunk, but would certainly not be in a receptive frame of mind. He looked at his aunt. She had no idea of finance or business affairs, but maybe if he could convince her his idea was sound she could influence his uncle. He waited until Yiorgo had left the house to spend the remainder of the evening at the taverna, where he would doubtless continue to complain vociferously to all who would listen to him.

'Mamma Anna,' he began tentatively. 'I went into Aghios Nikolaos again today.'

'I don't know what you find so attractive about the place.' She glanced at him sharply. 'Does Ourania know?'

Yannis smiled at her easily. 'I'm not going for the girls. I went in to talk to a man at the bank.'

'What for?' A bank held a great mystery for Anna. Her nephew had been quite unable to convince either her or Yiorgo that money in a bank could make more money.

'Well, it's partly to do with this road. That's why I didn't think it a good idea to talk to uncle Yiorgo tonight. You see, the government is planning to build a road, a proper road, all the way from Aghios Nikolaos to Plaka. I didn't know about the one over the hill, but I think it's a good idea.'

He held up his hand, as Anna was about to repeat that the land belonged to Yiorgo. 'I'll tell you why. If there's a proper road people will use it. In Aghios Nikolaos people are coming from other countries. Most of them want to see Knossos and then they travel down to Aghios Nikolaos because they've been told it's a pretty town and the site of Gournia is only a few kilometres further on. The bus goes four times every day to Heraklion now. The man at the bank told me that now is the time to buy land. There's a lot of land available because the widows of those who didn't come back from the war can't farm it. They're glad to sell and have the money.'

'But what would you do with it? Run more sheep?' Anna was not really following her nephew's reasoning.

'Maybe; for a while. Don't you see, Mamma Anna, if they

want some of uncle's land to build a road, they're going to want other people's land to do the same. Land is cheap now. People who can't farm it are willing to sell, but in a few years time they won't be. Then the price of land will go up. If uncle lets me have grandpa's money now I could buy a thousand square metres, that's a hundred times bigger than this farm, and I know that when I sold it I would make a profit.'

'But what would you do with the money? You'll have the farm when Yiorgo goes.' Anna crossed herself against the evil thought.

'I hope it will be a long time before uncle Yiorgo leaves us, but I'm a man now. I'm planning to marry Ourania and I want to give her a good life. I don't want her to have to work in the fields as you have or grandmother did. Do you know, in Aghios Nikolaos, they don't have to use the yard? They have a proper room inside the house.'

Anna wrinkled her nose. 'That would be a breeding ground for disease.'

Yannis smiled at her. 'No, each time you use the pan in there you pull a handle and water washes it away. There's no smell, well, not as much as in the yard. They don't have to go out to a pump to get their water. They turn a tap and water comes out. That's what I want for Ourania.'

'So you'll go and live in Aghios Nikolaos?'

'No, Mamma Anna, not yet. I want to build her a house where she can have all these things. It takes a lot of money, more than grandpa left me, but if I bought some land and then sold it, I would soon have enough.'

'Have you talked to Ourania about this?'

Yannis shook his head. 'I have to talk to uncle Yiorgo first. Do you think it's a good idea, Mamma Anna?'

'I don't know,' replied Anna doubtfully. 'I don't know about these things.'

'Please talk to uncle. He listens to you.'

'It's men's business.'

'But I don't have any other men to talk to. I only have you.'

Anna felt her heart go out to the orphaned boy. 'I'll see, Yannis, I'll think about it.'

Anna repeated her nephew's conversation to Yannis and the news of the proposed road the next time she visited the island. Yannis shook his head.

'I can't advise you, Anna. Nothing you did on the mainland would make any difference to us. I can understand Yannis's reasoning, he has a good head on his shoulders, and if the man at the bank feels it would be a good investment then he should take his advice. I just wish you and Yiorgo would put your money in the bank. If you'd done so originally it would be nearly doubled by now.'

'I don't see why the bank should give us money.'

'It's called investment, Anna. You lend the bank your money and they give you a drachma for each hundred you lend them.'

Anna shook her head. 'If they only give you a drachma for each hundred you must be losing money.'

'They don't take your money away from you.'

'I don't understand it, Yannis. It's better it stays in the cupboard. It's safe there.'

Yannis sighed in exasperation. 'I just wish I could convince you. Has Yiorgo decided to sell to the government?'

'He says he won't sell. He and Yannis have been arguing all week. Yannis says he should ask more money for the land than they are offering and Yiorgo insists they can't have it at any price.'

'He'll have to give way eventually. If they're determined to run the road through they won't let Yiorgo stop them. I asked Lambros, he used to be a lawyer, and he said they could use 'compulsory purchase' if the owner refuses to sell. Then they pay him a rock bottom price, less than the market value.'

'But it belongs to Yiorgo,' persisted Anna.

'That makes no difference, Anna, not to the government. I think he ought to go to Aghios Nikolaos and see a lawyer.'

Anna looked at her brother doubtfully. 'Would that make any difference?'

'Not to the final outcome, but Yiorgo would know what he could and couldn't do. Whether he sells voluntarily or waits for compulsory purchase he'll have to use a lawyer eventually. He might just as well take his advice in the first place.'

Much to Anna's surprise, Yiorgo did agree to see a lawyer; even more amazing to her was his insistence that she accompanied him.

'Why do you want me to come? It's men's business.'

'It might be men's business, Anna, but it's your farm too. I know Pappa said it was for me, but that was when he thought you'd get married like Maria. I work on the farm and you look after me. We'd neither of us be able to manage without the other so it's only right that you come along to hear what's said.'

Meekly Anna agreed, wondering how long they would be gone. Timidly she asked Yiorgo if she should take her nightgown and he gave her a withering look.

'I can't think what for. We'll go on the motorbike. You can ride on the back and we'll be there in no time.'

Anna's face blanched, but she did not argue. Whenever she saw either Yiorgo or Yannis astride the unwieldy, noisy machine she crossed herself. She had never ridden on it, and now she was expected to ride to Aghios Nikolaos.

Sitting side-saddle, as if riding a donkey, Anna sat rigidly on the machine, gripping her brother tightly, as they bumped over the ruts of the cart track. The dust blew into her eyes, nose and mouth, whilst the wind generated by their speed made her ears ache. At Elounda she begged Yiorgo to stop and he eased his foot off the throttle.

'What's wrong?'

'I can't breathe.'

'Pull your scarf over your mouth,' he answered, and continued unconcernedly on their way.

Just before Olous they lurched from the rutted cart track onto the smooth surface of the new tarmac road and Anna began to find the journey a little easier. She looked in awe at the monster machines that spewed out the raw materials that the men spread across the ground nonchalantly. It seemed incredible to her that the hot, black, sticky, mess could turn into something hard and smooth.

Feeling dirty, hot and stiff, she stood and watched whilst Yiorgo propped the unwieldy motorbike against the wall of a building. He ran his fingers through his hair and wiped them down the sides of his trousers.

'Upstairs,' he announced and proceeded to lead the way.

The flight of stone steps gave way to a small landing and Yiorgo peered at the names on the doors anxiously. 'Must be further up,' he muttered, hoping he had remembered Yannis's directions.

Another flight of steps and more anxious peering revealed to him the name he sought and he pushed open the door. Inside a small room sat a young man at a desk who looked up curiously at their entry.

'I've come to see Mr Standakis.'

'Do you have an appointment, sir?'

'Appointment?'

'It is usual for people to make an appointment. Mr Standakis is a very busy man.'

'And so am I,' answered Yiorgo.

'I don't think Mr Standakis has any free appointments for today, sir.'

Yiorgo sat down on a chair in front of the desk. 'I've come from Plaka to see Mr Standakis and I'm not going back until I've seen him.' He folded his arms and waited.

The clerk eyed him doubtfully. 'Mr Standakis never sees anyone without an appointment.'

'Then I suggest you ask him to make one for me now.'

'Maybe tomorrow, if you'd...'

'I want an appointment now.'

'But, sir...'

'Now!' Yiorgo's fist crashed down on the desk.

'Yes, sir.' The clerk hurried from the desk to an inner room where voices could be heard.

'Mr Standakis is willing to fit you in at two.'

'When is that?'

The clerk frowned. 'Today, at two.'

'I don't wear a time piece.' Yiorgo thrust his wrist beneath the clerk's nose.

The clerk consulted his own wristwatch. 'It's ten fifteen now. Three and three quarter hour's time.'

Yiorgo nodded. 'I'll wait.'

'For three hours!'

'Why not? I've nothing else to do.'

The clerk eyed Anna standing miserably in the corner. 'Maybe the young lady would like to go for some refreshment? I can recommend the coffee shop around the corner or the taverna up the road.'

'Yes, please, Yiorgo.' Anna spoke quickly before her brother could forestall her with a refusal.

Yiorgo glared at the clerk. 'We'll be back.'

'Yes, sir. At two o'clock.'

Once outside Yiorgo turned to Anna. 'So now what do we do for three hours?'

Anna looked at him in exasperation. 'Yiorgo, there would have been no point in sitting in that office for three hours. You wouldn't have seen Mr Standakis any earlier. Didn't you know you had to make an appointment?'

'Yannis didn't mention it.'

'Let's go to the taverna. I need something to get rid of the dust from my throat.'

'And then what do we do?'

'I know what I'd like to do.' Anna looked at Yiorgo shyly. 'I'd like to climb to the top of the hill where Yannis used to go with Annita. He says you can look down and see all of Aghios Nikolaos from there.'

Mr Standakis greeted them cordially, despite having had to curtail his luncheon and forgo his afternoon sleep to give them an appointment.

'What is so urgent, Mr Christoforakis, that you had to see me today?'

'They want to take my farm away.'

Mr Standakis held up his hand. 'Please, some facts first. Where is your farm and who is laying claim to it?'

'It's at Plaka and the government want the land for a road.'

'The whole farm, or just a part of your land?'

'They want some land that runs up over the hill so they can build a road.'

'Ah,' a smile spread across Mr Standakis's florid features. 'Have they offered to buy it from you?'

'They said if I wouldn't sell them what they wanted they would take it. They can't do that, it's my farm.'

Mr Standakis turned to the map pinned up on his wall. 'Can you show me exactly what they want?'

Yiorgo placed a grimy fingernail on the village of Plaka. 'They want from the cart track to the top of that hill. I run my sheep there.'

'Is there nowhere else you could run your sheep?'

'How am I going to get a flock of sheep and goats through a fence and across a road? The rest of my land is under cultivation.'

Mr Standakis nodded. 'I see. You feel the money offered is not sufficient to recompense you for the inconvenience incurred.'

Yiorgo looked at the lawyer blankly. 'It's my farm.'

'Of course. Now, the choice is yours.' The lawyer removed his spectacles. 'You have two options. You can refuse and eventually they will insist on purchasing the land, probably below the market value. Alternatively I can write to them, accepting their offer for the land and asking for inconvenience money due to having to move your sheep across the road. Personally I feel that the latter would be most advantageous to you, but, as I say, the choice is yours.'

Yiorgo shifted uncomfortably in his chair. He did not understand this kind of talk.

'I'll think about it,' he muttered. 'I'll speak to my nephew.'

'Would that be Mr Yannis Christoforakis? He has the makings of a fine business man. You could do worse than be guided by him. Now, shall we make an appointment for next week? See my clerk on the way out and he will let you know when I'm free.'

Yiorgo flung the motorbike against the side of the farmhouse with unnecessary violence. A whole day wasted! All the lawyer had suggested was to talk to Yannis, and he already knew Yannis's opinion.

Anna walked into the house miserably. She had disliked the drive to Aghios Nikolaos, but the return journey had been even worse, with Yiorgo travelling at a reckless speed. Her head ached and she was not sure what the lawyer had finally said. She would certainly not go next week, however hard Yiorgo tried to persuade her.

For the rest of the week Yiorgo was morose, hardly speaking a word to either Anna or Yannis.

Yannis ignored him. 'He'll come round,' he assured Anna. 'He has no choice.'

Yiorgo lit a cigarette and inhaled deeply. 'You'd better tell me what that lawyer fellow was talking about before I go and see him again tomorrow.'

326

Yannis smiled to himself. 'Of course, uncle. I think it's time we had a very serious talk.'

Yiorgo looked suspiciously at his nephew. 'What about?'

'Our future.'

'They're not taking my farm.'

'No one wants to take your farm. Listen, uncle, they only want a strip of the hill. If you agree to sell it to them now, you can ask them to pay the cost of the fencing and ask them for extra money because you have to take the sheep across the road. That way you make a good profit. If you continue to say no to them they'll come along with papers that say they can build the road and only pay you half of what they're offering now. You've nothing to lose.'

'Only my land,' grumbled Yiorgo.

'A very small piece. Besides, I've been thinking. You can always split the flock. Keep half one side and half the other. That way you don't have to take them across the road, but we don't tell them that.' Yannis grinned. 'Let me come in with you tomorrow, uncle, I'll make sure you get a good deal. Maybe we could settle some of my business at the same time?'

'Your business? What business do you have? It's not your land they're taking.'

'Uncle, I've asked you to take grandpa's money into Aghios Nikolaos and put it in the bank. If you won't take yours and aunties, at least let me take mine.'

'It's safe where it is.'

'I know it's safe, but it's not doing anything. Mamma Anna knows how the price of flour and soap went up during the war; you know that tobacco costs more. I know it also means we sell the carob for a better price now, but we don't know how long that will last. There could be a day when we have to spend more money to live than we have coming in from the farm. Then what do we do?'

Yiorgo smiled triumphantly. 'That's when we use your grandpa's money.'

'And how long would that last?'

'There's a good bit there …'

'But if you put it in the bank there would be even more if you needed it.'

Anna was struggling hard to follow the conversation and she dared to interrupt. 'That's what Yannis said when I spoke to him. He said it would almost be double if we put it in the bank.'

'What does he know about it? Stuck on the island he has nothing to spend his money on.'

Yannis smiled gratefully at his aunt. 'Uncle Yannis has had money in a bank since the government gave them a pension. When you gave him his share of grandpa's money he put it in the bank. He has it written down in a little book how much he has put in there and how much the bank has added to it.'

Yiorgo scratched his head doubtfully.

'Please, uncle. I know I don't come of age for another six months, but I'd like to have grandpa's money now. I've talked to the bank and I've talked to Mr Standakis. They both agree that if I had the money to buy land now it would sell for a good price in the future.'

'What do you want more land for? We've got enough. We could run a few more animals than we do now and still have enough grass for them.'

'I don't want land to run more sheep and goats. I want to sell it to someone else later on. If I buy land now, whilst it's cheap, and wait until it's wanted by the government I can make a lot of money.'

'And what would you spend the money on? If you're not going to run sheep there's not much point in buying land just to sell again.'

'Uncle, it's called 'speculation'. I just can't lose. The price of land will never go down.' Yannis looked at his uncle pleadingly.

Yiorgo shook his head. 'I don't know what you're on about, boy. You can have your money to put in the bank if you're so set on the idea, but when it's gone there'll be no point in asking me for more.'

'I'll not do that, uncle. I've gone into this very carefully and I'm sure I'm doing the right thing.'

'Suppose,' Anna spoke hesitantly. 'Suppose you put some of my money in the bank.'

Yiorgo watched as the men and machines moved onto his land. With each bite into the hillside and load of earth that was moved to one side he felt more bitter. He had stood by powerless to stop the Germans from burning whole villages, but had been willing to lay down his life to save his fellow Cretans from their domination, and all for what? So the government could take his land and use it as they wished.

Grudgingly he admitted that the tarmac road made it easier to ride the old motorbike, or even drive the donkey and cart to Elounda and beyond, but where was all this rapid change leading? He had given in to Anna's pleading that he buy a wireless now electricity had been brought to the farm and agreed it was interesting to hear of events in Heraklion, Athens or further afield, but the music that Yannis seemed inclined to turn to he thought quite unnecessary.

Anna told of the acquisition proudly to her neighbours and to Yannis when she visited. Yannis smiled at her fondly.

'I know about the wireless. Most of us have one over here, but have you seen a film, Anna?'

'What's a film?'

'Pictures of people moving around and doing things. Remember when you came over to watch us acting in "The Birds"?'

Anna nodded. She had understood very little of the dialogue, but the enthusiasm of the actors had held her spell-bound.

'It's like that, except it's not real people that you're seeing, it's photographs of them. You'd enjoy that. Ask Davros to bring you over next Wednesday evening. Yiorgo and Yannis can come if they want. You'd all enjoy seeing a film.'

Anna returned from the island full of the wonders she had witnessed. 'You must come next time, Yiorgo. It was so funny. There was a little man called Charlie Chaplin, and he fell over time and again without hurting himself. He had a little stick with him, and when he leant on it, it bent.'

Yiorgo listened to his sister patiently as she laughed at the memories of the comedian's antics. He had not seen her so happy for a long time.

'Why don't you take Ourania and Eleni with you next time you go? They'd probably enjoy it.' Yiorgo had no intention of going himself.

'Maybe I will. I'll tell them all about Charlie Chaplin tomorrow and ask Yannis when they're having another film. It was so funny.' Smiling happily she retired to the kitchen to tackle the supper dishes left by the men.

It became a regular weekly event for the three women to cross to the island with Davros to watch whatever film had been hired. Sometimes it broke down half way through and they had to sit in an agony of suspense before it could continue, they laughed, they cried and always applauded loudly at the end. Anna found excuses to visit the village shop where she could relive the entertainment, sitting with the two other women in the back room, drinking coffee and eating a sweetmeat.

'Yannis says he's going to have photographs taken at our wedding,' Ourania announced proudly.

Anna looked at her in disbelief. 'Moving photographs! Of your wedding!'

'Not moving ones. He says there's a man in Aghios Nikolaos who will come to the wedding with a camera and take a picture. If Marisa's not able to come over we can send one to her.'

Anna nodded. She had been torn in two by the news that her niece was expecting a child only a month after Yannis's wedding. Tentatively she had suggested that Yannis might be willing to delay his big event to enable Marisa to recover and attend.

'Not even for you, Mamma Anna. I'd like to have her and Victor here, but there's Ourania and her mother to consider. All the arrangements are made and I'm not having the villagers say I've had second thoughts.'

'Marisa might need me.'

'I'm sure Marisa would be delighted to have you there, and I'll be only too happy for you to visit her once you've been to my wedding. She's in good hands, Mamma Anna.' Yannis placed his arms around Anna. 'I know you're worried in case anything goes wrong, but there's no reason why it should.'

'There was no reason why it should go wrong for your poor mamma, but it did.'

'Marisa is going into hospital in Turin and she'll have the best of care.'

'If everything's all right she shouldn't need to go to a hospital.'

Yannis squeezed his aunt to him. 'There's no pleasing you, is there? If she stayed at home you'd be worried what would happen if she needed a doctor, and if she goes into hospital you think there must be something wrong. I don't know what you'll be like when Ourania and I start a family.'

'Is that why you won't change your wedding date?'

Yannis threw back his head and laughed. 'No, it isn't, Mamma Anna. You know Eleni hardly lets her out of her sight.' He frowned. 'I'm not sure I'm doing the right thing by agreeing to live there with her mother. She has far too much influence over Ourania.'

1955 – 1959

Anna sat with her brother in his tiny house. 'You'll soon be back,' she said confidently. 'Once they've declared you free from infection you'll be able come home.'

Yannis sighed. 'I don't like it, Anna. They're up to something.'

'This is what you've wanted ever since you found out there was a treatment. There's no satisfying you, Yannis.'

'I don't like the idea of going back to the hospital in Athens,' he admitted. 'Why can't they do it here?'

'The doctor explained all that to you. You told me yourself, they have to do tests and watch the results. It takes time.'

'It would be much easier to do them here.'

'You're being unreasonable, Yannis. You haven't got the equipment on the island.'

'They could bring it here, instead of taking us over there.'

'But you've always wanted to see Athens. You'll be able to visit all the museums and the Acropolis. You'll write to me, won't you, Yannis, and tell me all about everything?'

'I'll be back soon and be able to tell you all about Athens.'

'I'd still like a letter. By the time you return you'll have forgotten some of the things you've seen and done.'

Yannis snorted. 'I don't plan to be gone more than a few weeks.'

Yannis's letters reached Anna regularly. In each one he complained that he was still at the hospital, despite having a small room to himself, his meals provided and able to walk around the city as he pleased. He described his visits to the museums and sites in vivid detail to her, but always ending with a wish to return home to the island.

Anna would reply, covering pages in her misspelled, childish writing, giving him news of the completion of the road and complaining that very little traffic ever used it. She wrote of the difficulties their nephew appeared to be encountering with his mother-in-law. Eleni disapproved of him disappearing off to Aghios Nikolaos and even Heraklion for whole days at a time and Yannis refused to give her any explanation. Anna had also tackled him about his absences, only to be greeted with a secretive smile and been told to wait and see.

The numbers on the island dwindled as more and more people were transferred to the hospital in Athens for tests, and Anna no longer visited the forlorn and deserted village. She spent more time with Eleni and Ourania, whilst Yiorgo was occupied on the farm, and felt useless and frustrated with so little to do. To her surprise the money she had asked Yannis to place in the bank for her, more to show her support for him than with any clear idea of investment, had increased dramatically.

'Do you believe me now, Mamma Anna? What would you like to spend it on? A new dress?'

Anna shook her head. 'There's nothing I need.'

'Now that's where you're wrong. Remember I told you I wanted Ourania to live in a house where the water comes from a tap and you didn't have to go out to use the yard in all weathers?'

Anna nodded. Despite all Yannis's talk from a couple of years ago he and Ourania were still living with Eleni, his sheep running with his uncle's, his only personal acquisition a new motor bike.

'Have you seen the new buildings in Elounda? They have indoor facilities. The government has laid drains and eventually no one will have to use their yard. I've asked them to do the same here, but they've refused. They say it would be too expensive, so I'm doing it myself.'

'What do you mean, Yannis? If the government can't afford it, how can you? You can't dig drains yourself.'

'I'm not talking about being on a main drainage system. I'm going to pay someone to come and dig a cesspit for me. Then I'll build a little room on the back, have a toilet fitted and a pipe that leads to the cesspit. It's the next best thing to having drains. Why don't you do the same?'

Anna looked at her nephew doubtfully. 'It would be up to Yiorgo.'

'Why? Why should uncle have a say in how you spend your money?'

'It's his farm.'

'No, Mamma Anna. It belongs to both of you. Why shouldn't you make it more comfortable?'

'It would cost a lot of money, Yannis.'

'Not as much as you think, besides, you could pay half each. Suppose Marisa came back for a visit? What would she think, still having to use the yard?'

Anna sighed. She wished her niece would return. Two miscarriages between the birth of her first child and the second was worrying. 'I'll speak to Yiorgo, then maybe he could talk to you about it.'

Yannis nodded. It was a step in the right direction.

Yannis's letters from Athens continued to arrive. No longer did they contain descriptions of the marvels of Athens, they were now filled with his acrimonious wrangles with the doctors regarding the delay. He had written to Elias, Annita's husband, whom he hoped was attending an international conference in Vienna, and asked him to table a motion against the medical authorities.

Anna wrote back, each time making excuses for the delay he was having. She extolled the virtues of the new toilet that had finally been installed and wished they had thought of it years before. '*Even mamma would have been able to use it easily. It could have saved so much washing,*' she wrote wryly. '*Yiorgo insists there is nothing wrong with using the yard, but I noticed last week when it rained he used indoors*'.

Yannis had smiled over the letter and shaken his head. They had constructed toilets on Spinalonga where the waste soaked away into the ground and finally to the sea to avoid having smelly, communal areas. What did people do with obstinate brothers like Yiorgo?

A coat of white wash was given to the farmhouse and Yiorgo was persuaded to purchase a small cart with a motor at the front. It had taken weeks of persuasion by Yannis to convince him that the money would be well spent and recouped by the time saved in travelling to Aghios Nikolaos with goods to sell. Unbeknown to Yiorgo, Yannis had placed the money entrusted to him into his own bank account and arranged monthly payments at very little extra cost.

Anna wrote of the motorised cart to Yannis and received a reasonably happy sounding letter back. Elias had visited him at the hospital. Yannis went into a long account of the speech Elias had made in Vienna and he had high hopes that he would soon be returning to the island.

His next letter, although full of confidence for his return, showed annoyance that he had been asked to stay at the hospital to help the newcomers settle in. Spiro planned to return to the island in a couple of weeks, and Flora had already returned, but he had agreed to stay and now regretted the decision.

Anna replied comfortingly that the time would soon pass. She was also able to relay the good news that Marisa was expecting another child and so far all seemed to be going well, although there was no sign of Yannis and Ourania starting a family. In fact Anna was seriously worried about the state of her nephew's marriage. He seemed happier to spend his evenings with them than with his wife and mother-in-law, and she knew that on more than one occasion he had spent the night away from Plaka without giving Ourania any explanation. Eleni had told her that twice she had found him asleep downstairs in a chair and not in the bedroom where he should have been, yet Anna hesitated from tackling him directly.

'You would tell me if you had any problems, wouldn't you, Yannis?' she asked.

'I have no problems,' he assured her. 'I'm beginning to be very hopeful about my investments. Another few months and there could be some results.'

Anna hoped the situation might improve when Davros brought an invitation for the whole village to visit Spinalonga and celebrate Flora's wedding to Manolis. Maybe Yannis would remember how he and Ourania had slipped away during his sister's wedding and been found by Yiorgo, almost anticipating their own.

Once again Anna was destined for disappointment.

'I can't possibly go,' stated Yannis. 'I have a business appointment in Heraklion.'

'Couldn't you put it off?' suggested Anna.

'Certainly not. If I'm not there to sign I could miss the opportunity of a lifetime. Ourania and Eleni must go, but I can't.'

Nothing Anna could say would move him, nor could she get him to disclose the nature of the appointment. Ourania sulked, Eleni nagged perpetually, but he would not give way to them. He waved cheerfully to Anna as he rode past the farmhouse and up the new road towards Heraklion.

He felt elated. This was what he had been waiting for. Now he would show them all and give his ultimatum to his wife and her impossible mother.

Yannis did not return for three days, leaving both Anna and Ourania frantic with worry, whilst Eleni went about grim-faced. She'd give her son-in-law a piece of her mind when he returned.

He need not think she would put up with that kind of treatment for her daughter. Who did he think he was?

The small black saloon car swept through Elounda and continued on to Plaka, stopping outside the village shop. Knowing all eyes would be upon him, Yannis took his time. He fiddled with the dashboard, wound up the windows and locked the doors. He strode into Eleni's shop, immaculate in his blue pin-stripe suit, white shirt and new shoes. Ourania and Eleni gasped at the sight of him.

'I want to talk to you.' He grasped Ourania's elbow and led her through to the back room, Eleni following. 'No, not you. I want to talk to my wife in private.' Very deliberately he shut the dividing door in his mother-in-law's face.

'Sit down and listen to me.'

Ourania obeyed. This was a Yannis she did not know.

'I'm leaving Plaka and you can come with me or stay as you please. You have a week to think it over.'

'Where are you going?'

'Aghios Nikolaos.'

A pleased smile spread over Ourania's face. 'That will be lovely. Mamma and I…'

'Oh, no. There's no mamma. I'm asking you to come. I'm not living with your mamma a day longer. I'll not stop you seeing her and I'll provide for her, but I'll not live with her. You have to choose, Ourania, your mamma or me.'

'But, mamma…'

Yannis shook his head. 'No mamma. You and me, Ourania, or you and your mamma. I'll be back next week.' Yannis rose and pulled his wife to him. 'I do love you, 'Rani, but I can't live like this any more.'

He wrenched open the dividing door, almost knocking Eleni over where she was listening at the crack, and walked out to the car, unlocked the door and slipped behind the wheel. He drew a deep breath. He had done it, given Ourania the ultimatum he should have done long before.

He coasted round the corner, pulled up outside the farmhouse and hooted. He watched as his aunt look out, her eyes widening in surprise.

'Yannis!'

Not bothering to lock the doors this time he jumped out and swept Anna into his arms. 'What do you think of it? Would you like a ride?'

Anna ignored his invitation. 'Where've you been? Ourania and I have been worried sick about you.'

'I've just seen Ourania. It's you and uncle Yiorgo I want to talk to.'

'What have you done, Yannis? Are you in trouble?'

Yannis threw back his head and laughed. 'Not at all. Let's go inside and I'll tell you my news, but first, how was the wedding? Did you enjoy yourself?'

'It was beautiful, Yannis.' Tears came into Anna's eyes as she recalled the day. 'They were so happy. After all, they'd waited years.' She shook her head. 'I wish your uncle had been there too.'

'You'll be able to write and tell him all about it. Now, I'll go and fetch uncle whilst you get out the brandy. This is a celebration.'

'You'll not go walking up to the fields in those clothes. I'll fetch him.' Without more ado Anna left the farmhouse, happy that her nephew had returned and curious to know what there was to celebrate.

Somehow Yannis managed to contain himself whilst Yiorgo washed his hands and joined them in the living room. Yannis raised his glass. 'I'd like you to drink a toast with me. To the Andronicatis chain of hotels.'

Anna choked and Yiorgo lowered his glass in amazement. 'What was that?'

Yannis grinned. 'Remember all the land I bought? Well, I've just sold most of it.'

Yiorgo nodded. 'What's all this about hotels?'

'I have sold a prime site to a developer to build a hotel, and, what is more, we came to an arrangement whereby I lowered the price of the land in return for a controlling interest in the hotel.'

'What does that mean?'

'That means that when the hotel is completed I have a percentage of their profit each year.'

Yiorgo eyed his nephew warily. 'Suppose they don't make a profit?'

'They still have to pay me a basic price, and if they go out of business the hotel has to be sold up and I get a percentage of that price. I can't lose, uncle. I just can't lose.'

'There must be a catch somewhere. Nothing can be that easy.'

'Look, I took a chance. I bought land that crops wouldn't grow on and sheep would have turned their backs on, but it was cheap. Now some of it's wanted so badly that they were willing to agree to my terms. It could have gone the other way and I could have been stuck with that land for ever.'

'Where is it, Yannis?'

'Just outside Heraklion. I'll drive you up to have a look if you like.'

'When are you taking Ourania and Eleni?' asked Anna.

'I'm not.' Yannis's mouth set in a grim line. 'That's the other thing I have to tell you. I'm leaving Plaka.'

'Oh, Yannis.' The disappointment in his aunt's voice was obvious.

'I'm not going far, only Aghios Nikolaos, but I don't know if Ourania's coming with me.'

Anna stared at him. 'You mean you're leaving her? Leaving your wife?' The enormity of the implication was too great for Anna to comprehend.

'I've told Ourania that I'm going and I've given her a week to make up her mind if she wants to come with me, but only her. I'll not have her mother. She must choose who she wants to live with – a husband or a mischief-making tyrant.'

Yiorgo refilled Yannis's glass and his own. 'Decided to assert your manhood, have you?'

'I'd just like the opportunity! It's always 'we might disturb mamma', 'mamma's next door, remember'. It's inhibiting. She's lucky I have asked her to come with me and not gone off with some trollop.' Yannis drained his glass. 'I love Ourania, but the biggest mistake I ever made was to go and live in that house with her mother.'

Eleni descended on Anna, full of vituperation against her son-in-law, finally breaking down in tears and asking what would happen to an old widow woman left on her own. Anna waited until Eleni was mopping her eyes; it was time for plain speaking.

'You've brought this on yourself, Eleni. When a girl marries she's got her own life to lead. Her mother can't always be there to hold her hand. She has to fight her own battles with her husband and a good many of those take place in a bedroom, and that's no place for a third person.'

'What would you know about that, Anna Christoforakis? You've never managed to get yourself a husband.'

'Strange though it may seem to you, I've never particularly wanted one, but that's not the point. Face facts, Eleni. You keep your Ourania with you and that's the last she'll see of my Yannis. Let her go with him and she stands a good chance of being happy. Give them time on their own and you may even find you get an invitation to visit now and then. He's proved himself a good business man, now let him prove himself a good husband.'

Eleni sniffed. 'I'd like to know where he gets all his money from! A car, of all things, and a new suit.'

A smile twitched at the corner of Anna's mouth. 'Didn't he tell you? He owns a hotel in Heraklion.'

The dropped jaw of Eleni gave Anna amusement for the rest of the day.

Yannis wrote again from Athens, telling Anna that he was working in the hospital. He wrote an amusing description of his day, spent in the store room amongst rolls of bandages and bottles of disinfectant, and how he had searched frantically for items requested by the nurses on the wards. He congratulated his nephew Yannis on his success, and then reverted back to his work in the store room, how he had met Dora, a ward orderly, and found out she had leprosy also, but finishing as always by saying how much he missed Spinalonga and was longing to return.

Looking mutinous, Ourania climbed into the car and settled herself back in the seat. She wished there were more people still living in the village to see her. She and Yannis were hardly on speaking terms and she was determined that if she missed her mother she would return immediately, whether Yannis liked it or not. They drew up outside a new block of apartments in Aghios Nikolaos and Yannis led her up a flight of stairs into a spacious room with a view over the sea. A tiny kitchen, bathroom and bedroom led off the main room, bare and unfurnished.

'Well?' asked Yannis. 'What do you think?'

Ourania nodded. 'It would have been better on the ground floor.'

'There would be no view of the sea, besides, the ground floor will be the shop.'

'What shop?'

'Your shop.' Yannis took Ourania's hands. 'I've put a lot of thought into this and I'd like you to give it a try. I know that leaving your mother is a wrench and you're going to feel lonely. I don't want you running back there every day so you'll need something to occupy you. The shop is for you. Choose what you want to deal in. Walk around the town and see what the other shops are offering and let me know what you decide. Whilst you're looking you can choose some furniture for this place.'

Ourania pulled away from him. 'Suppose I say I don't want to live here and run a shop?'

'The choice is yours, Ourania, but it's the only time you'll have it offered. Say no and I'll drive you straight back to Plaka now.'

'And what would you do?'

'Keep the flat for myself and let the shop.'

'No doubt at a profit!'

'No doubt.'

'So why are you doing this for me, Yannis?'

'Because I think if we're given a chance our marriage can work. We need some time on our own and this is the only way we can get it. If you find you're really unhappy living here with me then I'll not hold you. All I'm asking is that you give it a try.'

Anna received a furious letter from Yannis. Had she heard – the government was putting a closure order on the island of Spinalonga. He was going to fight it. It was his home and he wanted to return. Anna replied that she had heard nothing of the proposal, but should it come into effect he was always welcome to return to the farmhouse and live with her and Yiorgo. She described Yannis and Ourania's new flat to him. She and Eleni had been driven there together to inspect and approve, and she had certainly found it most attractive, although small and there was no garden.

Eleni had criticised the moment she entered, complaining about the number of stairs there were to climb and wrinkling her nose at the plain white walls where a number of framed sketches, done by Yannis's mother, were proudly displayed.

'Where's your wedding photograph? That should be on that wall.'

'It's in the bedroom, mamma. Come and see.'

'Pink!' Eleni was heard to exclaim. 'Where's the patchwork quilt I gave you?'

Yannis smiled at Anna. 'I think I'm winning,' he said quietly. 'What do you think of it, Mamma Anna?'

'I think it's beautiful, Yannis. Has Ourania decided what she'll sell in the shop?'

'At the moment she wants to sell everything from furniture to ice cream. We're gradually whittling the list down and becoming practical.'

'You can't do better than a general store.' Eleni returned from the bedroom and picked up the conversation.

'A general store is no good in Aghios Nikolaos.' Ourania spoke firmly, then blushed at her own temerity.

'You're father made a good living from it. A general store is nothing to be ashamed of.'

'I'm not ashamed, mamma. It's just that in Aghios Nikolaos you would need an enormous shop to be able to sell everything. There are so many more people here. Some shops sell nothing but wine, and others just groceries, some even sell just books and newspapers.'

Eleni sniffed in derision. 'So what are you going to sell?'

'Something different. I'm still not sure.'

'You could always open as a general store until you did make your mind up. That's the trouble with you, my girl, always did have a job making up your mind.'

'No, mamma, better to keep the shop shut for a while yet. When it's open we'll invite you over again and it can be a surprise for you.'

Even Eleni had to recognise the snub.

The occasional car or lorry that drove carefully down the hillside on the new road was always watched with interest by Anna. Considering the fuss, which had been made about its construction, it was used very little, and usually by someone who had missed their way. The oncoming car was lost to sight as it rounded the curve of the hillside and Anna returned to stoning her plums, looking up in surprise as the car halted and a shadow fell across her.

'Anna?'

'Michael!' Her lips framed the word, but no sound came.

'It is Anna.' Michael advanced with outstretched arms and kissed her soundly on both cheeks. 'This is wonderful.'

Anna swallowed hard. 'Come in, never mind the fruit, I'll stone it later. Where have you come from?'

Michael hesitated. 'My wife and daughter are in the car.'

'Then bring them in. They can't sit there.' Anna fought to control the constriction round her heart.

Michael waved to them and they tumbled out, creased and weary. 'Anna says to come in,' he smiled happily.

'Has she got a... ?' the woman asked.

'Bound to have by now. I'll ask her.'

Anna smiled at his request. 'Yannis insisted we had one. It's round the back. I'll show you.'

Michael translated and the trio trooped round to the back of the house. Michael waited until the women returned, his wife wrinkling her nose just a little to disclose her distaste of the toilet they had just visited.

'Pooh, that stinks,' announced his daughter.

Michael laughed at the look of horror on his wife's face. 'Don't worry, Anna doesn't speak English. A few years ago you'd have used the yard and hoped the chickens wouldn't give you a peck. Let me introduce you properly.'

Michael drew Anna forwards. 'This is my wife, Heather, and my daughter Anne.'

'Please tell them I'm pleased to meet them. Now you must come inside.'

Anna led the way and took her mother's best white china from the cupboard. 'I'll make some coffee. Would your daughter like some orange juice?'

'I'm sure she would, but, Anna, please don't go to any trouble on our behalf.'

Anna fixed Michael with a reproachful look and left the room. He gazed around and shook his head.

'I only came in here once, but apart from her invalid mother sitting by the window and the bed that took up half the room, it's exactly as I remembered.'

'Not even had a coat of paint, I shouldn't think.'

'Now, Heather. Their ways are not ours. You agreed to come. Please be nice to her for my sake. Remember she saved my life at great risk to her own.'

'You said she doesn't speak English, so I'm not likely to offend her. The way you've talked of her in the past and this place, well, I just wasn't expecting such a – such a – hovel.'

'I always said it was a farmhouse, not a palace.'

'Yes, but this!' Heather's glance around the room said all her thoughts.

'Mummy, do we have to stay?'

'Yes, you do.' Michael spoke sharply. 'You'll eat and drink whatever she puts before you and look as though you're enjoying it. Afterwards you and Mummy can go for a walk if you want whilst we talk.'

Anne hung her head and examined her sandals. It was rare for her father to be cross with her and the tone of his voice said he was cross now.

Anna returned, carrying the steaming coffee pot and glasses of water. She placed a glass of orange juice before Anna and a plate of biscuits on the table, hoping they would none of them notice how her hands were shaking. No sooner had she taken her seat than Yiorgo stormed in.

'If it's that damned man from the government again he's not taking any more of my land.' He stopped at the doorway, covered in confusion when he saw Anna was entertaining his unknown visitors.

Michael rose and held out his hand. 'I'm not a damned man from the government. I'm a damned resistance worker.'

A slow smile spread over Yiorgo's face and he clasped Michael to him. 'You were here? Fighting with us?'

'I certainly was. Did Anna tell you how brave she was? We could always rely on her to come and bandage our wounds. She even saved my life.'

Yiorgo pointed to the man before him. 'Michael! You must be Michael!' He pumped Michael's hand vigorously. 'I saw you up at Lassithi. You came up there to convalesce just as we were moving out. Why are we drinking coffee, Anna? Fetch the brandy.'

'Were you part of the group who trapped the German commander?'

Yiorgo nodded. 'We got him.'

'So I heard, but it was expensive on your part.'

'That is war.' Yiorgo shrugged. 'We were all willing to give up our lives to get rid of him.' Yiorgo poured the brandy liberally.

Heather touched Michael's arm. 'Not too much.'

'I can hold my drink. Tell me, how's that boy Yannis, now? He had some courage, I can tell you.'

'He's married, and Marisa. Get the photographs, Anna.'

Anna obeyed, pointing out the various people who were in the wedding photographs, advising him who no longer lived in the village or who had died.

'Marisa was married on Spinalonga,' she said proudly. 'She had three weddings.'

'Three!'

'She married Victor, the Italian soldier who was here. Aah, I must tell you about that! She was married here, in the church, then on Spinalonga by Father Minos so her uncle could be there, and then in Turin. Such a party we had on the island. Flora was married over there a while ago, but Marisa's party was more splendid. Anyone is allowed over there now, but there are not many of our friends left. My brother, Yannis, he read about a cure for leprosy. For years he wrote to the government, begging to be allowed to take the medicine, until at last they agreed to take tests from the islanders to see if they were fit enough for treatment. Do you know what they found? Most of them no longer had leprosy. Burnt-out, Yannis called it. They've gone to the hospital in Athens now for more tests and Yannis says the island is to be closed.' Anna shook her head sadly. 'Soon there will be no one left.'

'So, Marisa married an Italian soldier. That must have caused quite a stir.'

'Do you remember the night on the cart? When I was stopped and questioned? It was Victor who told them to let us through. He thought you were Marisa's pappa.'

'When did he find out his mistake?'

'I told him the truth after Marisa was married to him. He laughed. He knew all along we were helping the resistance.' Anna turned the pages of the photograph album. 'There is Yannis with Ourania, Eleni's daughter. Marisa couldn't come to the wedding as she was expecting.'

'How many children does she have?'

'Only two. Two little boys. She has had problems and the doctors have said not to have any more. There they are, look.' Anna pointed to two cherubic faces, each with a mop of black curls.

'And Yannis and Ourania? Do they have any children?'

'No, not yet. I think Yannis has been too busy becoming a rich man. He owns land and hotels and shops.'

'What! Little Yannis?'

Anna nodded proudly. 'After the war he used his grandpa's money to buy land and he sold to a company who wanted to build hotels. Now he owns land and the hotel. He has a modern apartment in Aghios Nikolaos and his wife has a shop.'

'Really? You must give me his address so I can see him. Did your pappa come back from the mines?'

Anna shook her head. 'They should never have taken him, he was too old.'

'And your mamma?'

'She had another stroke a few years ago. It was to be expected.'

Heather cleared her throat. 'Anne and I will go for a walk along the beach. You obviously want to talk about the war and Anne is bored to tears. Please thank Anna for the coffee and the biscuits. You can drive along and pick us up later.'

Michael nodded, his face dark with anger when he saw his wife's coffee was untouched, although Anne had eaten a biscuit and drunk her orange juice. 'It's not far to Elounda. You'll probably find a taverna there to have a cup of coffee.'

Heather flushed. 'Come along, Anne. We'll go for a walk.'

Anne slipped down from her chair, uncertain what she should say. Michael pulled her to him and whispered in her ear. Triumphantly she said 'thank you' and 'goodbye' in mispronounced Greek.

Anna enfolded the small girl in her arms, stroking her blonde hair and sending forth a string of Greek until Anne pulled away from her. Heather took the child's arm quite roughly and pulled her towards the door.

'Come along now.' Without waiting to shake hands with Yiorgo and Anna she let herself out of the door and began to walk away.

Michael shrugged. 'I apologise for my wife's bad manners. It's the first time she's visited Greece. She doesn't understand our ways.'

Anna smiled. 'You still think of yourself as a Greek?'

'I do now I'm here. This is the first time I've been back since the war. I wondered if I'd remember the language! Now, tell me everything. What happened after I went up to Lassithi?'

For two hours they sat and reminisced, Yiorgo adding anecdotes Anna had never heard before about his time spent with the resistance until Michael looked at his watch in horror.

'Heather will think I've abandoned her. She'll never forgive me. I must go.' He held out his hand to Yiorgo. 'I'm so pleased to have met you.' Anna he kissed on both cheeks.

'You haven't got Yannis's address,' Anna remembered. She looked round for a pencil and scrap of paper.

'He doesn't need his address. We'll take him to Yannis.'

'I'm not sure if I can fit everyone in the car, maybe Anne could sit on her mother's lap.'

'There's no need. We have the cart.'

'It will take hours to get to Aghios Nikolaos by cart.'

Yiorgo grinned. 'Not now. It has a motor. Give me ten minutes to have a wash and put on a clean shirt. Anna, you ought to change your blouse, you've got plum juice on it.'

Heather was evidently furious with her husband when he finally drew up beside them. She pushed Anne into the back of the car and slammed her own door shut.

'I'm sorry, Heather. We were talking and the time just flew by. I didn't mean to stay so long.'

Heather did not answer. She took her lipstick from her handbag and tried to paint the line of her lips whilst they drove along. Michael tried again to make amends.

'When we get to Aghios Nikolaos I'll book us into a nice hotel.'

'If that village that we've just driven through is anything to go by I doubt if they know what a hotel is!'

'Aghios Nikolaos is quite big. Apparently her son lives there now. He was just a child, not much older than Anne when I last saw him.'

'I suppose that means you're going off to spend hours with him now.'

'I'd like to see him again. He seems to have turned into a very enterprising young man.'

'Well don't expect Anne and I to sit there like dummies for

hours on end whilst you gabble away to each other. That's if you can find him. It took you long enough to find that last dump!'

'That was because of the new road. I'll have no trouble finding Yannis. Yiorgo and Anna are coming with us.'

Heather turned and looked out of the rear window, turning back aghast to Michael. 'What is that thing they're driving?'

'It's a cart. All the farmers are getting them now.'

'Thank God none of my friends can see me,' replied Heather fervently.

'I don't know what's got into you. They're good, honest, farming folk.'

'They could also do with a good wash and some clean clothes.'

Michael laughed. 'They had a wash and changed their clothes before leaving. If you think they were a bit smelly I can tell you we stank to high heaven after living in the caves for a few weeks. All they smell of is honest toil.'

'Meaning that you prefer their smell to mine!'

'Meaning nothing of the kind. If you gave Anna a bottle of perfume she'd put it on the shelf to look at. They've never had those sorts of luxuries. I shall ask them to take us to a good taverna tonight. Yannis should know of one if he's living in the town, and I'm paying the bill. If you and Anne want some nice English food you'd better stay at the hotel and eat.'

'I have every intention of doing so,' replied Heather coldly.

Yannis was delighted to open his door and discover his visitors. 'Come in. Come in. This is wonderful. The most wonderful day of my life.'

'Well, well, well. Who would have thought that little Yannis who used to run up to the fields and tell me which Italian soldiers were going into town would be a married man now! I still think of you the way you were.'

Heather's eyes roamed critically around the small flat. It was certainly an improvement on the farmhouse. They even had some decent sketches on the wall. She moved a little closer to see if she could discern the signature.

'My wife is an art connoisseur,' explained Michael. 'I'm sure she would like to know the artist. I noticed the one at the farmhouse. There was no mistaking you and your pappa.'

Yannis frowned. 'There's no picture of me and my pappa there. Oh, you must mean uncle Yiorgo and grandpa.'

Michael shook his head in disbelief. 'It just shows how alike the men in your family are. Who drew them?'

'My mamma.'

Michael turned to Anna. 'You're very talented. I never knew you were an artist.'

'I'm not.' Anna felt herself go cold. 'I'm not Yannis's mamma.'

The colour drained from Michael's face and even Heather looked at him in consternation. 'You're not Yannis's mother?' The words seemed to be an effort for him to utter.

'What made you think I was? I'm his aunt.'

'But you never said, I always thought…'

'Yannis and Marisa are my sister's children. She died shortly after Yannis was born and they came to me to be looked after. They mean as much to me as if they were my own.'

'Yannis called you "mamma".'

'That was his baby name for me. He called me "Mamma Anna".'

'And Babbis? I remember you telling the Italians that you were his wife when I was in the cart.'

'My brother-in-law. I used my sister's papers. You didn't think he was my husband, did you?'

Michael shook his head. 'If I'd known; if I'd only known.'

Yannis began to point to the pictures. 'This was my mother and father. This is my father with Marisa. These show them up in the fields the summer my cousins came to stay. There's uncle Yannis, looking for pottery, and Mamma Anna talking to Annita, she's in America now. That's Andreas, Annita's brother, he's a priest in Heraklion, and that's uncle Stelios. There's grandma, sitting in her chair. There are none of me, of course, because mamma was dead. She just signed them 'Maria' and always tried to hide it somewhere in the picture.'

Michael was not looking at the pictures, instead his gaze was fixed on Anna. 'Why didn't you tell me?' His voice was an anguished breath and Anna did not meet his eyes.

'Well?' asked Heather impatiently. 'Do you know who the artist is?'

Michael jumped. He had entirely forgotten his wife's presence. 'It was Anna's sister. She's been dead a long time now.'

'That's a shame. They're very good. That kind of work is selling for a small fortune in England. Could you offer them a price?'

'They're not for sale, Heather.' He spoke more sharply than he meant to. 'They're family heirlooms.'

Heather gave a brittle laugh. 'They can't be that old,' her eyes slid maliciously towards Anna. 'Well, maybe they are.'

Michael felt the impatience with his wife welling up in him. 'We ought to find a hotel before it gets too late.' He reverted to Greek. 'Yannis, where is there a good hotel for us? I'd like to take my family there and get them settled, then I thought we could go for a meal and talk.'

Yannis grinned. 'I'll take you and get a special deal. The proprietor is a friend of mine. I can wait for you, then we can all meet at the taverna.'

'I think Heather and Anne would prefer to eat at the hotel. Heather feels a bit out of it, not speaking the language, and Anne must be bored. Anne? Where is Anne? Anne?'

'I'm here, Daddy. Look, isn't she beautiful? Please ask the lady what she's called.' Anne emerged from the kitchen, a small white Persian kitten in her arms.

Michael tickled the animal's ears. 'You don't often see a cat like this in Greece.' He looked at the young woman who had followed Anne from the kitchen. 'What's her name?'

'Omorfia, it means beauty,' she answered simply.

'Very apt. She is a beauty.'

'Put that animal down, Anne. It's probably got fleas.'

'She hasn't got fleas, have you, darling?' Anne buried her face in the cat's soft fur.

'Anne, do as you're told.'

Reluctantly Anne placed the cat on the floor where it rubbed around her legs.

'She likes me, Mummy.'

'I really think we should go.' Heather looked pointedly at her watch. 'Anne will be getting hungry.'

Michael returned to the hotel in the early hours of the morning. He crept into the bedroom hoping not to disturb his wife, but she was awake and waiting for him.

'Did you enjoy your evening with your friends?' Her voice had a sarcastic edge to it.

'Very much. How was your meal?'

'Barely edible.'

'You should have come with us. You would have enjoyed a traditional meal. They even got me dancing!' Michael smiled at the memory.

'Dancing!'

'Yes, like this.' Michael did a few steps across the room.

'You're drunk!'

'I am not. Have you ever seen me drunk?'

'Well, you're certainly not sober.'

'Now there I'll agree with you.' He dropped his shoes noisily on to the floor.

'I think we should go back to Heraklion tomorrow.'

'You haven't seen Aghios Nikolaos yet, and you said you wanted to visit Gournia and drive over to Ierapetra.'

'I've decided I've seen enough of this country. I'd be happy to go home tomorrow.'

'Go home? I could stay here for ever.'

'I'm surprised you didn't – with that peasant woman you seem so fond of.'

'I didn't know she wasn't married.' Michael's voice had a break in it.

Heather sat up in the bed. 'You mean you would have stayed – with her?'

'I loved her,' he replied quietly.

'You loved her!' Heather's voice had the ring of hysteria about it. 'You loved her! You mean you had a quick tumble whenever the Germans weren't about. You're no different from any other soldier who's away from home. A cheap piece of skirt and you'll take advantage.'

'It wasn't like that.'

'Of course it was. There's no need to lie to me.'

Michael shook his head. 'I'm not lying. I wanted to go to bed with her, but we never did more than kiss and hold hands. I thought she was married.'

'And what difference would that make?'

'All the difference in the world. You don't understand what it was like over here. Our lives depended upon the Cretans and their good will. We were like brothers in the resistance. You don't betray your brother.'

Heather let out her breath with a hiss. 'I don't believe you. You were quick enough to get me into bed with you.'

Michael shifted uncomfortably. 'I didn't hear you say no to me.'

'I was young and foolish.'

'Don't make me laugh. You were nearly thirty and I was your last chance. You grabbed me with both hands.'

'You think so? That just shows how wrong you were. I could have chosen any one of a number of men.'

'And I wish to God you had.'

'What's that supposed to mean?'

'You know as well as I do that the only reason we stay together is because of Anne. The only reason you agreed to come to Crete with me was so you could boast to your friends that you'd been to Greece. You'd have been happier in Bournemouth.'

'I came because I knew you'd had an affair with some black-eyed little bitch and I wanted to make sure you remembered you had a wife and child. Now I know why you insisted on calling our child Anne.'

'I did not have an affair with her.'

'And I wasn't born yesterday!' Heather lay back down on the bed and turned her back on her husband.

Michael slipped his feet back into his shoes and picked up his jacket.

'Where are you going?'

'Out.' The bedroom door closed behind him.

Michael walked back into the hotel, hoping the night porter would attribute his dishevelled appearance to a night carousing in the town and not to sleeping in the back of the car. With a self-conscious smile he walked past him and up to his room.

Heather was lying on her back, snoring loudly. Michael looked at her with distaste. Beside the bed was a bottle of sleeping tablets, and as usual, whenever they had a row, she had resorted to them by way of defence.

He shrugged and walked into the bathroom, stepped out of his clothes and treated himself to the trickle of warm water that passed for a shower. Having shaved, dressed in clean clothes and checked to see Heather was still deeply asleep, he left the room and went into the adjoining one in search of his daughter. Anne was sitting up in bed, reading a book.

'Hello, Daddy. What time is it? Mummy hasn't been in for me.'

Michael sat on the edge of the bed and took the book from her hands. 'What are you reading? Oh, a Doctor Dolittle; what a surprise!' he smiled and handed the book back to her. 'Mummy's not feeling very well and is staying in bed late. I thought you might like to go out somewhere with me this morning.'

'On our own?'

Michael nodded. 'Where would you like to go?'

'Could we go and see the lady with the cat again? I liked her – and her cat.'

'I don't know if she'll be in, but we could walk that way and see.'

Anne threw her legs over the side of the bed. 'I'll be ready in a few minutes.'

Michael left a note for Heather on the table beside the bed and explained to the hotel that she would not wish to be disturbed due to a bad headache. Full of sympathy the desk clerk assured Michael he would tell the maids to leave the room until later and offered to call a doctor.

'That's not necessary. She suffers from migraine and has taken her tablets. She'll probably sleep until lunch time.'

Anne skipped along happily beside her father, gazing into shop windows at statues and ornaments in bronze, onyx and alabaster, colourful embroidery and exotic items that she had never seen in England.

'I like it here,' she announced. 'I wish I could understand what the people are saying, like you can.'

'I suppose I ought to teach you. It could be useful to you one day. I was lucky. My mother always spoke Greek to me when I was little. In fact when I first went to school I knew very little English.'

Anne giggled. 'Did everyone think you were Greek?'

'No, just stupid.' Her father gave a wry smile. 'You can start learning now. If Ourania's there when we get to the apartments you can say good morning in Greek to her, and when we leave you can say thank you. Do you remember thank you from yesterday?'

Anne nodded. 'I said it to the old lady at the farm.'

'The old lady!' Michael looked at his daughter in amazement. 'She's not old.'

'She looked old, much older than mummy.'

'I'm sure your mother would be very pleased to hear you say that. Anna looks old because she's had to work very hard on the farm in all weathers. In countries like this where it's very warm your skin dries up and you get wrinkles.'

Anne lifted her face up towards the blue sky. 'I wouldn't mind getting wrinkles. I love the sunshine.' She studied her father carefully. 'Daddy, you know when mummy and I went to the toilet on the farm?'

'Yes.' Michael remembered Anne's comment.

'I could see a donkey up in the fields. Did it belong to them?'

'I expect so. When I knew them they always had a donkey. Yannis or Anna used to bring her up in the morning. One of them would collect her again in the evening and when Yannis came up for the sheep and goats he would tell me which soldiers were going into Aghios Nikolaos for the evening.'

'I suppose we couldn't go and see the donkey?'

Michael looked down at her eager face. 'I don't see why we shouldn't. Let's see if Ourania's in first and you can see her cat, then we'll go out to the farm.'

Ourania was delighted to see them, apologised for Yannis's absence, and produced her cat for Anne to play with.

'He should be back within an hour, then he's going over to see Yiorgo. He goes most days. His sheep are there and it's a good excuse to call on both lots of relatives and make sure they don't need anything.'

'Your mother still lives in the village then?'

Ourania nodded. 'A little distance between Yannis and mamma makes them better friends.'

Michael smiled. He knew just how trying a mother-in-law could be. 'I suppose Yannis wouldn't give us a lift? I left my wife not feeling very well and don't want to take my car in case she wants to go anywhere when she recovers.'

'Of course he will. You're sure your wife doesn't need a doctor? Doctor Stavros would see her. He's very good.'

'I know he is. He took my appendix out. I'll see him before we leave, but I'm sure Heather will be fine once her migraine has cleared. There's no need to trouble him on her account.'

Ourania looked at Anne, playing happily with the kitten and a piece of string. 'She loves my cat.'

'She loves all animals. It's her idea to go out to the farm. She spotted the donkey yesterday.'

Ourania smiled. 'There are some kittens in the stable. They're not like Beauty, but she'd probably enjoy seeing them. Now, would she like an ice cream? The place next door sells chocolate ones.'

Anna was relieved when she saw Yannis draw up in his car and that he had Michael with him. Eleni was with her, complaining that Michael had not been to see her the previous day, and she had helped the resistance just as much as Anna.

Michael spent time reminiscing with her, assuring her she was the main reason for his second visit as he had missed seeing her the previous day and could not bear to leave Crete without doing so. Innocently he spoke of his evening spent with Yannis and Ourania.

'How did you know where to find them?'

'Anna and Yiorgo took me in.'

Eleni turned to Anna immediately. 'Why wasn't I asked to go? Ourania is my daughter.'

'It was my fault,' Michael apologised. 'I didn't know Yannis had married your daughter, or of course we would have asked you.'

'You may not have known, but Anna knows. She should have told you and I should have been there.'

'Eleni,' Yannis placed a hand on her shoulder. 'I've come to take you back into Aghios Nikolaos with me now. Of course Ourania wants to see you, and she thought it would be nice if you spent some time together. There's usually so many of us around.'

A satisfied smile spread across Eleni's face. 'I'll get my shawl and I'll be ready.'

'Five minutes,' promised Yannis. 'I'll be down for you.' He waited until she had walked away. 'What a woman! Can't bear to think I've seen Yiorgo and Anna and she hasn't seen Ourania. I'll be bringing Eleni back this afternoon, so it's no trouble to pick you up then.'

'It was Anne's idea to come.' Michael wondered why it sounded like a lame excuse. 'She wanted to see the donkey.'

'I'll pick you up about three.' Yannis raised his hand and climbed back into his car. 'I shall be interrogated all the way back about last night.'

Anna looked at Michael. 'Why have you come?'

'Anne wanted to see the donkey and Ourania says you have some kittens in the stable.'

'Is that all, Michael?' She looked at him steadily.

'I needed to talk to you – alone,' he added.

'Where is your wife?'

'Not feeling very well. She decided to stay in bed and rest.'

Anna nodded. 'Take Anne to the stable. The kittens are in a box at the back. Tell her not to touch them. Their mother's very wild still and may scratch her. I'll make a lunch for us to take to the fields and join you.'

Anne knelt on the prickly straw and gazed entranced at the rough and tumble taking place inside the cardboard box. Every so often one would pause in its game, looking up at Anne to hiss and spit, before returning to attack its sibling.

'They're lovely, just like little tigers. Will they ever be tame?'

'I doubt it. Anna says their mother's very wild still and they'll not be encouraged to go into the farmhouse. Greeks don't make pets of their animals the way we do.'

'Ourania does.'

'Hers is a different cat, specially bought for her. These are just farm cats, kept to catch the mice.'

Anne teased one with a piece of straw. The mother arched her back and stretched, gazing steadily at Anne with her yellow eyes. 'I'll not hurt her,' Anne promised. 'Her or him? How do you tell when they're so tiny?'

'You tip them up and have a look, but I'm not putting my hand in there to find out for you. Here comes Anna. We can go up to the donkey now.'

Reluctantly Anne left the kittens and the trio trudged up the hill in silence.

'Would she like to ride her?' asked Anna. 'She'll be quite safe.'

'How about that, Anne? Would you like a ride?'

'How do I say 'yes, please'?' she whispered.

Michael laughed. 'Anna doesn't speak any English so you don't have to whisper, and you say 'yes, thank you,' remember?'

Shyly Anne spoke the words and her father lifted her on to the donkey's broad back. 'You're quite safe. She'll amble around with you as she crops the grass and you can give me a shout when you've had enough.'

Michael led Anna over to the wall. 'Shall we sit down? I can sit beside you at last, instead of having to lay behind it.'

'I must remember to milk one of the goats before we go down. Anne can give the cat her milk.'

'Anna, forget about cats and milking goats. There are more important things we have to talk about.'

Anna lifted troubled eyes to him. 'Why have you come back, Michael?'

Michael sighed. 'I'm not sure if I can answer that. I kept telling myself that I wanted to see Crete again, but it was an excuse to see you. I wanted to prove to myself that you were not the reason that my marriage is such a failure, that you meant nothing to me now.'

Anna did not answer.

'Why didn't you tell me you weren't married?'

'You never asked me.'

'I just assumed you were because of the children. What a fool I was!'

'It would have made no difference, Michael. You went back to England.'

'I would have come back for you. I swear it, as soon as the war was over I would have returned.'

'For what?'

'To take you to England.'

Anna smiled sadly. 'That would have been impossible and you know it. I had my mamma and the children. I couldn't leave them, and then Yiorgo came back.'

'I could have stayed here.'

'And what would you have done here, Michael? You're not a farmer.'

'I'd have found something, anything to be with you.'

Anna shook her head. 'No, Michael. You were in a strange land. Your life was always in danger and I was willing to help you. It was a fantasy.'

'I loved you, Anna. I still love you, and years ago I thought you loved me.'

'You're married Michael.'

'Only in name. I'm leaving her.'

Anna looked at him fearfully. 'Why?'

'We had words last night. I walked out on her and slept in the car.'

'Oh, Michael.'

'As soon as we get back to England I'll leave her and she can start divorce proceedings.'

'You can't do that, Michael. What about Anne?'

'What about her? She'd be better off with one parent than two who are always fighting. Half the time she dare not open her mouth for fear that she says the wrong thing and starts another row.'

'You must have loved her once.'

Michael took Anna's work-worn hand in his own. 'When I was shipped back to England I was still feeling pretty groggy physically and devastated at the thought of never seeing you again. As soon as I was fit I tried to get back out here, but they wouldn't have it. A nice quiet desk job was a suitable reward for all I'd done. I was stationed in London and although it was wartime there was a party every night if you could stand the pace. Everyone lived for that day, they refused to talk about tomorrow, because it might never come for them. I thought you were married and I tried to forget you with every pretty girl I saw. I met Heather at a cocktail party. She was pretty, vivacious, a social butterfly. Her father had money and she was involved in charity work. It was the thing to do if you didn't have to work. She soon showed she was interested in me. I drifted into a relationship with her which meant very little to me and then I found I was in too deep to get out. Anne was on the way. I suppose I could have left her then,' Michael sighed, 'but it was the coward's way out I thought. I was more of a coward to marry her than to face the fact that I didn't love her.'

Anna's hand tightened on Michael's. 'Poor Michael.'

'Daddy, Daddy, look!' Anne let go of the rein with one hand and waved at her father.

'You be careful.' He turned back to Anna. 'If she falls off I'll be in more trouble. When I went back to the hotel this morning I found Heather had dosed herself up on sleeping tablets. She always does if we have a row over anything. I left her a note to say I'd taken Anne out, but I didn't say where.'

Anna bit her lip. 'Anne will tell her?'

'Sure to, she's having a wonderful time, and I wouldn't ask her to lie for me.'

'She's all right, with these sleeping tablets?'

'She was snoring when I left. She's been taking them for years. When I come back, Anna…'

Anna placed her finger on his lips. 'We'll not talk about it now. Fetch Anne and we'll have some lunch.'

'You stand by the donkey and let me have a photograph of you both.' Michael helped Anna to her feet and looked deeply into her eyes. 'I love you, Anna.'

Anne placed the bowl of milk, still warm from the goat, beside the box in the stable and sat down on a bale of hay. The cat stalked forward slowly, mistrust showing in her every movement.

'There's a good cat, a lovely cat. Come and have some milk, there's a good cat.'

Anne crooned the words softly and hypnotically over and over again as the cat crept forward. Very slowly Anne moved her hand downwards until she was no more than an inch from the cat's back. She waited, then moved again, the cat looked up at her, then dipped her head back into the bowl. Anne lowered her hand the final fraction and touched the rough fur. For a moment the cat bristled and Anne expected her to run, then she seemed to relax, sensing she had nothing to fear, and bent her head back into the bowl. A happy smile on her face, Anne continued to stroke her.

Yannis arrived with Eleni just before three, she was full of her daughter, what she had said, what they had done together, until Anna could listen no more.

'I'm sorry, I'm not feeling well, Eleni. Come tomorrow and tell me.'

Eleni looked from Anna to Michael, a sly smile on her lips, but Anna did look rather pale.

'It's my fault,' Michael apologised. 'I made Anna walk on the hills with me and sit up there in the sun whilst my daughter rode the donkey. I should have been more thoughtful. I'd forgotten how strong the sun is at mid-day.'

'I'll walk you down the road, Eleni. Then I'll drive Michael and his daughter back to Aghios Nikolaos.' Yannis shepherded his mother-in-law out of the house.

'I have something for you before you go, Michael.' Anna went to the cupboard and took out a large, flat box. 'These are more of Maria's sketches. I'd like you to have this one.'

Michael looked at the drawing before him. It showed a family group having a picnic in the hills, much as they had done only an hour or so ago. He felt a lump come into his throat, knowing Anna was giving him one of her most treasured possessions.

He drew Anna into his arms and kissed her. 'I love you, Anna. I swear that nothing will stand in the way of me returning to you.'

With the precious sketch rolled in a piece of cloth they went to find Anne, sitting in the stable stroking a docile cat that lay at her feet.

Anna's eyes opened wide. 'The child has a gift. No one has ever touched her before.'

At their presence the cat arched her back and spat, jumping back to the security of the straw bales.

'You've spoilt it, daddy. You frightened her.' Anne turned reproachful eyes on her father.

'It's time to go. Yannis is here with the car.'

Anne's face fell. 'Do we have to? This has been the best day of the holiday.'

'Then say thank you to Anna.'

Without a second thought Anne threw her arms around her namesake. 'Thank you, thank you for a perfect day.'

Anna held her tightly. 'Look after her, Michael. She's a lovely child.'

'I'll bring her back when I come,' he promised and Anna felt her eyes brimming with tears.

Yannis studied the profile of the grim-faced man sitting beside him. 'Something wrong?'

Michael sighed. 'Very wrong, but I intend to put it right as soon as I'm back in England. Why didn't you tell me she was your aunt?'

Yannis shrugged, lifting both hands off the steering wheel. 'You never asked me – it never occurred to me that you needed to know.'

'I loved her.'

Yannis shot him a swift glance and slowed the car. 'Do you want to talk? We could stop at a taverna.'

'I could do with a drink.'

'From what I saw before I left Aghios Nikolaos you're going to need one!'

Michael groaned. 'Was she making much of a scene?'

Yannis grinned. 'Yes, but no one knew what she was carrying on about. Another half an hour won't make much difference to her.' He drew in to the side of the road. 'Not the best in town, but adequate.'

Michael turned to Anne who had been kneeling on the back seat, watching the road unwind behind her. 'Come on, ice cream time. Yannis and I have some business to discuss.'

Obediently Anne allowed herself to be led into the taverna where a grubby baby was playing on the floor. Anne squatted down beside him. 'Hello,' she said, and was rewarded by a quizzical look.

'He'll keep her occupied,' smiled Michael. 'Animals and babies and she's happy for hours.'

Yannis ordered brandy for them both, then looked at his companion. 'Are you trying to tell me that you and my aunt were lovers during the war?'

Michael shook his head. 'I don't know how much she's told you about events.'

'She never talks about the war.'

'She was fantastic. We could always rely on her if a man was wounded. I don't know what she used, but they always recovered and hardly a scar to show for it. We had a bit of a skirmish whilst trying to rid the world of that German commander and one of my men ended up with a bullet lodged in his thigh.

The doctor had been and removed it, and we were relying on Anna to come up and change the dressing. The Germans were everywhere, they'd been doing spot searches as they knew we were in the area, and also that we'd had a couple of casualties. I didn't dare leave the cave and meet Anna as usual. Unfortunately she was found by a soldier on patrol. He gave her a nasty fright. If one of my men hadn't been on watch she would certainly have been raped.'

Yannis sucked in his breath. 'She's never told me any of this.'

'Don't tell her I told you. She probably prefers to forget the incident.'

Yannis shook his head. 'Of course I won't.'

'Well, she was brought into the cave and they told me what had happened. She was shivering and sobbing, her clothes all torn, but unhurt. I sat there holding her in my arms and I realised just how much I loved her. If Takis hadn't clubbed that soldier and he'd…' Michael shuddered.

'So why didn't you tell her you loved her?'

'It wasn't the right time. Afterwards when we met we would kiss and hold hands, never anything more. I thought she knew how I felt about her. When my appendix flared up she insisted on taking me to Doctor Stavros, regardless of the risk she was running. I heard her shouting and screaming that her husband, Babbis something or other, needed a doctor. She told the soldier I was Marisa's father. I'd never really thought about her being married before.' Michael sighed deeply. 'I decided that I couldn't leave Crete without seeing her again. The wicked thought crossed my mind that her husband might have been killed in the fighting.' Michael shrugged and swallowed his brandy in a gulp and Yannis refilled the glass.

Yannis nodded. 'I remember. You frightened the life out of us as you came through the door, then I saw your eyes and recognised you.'

'I quite thought those Italian soldiers would realise I was a fake. We only had a few moments together. I told Anna I would come back, but I remember she shook her head and said she couldn't leave you children. How could I double cross a fellow resistance worker by persuading his wife to leave him? I'd already betrayed him by falling in love with her.' Michael sighed deeply. 'I decided that I had to forget her, but if we'd had longer…'

'So you went back to England and married, whilst Mamma Anna sat there hoping you'd come back. Why didn't you write to her?'

'I honestly thought she was your mother. So many soldiers returned home to find their wives had run out on them – and where could she have gone? She had her mother and you two children. It would have put her in an impossible situation.'

Yannis topped up his own glass. 'So why have you come back now?'

'I had to. Heather and I are finished, completely finished now. It didn't work from the start, but I blamed myself. I thought it was because I continually compared my life with Heather to the one I envisaged with Anna. I admit that can't have helped the situation, but it wasn't all my fault. All Heather wanted was a wedding ring. She didn't love me any more than I loved her. I had an idea that if I could come back here and see Anna living happily with her husband I'd be able to forget her and give my marriage another try. If it weren't for Anne I would have left Heather long ago.'

'So what are you planning to do?'

'Divorce. It's the only answer. I'm sure Heather will agree and I'll not contest it. Your aunt's name won't be mentioned, I'll see to that. As soon as it's absolute I'll come back and marry Anna.'

'And your daughter?'

'I'd like to bring her back with me, but I doubt if I'll be given custody. She'll probably be allowed to spend her summer holidays out here.'

'Does Mamma Anna know? Has she agreed to marry you?'

'She knows I'm coming back. Why? You don't think she'll refuse, do you?'

Yannis spread his hands. 'I can't say. She's never given any hint to me about her feelings for you. In fact, to be honest with you, Michael, I'd almost forgotten you. Now I think about it there were one or two occasions when Mamma Anna was most unlike her usual self, but I didn't associate those times with you.' Yannis frowned. 'I've been brought up from birth by her and only now do I realise what a private person she is. We all go running to her with our problems and she never complains. It would do her good to get away from the farm and have a life of her own.'

Michael drained his glass. 'I suppose I ought to go back and face the music.'

Yannis pulled a wry face. 'Rather you than me.'

Anna read Yannis's letter with pleasure. He seemed to be accepting life at the hospital now the closure had finally been placed on the island. Reading between the lines Anna discerned that Dora had a good deal to do with his change of heart. In almost every sentence her name was mentioned and Anna wondered just how much influence the woman was able to impose on her brother.

In her reply Anna once again offered him a home at Plaka with them and mentioned the surprise visit from Michael and how pleased they had been to see him and his family. Of her personal feelings she made no mention.

Each day her mood varied, sometimes elation, knowing Michael would be returning to her, other days she felt a black despair, convinced she would never see him again, and have to stifle all the long suppressed emotions that tended to surface and threaten to engulf her.

The news from Marisa a week later sent her into a frenzy of cleaning and polishing. In a month's time she and Victor would be visiting. They would bring the boys with them, they had to be seen to be believed, their photographs did not do them justice. Tentatively Marisa suggested they stay in a hotel in Aghios Nikolaos, but Anna would not hear of it. Mattresses could be brought downstairs and the family from Italy could have her room and Yiorgo's.

She approached Yannis with her money in her hand. 'I want you to buy me a bed. It must be a big one, it's for Marisa and Victor, but it has to be small enough to go up the stairs and through the doorway. How did you get your bed into your apartment?'

Yannis smiled at her. 'They come in pieces and then you fit them together. Put your money away and come into Aghios Nikolaos with me and choose one.'

Anna looked at him cautiously. 'You don't think I'm being foolish, do you?'

'Foolish? What's foolish about buying a bed?'

'Well,' Anna hesitated. 'They're only coming to stay for two weeks.'

Yannis smiled at her. 'I'm sure you'll use it after they've gone. You'll find it more comfortable than a mattress on the floor.'

Anna blushed and Yannis turned away so she should not see him smile. 'What about uncle Yiorgo? Are you going to buy a bed for him?'

'Of course. The baby will sleep with Marisa, but the older boy will need a bed.'

'Get your shawl. We'll go into town now before you change

your mind. What about pillows, sheets, and blankets, do you have enough?'

'I'm not sure. Maybe.'

Yannis smiled benevolently. 'We could always get some spares, just in case.'

Anna was in a flutter of excitement. The new beds had arrived and Yannis had suggested a coat of white wash to the bedroom walls before taking them up and erecting them. Grudgingly Yiorgo had agreed to help him, although he saw no good reason for the waste of paint. The beds, with new mattresses, sheets, blankets and pale green covers were Anna's pride and joy. The iron-framed double bed all but filled her tiny room, but she did not mind. It was worth it to have her niece visit, and maybe, when Michael returned...

Anna refused to accompany Yannis to the airport to meet Marisa, but now she regretted the decision. Everything was in readiness and she had nothing to do but wait. Yiorgo had glanced sourly at his mattress in his old bedroom beside the kitchen. It was such a lot of fuss about nothing. The way his sister was carrying on you would think someone important was coming. He did finally agree to return to the house to wash and change before their expected time of arrival, although he refused to don his Sunday suit.

The car drew up outside and Yannis placed his hand on the horn quite unnecessarily. Anna was out of the door as he applied the brakes, then she stopped. From the car stepped an elegant young woman wearing a cream linen suit, a baby in her arms, whilst Victor swung his other young son up into his arms.

'Marisa! I would never have known you.'

Marisa giggled. 'That's what Yannis said when he met us at the airport. Victor, take the baby so I can say hello properly.' Marisa enfolded her aunt in her arms. 'Oh, it's good to be back. I have missed you. Why haven't you come to see us? I've asked you a hundred times. Come and meet Angelo. He's feeling very shy.' The small boy released his father's hand reluctantly and stepped forward.

'Does he speak Greek?' asked Anna.

'Of course. He speaks Greek and Italian. Say hello to aunt Anna, Angelo, then to uncle Yiorgo.'

Anna studied the small, serious face. 'He's like your pappa.'

Marisa turned triumphantly to Victor. 'You see! I always told you so.'

Victor smiled at her indulgently. 'Of course, you are right. Always you are right.' He winked at Yannis. 'We could carry the cases in?' He handed Giovanni back to Marisa and picked up two cases. 'Where they go?'

'Upstairs. I'll show you.' Anna led the way and pushed open the bedroom door to show off the new furnishings.

Victor smiled at her. 'Is nice. Much more nice than the mattress on the floor.' He placed the cases beside the bed. 'Now I say hello.' He seized Anna and kissed her soundly. 'Marisa miss aunt Anna, I also.'

'I've missed you too. It's been such a long time.'

Victor frowned. 'My fault. Marisa want babies. I want babies.' He shook his head. 'Not well when babies on way.'

'You have two beautiful children.'

Victor smiled proudly. 'Two, we have, no more. Doctor say no to Marisa.'

Anna nodded. 'She told me.'

'Now we go down, see Yiorgo, be happy,' he beamed at her. 'Always I love aunt Anna and cheese and spinach pie.'

'What is wrong, Anna?'

Anna looked at Victor sharply. 'Nothing. Why should there be?'

Victor shrugged. 'I just feel there is something.'

'Only that you will be gone in a few days. I shall miss you all so much.'

'We miss too. Marisa miss very much, Angelo miss, even Giovanni miss aunt Anna.'

Unaccountably Anna's eyes misted. 'Everyone I love always has to go away.'

Victor looked at her quizzically. 'Man in cart hurt Anna? I know he visit. Yannis tell me.'

Anna felt a lump come into her throat. 'It was good to see him again.'

'He come back for Anna?'

'He has no reason to come back.'

'Love very good reason.' Victor's dark eyes seemed to penetrate to her soul and she felt herself colouring.

'Don't be silly, Victor.'

'I come back for Marisa.'

'That was different, you were both young. Besides, he's married with a little girl.'

Victor shrugged. 'He must decide. Come back to stay or go and not come back. But not come, go, come and hurt aunt Anna.'

Anna tried to smile. 'I shall hurt more when you leave.'

'Come back with us. Always we ask you, always you have good reason to say no. Now no reason.'

Anna hesitated. 'I'll think about it, Victor,' she promised, knowing her answer would be no. She must be there for when Michael returned.

Yannis returned from the airport to find his aunt sitting desolately in the living room, her hands lying idle in her lap. He squeezed her shoulders.

'They'll be back, or you could go and visit them.'

'It just seems so quiet and empty.'

Yannis looked around. 'Why don't you put the wireless on? That would be company for you whilst Yiorgo is up in the fields.'

Anna shook her head. 'They're just voices.'

'All right, come into Aghios Nikolaos with me and you and Ourania can wander around the shops.'

Again Anna shook her head.

Yannis squatted down beside her. 'You don't have to stay here all the time. He knows where to find you.'

Anna looked at her nephew. 'He told you he was coming back?'

'He was very definite about it. If you're not here he'll come to Aghios Nikolaos and find me.'

'It isn't right, Yannis.'

'What isn't right? Why should you be denied some happiness just because he made a mistake and married that stupid woman? If I'd had any sense I'd have insisted he stayed here and told her to go back to England alone.'

Anna shook her head. 'There's Anne to think of. She needs a father.'

'She'll still have one. He'll write to her and she can come to Crete for her summer holiday. Maybe he'd like to manage one of my hotels in the season?'

'That's grand talk, Yannis.'

'Not as grand as you think. This is a secret between us, just you and me. In two weeks time I'll have signed for the controlling share in two more. They're dilapidated and run down, they'll need a good deal of work done on them, but by next season they'll be bringing in some money.'

'Really? Where are they?'

'Both in Heraklion. Next time I go up I'll take you with me. We'll look at the two old ones, then I'll show you the one that was built on my land. That's how I shall want those to look.'

'Can I tell Yannis and Marisa about them when I write?'

'Of course. I just don't want Ourania to know yet. She gets worried when I spend money. I keep telling her I know what I'm doing, but I don't think she believes me. You know, you could really do me a big favour. I want her to sort the shop out. It's just a mess. She's selling guidebooks, maps, jewellery, ornaments, scarves, sweets, postcards – you name it and she's got it tucked away somewhere. If you could come up and help her for a few days it could make all the difference.'

'I've never worked in a shop.'

'I'm not asking you to work in it. She can see to the customers. I want you to sort out the rubbish, get rid of the sweets and cheap jewellery. I saw some beautiful onyx ornaments when I was up in Heraklion. I want her to start specialising in better quality goods.'

'Just give it a clean out, really?'

'That's it. When she sees how much space she could have to display the good items it will encourage her.'

'Well, I suppose I could do that.'

'Fine. I'll come and collect you tomorrow and bring you back in the afternoon.' Yannis kissed his aunt. 'I don't know what I'd do without you to rely on.'

Yannis left Anna in a happier frame of mind. His next hurdle would be to persuade Ourania. The idea for changing the shop had come to him on the spur of the moment as an excuse to take his aunt away from the farm for a few hours and stop her brooding. He was not at all sure how his wife would react. Fortunately for him Ourania was willing to be co-operative.

She looked steadily at her husband. 'I know there's something wrong. I'm not sure what it is, but it seems to stem from when that English family visited. You don't have to tell me, Yannis. If it will help Anna to come and fiddle around in the shop for a few weeks then I'll suffer the intrusion. All I ask is that we do something similar with my mother or we'll never hear the end of it.'

'I'll think of something,' Yannis promised her.

Surreptitiously Anna removed the box of sticky sweets to the back room, along with the cheap jewellery. She sorted the maps from the guidebooks and postcards and draped the scarves along one plain white wall. Ourania had to agree the change was for the better, making the shop look more attractive and less cluttered.

'I wish we could find something for the other wall.'

'We could hang some more scarves,' suggested Anna, but Ourania shook her head.

'We need something different.'

'Suppose we had some shelves and put some books up there?'

Again Ourania shook her head. 'They'd get too dusty and we'd have to keep climbing up for them.'

'I know, Yannis's pictures.'

'He'd never sell those.'

'I should hope not,' retorted Anna swiftly. 'They won't be for sale. If I brought in the box from the farm and Yannis had some of them framed we could hang them around. They'd look better than the scarves and people would come in to try to buy them and buy something else instead.'

'That's a good idea. Do you think we could?'

'We'll ask Yannis.'

Yannis thought the idea was excellent. 'There's one condition, 'Rani, you get rid of all the junk. I'll take you up to Heraklion tomorrow and I'll show you the onyx I've been talking about. If you had that on display with some marble statues it would be like an art gallery. You'd become well known for your quality.'

'I don't know anything about art,' protested Ourania.

'You don't have to know anything about it. I'm not asking you to sell masterpieces, just well crafted work. Nothing flawed or chipped, or badly made. You could have some really good, expensive items and some of the cheaper gifts that the tourists go for. Look at Yiorgo's up the road. You can buy an embroidered handkerchief for a few drachma or a tablecloth or shawl that costs hundreds, but you won't find a loose thread on anything or a stain.'

Ourania looked around her shop, at the battered wooden

counter, the box where she kept the money and the old chair where she sat. 'If we're going to sell high class goods we'll have to make some improvements in here.'

Yannis grinned. 'Why do good ideas always cost money? Come on, then, tell me what you want and we'll see what we can do.'

'I'd like glass. A glass counter, with sliding doors, like they have in Minos, the jewellers, so I could put the expensive items in there and they wouldn't get broken. I'd like glass shelves, some of them high and some lower, just little ones, to hold one or two pieces at a time. And the floor, something would have to be done about the floor. Black tiles, that's it, and a black chair.'

Yannis was calculating rapidly. The changes his wife had in mind were going to cost him a small fortune and then there would be the new stock to buy. He smiled at her confidently.

'I'll look around a bit and get some figures. You work out how many shelves you want and where you'll put them.'

Driving back to Plaka Anna noticed the worried frown on Yannis's face.

'Have you got enough money, Yannis?'

'Of course. Why?'

'It just seems rather grand suddenly.'

'I'll have a talk to the bank manager. I expect he'll lend me some.'

'You shouldn't ask strangers for money. Yiorgo and I could lend you some.'

Yannis smiled at her innocence. 'When you ask the bank manager to lend you money, he doesn't lend you his own. He lends money that other people have placed in the bank. If he gives you one drachma for every hundred you deposit, he charges me two drachmas for every hundred I borrow. That way he pays you and makes a profit.'

'But if Yiorgo and I lend you the money you won't have to pay any extra.'

'That wouldn't be fair, but you've given me an idea. I'll talk to uncle Yiorgo when we get to the farm.'

Yiorgo spread his hands at Yannis's request. 'I told you it would be no good you coming to me when you'd spent your money and wanted more.'

'It's not like that, uncle,' protested Yannis. 'I have plenty of money, but I don't want to use it. I've just signed a deal for these hotels and it's going to cost quite a bit to repair and decorate them. I don't want to have to sell one to finance the shop, but I also don't want to disappoint Ourania. She's got some good ideas. I was going to ask the bank manager for a loan, then Anna suggested I asked you. It will be worth your while. I'll pay you the same interest as if I was borrowing from the bank and I'll even give you my share of the sheep and goats as security.'

'Don't know why you don't sell the animals. You're too busy these days to be a farmer.'

'Then you keep them, uncle. Have them as a present from me for lending me the money.'

'I can't do that.'

'Then I'll tell you what. You look after them for me and I'll pay you for doing so. If I can't pay back the money I borrow from you within a year then you keep them.'

'I've been looking after them for you anyway.'

Yannis laughed. 'Now who's the businessman? How much do you want as a back payment?'

Yiorgo shook his head. 'I know you're making me a good offer. It just worries me when I hear you've bought land, hotels and the like. What happens if you don't make money and you've no farm to fall back on?'

Yannis smiled easily at his uncle. 'If the shop doesn't make money we can let it or sell it. There'd be no problem there. If the hotels don't make money I can sell my share back to the others, and I still have my father's land and a little more elsewhere. I do know what I'm doing, uncle.'

Reluctantly Yiorgo had to agree that his nephew certainly seemed capable of managing finance.

'There's a condition, uncle. When I pay this money back I want to see most of it going into the bank. You trust me as a business man, don't you?'

Yiorgo nodded.

'Then trust me on this. You will not only make money by putting it in the bank, but it will be safe. Just suppose you had a fire? You'd have nothing left.'

'Yannis is right,' agreed Anna. 'My money has increased since I put it in the bank. You ought to do the same, Yiorgo.'

Grudgingly Yiorgo agreed. Somehow money in the bank was not the same as having it in the cupboard where you could see it.

Michael drove steadily towards the airport. His mood alternating between sadness and elation. The bitter and acrimonious words that had passed between him and Heather were best forgotten; he would never need to see her again. The final hurt had been when she had refused to let Anne visit him.

'Let her fly out there on her own? Now I know you're mad.'

'She'd come to no harm. The stewardess would look after her. Plenty of children fly on their own. I'd be there to meet her at the airport. If you don't like the idea of her flying alone come with her. You could always stay at a hotel.'

'I have no intention of ever setting foot in that country again, and if I have my way nor will she.'

'Don't you think you ought to ask her about that?'

'Anne is a child. Whilst she's under age she'll do as I say,' snapped Heather.

'Suppose the courts gave me custody? I'd let her come back to England to see you.'

'No judge in his right mind would give the custody of a child to a man. Besides which you'd have to say you were planning to take her to a foreign country where she doesn't even speak the language. What kind of schooling could she expect to have in that awful village?'

'She could go to school in Aghios Nikolaos.'

'And then what? Work on a farm or in a taverna? What a prospect for a bright child. No, it's far better that she stays here with me and goes off to boarding school as we'd planned.'

The evident pain in Michael's face gave Heather a malicious pleasure.

Michael consulted a firm of solicitors and was advised not to fight Heather's application for sole custody.

'It's in the interest of the child,' the lawyer explained. 'It can scar them emotionally for ever if they are questioned over which parent they want to stay with. They suffer the most tremendous feelings of guilt for the parent they have to reject. I've even known some who have needed psychiatric help to recover from the trauma. No, it's far better for you to say goodbye to her and wait until she's of age before contacting her again.'

'I can't even contact her?'

'Better not to. I've seen it all too often.' He tilted his chair back and placed the tips of his fingers together. 'Just as the child is accepting the loss of a father and re-adjusting to life with one parent along comes a birthday card or letter and they're thrown into a turmoil of indecision again. Very disruptive and distressing for them.'

Michael frowned. 'Anne's a very well-balanced child. I don't think it...'

'And that's how you'd like her to stay, isn't it, sir? Well-balanced. Take my advice, just say goodbye to her as if you were going to your normal place of work, no distressing scenes, just a quick, clean break.'

He had watched with a satisfied smile on his face as Michael walked away from his office. Heather had told him her husband knew nothing about custody laws and she had been right. That had been the easiest thousand pounds he had ever earned in his life.

Now the long letter he had written to his daughter, trying hard to be fair to her mother, yet convey his deep love for her, sat in the strong box at the bank, along with the picture Anna had given him. It was to be given to Anne when she reached her twenty-first birthday, and the choice would then be hers. Eleven long years without sight of her, not knowing what she was doing, if she was happy, whether she missed him. Tears misted his eyes as he swung towards the turn off, completely obliterating the lorry bearing down on him and giving neither of them the chance to take avoiding action.

Anna hugged the letter to her. Michael was coming. It was true. He did love her. Reverently she placed the letter between the folds of his shirt, which had sat for so long in her chest of clothes, and sighed with happiness. Whilst Yiorgo was in the fields she cleaned the house through, insisting he provided her with white wash to freshen up the kitchen and living room walls. Michael could arrive at any time and she wanted to be prepared for him.

To pass the interminable days of waiting Anna wrote long letters to both Yannis and Marisa, telling them about the changes to Ourania's shop. How she had helped, and then visited the suppliers with Yannis and Ourania selecting the goods they would sell. She tried to describe every detail of the glass shelving and the beautiful onyx vases that sat on it, the black shelves, which Ourania had decided would show off white marble statuettes to their full advantage, and how fine Maria's pictures looked up on the walls. She also added that Eleni had had no hand in it, and to mollify her Yannis had promised she should choose the covers for the beds in his new hotels when the refurbishment was complete.

Marisa replied that she was so glad Ourania had taken her advice and styled the shop on some of the most select establishments in Turin, and how she was sure some of the other shopkeepers would follow her lead or find they were losing trade. Anna took the letter in to Aghios Nikolaos and showed Ourania.

'Did Marisa really suggest you displayed the goods like this?' Anna asked.

Ourania smiled and nodded. 'You saw how smart she was. She said everyone in Turin dressed the way she did, and she described the shops to me. She said if I wanted to sell high-class goods, then the shop had to look high-class to start with or people with money to spend wouldn't come in. I think she's right. People come in to look because it's different and they always buy some little thing.' Ourania's eyes took on a dreamy look. 'I want Yannis to take me to Turin to see for myself all the lovely shops they have there.'

To Anna's surprise Yannis hardly mentioned Ourania's shop when he replied to her letter. He was full of his own news. He had had a letter printed in a medical magazine and the editor had suggested he should write some articles and send them away. Spiro and Dora had encouraged him and finally he had done so. The amazing thing was, whilst he was in the post office he was sure he had seen Stelios. He had tried to catch up with him as he left, but been unable to do so. He was now hoping he would bump into him again and be able to speak to him. He ended angrily that he wanted an explanation of Stelios's behaviour towards his family.

Anna sighed. Life never seemed to run smoothly for Yannis. He would never accept the inevitable, as she had, with her youngest brother. If he did not want to acknowledge them there was nothing she could do but accept the fact, as she was beginning to accept that Michael would not be returning to Crete.

It was more than six months since his letter and there had been no sign of him and no further word. Purposefully she kept herself busy, stifling the emotions which she had allowed to surface for such a short time, interesting herself in Ourania's business, tending her herb garden and ministering to the few people who still lived in the village.

Yannis wrote again, he was tired of living at the hospital, tired of his cramped accommodation, not having anything to do all day except visit museums and wander around Athens. He was still waiting to hear if his anecdotes about his life on Spinalonga had been accepted and he had not seen any sign of Stelios.

Anna wrote back, begging him to return to Plaka where he would be welcome to live on the farm, but knowing in her heart that however much he complained he would never be able to forsake the wonders of Athens for the huddle of dilapidated houses which made up the village, or be able to face living opposite the island that held so many memories for him. She suggested he visited Marisa and Victor where she knew he would receive a warm welcome.

The return letter she received confirmed that both her suggestions had been rejected. He would not go and live off relatives, being a useless burden to them and an embarrassment. At least he did not have to explain his condition to people at the hospital or make the excuse that he had been burnt in a fire and receive sympathy for his injuries.

Anna sat in Ourania's shop sipping coffee. She never tired of looking at the elegant and beautiful items displayed, although she declared she saw no point in having such useless objects around. Ourania had smiled and continued to stroke her Persian cat.

'You like looking at them here, so why not at home? Down you get, my Beauty. Here comes a customer.'

Ourania charmed them, offering them her lower priced wares, gradually bringing out the better pieces until she showed the most expensive. With a look that said she doubted if they could afford it, but they could admire, she skilfully talked them into parting with far more money than they had originally intended. She always boxed and wrapped the pieces before them so they knew they were in perfect condition when they left the shop, and not been exchanged for a damaged article.

'Do you always talk people into buying the more expensive goods?' asked Anna.

'I try. That's business. Sometimes a customer comes in who knows just what they want and nothing else will do, but usually they're just browsing and then I have to persuade them without appearing to influence them at all.'

'You and Yannis are such clever people,' sighed Anna.

'You're clever too. You know all about herbs.'

'That's just common sense. I could never run a business.'

'I'm sure you could. Think how you ran the farm whilst Yiorgo was away, and looked after your mother and the children. It can't have been easy for you.'

Anna sighed deeply. 'It's a good deal easier now, but I'd give a lot to have those days back again.'

Yiorgo was annoyed. Yannis had promised to pay him back the money he had loaned him within a year and it was thirteen months now. For the last two weeks Yannis seemed to have been avoiding him, and he was sure he would never see his savings again.

'Are you going into Aghios Nikolaos today?' he asked Anna.

'Yannis said he'd collect me during the morning.'

Yiorgo nodded. 'I'll stay around. I want a word with him.'

When Yannis arrived Anna relayed her brother's message and a broad grin spread over Yannis's face. 'I know what he wants to see me about. Quick, get in the car. I don't want to see him for two more days.'

'Why not? You haven't quarrelled with Yiorgo, have you?'

'Of course not. He wants his money repaid, that's all.'

'You haven't lost it, have you, Yannis?' asked Anna in horror.

Yannis looked at his aunt scornfully. 'No, I just want to see his face when I present him with the bank book and he sees how much interest he's earned. I want to have this month's put in, and it's due in two days time.'

Yannis skilfully avoided seeing his uncle until he was ready, then he sat easily at the table and passed the book across. Yiorgo opened it and frowned.

'What does this mean? I didn't lend you nearly as much as this.'

'I told you if you put your money in the bank you made money. I divided the money you'd lent me into twelve amounts and repaid the same amount, with interest, each month. The bank also gave you interest and look how it's mounted up.'

Yiorgo studied the small blue book. It didn't give him the same feeling of security and satisfaction as looking at a pile of drachma notes.

'Suppose I wanted some of this money? What would I have to do?'

'It's simple. You just go along to the bank, tell them how much you want and sign a form. They take the amount from your account and give you the cash.'

Yiorgo continued to look at the figure entered in the book in disbelief. 'Where did you get the money from each month to put in here?'

'From the shop. Thanks to you it's doing really well. I'd like to open another one, but I've no one to run it.'

'Anna could do it,' offered Yiorgo for her.

Yannis shook his head. 'Not on a full time basis, it would be too much. Ourania's open from early morning until late at night. We live above so it's no inconvenience. Anna would have to return to Plaka, and then she'd have the cooking and cleaning to do. She'd be worn out within a couple of weeks. I'm sure I'll find someone if I need them.'

As Yannis left Yiorgo followed him out to his car. 'I'd like to say thank you.'

'Don't mention it. I only forced you into doing something you should have done years ago.'

Yiorgo scratched his head. 'I'm proud of you, Yannis. I'm as proud of you as if you were my own son.'

Yannis felt a lump come into his throat. It was rare for Yiorgo to show any emotion. 'I hope I can continue to make you proud of me,' he said roughly and held out his hand for Yiorgo to shake.

Anna thought about Yannis's idea of opening another shop. She had no desire to spend all day sitting waiting for customers and was pleased that Yannis had turned Yiorgo's idea down out of hand, but there was Eleni. As Yannis drove her in to visit Ourania she tentatively put the suggestion to him.

'It would be as difficult for her as it would be for you. I'd have to collect her in the morning and bring her back each night. She'd be worn out in no time.'

'Not if she lived in a flat near you.'

Yannis looked at his aunt. 'You've got it all worked out, haven't you?'

'It just seemed like a good idea. She's lonely. She misses Ourania and if you set her up in a shop she'd feel really useful.'

'It's not the shop I'm worried about; it's having her live so close to us. It wouldn't work. She was the reason we moved to Aghios Nikolaos. Before I knew it she'd be running Ourania's life again. She almost managed to turn the shop into a general store and I'm not having that. We're becoming quite well known now. People come down from Heraklion and ask for us.'

'So why don't you open a shop in Heraklion?'

'Have you any idea how much a shop in Heraklion would cost? I managed to rent this one and the flats for next to nothing for the first few years. Now the rent's trebled and the rents are even higher in Heraklion. I can't afford that at the moment, not until the hotels start to bring in some extra money.'

'Why don't you open a shop in a hotel? You must have plenty of space.'

Yannis considered the idea. 'You know you might just have something there. Not everyone wants to come down to Aghios Nikolaos, but if there were some goods on display at the hotel they'd either buy there or want to see a wider selection.'

'There you are then.'

'I'd still need someone to run it, and Eleni would never agree to live in Heraklion.'

'For that I don't blame her.'

Yannis laughed. 'You've never even been to Heraklion.'

'And I've no wish to. Aghios Nikolaos is quite big enough for me.'

1960 – 1979

Anna read the letter from Yannis a second time. There was no mention of Stelios; all he wrote about was the acceptance of his articles. He planned to write more and wanted Anna to remember everything she could about her visits to the island and relate them to him. Spiro was reminding him of incidents which had happened and he was spending time with the few who had stayed at the hospital and cajoling them into helping him.

Anna smiled. Yannis had something to occupy him; the time would not hang so heavily on his hands now he had a new interest. She wondered if he would become famous and she would see his name on the covers of books displayed in the bookshop in Aghios Nikolaos. She would buy them, of course, but she doubted if she would read them.

The letter she had in reply to her own was not as happy as the previous one. Once again Yannis was fretting about living in the hospital. He had decided to ask Andreas about the money that had been deposited in the bank on behalf of the original hospital patients from Heraklion. Hoping that he would have enough he was looking at apartments in Athens to get an idea of the prices.

Anna suggested he returned to Crete, extolling the virtues of their nephew's apartment, which would surely be cheaper than anything he could rent in Athens. It was a forlorn hope and she knew as she wrote of the idea that it was doomed to failure.

Yannis turned the suggestion down out of hand. He had no

387

intention of renting; he planned to use his capital to buy and was relying on his small pension and the income from his writing to live on. He had seen a small apartment that he thought would be ideal, and was only waiting for the formalities to be completed to release his share of the money.

Before Anna could reply to him he wrote again. He had purchased the apartment and would be moving from the hospital in a few weeks, as soon as Dora had finished choosing the decoration and the furniture. Now he had somewhere decent to live he had asked Dora to marry him and she had agreed. Once they were settled Anna must come and visit them, to meet her new sister-in-law.

Anna had smiled to herself. She was certain nothing would ever get her to venture so far afield.

Yannis's disappearance to Heraklion for two or three days almost every week to check on the running of his hotels had become a common occurrence, but when he announced he would be staying away for a week, as he had to meet his business partners, Ourania objected.

'I don't see that you need to be gone a week. Suppose anything happened to your aunt or uncle whilst you were away, or even to me?'

'What do you think is going to happen to you? If you don't feel well you don't open the shop. You have friends and neighbours who would look after you until I could get back if you were really ill.'

'Why do you have to be gone a whole week?'

'It may not be a week, but I'll need the usual few days to inspect the hotels, then I have to go to Chania. I told you, Kyriakos has hurt his back and can't move from his chair. It's a good morning's drive from Heraklion, business in the afternoon, stay over night and drive back down here the following day. Would you like to come with me?'

Ourania considered her husband's offer. 'Not really. I'd like to go to Heraklion again, but not if you have business meetings to attend.'

'If you're worried about staying on your own you could ask your mother to come up for the week.'

'She would love that, Yannis.' Ourania slipped her hands behind her husband's neck. 'You are a kind and thoughtful person. I'm so glad I married you.'

Yannis kissed her. 'And I'm glad we moved to Aghios Nikolaos. You make sure your mother is ready to go back to her own home when I return.'

'I promise.'

Driving to Heraklion Yannis thought about Ourania's worries over his aunt and uncle. How would they send a message to Aghios Nikolaos if they needed help? Davros was the most practical messenger, and he would have to sail his fishing boat to Olous and row through the canal to get to the town; a major undertaking for a man of his age. Maybe it would be a good idea to talk to his partners about having telephones installed in their homes. It would save a considerable amount of time, just being able to talk to each other without having to drive to a meeting. All the hotels were wired for telephones and it seemed foolish for their owners to be without.

He smiled as he pictured Anna's face when he installed a telephone and instructed her how to use it. She would be as enthralled with that, as she had been when the electricity was first generated on Spinalonga.

The black implement sat on the windowsill in the living room and Anna regarded it warily. Yannis had told her that when it rang she was to lift the receiver and say hello and he would talk to her. She had been waiting ever since he had driven away and nothing had happened yet.

When the shrill sound came Anna was paralysed with fear. She stood and looked, not daring to touch or lift the receiver. It stopped and she breathed a sigh of relief, then the noise came again, an insistent, penetrating ring, which seemed to be inside her head. She stretched out a trembling hand, placed it on the telephone and curled her fingers round the receiver. Lifting it just off the rest she whispered, 'Hello.'

There was a crackling and slight noises, but she could not hear Yannis's voice, so she replaced it. Four more times in the next ten minutes she repeated the procedure, then the annoying noise ceased. The next thing she knew Yannis had drawn up outside.

'What's wrong with the telephone? Why haven't you been answering me?'

Anna looked puzzled. 'I have. Each time it rang I picked it up and said hello like you told me.'

'I couldn't hear you. I've asked Ourania to telephone here. If she can't hear me there must be something wrong with it.'

Yannis paced the room impatiently, snatching up the receiver on the first ring and placing it to his ear. 'I can hear you perfectly, 'Rani, can you hear me?' A pause. 'Fine. I'm going to ask you to talk to Anna now.' Yannis handed the receiver to his aunt. 'Say hello to Ourania.'

'Hello,' whispered Anna, holding it at arm's length.

With an effort Yannis controlled his amusement. 'No, not like that. Hold it up to your ear so that the other piece is by your mouth and talk into it the same as if Ourania were in the room and you were talking to her. Now can you hear her?'

Anna nodded.

'Then tell her. Say "hello, Ourania, I can hear you."'

Obediently Anna repeated the words, then handed the receiver back to Yannis.

'It's obviously working all right. I'll get Anna to telephone you back, then I'll come home.'

Yannis turned to his aunt with a smile. 'Now, when it rings, pick it right up and put it to your ear. You won't be able to hear otherwise. This is our telephone number and I want to see you dial it before I go. Ourania will answer and you can tell her I'm just leaving.'

It took some weeks before Anna felt at home with the new telephone and could answer it without her hands shaking. Each time he telephoned Yannis insisted she also telephoned him back, finally telling her she was to telephone him the next day at a certain time, breathing a sigh of relief when she did so. It would be comforting to know that as his aunt and uncle grew older they would be able to contact him at any time of the day or night if necessary.

Anna wrote to Yannis and Marisa and told them both at length how the telephone allowed her to speak to Yannis or Ourania at their shop just by dialling a number. Marisa replied that many people had them in Turin, but as yet Victor had not seen the need to invest in one. She would have to talk to him seriously about it as she was unexpectedly having another baby. Having been advised by the doctor to have no more after Giovanni, they had been very careful, but this one had "happened" and all seemed to be going well at present. Victor was delighted, and she hoped her sons would be when she finally told them the news. She had no doubt that once over the first shock of a new baby they would dote on it, despite the large age gap.

Marisa pressed her aunt to visit her in Turin as she would be unable to travel to Crete that year but Anna refused. It would be impossible for her to travel so far, particularly as she had no idea of the language. Each year, when they visited, she had seen Marisa's sons developing, and in some small way this had made up for the lack of offspring from Yannis and Ourania. This year she would not be able to have that pleasure.

Yannis had been most off-hand about the telephone, saying he frequently used one in Athens and was thinking of having one installed in their apartment. It could be useful, saving him long journeys across the city to consult with his publishers. He and Dora hoped Marisa would keep well during her pregnancy and asked Anna to keep him informed over the months.

He repeated his invitation to Anna to visit them, but as usual she declined. She was needed at Plaka to look after Yiorgo. He could not be expected to run the farm and also cook for himself. Yannis had smiled thinly, recognising this as an excuse almost as transparent as his own when he said he was too busy to visit Plaka.

Anna still jumped whenever the telephone bell rang, but she had lost her fear of the implement and would chat happily to Ourania two or three times a day. It was rare for it to ring during the evening, unless it was Yannis to let them know he had returned safely from Heraklion, and when it rang stridently, cutting across the wireless programme, she felt her heart racing.

'Hello?'

'Hello, aunt Anna, is Victor here.'

'Victor! What's wrong? Where are you? Is it Marisa?'

'All is good. Marisa have baby boy.'

'Where are you?' Anna looked around the room as if expecting Victor to materialise there.

'In Turino.'

'How is Marisa?'

'Very good.'

'So why are you telephoning, Victor?'

'To tell you good news. You understand, baby boy, today.'

'And Marisa really is all right?'

'Of course. Soon she will talk with you, next week maybe.'

'You mean you have a telephone?'

'Marisa want telephone to aunt Anna so I get telephone.'

'Oh, Victor.' Unaccountably Anna's eyes filled with tears. 'How are the boys?' she remembered to ask.

'Very good. Very happy with the new brother. His name Joseph.'

'I'm so pleased, so happy for all of you. Give me your telephone number so I can call Marisa.'

'No, Marisa call you when home from hospital. No good before. No one here.'

'Why is she in hospital?'

'Doctor say better in hospital.'

'Are you sure she's all right?'

'Marisa very good. Never I lie to aunt Anna, believe me, all is good.'

Heather opened the letter from the bank that was addressed to her daughter. It would probably be the usual reminder that she was overdrawn on her account and a request that she put matters to rights immediately. She knew Anne took little notice of such regular correspondence.

'They'll just have to wait,' she would shrug. 'How do they expect students to live on their grant? It's impossible.'

This letter was different and Heather sat down to read it again. The request was not for a repayment of an overdraft, but that Anne should call in and collect some papers that had been deposited there by her father. Heather sucked in her breath. All day she thought about it, finally deciding to telephone the bank and offer to collect them herself.

There was the usual delay whilst she was put through from the junior to a clerk to the manager. Heather explained; Anne was at University, not expected to return home until the end of term, so she would collect the papers on her daughter's behalf. The clerk refused and Heather insisted imperiously that she was to be put through to a higher authority. The bank manager was adamant. He had strict instructions. The papers were to be handed to Anne in person and signed for by her. Heather tried to be charmingly persuasive, but to no avail, finally slamming down the telephone in annoyance. She would keep a sharp eye on

Anne's post and anything that had the bank logo on the envelope would be opened.

Anne looked at her mother with distaste. Each holiday spent at home from boarding school had seen a different uncle in residence and Anne had felt unwanted and unloved. Having finished her University course the idea of living permanently in the same house for an indeterminate amount of time with her mother and her latest boyfriend did not appeal.

'I've made up my mind. I don't want to settle down yet. I want to travel and get some experience of the world.'

'So where would you travel? You went to France last year,' protested Heather, seeing her additional source of income disappearing.

'I mean really travel. I'm going to a Kibbutz for two months; then I'll see. I may stay on if I enjoy it.'

'All those years of education wasted.'

'They're not wasted. As a vet I can get a job anywhere in the world. I may decide to go to America or Australia eventually. I've heard you can earn better money there than in England.'

'So why go off to a Kibbutz?'

'To gain a bit of experience, see how other people live. You're very sheltered at University.' Anne hesitated. Should she tell her mother or wait until she returned from Israel? She decided to take the plunge. 'I've applied for overseas work in a third world country and they're considering me. I shan't hear for about three months, so I thought a Kibbutz was a good idea, get some idea of conditions outside England.'

'You won't be living at home at all, then?'

'No,' replied Anne cheerfully. 'As from next week you can let my room if you want. I'll pack up my stuff and put it in the loft.'

'The extra income would help. Your father certainly didn't leave a fortune, most of it was in trust for your education.'

'And I'm truly grateful to him.' Anne's face saddened. 'I do wish he had been able to see me on Graduation Day. He would have been so proud.'

Heather fixed Anne with a stony look. 'I doubt he would have been able to attend. He always put his own affairs before yours and mine.'

Anne returned from the Kibbutz, happy to have finished her stay there.

'I enjoyed it,' she told her friend, 'but I didn't feel very necessary. They're so well organised. I just hope I get chosen to go somewhere I can be really useful.'

'Maybe you should have been a nurse. They're always wanted in every country.'

Anne shook her head. 'I prefer animals. I always have. They seem to trust me.'

James looked at her sadly. 'You won't reconsider my offer?'

Anne kissed him on his nose. 'I'm very fond of you, James, but I don't want to settle down with anyone yet. You'll meet another girl and it will be my loss.'

James sighed. 'I'll not be looking very hard. You will write to me, won't you? I shall want to know all about the heathenish place you end up in.'

'Of course, but I've still got to be chosen yet.'

'You'll be chosen. No one in their right mind would turn down a vet who was willing to go to the ends of the earth to stick a needle in a sick cow.'

Anne giggled. 'If that's all there was to it anyone could do the job. You have to know what's wrong with them first. I'll have to do some swotting now I've been called for an interview.' She frowned. 'It would help if I knew before hand what country they had in mind. Different countries have different endemic diseases.'

The routine days passed monotonously for Anna. No longer did her heart jump whenever a vehicle passed the house. On Mondays she would go to Aghios Nikolaos with Yannis and spend the day sitting in Ourania's shop, Tuesday she tackled the weekly washing, Wednesday was cleaning day, Thursday was spent baking and Friday saw her back in the shop with Ourania. There was more than enough time to write long letters to her brother in Athens and her niece in Turin over the weekend, along with the customary visit to church.

The only time her routine differed was when Marisa, Victor and the boys came to stay. Even that she realised was coming to an end. Angelo was not coming with them that year. He was at University, studying to be an architect like his uncle, and had been invited to Rome by a friend, an invitation too good to refuse.

Anna smiled sadly as Marisa told her the news over the telephone. This year it was Angelo, in a couple of years it would be Giovanni, at least Joseph was still young enough to accompany his parents on their annual visit for a number of years.

She was surprised when they arrived to see Giovanni was now taller than his father and certainly more handsome than she remembered Angelo at that age. His voice was deep and melodious as he alternated between Greek and Italian.

'What do you plan to do now you're no longer at school?' she asked him. 'Are you going off to University?'

Giovanni seemed ill at ease for the first time. 'It depends. I really want to talk to uncle Yannis.'

Anna smiled. 'You want to have a shop like Ourania's?'

Giovanni shook his head and shuddered. 'I can't think of anything worse. I want to ask him if he'll let me work at one of his hotels.'

Giovanni glared defiantly at his father.

Victor shook his head. 'I tell him, he has good brain. Go to University.'

'I don't want to go to University, Pappa. What would I study?' Giovanni had reverted to Italian.

'Languages. You're obviously fluent in Italian and Greek, your English is good and so is your French.'

'And then what would I do? Become a teacher? I want to use my languages. We've been through all this before, Pappa.'

Anna looked from one to the other. 'Why do you want to work in a hotel?' she asked Giovanni.

Giovanni sat forward on his chair. 'I want to learn to become a manager. Not the kind of manager that uncle Yannis is. I don't want to go round and spend a day making sure the rooms are booked and the bills have been paid. I want to be the kind of a manager who talks to the guests. The one person they can rely on if they have a problem. You may have noticed when you go into Aghios Nikolaos the amount of foreigners there are over here. They don't speak Greek and the shopkeepers and hoteliers are beginning to pick up a bit of their language. I can do better than that. I can speak four languages, properly speak them, not just say "hello, how are you?" If there were foreign people staying in the hotel I could help them with their travel arrangements or anything else. Word would get round and visitors would want to stay in a hotel where they knew they would be understood.'

'And your Pappa doesn't like the idea?'

Victor shook his head. 'Good idea, but University first.'

'No.' Giovanni set his lips firmly. 'If I wait that long other people will have had the idea, besides, I don't need to know all the intricacies of a language to be able to speak to tourists.'

'And your Mamma, how does she feel?'

'Mamma always agrees with pappa.' Giovanni spoke somewhat scornfully.

Anna looked at Victor who shrugged.

'Suppose you ask Yannis his opinion?' she suggested. 'If he said University first would be a good idea would you agree?'

Giovanni shook his head. 'If uncle Yannis won't give me a chance at one of his hotels I'll ask elsewhere. Someone will realise the sense of what I'm saying.'

Giovanni was up in the hills with his younger brother and uncle Yiorgo when Yannis called in on his way back to Aghios Nikolaos from Heraklion. Anna took him to one side and told him of the boy's ambition. Yannis was full of enthusiasm.

'It's a brilliant idea! Why didn't I think of it? He'd have to start at the bottom, though. Long hours and little pay. He needn't think he could walk into a top job straight away.'

'Victor doesn't like the idea. He thinks Giovanni should go to University first.'

Yannis smiled. 'Leave Victor to me. I'll have a few words with Marisa, remind her how she threatened you she would run away with Victor if she didn't get her own way. She wouldn't want her son to leave home and she not know where he was. Once I've talked her into the right frame of mind, she can soon twist Victor round her little finger. In fact, I've got a really good idea. Suppose Giovanni stayed here and worked for the summer? If he changes his mind or I find he's no use he would still have time to go back and apply for University.'

Giovanni felt very pleased with himself. He had agreed to his uncle's suggestion and now he was thoroughly enjoying himself. The teeming life of Heraklion appealed to him far more than the solitude of the farm, or even the bustle of Aghios Nikolaos, and everywhere was fresher and cleaner than his home in Turin. He had listened intently as Yannis had explained how the bookings for the hotel were made and the rooms allocated, and agreed to work under the instruction of the elderly man who had been in charge since the hotel first opened.

Now left on his own to learn and expand his own interest he was making good use of his free time. Systematically he toured the hotels in the town, pretending to speak only Italian, and was amused at the puzzled reception he met with. At only one hotel was a porter called, who could speak a little of the language, and an attempt was made to understand his request.

He reported his findings to Yannis, who was suitably impressed. 'I've been doing a bit of research of my own,' he admitted. 'There's a school opening up to teach English. How about you enrolling for an advanced course?'

Giovanni agreed willingly. 'That should help reconcile Pappa a bit,' he grinned. 'If he thinks I'm continuing my studies he'll be less persistent about University. Do they only teach English? I'd like to keep my French going and maybe learning German would be useful.'

Panyotis gave a glowing report to Yannis. The boy was a real find. He was obliging, willing, and quite charming to the visitors. Nothing was too much trouble for him, and when he was not on duty at the reception desk people would ask for him and wait until he arrived. The notice Giovanni had placed in the window of the hotel made Yannis smile. Written in four languages was the statement 'In this establishment we speak Italian, French and English'.

'Is that really necessary?' Yannis asked.

'Of course. How do people know they'll be understood otherwise? I've had another idea, uncle. Suppose you advertised.'

'Advertised? What would I advertise and where? Local people don't want to stay in a hotel.'

Giovanni pulled a glossy brochure from beneath the counter. 'Look at this. I know you can't read it because it's in Italian, but look at the pictures. It's a magazine you get from a travel agent. It shows a picture of the hotel, says how much it is to stay there and all the local attractions. If we asked to be included and said the language was spoken here it would encourage tourists to book with us before they arrived. That way we have guaranteed custom and don't have to depend on people finding us by accident. We could also advertise the gift shop and mention Ourania's.'

Yannis looked at the lurid pictures. 'What are these offering?'

Giovanni pointed to one. 'They only show the outside of the hotel and a view of the town. We could show the bedrooms, have a picture of the gift shop and show Knossos. People would really know what to expect when they arrived.'

'Make up an example for me, Giovanni, in Greek, then I'll discuss it with my partners and let you know.'

Yannis returned to Giovanni with approval from his partners. 'You're in charge,' he announced. 'Find out the procedure and let me know the cost. Everyone agrees we should go ahead.'

Giovanni grinned broadly. 'I've had another idea. I don't know how you'll feel about this one.'

'How much will it cost?' asked Yannis.

'Not much. How many of your mother's sketches do you have?'

Yannis shrugged. 'I'm not sure. There are about twenty framed, but Anna has the rest. Why?'

'If you had them framed we could hang them in the hotel foyer. I could do a notice that said they are sketches executed by the hotel proprietor's mother and the rest of the collection is at Ourania's in Aghios Nikolaos. It would encourage them to visit the shop.'

'They might think they're for sale, then find they've had a wasted journey.'

Giovanni shook his head. 'I've thought of that. Before they're framed we have them copied. I could do a notice to say that copies are for sale.'

'You and your notices!'

'People like to know about things. I've started writing out the menus in other languages now and it's really popular. The people have some idea of what they're eating.'

Yannis nodded. His nephew certainly had a good head on his shoulders. He must think seriously about making him a partner in a few years, maybe when Kyriakos finally gave in to his ill health would be the right time.

Giovanni telephoned his parents from Heraklion, speaking first to his father in rapid Italian. 'Pappa, I've the most wonderful news. I'm sure Yannis will telephone you, but I wanted to tell you first. He's asked me to become a partner in the hotels. Isn't it wonderful?'

Victor digested the news in silence as Giovanni continued to enthuse. 'Yes,' he said finally. 'I'm very pleased for you.'

'You don't sound very pleased.'

'How much is it going to cost, Giovanni?'

'Cost? Nothing. Why?'

'Usually to buy yourself a partnership costs money.'

'This is different. Uncle Yannis says I'll be a junior partner to begin with. I can't make decisions, but I can attend business meetings. If I think their ideas won't work I can say so, and I can put forward ideas of my own. Is Mamma there? Let me tell her.'

Victor handed the telephone over to his wife, covering the mouthpiece with his hand. 'He has good news, don't spoil it for him.'

Marisa finally replaced the receiver and looked at her husband. 'I'm so pleased for him. He sounded so excited and happy.'

Victor took her hand. 'We'll see the lawyer this afternoon. He should know by now what they plan to charge Joseph with and when he'll be brought to trial.'

Victor and Marisa sat miserably in the lawyer's office. He would do his best, he assured them, he would play on the youth of their son and stress how he had been led astray by older, experienced criminals, but he could give no promise that Joseph would escape a prison sentence for his part in the robbery.

Marisa twisted her fingers in anguish. Joseph was young, only eighteen, but very young for his age. When she thought of Angelo, who was preparing to go to University at that age, or Giovanni, standing out against his father and asking his uncle for a job in his hotel, she was struck anew by the immaturity of her youngest son.

Victor was scowling. The disgrace, the shame, that his son should be a criminal. How would he be able to hold his head up again and face his relatives and friends?

'Can we see him?' he asked.

The lawyer nodded. 'I can arrange a meeting, but be prepared for him to be hostile towards you. Juveniles usually are. They seem to feel the world is against them.'

The lawyer was right. Joseph sat sullenly before them, refusing to answer their concerned questions. Finally Victor lost his patience.

'Very well, Joseph. You don't appear to care about us, so we won't care about you. When you're released from prison you can find somewhere else to live. We'll not take responsibility for you any more.'

Victor took his wife's arm and pulled her to her feet.

'No, Victor, you can't...' Marisa began to protest.

'Yes, I can. He's obviously old enough to get himself into trouble, let him get himself out of it.'

For the first time Joseph looked frightened. 'Pappa, you wouldn't throw me out. Pappa, I don't want to go to prison. Pappa ...' His voice rose hysterically as his parents left the room.

Once outside Victor took Marisa in his arms. 'I'm sorry, so sorry, but something has to be done to make him come to his senses.'

Marisa gave a shuddering sob. 'He's such a little boy.'

Victor shook his head. 'No, he's not. That's where we've made a big mistake. He's not a little boy any longer. He's a spoilt young man and I know just what will happen to him when he's released from custody.'

'You won't beat him?' Marisa asked fearfully.

Victor laughed harshly. 'It would be a good thing if I'd beaten him a few times when he was younger. No. I shall arrange for him to go into the army. He'll soon find out what life is all about in there.'

'But, Victor, you hated it.'

'And I hope he does!'

'Six months deferred sentence, as the accused is entering the army. Any further criminal offence will be dealt with by them and the six months sentence will also be served in a civilian prison.'

Joseph's face blanched as he heard the judge read out his sentence and he sought his father's grim face across the courtroom. This was his doing. Six months in a civilian prison would have been like a hotel compared with life in the army.

Anna read Marisa's letter sadly. Poor little Joseph. She was sure it was not his fault that he had mixed with bad company and been persuaded to help rob a factory of the pay roll. She read Marisa's words again.

"Victor has taken this very badly. He feels it must be his fault if Joseph is bad. Why it should be his fault and not mine I don't know. I know he thinks the army will be good for him with all the discipline, but I'm not so sure I shall write to him every week, and I'm sure he'd like a letter from you, but Victor says we are not to sympathise with him. He has to learn his lesson."

Anna sighed. They were being very harsh with the poor little boy.

Yannis decided it was time to review his financial position. His bank manager greeted him with pleasure. A visit from Mr Andronicatis usually meant profitable business.

'What can I do for you? A loan, maybe, for another property investment?'

Yannis shook his head. 'Advice, mostly. I have a good income.'

The manager permitted himself to smile – he wished his own income were as good.

'I'm negotiating to buy the shop and block of flats where we live. The previous owner has died and his widow is willing to sell provided she can live rent free for the rest of her life. I'm happy with that arrangement and I've told my solicitors to draw up the contract. There's no problem there. I want you to tell me whether I should hold on to my last bit of land and build on it or whether it would be better to sell. I also want to give my sister a present without her knowing it has come from me.'

The manager looked puzzled and Yannis went on to explain.

'My sister and brother-in-law have just had an expensive court case in Italy. I wondered if my sister still had an account here with you?'

'Mr Andronicatis, I'm not at liberty to disclose which customers have accounts here.'

Yannis shook his head. 'I just thought if she had one I could give you some money which you could add to her balance and simply say it was an error in bank interest rates.'

The bank manager smiled. 'Banks do not make errors.'

'Surely you could make some excuse and credit it to her without mentioning my name?'

'I'm sure we could arrange something. Of course, if we have to send the money to Italy the commission charge would be a little high,' he spread his hands.

'What you mean,' said Yannis dryly, 'is that it will cost me for a favour.'

The manager smiled. Mr Andronicatis understood business. 'As to your other query I can't help you. Land will always increase in price, but a building on it could add to the value. What did you have in mind? Another hotel?'

Yannis shook his head. 'My aunt and uncle are not getting any younger. The day will come when they're quite unable to stay out there on that farm alone. I thought a new house, between Olous and Aghios Nikolaos could be the answer eventually, and when the time comes Ourania and I will have a retirement home.'

Yannis replaced the telephone receiver thoughtfully.

'What's the problem?'

'That was Andreas. He says uncle Stelios is very ill and asking for Yannis and Anna. He wondered if he meant me, but I'm sure he doesn't. I can hardly remember him. He must mean uncle Yannis in Athens.'

'So what are you going to do?'

'Well, I'm certainly not going all the way to Athens on the off chance that some old uncle wants to see me on his deathbed. I'll drive out and see Anna and Yiorgo. He's their brother and if they want to go I'll make the arrangements for them. On the way back I'll stop off and see how the house is progressing.' He kissed his wife. 'And I'll call on your mother and make sure she's all right.'

Ourania smiled. 'Life would be so much easier if they weren't rivals for our affection and time.'

Yannis did not answer. He was not going to point out that it was Ourania's mother who had started and continued the rivalry over the years.

Anna was also surprised by Yannis's message.

'I'll ask Yiorgo. Maybe we should go. It's such a long way, but he is our brother.' Anna turned distressed eyes on her nephew. 'I don't know what to say.'

'Walk up to the fields with me and we'll ask Yiorgo now.'

Yiorgo looked at them in disbelief. 'You expect me to leave the farm and run off to Athens because Stelios suddenly decides he wants to see us after all these years? He's got another think coming. Anna can go if she wants, but I'm certainly not wasting my time.'

Anna walked back to the farm in an agony of indecision. 'What shall I do, Yannis? I feel I should go.'

'You think about it and let me know this evening. Talk it over with Yiorgo and see if he has a change of heart.'

Anna shook her head. 'He'll not change his mind. You know your uncle as well as I do. Once he says something he means it. I'll have to go. He's my brother and someone should be with him.'

'I'll take you up to Heraklion and you can stay in my hotel if you like.'

Anna turned fearful eyes on her nephew. 'I can't stay in your hotel. I wouldn't know how to behave.'

'Giovanni's there. He'll look after you.'

Anna shook her head. 'Ask Andreas if I can stay with him. How will I get to Athens, Yannis?'

'You can leave all the arrangements to me. I'll book a flight for you. Giovanni can take you to the airport in Heraklion and uncle Yannis can meet you in Athens. Have you got a suitcase?'

Anna looked round the living room. 'What do I want one for?'

'For your clothes. You'll have to stay a few days.'

'There's a clean sack out the back.'

Yannis shook his head. 'You're not going off to Athens with your clothes in a sack. Leave it to me. I'll telephone Andreas, buy you a suitcase, and Ourania can come and help you pack this afternoon. I'll sort out a flight for you and telephone to say what time I'll collect you tomorrow.'

The enormity of her proposed action suddenly dawned on Anna. 'Oh, Yannis, it will be all right, won't it? To go to Athens, I mean.'

'Of course. Yannis has been asking you to go for years. You'll be able to meet his wife and see the city. When you get back Ourania and I will want to hear all about it, and just think,' he winked wickedly at his aunt, 'how jealous Eleni will be.'

Anna was petrified. Her knuckles were white as she gripped the arms of the aircraft seat. No one had told her of the noise and the speed with which it ran along the ground. With a final thrust of the engines the plane left the ground and Anna felt her stomach lurch. She dared to release her grip on the armrest to cross herself hurriedly and screwed up her eyes. Giovanni has said the flight lasted less than an hour, but it seemed to be going on for ever.

'Would you like something to drink?'

Anna groaned.

'Are you not feeling well, madam?'

Anna shook her head.

'What's wrong? Do you feel sick?'

'When are we going to land?' she whispered.

'About three quarters of an hour's time. It's only a short flight.'

'I want to get off.'

'You can't get off now. We're up in the air.'

'That's why I want to get off.'

The stewardess patted her shoulder. 'There's absolutely nothing to worry about. You're quite safe. Is this the first time you've flown?'

'Yes.'

'If you relax I'm sure you'll enjoy it. Let me bring you a drink. What would you like? A fruit juice, water, or something stronger?'

'Water, please.'

'I'll be back in just a moment.' The stewardess retreated to the rear of the aircraft. 'There's always one!' she remarked. 'There's an old girl down there who wants to get off! Never flown before. What does she think she's on? A bus?'

Anna stepped from the aeroplane onto the hot tarmac. Her legs were shaking as she was herded towards the passport control building with the other passengers. Frantically she looked around for her brother. He had promised he would be there, but she could see no sign of him. The official gave her picture a quick glance and stamped her papers, slapped them on the desk in front of her and held out his hand for the next person in line. Anna handed her papers back to him.

'What's the problem?' he frowned. 'I've stamped yours. You can go through.' He pushed them back at her and she gathered them up.

'My brother said he would meet me.' She looked around her in gathering despair.

'He's not allowed through here. When you've collected your luggage you can go through and look for him. Next!'

Still Anna hesitated and the passenger behind placed his hand on her arm. 'I'll help you find your case. Follow me.' He guided her over to the conveyor belt and waited until there was a gap in the press of travellers.

The man retrieved his own case and waited until Anna's came into view. He caught it and held the label for her to read. She nodded in relief as she recognised her name that she had printed carefully.

'I'll carry it through for you.'

'Thank you.' Anna shuffled along by his side, scanning the faces of the men and women who stood behind a barrier awaiting the arrivals. He deposited her case beside an empty chair and urged her to wait until her brother found her.

'Give him half an hour and if he's not shown up ask them to put out a call for him. The desk is over there.'

Anna was still stammering her thanks as he was swallowed up by the moving mass of people.

'Anna!'

She looked up to see her brother standing before her, despite the years his disfigurements seemed no worse than before.

'Yannis! Thank goodness you've arrived.'

'I said I'd meet you. What's the problem?'

'I didn't know what to do.'

Yannis smiled at her. 'Your flight was a little earlier than I had expected. I didn't allow quite enough time for the traffic.' He looked at her case. 'Are you able to carry your luggage?' His fingers were far too misshapen to slip through the handle.

Yannis led the way to a taxi rank, signalled to a driver and helped his sister inside. The drive was a nightmare, almost as petrifying as the flight for Anna, as the taxi sped through the streets, weaving its way through the traffic with only centimetres dividing it from other vehicles. She was relieved when they finally drew up outside an apartment block and the driver opened the door for Yannis and placed her case on the pavement.

Anna sat on the side of her bed in Yannis's apartment. At first she had been completely over-awed at the magnificence, although he had assured her it was very ordinary by Athenian standards. Dora had fussed over her and Anna wished they lived closer. She felt she and Dora could have become good friends. Despite the attention Yannis and Ourania gave her she was lonely. The few women who remained living in Plaka were as reclusive as she was, without their men folk they were just passing their days aimlessly until their lives ended.

She grappled mentally with the new situation she had been presented with. On visiting Stelios in the hospital she had also met his wife and children. She shook her head sadly. Stelios had denied their mother her grandchildren and his children had been denied half of their family. Daphne had been well educated and brought her children up well. Nicolas was a school teacher and Elena was a secretary. Had Stelios been ashamed that his family were farmers? Indignation rose in her. There was nothing wrong with being a farmer. Now he was dead. She was not sure if the tears that were dribbling down her cheeks were for the death of her youngest brother or sadness at his denial of his family.

The two weeks that Anna spent in Athens passed quickly for her. Dora took her into the centre of the city and they walked from shop to shop, Anna admiring and wondering at the variety and quality of the goods on display. Yannis escorted her to the Acropolis, telling her the history of the site in minute detail, leaving her bewildered. She had been more impressed by the view she had of Athens sprawled before her, unable to comprehend how so many people could possibly live in one place.

Now she sat at the kitchen table in the farmhouse with her brother Yannis whilst they waited for Nicolas and Elena to arrive from Aghios Nikolaos where they had spent the night in one of her nephew's hotels. Davros had agreed to take them to visit the island of Spinalonga and Yannis had promised to give them a conducted tour. Whilst they were gone she planned to tell Yiorgo of the wonders and splendours she had seen and then Yannis and Ourania were coming for lunch. There would be time enough to tell Eleni when they had all returned to Athens and she was once more alone during the day.

'I'll have a special meal prepared for when you return,' she promised as she waved the boat away from the shore.

Nicolas and Elena walked slowly round the corner towards the farmhouse, their faces white, Elena's streaked with tears. To their relief they saw a car drawn up outside and guessed Yannis and Ourania had arrived.

'How do we tell her?' she asked her brother.

'Leave it to me. I'll try and be gentle.'

Nicolas led his aunt into the living room. 'Leave the cooking for a while. Come and sit down. We have to talk to you.'

'Where's Yannis?'

Nicolas did not answer until Anna was seated. 'I don't know quite how to say this, aunt Anna, but he's not coming back.'

'Don't be silly. He can't live over there on his own. What about Dora? I'm sure she wouldn't be happy living there.'

'Aunty, he can't come back.'

Ourania moved swiftly to Anna's side, understanding what Nicolas was trying to say.

Anna frowned. 'Can't come back? Of course he can. Yannis, you go over there and talk to him. Make him realise what a silly idea it is.'

Yannis shook his head. 'What Nicolas is trying to tell you is that uncle Yannis is dead.'

Nicolas nodded as Ourania placed her arms around Anna.

'Yannis? Dead? He was all right this morning. What happened?'

'I'm not quite sure. Elena and I climbed up to the top of the fort. He said he would wait for us and sat down by the house at the graveyard. When we came back he'd toppled over and was dead.'

Anna took a deep breath. She seemed to be struggling hard with her emotions. To everyone's amazement she gave a small, sad smile.

'Poor Yannis. He never did want to leave his Phaedra. Now he doesn't have to.'

Nicolas looked at his sister. This was not the reaction he had expected. Ourania withdrew her arms and looked at her husband.

'What do we do?'

Yannis sat down heavily on a chair. 'I don't know. I must think. Yiorgo must be told.'

'I'll go,' offered Nicolas quickly. Having done his duty he wanted to escape before the weeping and wailing began.

Anna continued to sit and talk calmly. 'We have to tell Dora. Maybe your mother could come with her?'

Elena looked at her aunt in surprise. 'Come where?'

'Here, of course, for the funeral.'

'But surely he'll be taken back to Athens? There'll be no point in aunt Dora coming here.'

Again the small smile played at Anna's lips. 'He's come home. He's come home to be with Phaedra.'

Yannis shook his head at Elena, warning her not to argue. 'Shock,' he mouthed above his aunt's head. 'Maybe you could make us some coffee, Elena? I think we could all do with a cup.' Yannis moved his chair round to face his aunt and took her hand. 'We have to think clearly and make some arrangements. We'll have to call a doctor to find out how he died and get a certificate. Maybe he could be buried in the churchyard here if Dora is agreeable.'

Anna looked at her nephew. 'Go and fetch Doctor Stavros, then I'll go over to the island with him and wash Yannis.'

'There's no need for that. I'll ask the undertakers to collect him and they'll wash and lay him out.'

'They will not.' Anna spoke vehemently. 'Yannis is going to stay on the island.' She leant forward in her chair. 'Don't you see? This is why he came back. Something told him he was near the end and he came back to be with Phaedra. You can't take him away now.'

Yannis shifted uncomfortably and looked at his wife. 'I don't know that he will be allowed to be buried on the island.'

'He doesn't have to be buried. He can go in the tower.'

Ourania caught her breath. 'You can't! It wouldn't be right.'

'It would be more right than burying him here or in Athens. Yannis lived on that island longer than anywhere else.'

Yannis looked at his aunt wonderingly. 'You're serious, aren't you?'

Anna nodded. 'He can be placed in the tower and a headstone put in the village churchyard.'

'What will Dora say?'

'I think Dora will understand. Now, Yannis, go to Aghios Nikolaos for Doctor Stavros. I'll telephone Dora, then Andreas.'

Ourania looked helplessly at her husband who shrugged.

'Mamma Anna, will you be guided by Andreas and Doctor Stavros?'

'Guided by them? Whatever for? I know what Yannis would have wanted, and that's what he'll get.' Anna's mouth set in a determined line.

Anna sat stiffly in her chair. She had accompanied Doctor Stavros to the island where he confirmed Yannis's death was due to a heart attack and no blame could be attached to Nicolas or Elena.

'You have to understand how leprosy can weaken the heart. It's a miracle he lived so long. I think he was just waiting to come home. I understand his widow is attending the funeral. Do you know how she's taken the news?'

Anna shook her head. 'Nicolas and Elena will meet her and look after her. She's travelling with her sister-in-law. They should be here tomorrow. So sad for Yannis and Stelios to have met again after all these years and die within a month of each other.'

Doctor Stavros looked at the elderly woman and her brother. They seemed to be accepting the inevitable just a little too calmly. Maybe it would be as well if I was here the following day when the other relatives arrived.

Elena drew up in her car and Nicolas helped out the two women and an elderly man.

'Who's that?' asked Ourania, as the man tottered forwards unsteadily, leaning heavily on a stick.

Anna drew in her breath. 'It's Spiro. It has to be. There's no one else left except Flora.'

For the first time Anna began to cry.

1980 – 1988

Anne settled herself comfortably in her seat. She was not sure if she was relieved to have said goodbye to James and be alone again. He was so intense, so concerned about her welfare and so thoroughly dependable. She was going to miss him for the first few weeks that she was back in Africa. She was sure he would enjoy the primitive wildness of the country if only she could persuade him to visit her.

Without much interest she drew the travel brochure advertising the airline from the pouch in front of her. This would do to pass the time until the stewardess arrived with drinks. She flipped the pages over idly. A weekend in Paris, honeymoon in Venice, historical tour of Greece, cruise around the Greek islands. She smiled ironically as she read the glowing descriptions. She could make Malawi sound like paradise on earth if she tried.

"Visit Knossos on the sun drenched island of Crete".

Crete – that was where her father had taken them on holiday the year before he died. How sad he should have been killed in a car accident after all the narrow escapes he had had during his work with the resistance.

The woman he had taken her to visit, the one with the donkey and the cats, she had helped him during the war. Anne wondered what had become of her. One day, maybe she would go back and see if she were still there. At least James should be willing to venture as far as Greece.

Anne wrote regularly to James during her years in Malawi. She found it hot, dusty and depressing. Outbreaks of disease amongst the cattle never seemed to end. She was sure it was due to lack of nourishment during the continual drought, but she could not provide rain. She wrote heart-rending accounts of the starvation faced by the people as their animals died and with them their living. How whole communities would be faced with starvation and would be seen straggling across the countryside in search of a better life in the town, or those who decided to stay and wreak some kind of living from the land and ended up starving like their animals.

James would shudder. How could anyone bear to live out there; surrounded by such poverty and misery? He urged her to return to England, but she was adamant. She had no leave due until she had completed a two year spell, then she wanted to travel back over land if possible, which would give her no more than four weeks in England. She urged James to visit her, but he declined. The Italian lakes with their lush scenery were far more attractive to him than the barren wilderness Anne described.

To her mother Anne wrote once a fortnight, barely a page, simply stating that she was well, happy and working hard. She knew Heather had no interest in the diseases of cattle or the hardship of the people. Occasionally Heather replied, usually to say there was a new lodger in Anne's room and mention how hard it was to make ends meet. Anne knew her mother felt it necessary to have at least one new outfit a month and keep a well-stocked bar in the lounge, so she ignored the hints, ensuring that the bulk of her money was safely transferred to a London bank. She knew exactly what she wanted to do when she was tired of working in the third world.

Annita and Elias arrived at the airport in Heraklion and collected the hire car they had arranged. 'Shall I drive?' offered Annita.'

Elias shrugged. 'If you want. I'll read the map?'

Annita drove slowly. It was nearly fifty years since she had visited the city and she felt a total stranger. She was relieved when Elias finally said they should turn to the left and the church where her brother was the priest should be a short distance down the side road with his house next door. She drew to a halt and allowed Elias to climb out before she parked the car on the narrow pavement as close to the wall as she dared.

Andreas had been watching for them and he opened his door before they had a chance to knock. He eyed his sister with disapproval. She was wearing trousers!

Annita threw her arms round his neck before he had a chance to say a word. 'It's good to see you again, Andreas.'

Gently he disentangled her arms before shaking hands with his brother-in-law. 'Come inside. I can't greet you properly out here.'

They followed him in to his small living room and Andreas hugged his sister to him. 'I'm so pleased you were able to come. I never thought I'd see you again.'

'You know you could always visit us. I've asked you time and again, but you've always made some excuse,' Annita reproached him.

Andreas spread his hands. 'If you were in Athens it would be different.' He shuddered, 'America is so far away. What brings you back to Crete? Have you decided to come home?'

'Don't be silly, Andreas. America is my home now. No, we decided we needed a holiday and it seemed a good idea to visit Elias's sister as she can't come out to us this year. She's waiting for an operation on her hip and is in so much pain. Elias suggested that as we were so close I might like to visit my relatives, those that are left,' Annita finished sadly.

Andreas sighed. 'I don't see them very often. Anna stayed the night with me before she went over to Athens when Stelios died. When she returned she and Yannis visited me with Stelios's children, and of course, I took the funeral service for Yannis.'

Annita gazed at her brother sharply. 'You held it on Spinalonga, I understand.'

Andreas nodded. 'That's what Yannis would have wanted.'

'You're able to visit the island?' asked Elias.

'Boatmen take people out every day. It's become quite a tourist venue.'

'I'd like to go over. I met Yannis once in Athens at the hospital and I'd be interested to see the island.'

'I'm sure it can be arranged. Speak to Manolis.'

'I'll do that,' nodded Elias. 'Where can I find him?'

'Annita should be able to find him easily enough. He and his wife live in our old house in Aghios Nikolaos.' Andreas smiled at his sister. 'Flora has a penchant for geraniums. Now some refreshment for you.' Andreas looked at his watch. 'I have to take a service shortly, but after that I shall be free for the rest of the day.'

Annita frowned. 'How long will it take us to drive to Aghios Nikolaos? We want to book into a hotel for the night so we mustn't leave it too late.'

'No more than a couple of hours. We have plenty of time to spend together.'

'You have chosen an unfortunate time to visit. Yannis and Giovanni are in Athens for a few days and Ourania is in Turin.' Anna looked at her cousin. She would never have recognised her as the girl she used to know. She was dressed in a pair of black trousers and scarlet blouse, her hair raven black and her face made up. She no longer wore the stud earrings that Yannis had give her as a betrothal gift, instead a large diamond sparkled in each ear, matching the ring on her finger.

'It doesn't matter a bit. I don't know any of them. I came to see you and Yiorgo. I know you understood that I couldn't be here for Yannis's funeral, but I wanted to come – for old time's sake.' Annita took in the plain black dress of her cousin and hoped she did not look as old and careworn as the shapeless figure before her. If she had married Yannis and stayed on Crete she would probably look much the same.

Anna shook her head sadly, her gaze travelling to the sketch that hung above the fireplace. 'It seems so long ago. So few of the family left now.'

Annita followed her gaze. 'I didn't realise how like his father Yiorgo had become.'

'And Yannis is just like Yiorgo to look at. He's very different in his ways, not so restricted in his outlook. Always has such plans. He went over to Athens for two days last year to see Dora about Yannis's memoirs. He stayed for five days and in that time he had made an investment in another hotel. That's why he and Giovanni are over there now, making sure all will be ready for the opening. Do you know,' Anna spoke in a hushed voice, 'they even have a swimming pool on the roof.'

'How lovely. You must give me the address and I'll recommend it to all my friends who visit Greece. Athens is stifling in the summer months.'

'That was Giovanni's idea,' announced Anna proudly. 'He always has good ideas. He's planning a night club in the basement.'

'He's Marisa's middle son, isn't he?'

'That's right. Angelo, the eldest, is an architect, like his uncle, and Joseph went into the army.' Anna did not add that the whereabouts of Joseph was unknown. 'I have some photographs of them here.'

Anna placed a pile of snapshots on the table and Annita dug into her purse for her spectacles before proceeding to leaf through them.

'Now, tell me about your family. You're fortunate to have so many grandchildren. Children keep you young, I always say.' Anna sighed heavily. 'I wish Yannis and Ourania had been blessed, but,' she shrugged philosophically, 'it was not to be.'

'They're not always such a blessing.' Annita spoke grimly, thinking of the problems her youngest daughter had caused them. 'I really wasn't prepared to have such a large family. I found it very difficult until my Mamma came to look after them. I hated being at home all the time, not knowing what was going on in the laboratory.' Annita shrugged resignedly. 'Elena and Matthew are fine, and their girls are doing very well at college. I have a feeling one of the twins will be pestering them to get married shortly. She met a nice young man at High School and they have dated regularly ever since. Marianne, now, she's different again, only interested in her studies. Says she wants to be an international lawyer. She's never been out seriously with anyone. Andrew has just started his college course. It will probably take him a while to find his feet.'

'What does he want to do?' All this talk of college was beyond Anna's limited knowledge, but she felt bound to take an interest.

'He says he wants to be a graphic artist. I would have said he would do better as a cartoonist. He draws such funny pictures of the family. Elias has one framed in his office. It's of a microbe looking back at Elias through the microscope. He's caught Elias's surprised expression perfectly.'

Anna smiled politely – what was a microbe?

'Poor Maria, she has no children, of course,' Annita continued. 'Bernard's accident was such a tragedy. All he was doing was changing a light bulb for a friend. To fall only a few feet and fracture your skull seems incredible. Other people have far worse accidents and get up and walk away. Such a shame Maria didn't have a child to console her. For the first five years she would hardly leave the house. I'm sure she cried herself to sleep every night.'

Anna gave her cousin a withering look. 'She needs to keep herself busy.'

'Oh, she's better now. She goes to self improvement classes.' Annita sighed. 'She never seems to stay at one subject for very long. She says she gets bored. She started with flower arranging and thought she might become a florist, but after a few weeks she dropped that and went for gardening. When it turned cold and wet she decided she didn't want to do outdoor work so she tried painting. She had no talent, but she went from one art form to another, sculpture right through to batik until she realised the truth.'

'So what's she doing now?'

'Learning Portuguese.'

'What good will that do her?'

Annita shrugged. 'Probably no good at all, but she says she's planning to go to Brazil to work with the poor. At least it keeps her mind occupied for a few hours a week.'

'And what about your other two?'

'Andreas is fairly successful. He's had two plays put on in New York now. He's hoping the film rights might be bought for his latest one.'

'Is he married?'

'No.' Annita felt herself blush with embarrassment. 'He prefers a bachelor existence.'

Anna made no comment. Yiorgo had never shown any inclination to be married. 'And my namesake?'

'She has three girls.'

'Oh, yes, the ones with the outlandish names. What are they?'

'Sorrell, Bryony and Saffron.' Annita deliberately omitted that her youngest daughter had a fourth child. 'I brought some photographs with me.'

Anna picked up the photographs, looking at them curiously. In some the girls seemed to be very scantily dressed and the older ones were wearing make-up. She could certainly not tell which girl was Marianne and which was Helena and even Sorrell was so like them she could have been their sister.

'What are Anna's daughters doing?'

'Oh, they're at school and college,' replied Annita airily. 'We don't see much of them now. They always seem to be so busy out and about.' She did not wish to admit that she only knew the whereabouts of Bryony, who was at school. Sorrell had disappeared saying she wanted to travel and Jeremy had taken Saffron away when he and Anna had divorced. No word had been heard from them since. Anna had led such a secluded life that she would never understand that young people seemed to do exactly as they wished these days. 'I brought some photographs of the house. I thought you might be interested.'

Anna looked at the snapshots of a large house standing in its own grounds. 'Which apartment is yours?'

Annita smiled with amusement. 'We haven't got an apartment, it's all our house.'

'All yours? Why is it so big? Surely you can't use every room?'

'You'd be surprised how much space you can occupy when you have it available. We also keep rooms ready for when Elias's sisters visit or the grandchildren come to stay over.'

Anna did not reply. She and Yiorgo had a bedroom each instead of sharing with another member of the family as they had for years; the room that had been built on at the back when Yannis was a baby had become a storage room for unwanted bits and pieces of furniture; there was more than enough space in the farmhouse. 'Did you stay with Andreas or at a hotel in Heraklion?'

'A hotel on the outskirts of Aghios Nikolaos; it was certainly very comfortable. I was pleasantly surprised.' Annita looked round the living room of the farmhouse. 'Why do you stay here, Anna? You could have somewhere more comfortable if you went to Aghios Nikolaos.'

'Yiorgo likes to live here.'

'But he could drive in every day. Surely you'd prefer to be closer to Yannis and Ourania?'

'I'm happy enough here. I've always lived here.' Anna's mouth set in a stubborn line. 'I wouldn't want to live in an apartment where there are other people going in and out all the time.'

'But it's so isolated. There's hardly anyone left in the village.'

Anna shrugged. 'It's my home.'

Annita looked at her cousin in exasperation. She was even worse than her brother, Andreas, who lived so sparsely that he could easily have been a monk. There was nothing wrong with having a comfortable home and pleasant surroundings.

'If it's a question of money,' she began tentatively.

Anna laughed. 'I've plenty of money; besides, Yannis would see I never wanted for anything. I'm just set in my ways now. What's the point of changing anything when you're nearly seventy? No, the farm is good enough for me.'

'Would you like to come back to America with me? You could meet the family and I could drive you around. We have the largest supermarkets you can ever imagine. They sell everything, and I do mean everything. You wouldn't be able to believe your eyes if you saw the goods on their shelves.'

Anna shook her head. 'I went to Athens when Stelios died. That was enough for me. Believe me, Annita, when I say I'm happy living here.'

Annita shrugged. 'We're all different. If you ever change your mind just pick up the telephone and I'll be at the airport to meet you. Now,' Annita looked at her small gold watch. 'I told Elias he should be back here by two. Manolis promised he would remind him and bring him over. I'll drive us back to Aghios Nikolaos to check out of our hotel, then we have to drive back to Heraklion. We really should leave here by four if we're going to say goodbye to Andreas and catch the night ferry back to Athens.'

'You didn't want to go over to the island?'

Annita shook her head. 'I prefer to remember Yannis as he was when we were in Aghios Nikolaos together. I don't belong over there.'

Anna looked at the immaculate woman in front of her. She was not sure she belonged in Plaka either. 'Yannis was very grateful to you for sending the results of all your work. The government finally had to listen to him.'

'We were happy to help. It was the least I could do for him.' Unexpectedly tears glistened in Annita's eyes as she remembered Father Lambros's words from so long ago. *"One day Yannis will thank you from the bottom of his heart."*

'I'll go and tell Yiorgo Elias will be here shortly. We're both looking forward to meeting him. You've been happy with him, haven't you?'

Annita nodded. 'We've been very happy together. I made the right decision all those years ago. I'd like to go to the cemetery before we leave and pay my respects to Yannis.'

'He has a very nice headstone in the cemetery,' Anna assured her.

Anna sat outside in the sunshine shelling peas. There was only Yiorgo and her left. Who would have thought that Stelios would have died before Yannis? He had been nine years younger and Yannis so ill for most of his life. Her thoughts ranged back and forth across the years, remembering incidents from her childhood, the happy summer when her cousins had come to stay, the children when they were small, her visits to the island, but her war time memories she shut away, not daring to approach them.

Marisa was so happy with her Victor. That was a happy memory from the war years. She had two young men to be proud of, serious, hard working Angelo and happy, fun loving Giovanni. He worked hard too, in his own way. It was a shame about Joseph. After his father had managed to get him a second chance in the army as well. He had been a foolish boy to run away and get mixed up with the wrong company again. He was a black sheep. Anna sighed. Had Stelios also been a black sheep? No one seemed to know what he had been up to in Athens before he married Daphne.

It was a shame Yannis and Ourania had no children, but Yannis had done well for himself. So sad that his mother had not lived to see the success he had made of his life, or his father for that matter. He had wanted his father to be proud of him. He knew how to make money. A businessman through and through. The grand new house he was building was proof of that. It would be the richest for miles around, as luxurious as Stelios's and Daphne's apartment in Athens had been.

She had been blessed to have the children to look after. It had made up for having none of her own, and she had enjoyed having Marisa's boys to visit. It would have been lovely to have… no, she would not think of that. She must put the memory of that day in the same compartment as her war memories. She would only remember the happy times, but she had been happy the day when… no, forget it, pack it away with the carefully folded shirt, the only letter tucked safely in the pocket.

Anna picked up the bowl of peas. Did Yiorgo like peas? She couldn't remember. Either Yiorgo or Yannis liked them, but Yannis wasn't there any more. Did she mean her brother Yannis or her nephew? She was no longer sure. She would cook them anyway. She placed them on the kitchen windowsill and there they sat, forgotten.

Yannis walked through his new house with pride. It was really taking shape now. There was a well-appointed kitchen leading into a dining room and through an archway there was the lounge. A spacious balcony ran the along the back of the house, giving a spectacular view across the bay to Spinalonga. Upstairs there were two large bedrooms sharing a bathroom that would have graced any film set. Above the double garage were two spare bedrooms with bathrooms en suite. Adjoining the main building was another, long and low, which had two bedrooms; again with bathrooms en suite, a kitchen and lounge. He hoped to persuade his aunt and uncle to move to the specially designed apartment as soon as the decoration had been completed.

They were both of them growing old. Yiorgo still rose early and walked up to the hills to release the sheep and goats to graze, but the flocks had diminished considerably. No longer were replacements bought for those that had ailed during the winter, and the majority of the lambs and kids were sold for their meat. The carob trees were completely neglected, the crop not being picked from one year to the next, and the olive trees were allowed to drop most of their fruit to the ground. Yiorgo tended the vines, but his sight was poor and signs of blight or leaf mould went undetected for weeks, often killing the plant altogether, and the yield was only sufficient for the family.

Anna tried to keep her vegetables and herbs growing, although the effort of kneeling for any length of time was beyond her. Each day when Yannis visited he left a selection of vegetables in the kitchen and cooked meals in the refrigerator, which Anna accepted unquestioningly. He took it upon himself to check her stock of flour, rice, lentils and coffee and replenish them as necessary without a word.

He was thankful he no longer had to worry over Eleni, who had become so senile that the hospital was the only place able to cope with her. She had been found wandering along the road in her nightclothes with no idea where she was going or why. After three such occurrences in the space of a few days Yannis had decided she was not safe to be left alone at night and as a temporary measure Ourania had gone to stay.

Within a week she was back, distraught at the depths to which her mother had sunk and accepting the fact that her mind had gone. For hours Eleni would sit in her chair mumbling to herself, then rise and thrash out wildly, shouting and using language Ourania had never guessed her mother knew. She suffered a bowl of cold water poured over her, food, cups and plates thrown at her, but when a knife narrowly missed her she decided it was time to leave.

Yannis wondered if his sister was having the same problems with Victor's elderly parents, but decided not to ask. She had enough trouble with Joseph. After absconding from the army he

425

had been caught pilfering by the military police and sent back to his camp for punishment duty. He had completed his term and promptly run away again, and since then it had been one long catalogue of petty crime and imprisonment. He was undergoing a lengthy psychiatric rehabilitation programme at the moment and Marisa had begged her brother to find him a job at one of his hotels to keep him out of trouble when he was released. Yannis had refused outright. He could not afford to employ anyone of a dubious reputation. Let the boy prove his worth and he would reconsider.

Anne had cabled James and asked him to meet her at the airport although it was not the time when she usually took her annual leave. She had been ill and ordered back to England to recuperate. He looked at her with concern as she pushed a loaded trolley through the barrier and gazed around as if disorientated.

'Let me take that,' he said, and proceeded to manoeuvre the unwieldy load. Anne transferred her hands to James's arm and walked slowly. 'Straight home?' he asked.

Anne nodded. 'All I want to do is go to bed. James. Would you mind awfully if I stayed at your flat? I can't possibly face my mother until I'm feeling better.'

'Is she expecting you?'

'I didn't cable her, only you.'

'No problem.' Slowly he led her to where his car was parked, settling her inside before he dealt with the luggage and returned the trolley.

'What's wrong?'

'Probably a touch of malaria. I'll be fine in a few days. Could even be gone by tomorrow now I'm back in England.'

James nodded. She looked ill, desperately ill and the first thing he intended to do was to call a doctor. They drove in silence, Anne appearing to be asleep most of the time.

'Where's mummy?' she asked suddenly. 'Will she be at home?'

426

James looked at her in surprise. 'I don't know.'

Anne snuggled herself close to him. 'It was nice of you to come and meet me. I've missed you so much, Daddy.'

James took another look at his passenger and swung to the right. The hospital was nearer than his flat.

James sat in the small office, answering the questions put to him by the young doctor as best he could. He gave Anne's name and what he thought was her correct date of birth.

'Have you any idea what could be wrong with her? Is she on any form of medication that might disagree with her?'

James shook his head. 'I've really no idea. I'm pretty sure she isn't diabetic, but apart from that she could be on anything. She only comes home once a year. I always meet her, and she's been fine before.'

'Comes home from where?'

'Malawi.'

'What's she doing in Malawi?'

'Something with cattle, I think. She's a vet.'

The doctor rose. 'That could answer a lot of questions. I suggest you go home and get some rest, sir. Call us in the morning and we will be able to let you know how she is.'

'What do you think is wrong with her?'

'I really don't know. It could be a bad case of malaria, but I'm going to call up our colleagues in Tropical Medicine and see if they can give us any pointers. You've been very helpful.'

James felt himself dismissed. He walked out to his car and sat inside in the darkness, drawing hungrily on his cigarette.

After a sleepless night James telephoned his office. 'I can't come in today. No, I can't talk now. I'll explain tomorrow. To hell with the contract. I've told you, I can't talk now. I'm on my way to the hospital.' He replaced the receiver and rubbed his hand across the stubble on his chin. He should have shaved earlier.

The doctor, also looking hollow-eyed and unshaven greeted James quietly.

'Come into my office. I need some more information about this young lady.'

James sat nervously. 'She – she is all right?'

The doctor nodded. 'We're doing everything possible. Thanks to your prompt action in bringing her here she has a fighting chance. She should have hospitalised herself in Malawi.'

'What's wrong with her?'

'We're waiting for the results of tests, but according to our colleagues the symptoms show that she's been bitten by a tsetse fly. Did she say anything to you about the length of time she'd felt ill?'

James shook his head, trying to recall their conversation. 'I met her at the airport and she asked if she could stay at my flat until she felt better, rather than go home to her mother. She thought she had malaria and would recover in a couple of days.'

'Wishful thinking on her part. Why didn't she want to go to her mother?'

'They don't get on terribly well, different life styles.'

'And you and she...?'

'We're friends. Have been for years. We met at University. Could I see her?'

'There's not much point. She won't know you.'

'I'd like to stay with her, if I may.'

The doctor shrugged. 'I think you should carry on with your own life, but it's up to you. You can stay if you want. Do you happen to have the address or telephone number of her mother? She ought to be informed.'

'I'll do it.' James sighed. He did not relish an encounter with Heather.

James stayed at Anne's bedside for three days, praying she would regain consciousness and recognise him. Heather had paid a brief visit, and left, asking James to keep her informed. Now the doctor beckoned him outside the tiny private room and James felt fear clutching at his heart.

'I'm ordering you home to get some proper sleep.' The doctor spoke sternly. 'She's out of danger and another twenty-four hours should see an improvement. Come back tomorrow and she might even open her eyes for a moment.'

James swallowed. 'Are you telling me the truth?'

'Certainly I am. I'll give you something to help you sleep.'

James permitted himself to smile. 'After so long without I shouldn't need anything but a bed.'

'You'll be surprised how strung up you are.' The doctor placed a small bottle in James's hand. 'There's a couple in there. Take them. They'll put you to sleep, but not knock you out.'

In the distance James could hear the telephone ringing, he rolled over and groped clumsily at the table beside his bed. It was too much effort; he rolled back the other way, hoping to shut out the persistent ringing. Then he was awake – the hospital – Anne. He sat up with alacrity and snatched the receiver.

'Doctor?'

'James, Edward here, how are you? They told me at the office you were sick. Thought I'd give you a call. Will you be well enough to get in tomorrow?'

James ran his hand through his thinning hair. 'I hope so. Thanks for calling, now do me a favour and get off the line. I need to 'phone the hospital.'

'Hospital? You're not that sick, are you, old man?'

'Not me. I'll explain when I see you. Now get off the line.'

'Can I…?'

James replaced the receiver. No doubt he would have offended Edward, but that could be rectified at a later date. He dialled the hospital number and asked for the doctor, only to be told he was off duty. Cursing, James showered and dressed, had two cups of black coffee for his breakfast and was on his way to the hospital within half an hour.

Anne's progress was slow. Most of the time that James spent beside her bed she was asleep, and when she did open her eyes they had little recognition in them. The doctor assured him she was progressing satisfactorily, but it would take a long time before she would be well enough to leave the hospital, then a long period of convalescence and certainly no possibility of a return to Africa.

James had returned to his office and explained his absence. He offered to have the week deducted from his pay or holiday entitlement. He really did not mind, relieved to know Anne would recover, and hoping she would change her mind about marrying him now that she could no longer work abroad.

Anne lay on the sofa, a rug over her legs and a cushion beneath her head. 'I'm not an invalid any more, James. I could easily get the lunch.'

'You know what the doctor said. You were to do next to nothing for three months. Times not up yet. I don't mind getting the meals. I've cooked for myself for years and the amount you eat doesn't make much difference.'

Anne looked at him gratefully. 'Let's strike a bargain, James. Next week I get supper every night. I've got to start sometime. I can't just lay here for ever more.'

James regarded her anxiously. 'What will you do, Anne? You refuse to marry me, and you can't return to Africa.'

'I haven't said I won't ever marry you. I've said I won't marry you now. I need to get my life together again before I start making major decisions like that. I want to see my bank manager in a couple of weeks, then I can start making plans.'

'What kind of plans?' asked James suspiciously.

'I'm still a vet,' Anne reminded him. 'I'm hoping I'll have enough saved to buy into a partnership or start up on my own.'

'Is that wise? With animals again.'

'If I have a town practice I'm hardly likely to be called upon to treat a sick cow! And we don't have tsetse flies, thank God.'

The bank manager looked at the thin, sallow-faced woman in front of him. She hardly looked strong enough to sign her name, let alone open a veterinary practice.

'Are you sure you're ready for this step? A little longer to recuperate, maybe?'

Anne shook her head. 'I need something to occupy me. If I lease the premises now I can take my time fitting it out and then build the practice up gradually. I just want to know that you'll be patient with me if I go overdrawn for a while when I first start.'

The bank manager was wary. 'We'd make arrangements for an overdraft. Do you have any other security?'

'Well, I've always assumed my mother's flat would come to me eventually.'

'Would she guarantee you?'

'I doubt it. I wouldn't want to ask her. I have a friend who would stand by me, but if I'm careful I should be able to manage. It's just that initial period whilst I'm getting established.'

'Of course. Don't hesitate to come to me again if you run into any problems.' The manager showed her out, then handed the papers to his secretary for filing. She looked at the name and frowned.

'Did you give Miss Castleton her papers?'

'What papers?'

Mrs Hunt looked at him in exasperation. He had not the grasp of affairs that his predecessor had shown. 'In the strong room there are some papers left for her by her father. He was killed in a car accident years ago. Mr Johnson wrote to her when she came of age, but she's never collected them.'

'Maybe she knows what they are and isn't interested.'

'Then I suggest you get them to her so she can dispose of them. Shall I write and make an appointment?'

Mr Clarke sighed. It was a great pity that elderly secretaries were not forced to retire with their managers.

Anne unrolled the sketch and looked at it curiously. What was so important about it that her father had deposited it with the bank? She could not even see a signature on it. She tossed it to one side and opened the bulky envelope.

My darling Anne,

When you read this letter you will not have seen me for eleven years, eleven long years they will have been for me, when I will have thought of you every day. I am sure you will ask why, if I loved you so much, did I leave, and that is what I will try to explain to you.

I expect our holiday in Crete is no more than a dim memory to you now. Maybe you remember your 'perfect day' when you and I visited a farm and you rode a donkey and played with some kittens. That was when I finally made the decision to leave your mother and return to the only woman I have ever really loved.

To help you to understand I have to go back to the war years when I was on Crete. Anna, the woman on the farm, risked her life time and again to help the resistance. For weeks I would see her almost every day, then I would disappear into the hills, but each time I returned, she was there, ready and willing to help us.

Foolishly, but who can control their heart, I fell in love with her and now I know she loved me in return. We had little time alone together, and I never declared my feelings for her in words. It was the most disastrous mistake of my life.

On the farm were two children and I assumed them to be hers. The night she took me to the doctor in Aghios Nikolaos she pretended I was her husband to get me past an Italian checkpoint. The boy had spoken to me of his father, Babbis, who was with the resistance, so I had no reason to doubt the genuineness of the papers.

I knew I had to forget her, whatever the cost to myself. The resistance was a brotherhood, each man willing to lay down his life for the next. I could not fight alongside a man and then steal his wife away from him. Cretan family ties are very strong and they are a very moral people.

Had the villagers thought she was having an affair behind her husband's back they would have stoned her to death, even her own relatives joining in.

I thought I had no choice, Anne, believe me, but to leave her. Once back in England I tried to forget her. There were so many distractions taking place for service men that I was out every night. I have to admit that I enjoyed being something of a celebrity, a returned resistance worker. I was invited to every party and I usually went. After a while it seemed that your mother was at every party too, and she was attractive, witty, amusing, good company for a lonely man.

I should never have married her. I thought I should for your sake, to give you a father and save her reputation, but, Anne, never, ever marry anyone if you do not love them whole-heartedly, however good you think the reason might be.

Within weeks we realised our mistake. We tried, I have to give your mother credit for that, the faults were not all on her side, or mine, for that matter, but our marriage was doomed to failure from the start. I blamed myself and finally persuaded your mother to visit Crete. I thought if I could see Anna, happy with her husband, I would be able to put her out of my mind and make a fresh start with your mother.

As soon as I saw her I knew I still loved her and your mother guessed immediately. I thought Anna was married (although I was too dazed to ask about Babbis) until we reached her nephew's flat. Her nephew, Anne, not her son. I asked about the sketches, which your mother had admired, and that was when I found out. Anna's sister had died long ago and Anna had brought up the two children as her own.

Your mother behaved very rudely towards them, and I was thankful they did not understand English. Of course, your mother and I had one of our usual rows, but this time it was final. I walked out on her and spent the night in the car. When I returned that morning she had taken refuge in her sleeping tablets, so I took you out with me.

Whilst you were riding that old donkey I had a long talk with Anna. I told her I was going to ask your mother for a divorce and would be returning to Crete as soon as possible. It took a little time to put my affairs in order and wait for my divorce to become absolute, but I'm leaving tomorrow.

Please don't think too badly of me, Anne. The solicitors told me I had no hope of gaining custody of you under the circumstances and it would be better for me not to fight the decision or you could be dragged through the law courts. I wanted you to come to Crete to spend your holidays with us and get to know your namesake, but they wouldn't entertain that idea either. It had to be a clean break, for your sake, not even kiss you goodbye, and not to contact you until you were twenty-one.

Well, if you've just read this, you must be twenty-one, and in the eyes of the law an adult and capable of making up your own mind. I will understand if you decide never to see me again. All I ask is for you to remember that your father loves you dearly.

I am leaving with you the picture Anna gave me before we left. It was done by her sister, showing them having a picnic up in the fields. If you study it carefully you will find the name 'Maria'. I know her sister's pictures were Anna's most treasured possessions and your mother considered the sketches she saw to be collectors' items. You can always sell it if you don't want it.

Goodbye, my darling daughter, for eleven years – I hope and pray that when you have read this you will understand and not think too badly of me.

You know where I am if you want me.

> *Your loving father.*

Anne let the letter slip from her fingers. Poor daddy. Poor, dear daddy. Her tears began to flow and she was still sobbing when James returned from work.

James took Anne in his arms and waited until she quieted.

'Are you feeling ill? Have you had a relapse? The doctor said it could happen if you over did it, you know.'

Anne shook her head. 'I collected the papers from the bank. I'll never forgive my mother for this. Never.'

'What's she done?'

'She didn't tell me. All these years and she never said a word. Poor daddy – and poor Anna too.'

James sat down beside her. 'You've lost me completely. I've no idea what you're talking about. Are you feverish?' He tried to place his hand on her forehead, but she brushed him away impatiently.

Anne thrust the letter into his hands. 'Read that. Mummy never told me they were divorced. I thought his car had crashed on the way to work. Why didn't she tell me?'

James tried to concentrate on the letter despite Anne's continual tirade.

'Are you sure you want me to read this? It's very personal.'

Anne nodded. 'I'll have to see her. Somehow I have to tell her.'

'Why not just leave things as they are? You're mother thought she had good reason for not telling you, and you've been none the worse over the years.'

'Not my mother! I'm talking about Anna.'

James took her hand. 'Now, just quieten down a minute. Let me finish reading this, then we'll talk.' He turned the pages, reading slowly, then handed it back to Anne before he lit a cigarette and inhaled deeply.

'Poor devil. Somehow one doesn't think of one's parents as having love affairs.'

'What am I going to do, James?'

'I don't see there's much you can do. Your father's dead.'

Anne's mouth set in a stubborn line. 'I owe it to her, to Anna, to tell her what happened. She must think he changed his mind about going back.'

'Suppose she is married now? You could upset things pretty badly.'

'If I find she's married I don't need to say anything.'

'How are you going to find her anyway? There's no address on this letter. She may not be alive still.'

Anne took the letter back. 'He mentions Aghios Nikolaos. We stayed there. It wasn't very far from their farm. We drove out there with a man who had a gift shop.' Anne's eyes took on a dreamy look. 'We went to their flat, I remember. There were pictures all round the walls, like this one, and she had a cat, a white Persian called Beauty.'

'You can't walk into every gift shop in the town and ask the owners if they have pictures on the walls in their flat. The chances are they'll all say yes, and the cat's hardly likely to be alive after all this time.'

'I have to go, James.'

'You're not fit enough to go travelling abroad again yet. The doctor said a year at least, and then only Europe.'

'Crete is in Europe.'

'Only just. Let me have a look at that picture. Who are they?'

'Anna's family, I presume, but I don't know. I wonder which one of the girls is her?'

Anne leased the ground floor of an old Victorian house and set about the conversion from a mediocre flat to a smart, efficient, veterinary surgery. The kitchen, at the back of the house, she had stripped of all fitments and instead a series of cages of varying sizes were fixed to the floor, above them a wide wooden shelf ran the length of the wall. The bath was removed and the room partitioned to form a tiny kitchen, suitable for hot drinks or a snack lunch, and a new toilet fitted.

The two other rooms had their dividing wall removed and three rooms made in their place. The back room had a tiled and fully equipped theatre for animal surgery, the middle room was designed as a treatment and consulting room and the front room was the waiting room, furnished with a desk and filing cabinet to cope with the resulting paper work.

James admired the alterations and her attention to detail. 'All you need now is to decide on the décor. What colour carpet will you have?'

Anne eyed him with amusement. 'You don't have carpet in a vets. You've no idea how nervous some pets are when they come and it would be such an embarrassment to their owners to see a ruined carpet and know it was their animal's fault. A hardwearing vinyl will be in all the rooms, grey probably, with cherry red blinds or curtains and grey seats. I want a décor which is easy to replace if it does get damaged.'

'And the walls?'

'White,' said Anne firmly. 'They can be touched up when they get grubby without having to worry about colour matching. I'll have a piece of cork on that wall for notices and probably a poster or two around for people to look at whilst they wait. I'm not wasting money on magazines because I'll be working mostly to appointments so no one should have to wait very long.'

'All you need is a brass plate and some advertising and you'll be away. You won't overdo it at first, will you? I don't want you to get overloaded with work so that you come home exhausted and have a relapse.'

Anne twisted her fingers in embarrassment. 'I wanted to talk to you about that, James.'

'About what?'

'You've been terribly good to me. For six months I've lived in your flat and you've looked after me wonderfully. I know I've paid my share of expenses, but it's time I stood on my own two feet and allowed you to get on with your life.'

James regarded her sadly. 'You mean you've had enough and want to leave.'

Anne shook her head. 'I feel I've taken advantage of your good nature and hospitality long enough.'

'Forget any silly ideas about taking advantage. I enjoy having you there. Most evenings I would come home from work, have a drink, think about a meal, have another drink and then go for a take away or fish and chips. Now I eat properly and look forward to coming home and spending the evening with you.'

'But it can't go on for ever, James.'

'Why not? We could get married, then you wouldn't feel you were taking advantage of my hospitality.'

'I can't marry you, James.'

'I don't see why not. You know I love you and you obviously don't dislike me.'

Anne drew James towards her. 'You are the most wonderful, patient, kind and loving man I've ever met. I love you dearly, but I'm not ready to get married.'

James's brow creased. 'I don't see the problem.'

'The problem is me. At the moment I can go where I want, when I want. At any time I can pack my bags and wave you goodbye. If we were married I couldn't do that. This may sound strange, but all the time I know I can walk out on you I don't want to, but if I were married I'd feel trapped and resentful. I need to be free. Free to make my own decisions without having to consider anyone else, their feelings, their opinions.'

'I wouldn't make you feel trapped.'

'You wouldn't intend to make me feel trapped. Putting a ring on my finger would do it. I'd feel like a wild animal in a cage, desperately searching for a way out and becoming more miserable because I'd know how much I was hurting you. It just wouldn't work, James, not at the moment, with you or anyone.'

James kissed her lightly on the forehead. 'That doesn't mean you have to move out.'

'It's not fair on you if I stay. You'd like to be married, comfortably settled, the slippers warming by the fire bit and the little woman asking if you've had a good day at the office. One day you'll meet that woman and you'll wish I wasn't around, hanging wet undies in the bathroom and borrowing your razor.'

James laughed. 'You always use the tumble dryer. If you won't marry me I'm still not looking for anyone else. I'm happy with you around. You're all I want, Anne, married or not.'

Anne looked at him with troubled eyes. 'Suppose one day I met someone else and married them? Wouldn't you feel I'd been taking advantage of you?'

'That's a chance I have to take. It could happen if we were married. I'm willing to take that risk if you are. I could suddenly see the attractions of Miss Shaw tomorrow, buck teeth and all.'

Anna giggled and hiccupped at the same time. 'This is supposed to be a serious conversation.'

'And Miss Shaw is a serious threat. She's been after me for years. You should see how her hand shakes when she passes me my coffee. Come on, get your coat. I'm taking you out to dinner.'

'Why? I took some chicken out this morning.'

'It will keep until tomorrow. This is a celebration.'

'What are we celebrating?'

'The completion of your new surgery and of our new understanding.'

'I'm not sure we've come to one.'

'Yes, we have,' said James firmly. 'You are living at my flat, expenses shared for as long as it suits us both. You're free to leave and I'm free to kick you out.' He drew Anne back into his arms and kissed her gently. 'In the meantime, I love you very much.'

Anne looked up from her accounts. 'Not bad, I suppose, for the first year. If you take off the cost of the alterations and decorations I've broken even. Give it a couple of years and I might even show a profit.'

James looked up from his newspaper. 'Enough to go on holiday?'

Anne made a face. 'Margate, maybe.'

'I couldn't face the excitement.'

'I'll not go on holiday this year. If I find I've a lull I might drive out into the country for a day.'

James nodded. 'Edward's quite keen to go to Lake Como again.'

'Then go. No strings, remember.'

'I probably will. I just wanted to find out your plans first.'

Anne shut the books.

'Well, unless my accountant finds I've made a massive error in my favour it will definitely be day trips – if I can afford the petrol.'

'You won't mind being on your own for a couple of weeks?'

'Of course not. You make your arrangements and go off and enjoy yourself. What does Edward find so attractive about Lake Como?'

James grinned.

'He enjoys playing tennis and making me look stupid in front of the local girls. He's also learning Italian.'

Anne raised her eyebrows. 'What for?'

'So he can impress the locals. Judging by their expressions whenever he tries to make himself understood he's been learning Chinese.'

'There must be more to it than that.'

'There is, he likes to know the difference between spaghetti and macaroni when he sees it on the menu. It's quite a laugh going away with him. He's such a fool. Thought he'd ordered fish and a side salad and when it arrived it was tiny whole fish and crabs cooked in batter sitting on lettuce leaves, all watching him with little black beady eyes. He tried to tell me it was delicious and was violently sick afterwards. Actually you ought to come with us. The scenery is beautiful, you'd enjoy it.'

Anne shook her head. 'Three's a crowd. I wonder if I'll have time to get these books to the accountants before my first appointment tomorrow?'

James placed the tickets on the table, along with a travel brochure. 'Before you say you can't afford it, this is my treat.'

Anne looked at him suspiciously.

'Edward can't go away as we planned. He's been waiting for a hernia operation for over six months and they've offered him a bed for the day after we were due to leave. He managed to get his money back, but I couldn't. After quite a bit of talking I managed to persuade the travel company to change the arrangements. I didn't fancy Lake Como on my own and I remember you said you wanted to go to Crete, so here we are, two tickets.'

'I can't accept that, James. It's far too expensive.'

James shrugged. 'Call it an early birthday and Christmas present if you like. I'd rather pay for you to go away with me than lose it all to a company that doesn't need it.'

'Are you sure, James? I can't pay you back yet.'

'I told you, early birthday and Christmas present. You don't have to repay me.'

Anne hugged her partner. 'You are so good to me, James. I'll have to think of something special for you.'

Breakfast over and the hire car outside the hotel, Anne and James consulted the map.

'There's Aghios Nikolaos,' James pointed.

'I don't know which way we went – up or down from Aghios Nikolaos. I know when we were at the farm you could see an island not far off shore.'

'I hope you knew your way round Malawi better than this! There are any number of islands. Let's start from Aghios Nikolaos. When you get there something may jog your memory.'

441

They drove through the dusty, suburban sprawl that was now Heraklion and on to the main coast road.

'This doesn't look anything like the way I remember. I seem to think there were hills going up and we were driving right by the sea most of the time.'

'Well, there's only the one road shown. They've probably done a tremendous amount of rebuilding since you were last here. Think what it's like at home. If you don't visit a town for a couple of years it looks totally different and everywhere is one way streets.'

'I suppose you're right.' Anne did not feel convinced by any means. 'What's this place? Oh, Malia. Doesn't mean a thing to me, but I'd love a coffee. Let's park up somewhere and have a wander.'

James complied happily and they spent the next couple of hours meandering up and down the main road, investigating the dark interiors of the shops and admiring the colourful clothing hung outside. Coffee and baklava were ordered at a café set a short distance back from the road and they watched the continual stream of traffic passing in front of them.

'Obviously a road to somewhere,' James observed. 'Do you want me to check that we're going the right way?'

Anne shook her head. 'Even I know that sign says Aghios Nikolaos. I do wish daddy had taught me Greek. He planned to. I can't even remember please and thank you now.'

'They all seem to speak English so I wouldn't worry about it. Ready?'

They continued on their way, drawing into Aghios Nikolaos shortly after mid-day. As they drove across the bridge Anne screwed her head round.

'There's the pool. I remember now. Daddy told me it's supposed to be bottomless.'

'Well, at least we know we're in the right place to start with. Where does one park here?'

James drove up the hill and down past the bus station, to where the shops petered out and the more residential area began. Cars and vans were parked at the side of the road and they drew in behind a small three-wheeled cart.

'They had one of those,' mused Anne. 'Mummy was disgusted.'

'Practical, I should think, if they were farmers. Dump everything in the back. I suggest we make our way back to the centre. I can't see any signs saying parking is for a limited amount of time and if we do get a parking ticket I can honestly plead ignorance at reading the sign.'

'Where do you want to eat?'

'I'm not that hungry yet. How about looking around generally, not just for your shop, then finding somewhere that has a menu that looks interesting. When everything starts to open up again we can start searching.'

Anne toyed with her food. 'I'm not sure this is a good idea, James. It all sounded so easy when we were in England, but now I've got my doubts. The shop may be a grocer now or a taverna. I know it was in the centre of the town, we don't have to go more than about three streets either way from the main road, but it could be anything.'

'Maybe the Tourist Information could help us. We passed it on the way in. Are you sure you can't remember their names?'

Anne shook her head. 'I've thought and thought. I've read daddy's letter again, but he only mentions Anna, no one else by name.'

'Right then; plan of campaign. I'll buy a map from the kiosk that shows the town and we'll mark off the streets as we cover them. We could even ask the waiter if he knows of a gift shop with a white, Persian cat,' James grinned.

'You're laughing at me, James. I know it's not much to go on, but someone must remember it. Have you seen a Persian cat anywhere? If you had you'd remember, wouldn't you?'

443

'Cats don't live to thirty odd years, so it's only the older people who'd remember it, and they're the ones who speak least English.'

'So we ask the younger ones to ask the older ones.'

'I give in. Another ouzo?'

Anne shook her head. 'Two make me feel sleepy, a third would be fatal.'

'We could copy the Greeks, book into a decent hotel and sleep for a couple of hours,' suggested James.

'I know just what you have in mind.'

'Well, we are on holiday.'

'No, let's pay the bill and start looking. You could ask the waiter when he comes.'

The young waiter shook his head. 'This my first season in Aghios Nikolaos, before I work Heraklion.'

'Blank number one,' murmured James. 'Do you want to start here by the pool?'

'No. I'm sure it wasn't here. I would have remembered. Let's go to the main street first and work our way up the right hand side to the square. If we don't have any luck we can work our way back down to the quay again.'

'Are we concentrating just on gift shops?'

'No, every shop.' Anne walked into the first one on the right hand side and looked at the bales of material stacked high on shelves and the decoratively draped displays. 'Excuse me, do you speak English?'

The man nodded. 'I speak good.'

'Is there a gift shop near here, with books, postcards, scarves and the lady has a white cat?'

'Kiosk. Very good books, postcards, stamps. Round corner.'

'Thank you.' Anne pulled a face. 'Not a very auspicious start.'

Up the right hand side they trudged, each person they asked shaking their head or directing them to a shop higher up or lower down. The left hand side bore no better result. James slipped his hand into hers.

'We'll go on to the next road and up on the right as far as the first café. I think we've earned a drink and a rest.'

With no better results they had almost reached the top of the hill before Anne spotted a café, as relieved as James to see the welcome sight. They ordered lemonade and pored over the map again, James marking off the road they had covered with his biro.

'There don't seem to be as many shops in this road, there seems to be more offices.'

'I suppose theirs could be an office now,' Anne spoke gloomily. 'I suppose we should be thankful Aghios Nikolaos is a small town. Just imagine trying to do this in London.'

For the rest of the afternoon they trudged wearily up and down the streets to no avail, until James insisted they booked into a hotel for the night and continued their search the following day. Anne did not protest. Her legs ached, her feet were sore and she was depressed and dispirited.

The morning was overcast which did not help Anne's depression. Added to the frustration of being unable to find the shop, she was having serious doubts about her ability to communicate with the woman if she did find her. Although the shopkeepers and waiters all spoke English, their vocabulary was limited and she was frequently misunderstood.

'Might as well ask at the hotel before we leave. Then we could start down here and gradually work our way back up from this side of the square.'

'If you like.' Anne spoke unenthusiastically.

'It's up to you. We can always give up and drive off somewhere else.'

'No,' Anne shook her head. 'I've got to try everywhere.'

The morning proved as fruitless as the previous day and Anne was tempted to succumb to a siesta when James made the suggestion. She swirled the ice in her ouzo contemplatively, then looked at him, surprise and delight showing in her eyes.

'James, we're in the wrong place.'

'What?' James almost choked on his drink. 'Don't tell me all of this has been for nothing.'

Anne nodded. 'We're the wrong side of the pool. We need to go across the bridge and up the hill that side.'

'Are you sure?'

'Certain. I remember daddy bringing me down the hill from the hotel to look at the pool, then we crossed the bridge to go up to the shop.'

'Why didn't you remember this before?'

'I don't know. It just suddenly came to me. Maybe we sat here whilst I had an ice cream or something.'

'Was it on the waterfront? There doesn't seem to be much up the side roads.'

'You can't possibly see from here. Let's go and look.'

The taverna owners tried to tempt them with their menus as they walked past, each claiming to be serving a speciality, but they waved them away. James consulted the street map.

'We'll start at this one with the Tourist Information at the bottom.'

The road appeared to be residential, large houses standing back in their own gardens, aloof from the tourist invasion and secure in the privacy of their high walls and iron gates. Three quarters of the way up they cut through the cross road to walk back down towards the pool. On the corner was a shop selling marble and bronze statuettes, onyx and crystal ornaments, the metal shutter across the door firmly locked. Anne and James stopped to peer inside.

'Worthy of Bond Street,' commented James. 'I wonder when they open? I'd like to have a look inside.'

They turned to go and as they did Anne clutched James's arm. 'Look, look in there. On that chair.'

Looking at them from pale green eyes was a large, white Persian cat.

'James, it has to be. It just has to be.'

'Don't get too excited. You told me it was a general gift shop.'

'It was, but you were the one who said it could be anything now. What time do they open?'

'It doesn't say. Do you want to wait?'

Anne gazed round her desperately. 'They could be away. They could be ill. Where can we find out?'

James stood back from the pavement. 'What's the name? "Oo-rani-ers". We could see if the Tourist Information office can help us.'

Gleefully Anne tucked her hand into his arm. 'I'm sure it's the one.'

The Tourist Information Centre was more helpful than Anne had dared to hope. Ourania's would be open later that day. It was usually open from nine until twelve and again from three until nine. Was there something particular they had seen in the window?

Anne nodded. 'I hope it will turn out to be very special.'

The receptionist looked after them speculatively. Was it worth her while to telephone Ourania? She decided against it, she was due to be relieved soon and Ourania was bound to keep her chatting.

James and Anne strolled back slowly towards the pool. 'So what do you want to do whilst we wait?'

'Write our postcards. Everyone seems to do that whilst they're drinking. What are you having, lemonade or coffee?'

'Ouzo,' replied Anne firmly. 'And I think your idea of a siesta isn't such a bad one.'

It was past five when James and Anne stood outside Ourania's shop. A smartly dressed woman was flicking over the pages of a magazine and speaking over her shoulder to someone in the back room.

James squeezed Anne's hand. 'I hope you're right.'

'There's only one way to find out.' Sounding far more confident than she felt, Anne stepped towards the open door. 'Let's just look round first.'

Ourania kept her eye on the two customers as they wandered around admiring her goods, whilst she appeared to look at her magazine. From the rear of the shop the cat walked languidly towards the door, and Anne bent down to stroke her.

'*Omorfia*,' she said, the Greek word coming unbidden to her tongue.

Ourania looked at them. 'That's her name. She is beautiful, isn't she?' she said in Greek.

Anne blushed. 'I'm sorry. I don't speak Greek.'

'Inglis? Name Beauty, you say.'

Anne felt tongue-tied. 'Do you know an old lady called Anna?' she asked in a rush.

Ourania frowned. 'Please?'

'Anna. Old lady from a farm, called Anna.'

'Anna?' Ourania looked round at her goods. 'You show, in shop. I give good price.'

'No,' Anne shook her head. 'Anna,' she repeated slowly.

Ourania turned and let forth a stream of Greek, which brought a man through from the back room of the shop.

'Problem?' he asked.

'I'm looking for Anna.' Anne spoke the words slowly and clearly.

'Anna?'

Anne nodded. 'Anna, old lady, from a farm near here.'

'Anna!' Yannis spoke to his wife in Greek who turned her surprised gaze on the couple and repeated the name.

'Do you know Anna?' Anne tried again.

'I know. Why you want Anna?'

'I need to speak to her – about my father.'

'Father?' Yannis looked at James.

'Please, it's very important. I must tell her about my father.'

'Who father?'

'Michael, Michael Castleton.' Anne took a photograph of herself and her father from her purse.

Yannis sucked in his breath. 'Michael? Where Michael?'

'He died a long time ago. I must tell Anna.'

'Wait. You wait.' Yannis turned to his wife. 'Get Giovanni on the telephone. I don't care what he's doing I must speak to him.'

'What do you think he's doing?' asked Anne.

'Telephoning her, I imagine.' James's eyes roved round the walls. 'I think I've found your sketches. Look.'

As he pointed Ourania switched on the light above each frame, illuminating the clear-cut lines. Anna gazed at them in delight.

'It is the right place. Look, there's the girl who's in my picture.'

Yannis began to speak rapidly down the telephone, finally replacing the receiver with a pleased smile on his face. 'Giovanni, come, maybe one hour. Please come.' He spoke to his wife again in Greek, who nodded and turned back to her magazine.

Anne and James followed Yannis back to the pool where he led them to a taverna and ordered a bottle of wine. The conversation between them was stilted and awkward, Yannis's English being very limited, and he glanced at his watch continually.

'What are we waiting for?' asked Anne in an undertone.

'Anna, presumably. What's he trying to tell us?'

'I've no idea.'

It was nearer to two hours before Giovanni drew up, leaving his car parked in front of the taverna, ignoring the shout from the owner to move it. He greeted his uncle with a frown.

'What was so important I had to drop everything and rush down here?'

'These people are English. I'm not sure what they want, but they keep on about Anna, wanting to tell her something. I think it's to do with the war, a resistance worker who was down this way. The woman is his daughter.'

Giovanni raised his eyebrows. 'What was aunt Anna up to with a resistance worker?'

'Helping him stay alive,' replied Yannis grimly. 'Ask them about it in English and tell me what they say.'

Giovanni shrugged. 'Good evening. I am Giovanni, this is my uncle, Yannis.' He stopped to give them all the opportunity to shake hands. 'He says you need speak with his aunt Anna. She very old lady now.'

Anne nodded. 'I – I don't quite know how to begin. My father, Michael Castleton, was here with the resistance. He was in the hills, near a farm and the woman there saved his life, her name was Anna. He was coming back to her and he was killed.' Anne's voice broke and tears began to course their way gently down her cheeks. 'This is silly,' she mumbled as James passed her his handkerchief.

Whilst she wiped her eyes Giovanni translated rapidly for his uncle. Yannis looked around. Curious eyes, both English and Greek, were on the party.

'We can't talk here. We'll go out to the house.'

Giovanni nodded. 'Please, my uncle ask you to his home. There we can talk.'

Giovanni swung the car easily down the side road and Anne looked in awe at the beautiful house where they stopped.

'The garden still to be finished, then look good,' Giovanni observed.

'It's wonderful.'

A fresh bottle of wine was produced, of far better quality than they had drunk in the taverna, and they sat on the veranda overlooking the bay.

'Please, you tell Giovanni.'

Anne took a deep breath. 'Maybe if you read this letter. You can read English?'

Giovanni nodded. 'I tell uncle Yannis what I read?'

Anne nodded and took another sip of the wine. Giovanni opened up the pages and read slowly, finally handing the sheets back to Anne. He drained his glass of wine and poured another.

'I tell.' Carefully he related to Yannis the contents of the letter, his hands moving expressively and his eyes gleaming with unshed tears. 'Your father love aunt Anna.'

'Very much.'

Yannis shook his head. 'Tell them Anna is old, confused, she may even have forgotten him. I'm glad I know what happened to him, but better not to tell her.'

'You can't do that,' remonstrated Giovanni. 'How do you know whether she has forgotten him or not? They've bothered to come all this way to tell her and you say they shouldn't. You have to tell her, uncle.'

'Why didn't they come before? She must have had this letter a long time.'

'I'll ask her.'

'I was working abroad and my mother never told me about the letter or the picture in the bank and it was just forgotten. After I was ill I was told I couldn't return to Africa. I went to the bank to arrange some money to open a veterinary practice and that's when it came to light. I wanted to come straight away, but I wasn't well enough to go abroad for a couple of years – and I couldn't afford it either.'

Giovanni translated and Yannis looked sharply at Anne. 'If she's after money she'll get none from me.'

'She hasn't mentioned money, except to say she couldn't afford to come earlier.'

Yannis scowled. 'I don't know what to do. I must talk to Ourania. Where are they staying?'

'At the Plaza.' James gave the information.

Yannis shrugged. It was not the best hotel in town, but certainly respectable. 'Tell them I'll telephone tomorrow.'

Anne woke early and stood out on the balcony watching the

early morning bustle of the town. She wondered when the telephone call would come and hoped it would be the young man whom she had no difficulty in understanding who would speak to her.

'Penny for them.' James stood beside her.

Anne shrugged. 'I was just wondering what time he would telephone.'

James looked at his watch. 'I know they rise early over here, but I'm sure we have time for breakfast. We can sit in the lounge afterwards and if we've heard nothing by eleven we could walk up to the shop and ask.'

'Suppose he doesn't telephone and there's no one at the shop?'

'We can always go to his house. Why shouldn't he telephone, even if it's to say we can't see Anna? We don't know where she is and would probably never manage to find her on our own.'

Anne sighed. 'You're right, of course. Could we have breakfast up here on the balcony do you think? We could watch what's going on.'

'I don't see why not. I'll get on to room service.'

Sitting in the lounge, in view of the reception desk, Anne jumped each time the telephone rang. James ordered more coffee for them and was wondering if they should have yet another pot when the telephone rang and the receptionist beckoned to Anne.

'Miss Castleton? Is for you.'

Anne's voice was shaking as she spoke to Giovanni. 'Yes, yes, of course. We're ready in the lounge now. We'll wait for you.' She replaced the receiver and let out a deep breath. 'He's going to take us to see her.'

Giovanni drove slowly out of the town and along the road towards Olous.

'We go to the farm. Please, remember, aunt Anna very old. Maybe not remember your father. Maybe big disappointment.'

'I just want her to know my father did love her and planned to come back. She must think he didn't care after all. I know he did.'

They passed Yannis's house and James was struck anew by the size. 'Do all the family live in that house? It's enormous.'

Giovanni smiled. 'Uncle Yannis build specially big. My parents, my brother visit from Italy, and there is room. Aunt Anna and Uncle Yiorgo come to live one day. There is plenty room.'

'So where do you live?'

'In hotel in Heraklion.'

'In a hotel!'

'I am manager. I live in hotel.'

'And your family? Do they live in the hotel with you?'

'No family. No wife.' Giovanni grinned widely. 'I prefer to have variety.'

They drove over the hill at Olous and dropped down towards the bridge, Anne looking desperately for a landmark she would recognise. They climbed steadily, wound their way down the hill into Elounda and continued on to Plaka..

'The church,' exclaimed Anne. 'I remember the church, and there's the island.'

Out in the bay Spinalonga shimmered in the morning sunshine and a small boat crammed with tourists could be seen progressing towards the mooring place.

'Island Spinalonga. Very sad island. People with leprosy live there for many years. Anna's brother live there, he come back and die there.'

'What do you mean?' James had read about the trips to the island and was not sure if he wanted to visit.

'Old uncle Yannis sent there as young man. Live for many years, then told he going to Athens with all other islanders. Hospital in Athens say no more leprosy. You go where you want.'

'So he came back to the island?'

'No. He live in Athens and write about the island. He visit once more and die.'

'When was this?'

Giovanni shrugged. 'Eight, nine, years ago.'

'From leprosy?'

'No. He had bad heart. No one knew. He sat in sun and died.'

James looked at the island with renewed interest. 'What is there to see over there?'

'The houses, church, hospital. They build.'

'They built them?'

'When they go all houses very old, falling down. Uncle Yannis make people build good houses from old houses.'

'That could be worth a visit, then.'

'I find you good boatman in Elounda.'

They drove along the winding road until a huddle of derelict buildings came into sight.

'This Plaka. No people now. Aunt Anna, uncle Yiorgo, two, three more is all.'

They swung round the curve of the road and drew up outside a neglected farmhouse where two elderly people were sitting outside. The woman was shredding the seed from some old cauliflowers, whilst the man sat apathetically, his hands dangling between his knees.

'Aunt Anna, uncle Yiorgo. Very old now,' said Giovanni by way of explanation.

Anne climbed from the car, her legs felt weak now the moment had come. Yannis walked from the house and came forward to greet them.

'Uncle Yannis bring food, every day he bring and aunt Anna think she make.' Giovanni sighed. 'One day must go to live with uncle Yannis.'

Ourania appeared, carrying a tray of pastries and coffee, and beckoned them in through the doorway. She placed the tray on the table and went outside to the old couple.

'Aunt Anna will think she make,' murmured Giovanni.

They stood and waited until Anna and Yiorgo entered, then

took their places at the table, accepting the cups of coffee and glasses of water from Anna as she tottered from one to another and finally handed round the pastries.

'Please thank her and tell her they are very good.'

Giovanni nodded and opened his mouth to comply when Anne placed a hand on his arm. 'No, wait. Tell her I remember how good they were the last time I was here.'

Giovanni did so and Anna smiled. When was this young woman here? She did not remember her.

Anne started again with Giovanni interpreting. 'I came here when I was a little girl. I rode the donkey up in the field and there was a family of kittens in the stable.'

A spasm of pain seemed to cross Anna's face.

'She does remember,' thought Anne hopefully. From her purse she took the photograph of her father and herself and passed it to Anna.

'Ask her if she remembers my father and his daughter.'

Anna turned troubled eyes on her guests. The man in the photograph looked like Michael. 'Tell her I'm the girl in the photo,' urged Anne.

Anna shook her head and touched her own hair. 'This little girl had yellow hair. Long yellow hair.'

'It was a long time ago, aunt Anna. Do you remember Michael coming here to visit you with his daughter? She's grown up now and come back to see you.'

Anna smiled and patted Anne's hand.

'Please explain to her what happened. Tell her my father loved her very much, more than anyone else in the world.' Anne felt a lump in her throat.

Giovanni nodded and talked quietly, whilst their coffee grew cold in front of them and the pastries sat uneaten. Tears ran in a river down the lines of Anna's face. She looked at the photograph and back at Anne.

'The little girl who loved animals.'

'You understand why Michael didn't come back, aunt Anna?'

Anna nodded. 'Poor Michael. I knew there had to be a good reason why he didn't come. He wrote to me and said he was coming. I never heard from him again.' She shook her head sadly.

Giovanni turned back to Anne. 'She understands.' Tears were glistening in his eyes and Ourania was crying openly.

'Please tell her to keep the photograph.'

James drew in his breath sharply and Anne glared at him.

'Anna gave my father a sketch of her family having a picnic. This is all I have to give her.'

Giovanni nodded. 'You have given her the knowledge.'

Anna continued to gaze at the photograph; her memories so long shut away were coming back. She smiled at Anne through her tears.

'He was a good man, a kind man. There was never anyone like Michael.'

Anne rose from her seat and placed her arms round the old woman, planting a kiss on the weathered and wrinkled skin of her cheek.

'I shall always love Anna because she has shown me what real love is.'

Giovanni looked puzzled and interpreted only half the sentence. Ourania wiped her eyes and began to clear away the cold coffee.

'I will make some fresh.'

'No, coffee isn't good enough. I'll see if Yiorgo still has some brandy in his cupboard.'

Anne looked back as they drove away from the house. Yiorgo and Anna had resumed their former positions as if they had never been interrupted. Anne felt for James's hand.

'I'm so glad I managed to tell her.'

'It must have meant a lot for you to give her your father's photo. It was the only one of the two of you together.'

Anne shrugged. 'I don't feel I need him any more. I have you. Do you still want to marry me, James?'

'You know I do.'

'Then why don't you ask me again? I feel ready now.'

Anna watched until the two cars were out of sight. Slowly she climbed the stairs to her bedroom and opened the chest, searching amongst her belongings until she found the shirt that had belonged to Michael, carefully folded with the letter in the pocket. She laid it on the bed, smoothing it gently with her hands, then placed the photograph between the pages of the letter. She must begin to sort out her possessions. There was no need to stay at the farm any longer in the hope that Michael would return.

The first few pages of the next book in the series, *Giovanni*

1976

Annita laid the finishing touches to the table. Each year there seemed to be more people to join them for the annual Thanksgiving dinner. She hoped she had ordered enough ice cream, crisps and Coca-Cola to satisfy Anna's younger girls. They always seemed to have such enormous appetites until they reached puberty and suddenly became weight conscious and worried her by not eating enough to keep a fly alive.

She counted the places again, Elena and Matthew, Helena, Marianne and Andrew, Maria she would put next to her father and he would stop her being maudlin, Andreas, Anna, Jeremy and the three girls, Sorrell, Bryony and Saffron. She hesitated. Maybe Helena would bring the young man from High School. She sensed there would be an announcement there eventually. Annita rolled a spare set of silver cutlery in a linen napkin and placed them on a plate at the end of the table. Either way she would have time to lay the place or remove the articles from sight when her family arrived.

Andreas arrived first, greeting her effusively before removing his overcoat and handing her a sheaf of flowers. 'For my favourite hostess. Only once have I missed Thanksgiving at home and I vowed it would never happen again. You're looking as young as ever, Mamma. I swear my current leading lady looks years older than you – and she claims she's not yet thirty.'

'Oh, Andreas, you always were a flatterer.' Annita caught the

458

odour of alcohol on his breath as he kissed her. 'Come on in. I need your opinion on the table.'

Andreas surveyed the large, oval dining table with approval. 'I'll have to write a play that revolves around a Thanksgiving meal and use your table. It's magnificent as always. It's so delightful to have a proper napkin and not those awful paper things you get at most places.'

Annita smiled happily at him. He always knew how to please her.

'I'll have these arranged in a vase. Help yourself to a drink. Your pappa should be down any minute.'

'You mean he's prepared to give up an evening with his beloved microscope to spend it with the humble likes of his family?' Andreas raised his eyebrows in mock amusement. 'He'll spend the whole evening wondering what developments have taken place in his latest experiment and trying to think of a good excuse to return to the lab.'

'No, he won't.'

The voice from the door made Andreas turn. 'Pappa! It's good to see you. What's new on the lepromatus front?'

'Very little, I'm afraid. Last month I wrote a paper and...'

'Elias! You promised not to talk shop tonight and you know Andreas is teasing you.'

Andreas looked sorrowful. 'You always did see through me, Mamma. Now, I've helped myself, can I get either of you a drink?'

Elias eased himself into a chair. 'I'll wait until the others arrive.'

'Well, you won't have long. There's a car just pulled up. Oh, God, it's Anna and her tribe.' Andreas dropped the curtain back in place. 'We could pretend there's no one in,' he suggested.

'Don't be so silly.' Annita felt herself almost giggling. Andreas always had this effect on her and she refused to accept that the slights and gibes he made at and about his youngest sister were serious.

Anna swept into the room, Jeremy and her three girls bringing up the rear. Andreas watched as they dutifully greeted and kissed each other. That was a very flowing dress his sister was wearing. There was another on the way! He looked at his nieces, Sorrell, only sixteen, was a striking figure in her skin-tight dress. Bryony had obviously been influenced by her sister, wearing a scarlet evening gown and her plump, childish face looked ridiculous covered in make up. Thank goodness Saffron still looked like a child. He poured himself another drink and nodded towards Jeremy who smiled vaguely back at him. Maria crept in through the door and Anna turned her attention towards her, commenting on her wearing widow's weeds at a Thanksgiving and so many years after the death of her husband.

'I always wear black,' sniffed Maria, near to tears. 'If you lost someone you loved as much as I loved Bernard you'd know how I feel. It would be sacrilegious to wear anything else. He would still be mourning me if the position had been reversed.'

Andreas did not hear Anna's reply, but by the way Maria's eyes filled with tears and she tried to dab them away without ruining her makeup he knew it had not been kindly.

He helped himself to a handful of peanuts from a small glass bowl and topped up his glass. No doubt the evening would be spent with Maria alternating between tears and putting on her 'brave face'. Someone should rescue her from Anna, who would certainly not help the situation.

Andreas moved over to where Sorrell and Bryony stood, Sorrell grimacing over the coca-cola she had been given.

'Well, well, Sausage and Bacon, how are you both. Trying hard to grow up, I see.'

Sorrell glowered at her uncle. 'Actually I am grown up. Rather too old to be called by the childish name you seem to like to give me.'

'Oh, ho, touchy in our old age! Maybe it would be more fitting to call you Sage and Onion.'

Bryony giggled. 'That would make us sound like a stuffing.'

'So it would,' agreed Andreas. He raised his voice deliberately.

'And talking of stuffing, am I correct in thinking my dear sister is in an interesting condition yet again?'

Anna blushed. 'You may call it interesting.'

'Personally I call it fascinating.'

'I don't know what you're on about. Jeremy and I...'

'Jeremy?' Andreas raised his eyebrows. 'I thought his name was Rudi.'

Anna's face was scarlet and a hush seemed to have settled on the room.

'I don't know what you mean.' Anna spoke through clenched teeth, her eyes glittering dangerously.

Andreas swallowed the last of his drink. 'Come, come, my dear. He's quite a striking figure. What will you be calling this little addition? Something appropriate, I hope.'

'You bastard! You out and out bastard!'

Anna flung herself at her brother who fended her off easily.

'Now that I'm not – unlike some.'

'How dare you, you pervert.'

Andreas shook his head. 'I'm not a pervert. Perverts tend to corrupt the innocent. I am quite innocent of corruption, or population for that matter.'

Jeremy stepped forward, his face and neck a dull red. 'I think you should apologise to my wife. You have been most insulting.'

Andreas laughed. 'I'll not apologise for speaking the truth. Ask her about her friend Rudi. Accept what lies she likes to tell you, but don't start playing the innocent injured husband in a few months time when you find the truth staring you in the face with a pair of big brown eyes.'

Jeremy sucked in his breath. 'What's he talking about, Anna?'

'He's seen me a couple of times with Rudi. His nasty perverted little mind has worked overtime.'

'Not my mind, but a certain piece of Rudi's anatomy has been, if his description is to be believed.'

Anna's face was as white as the napkins. 'You're disgusting.

461

I'll not stay here and be insulted. Take me home, please, Jeremy. Girls, come along.'

Saffron looked up at her father's furious face. 'Do we have to go, Daddy? We've not had anything to eat yet.'

'I think it might be better. Your mother's not feeling very well.'

Sorrell looked at her mother and stepfather. 'Well, I'm staying and so is Bryony,' she spoke defiantly.

Jeremy shrugged. 'You and your sister can do as you please.'

Sorrell's jaw dropped. She had expected to be ordered home and was prepared to add to the scene by declaring that she was not a child to be told what she was going to do.

Elena and Matthew entered, their arrival unnoticed by those already in the room until they began to call greetings and make apologies for being the last.

'Just about everything went wrong. Elena was searching for her earring, Marianne had lost her gloves, Andrew couldn't decide whether to wear a bow tie or a cravat, the traffic was heavy, to name but a few of the crises I've endured during the last hour. Still, we're here now, so the party may commence.'

'I think you've just missed the best bit,' murmured Andreas and refilled his glass.

'Andreas,' his father's voice cut across the room like a knife. 'I think it's time you left. You have an appointment, remember.'

Andreas gave a mock bow. 'How good of you to remind me.' He swallowed the contents of his glass. 'I'm so sorry not to be able to stay longer. You're party has been sadly depleted, Mamma, and that was not my intent.'

Annita shook her head sadly. Surely Andreas had been venting his spite on his sister unnecessarily. She would have to talk to Anna and see if she could smooth things over between them.